PRAISE FOR THE ALEX MARTEL THRILLERS

"*Perfect Shot* was a fantastic ride. Steve Urszenyi rolls on the throttle in *Out in the Cold* to make it even better! Alexandra Martel is one terrific protagonist!"
—Marc Cameron, *New York Times* bestselling author of
Tom Clancy Shadow of the Dragon

"With *Out in the Cold*, Steve Urszenyi delivers another electrifying, world-class thriller. The writing is precise, poignant, and utterly compelling. A jaw-dropper from start to finish." —Simon Gervais, former RCMP counterterrorism officer and bestselling author of *The Elias Network*

"In the world of espionage and high-stakes thrillers, few authors can match the adrenaline-fueled intensity and pulse-pounding action of *Out in the Cold*. He's only two books in, but if Urszenyi can keep this pace, his name will soon be mentioned among the pantheon of today's master storytellers. Prepare to be captivated from the very first page!" —Ryan Steck, The Real Book Spy and author of *Out for Blood*

"Alexandra Martel is the heroine readers are clamoring for, and *Out in the Cold* delivers the goods. Steve Urszenyi skillfully crafts a narrative as chilling as the Arctic winds, brimming with action that grips readers from start to finish."
—Jack Stewart, retired Navy fighter pilot and bestselling author of
Unknown Rider: A Battle Born Thriller

"Opening this book is like trying to jump onto a fast-moving train. Urszenyi is the real deal." —Linwood Barclay, *New York Times* bestselling author of
Take Your Breath Away on *Perfect Shot*

"Gripping and on target, *Perfect Shot* hits with maximum impact. Steve Urszenyi's debut thriller never lets up from the first page to the last."
—Jack Carr, *New York Times* bestselling author of *The Terminal List*

"A stunning debut heralding an extraordinary new character and series. Alex Martel is a kick-ass special agent in an action-packed, on-the-edge-of-your-seat espionage thriller with a jaw-dropping finish."
—Robert Dugoni, *New York Times* bestselling author of
the Charles Jenkins espionage series on *Perfect Shot*

"Steve Urszenyi's powerful debut starts fast and finishes faster. Full of high-octane thrills and intricate details that bristle with authenticity." —Mark Greaney, #1 *New York Times* bestselling author of *Burner: A Gray Man Novel* on *Perfect Shot*

"*Perfect Shot* is a highly accomplished debut—the most gripping opening chapters to a novel I've read in a very long time. You have to read on...."
—Peter James, *Sunday Times* #1 bestselling author of the Roy Grace series

Also by Steve Urszenyi

Perfect Shot

OUT IN THE COLD

AN ALEX MARTEL THRILLER

STEVE URSZENYI

MINOTAUR BOOKS
NEW YORK

OUT IN THE COLD. Copyright © 2024 by Steve Urszenyi. All rights reserved. Printed in the United States of America. For information, address St. Martin's Publishing Group, 120 Broadway, New York, NY 10271.

www.minotaurbooks.com

Designed by Meryl Sussman Levavi

USSR sickle and hammer symbol©Sutana4/Shutterstock

Library of Congress Cataloging-in-Publication Data

Names: Urszenyi, Steve, author.
Title: Out in the cold / Steve Urszenyi.
Description: First edition. | New York : Minotaur Books, 2024. | Series:
    An Alex Martel thriller ; 2
Identifiers: LCCN 2024029420 | ISBN 9781250879141 (hardcover) |
    ISBN 9781250387110 (international, sold outside the U.S., subject to rights
    availability) | ISBN 9781250879158 (ebook)
Subjects: LCGFT: Thrillers (Fiction) | Novels.
Classification: LCC PR9199.4.U78 O98 2024 | DDC 813/.6—dc23/eng/20240628
LC record available at https://lccn.loc.gov/2024029420

Our books may be purchased in bulk for promotional, educational, or business use. Please contact your local bookseller or the Macmillan Corporate and Premium Sales Department at 1-800-221-7945, extension 5442, or by email at MacmillanSpecialMarkets@macmillan.com.

First U.S. Edition: 2024
First International Edition: 2024

10 9 8 7 6 5 4 3 2 1

For Lynne. Always.

OUT IN THE COLD

CHAPTER 1

Alexandra Martel turned, spotting her approaching quarry weaving through the crowd.

Got you now.

All around her was the smell of the sea, the briny scent cutting through the cologne and perfume of the well-heeled guests aboard the luxury megayacht *Aurora* as if to remind them that, for all their wealth and refinement, the sea was more formidable. *Aurora* and all she represented were merely transitory things bobbing on its undulating and unforgiving surface.

As her target breezed past, Alex exchanged her empty glass with a new flute of champagne from atop his tray. *Mission accomplished.* She sipped as the tuxedoed waiter smiled and moved on. Her mood was light, buoyed by the atmosphere of celebration and, perhaps, the champagne.

The spacious enclosed salon pulsed with music as multicolored lasers slashed through the darkness. Fog machines belched mist from an elevated stage. An ornate starfish mosaic encrusted with thousands of LED fibers seemed to scuttle across the dance floor as she strode through a pair of sliding glass pocket doors into a much quieter corridor.

The guests had boarded the ship at its home port in Antibes, France, the coastal town situated on the Mediterranean Sea between Cannes and Nice. At 148 meters—more than 485 feet—*Aurora* wasn't short on private spaces. Somewhere in one of the many salons on this deck, Alex would find the person she was actually looking for.

Madame Celeste Clicquot, secretary general of Interpol, had excused herself twenty minutes ago, telling Alex she had to meet with someone. But she had been evasive when Alex inquired further. That was out of character for Clicquot, who, since the events in Paris in the early summer, had been more open and forthright with Alex about her work affairs.

Alex opened a door into a lavish sitting room filled with plush velour settees, Persian rugs, vases, and sculptures from the Far East. Across from her, a man emerged from a doorway to what appeared to be a small private salon. He was older and unfamiliar to her, wearing a business suit that gave him the air of an outsider on this boatful of merrymakers. Stepping out from behind him was Celeste. Alex thought better of calling out to her and instead receded into the darkness. She watched as the man turned and shook Clicquot's hand, then hurried down a hallway toward the vessel's bow.

When Clicquot had taken a few steps in her direction, Alex stepped out of the shadows into the salon, taking a long sip of champagne for effect.

Clicquot spotted her and called across the room. "There you are!"

"Oh, hey! I thought I'd never see you again," said Alex.

"It is this boat, my dear. It's so massive."

She took Alex by the hand and led her back toward the dance hall. They emerged into the crowd of guests showing off their moves on the dance floor, where Clicquot found another waiter and relieved him of two fresh glasses of bubbly.

"I'm still working on this one," Alex protested, shouting to be heard above the din.

"Who said either of these is for you, my dear?" Clicquot replied, draining one in a single gulp.

Oh, what the hell. Live a little, Alex thought.

She polished off her own glass and seized another from the waiter's tray.

"You are a devil," Clicquot said conspiratorially. "Come. Follow me."

She led Alex up a highly polished chromium spiral staircase, her midnight-blue silk dress billowing in the breeze like the spinnaker of a grand sailing vessel as they climbed the stairs.

The deck they entered was open to the sea and as dark as its murky depths. A warm breeze wafted over the ship's gunwales as it steamed ahead. Clicquot guided them to a terrace overlooking the vessel's stern and dropped into a cushioned rattan deck chair. A glass-bottom swimming pool two decks below in the ship's beach club shimmered like sky-blue plasma. Behind them, a ribbon of luminous white foam split the sea, illuminated by a waxing gibbous moon hovering over La Baie des Anges—the Bay of Angels.

Clicquot continued to sip her champagne, staring ahead blankly, looking pensive. Maybe it was the champagne, but tonight she seemed troubled by some unspoken angst—one moment, she was a lively flame; the next, a smoldering candle doused by some foreboding from within.

"Madame—"

"*Madame?*"

Oops. Not a flame—a flame*thrower.*

"I'm not your boss anymore, Alex. And outside of office hours, I cease being the secretary general of Interpol. Well, mostly. So tonight, here on this boat, I am simply *Celeste.*"

Alex waited a beat before speaking. "Celeste, is everything okay?"

Clicquot leaned back in her chair and stared out to sea, taking another sip of champagne. Finally, the edges of her mouth curled up slightly.

"You are an impressive woman, Alex. Before Interpol snapped you up—*borrowed* you from the FBI—you had already established yourself as a formidable investigator. And, of course, your military accomplishments are legendary. But we still had no idea what we were getting into when you signed on to your secondment."

Alex leaned back against the pillowy seat cushion and kicked off her boat shoes.

"Despite your actions being what your former FBI handlers called *insubordinate,* what you did in Paris helped establish Interpol as a preeminent policing organization, not merely one that acts as an administrative liaison among its member agencies. You single-handedly advanced global policing by a decade. We're going to miss you, Alex. In fact, I already do."

For what the FBI had labeled *insubordination*, Alex's employment was terminated, and, with it, her secondment to Interpol had ended. The Department of Justice didn't subscribe to her *exigent circumstances* defense or appreciate the Machiavellian methods she had employed in Paris. For Alex, though, a morally imperative goal justified any means to achieve it. And a soon-to-explode nuclear warhead fit within that definition.

Alex wanted to ask her friend what was going on, but sensing the looming question, Clicquot silenced the thought with a gently waved hand.

"Chief Bressard lobbied hard to bring you into the organization," Clicquot continued. "I am indebted to him for his foresight. From the outset, I had reservations about your hard-charging methods. But despite my more conservative inclinations, Martin convinced me you would be a strong asset to Interpol. You have proved him most perceptive."

"Well, I'm glad. Chief Bressard became like a second father to me. I never wanted to leave Interpol, but my actions had consequences."

"Who knows? Maybe you'll be back one day."

Madame Clicquot's mood was lifting, so Alex quelled the urge to ask about it further. And though she was curious, now wasn't the time to ask about her downstairs secret rendezvous with the stranger.

All in good time.

The lights from shore off their port side shone in the distance. Higher above, the shape of a rocky peak capped in shimmering lights stood backlit against a star-filled sky.

Clicquot followed her gaze. "Everything is more beautiful when seen from the deck of this incredible yacht. My dear friend Valtteri, her owner, asked that I invite you and Caleb aboard for this little party following your investiture into France's Legion of Honor."

"I've yet to meet the elusive Valtteri."

"Tonight, you will. I promise." Her face lit up in a devious smile. "He's quite something. And as you can see, he is very successful."

Looking around them, that might have been the understatement of the evening.

As if on cue, a man's voice drifted in out of the darkness. "There you are. I thought I'd never find you again."

"Valtteri! Finally," Celeste replied. "I thought you might never break free."

"I'm sorry," he said, stepping from the shadows. "Investors."

"Ah, yes. The important people," she teased.

"None more so than you." Valtteri bent and kissed her on the cheek. He perched on the arm of Clicquot's chair and took her hand in his. This wasn't the same man Alex had seen her friend with moments ago.

So, if this is Valtteri, who was the other guy?

* * *

Caleb Copeland leaned over the ship's railing, looking on as the trio below sipped champagne and chatted under a string of lights that offered scant illumination. Alex was half turned away from him, looking remarkable in a summer dress, her tanned, bare shoulders drawing him in like a moth to a flame. The allure was intoxicating and impossible to ignore. Her pull on him was undeniable, whether she wore a ghillie suit, tactical gear, or a bare-shouldered dress.

They first met on a mission in the Netherlands involving a high-octane helicopter chase where he witnessed firsthand her world-renowned sniper skills. He was there in his capacity as a CIA paramilitary operations officer and branch chief, offering tactical support on a matter of national security deemed to be of the highest priority to the United States. To that end, he was there to enlist Alex into the Central Intelligence Agency and onto his team. She was an FBI special agent on loan to Interpol and a decorated soldier. He needed her unique skill set, so was determined to alter that arrangement. But Alex being Alex, she had rebuffed his recruitment efforts.

At the time, no one could have predicted that Alex would become the central figure and hero in a story fit for Hollywood. Most of the details of that operation would remain classified for decades to come, but the hunt for a stolen thermonuclear bomb had almost ended with the destruction of one of the world's greatest cities. Paris was still recovering from its near miss with catastrophe. If not for Alex's stubbornness and disregard for her personal safety, the powerful nuke would have detonated below the City of Light. Not only would Paris have been obliterated, but the global order would have been forever altered.

Alex, he learned, was a force of nature greater even than the nuclear weapon she had saved Paris from. Following the incident, his recruitment of her to his team within Ground Branch had been a success, even if it had taken some secret backroom brokering from CIA deputy director Kadeisha Thomas to finish the deal.

Alex was now a CIA contractor, a paramilitary operations officer on Caleb's elite team inside Ground Branch. And yet there she sat—her inner warrior concealed beneath the camouflage of a floral dress.

Reality is merely an illusion.

Madame Clicquot sat to Alex's right: the shepherd dog next to the lamb. Who was who depended on the circumstances. The man with them was Clicquot's boyfriend and the multibillionaire owner of *Aurora*. Caleb had yet to make his acquaintance but recognized Valtteri from his file.

As he watched the threesome chatting below, he heard someone approaching from behind.

"Are you ready, Mr. Copeland?" a man said. Caleb nodded. "I'll give you that tour now, starting with the security office and armory. My boss tells me that's what you were hoping to see first."

"It is," Caleb replied.

"I'm Jocko. Mr. Street mentioned you're Special Forces."

"Ex, but that was a long time ago."

"And now?"

"And now I'd be very interested in looking around this amazing vessel."

The security officer nodded. Caleb acknowledged his discretion with a smile and a clap on the back. "Lead on, Jocko."

* * *

"Alex," said Celeste. "I'd like to introduce you to Valtteri."

His bearing was bold, confident. A breeze tousled his wavy blond hair, and his smile revealed shallow dimples and laugh lines that gave him an amiable appearance. As he leaned forward, the patio lights illuminated his fiery eyes.

"It is great to finally meet you, Alex. Celeste has told me so much about you."

"I'm afraid she has kept you a secret until now."

"Not a secret," Celeste corrected. "We're just being discreet."

"Celeste detests the mere whiff of a scandal," said Valtteri.

"And would this be one?"

"Not in the least," said Celeste. "But one's personal life should be just that—personal."

Alex couldn't have agreed more.

"Shall I refresh our drinks?" Valtteri asked, raising a bottle he held at his side. But before he could refill their glasses—

BOOM! BOOM! BOOM!

The ship rocked as a series of concussive blasts echoed across the sea.

CHAPTER 2

Champagne flutes tumbled as multiple explosions jolted *Aurora*. The ship shuddered as her active stabilizers seemed momentarily confused by the irregular shockwaves and labored to compensate for the unanticipated disruption to her equilibrium.

"What was that?" asked Celeste.

Alex said nothing, but even with the din of the music from the deck below, she recognized the cracking resonance of military-grade high explosives. A gray-blue cloud of smoke rolled over the ship's gunwales, engulfing them in a pungent, slightly sweet odor that she tasted as much as smelled. It brought with it a long-ago memory of a grape hut on the side of a mountain in Afghanistan.

She caught a flash of light out of the corner of her eye. "Incoming!" she shouted. "RPG! Get down!"

A fiery streak of light illuminated the deck as it passed. The projectile's path ended in another cracking explosion somewhere on a deck above them, confirming her suspicions.

What the hell?

She ran to the side of the ship and saw the shadowy outlines of multiple rigid-hulled inflatable boats—RHIBs for short—not far from the megayacht.

"What's happening? Why are we under attack?" Celeste's questions weren't directed at anyone in particular.

The *what* was easy—multiple bogeys were assaulting *Aurora*. The *why* was less important for now. All that mattered was getting Madame Clicquot and Valtteri Lehtonen to safety.

"Do you have a panic room?"

Valtteri stared straight ahead, wide-eyed, mouth agape, but he didn't answer.

"Valtteri!" She raised her voice to punch through the fight-or-flight response his autonomic nervous system was eliciting.

Around them, lightning flashed, except it wasn't lightning. More explosions thundered from below. Panicked screams from the ship's guests, who until a few moments ago had been enjoying the percussive beat from the DJ's playlist, filled the night.

"A panic room," Alex demanded again, finally catching Valtteri's attention. "You must have a secure room on a ship like this. Where is it?"

They had to get moving. They were sitting ducks out here in the open. She grabbed Celeste by the hand and pushed Valtteri toward the ship's bow and the staircase they had ascended earlier. Another flash of light appeared off the side of the ship. She recognized it as the blowback of an RPG launch from one of the small boats encircling them.

"Get down!" she yelled.

They hit the deck as a rocket-propelled grenade shot past, impacting less than a hundred feet behind them before exploding in a blinding splash of fire and melted steel. The overpressure wave hit her in the chest like a Lennox Lewis punch. Her sinuses hurt. Her ears were ringing. She kept Celeste and Valtteri on the deck long enough for the debris to finish showering down around them.

"Anybody hurt?" she asked, checking them over for shrapnel injuries, seeing none. "Let's move," she said, calmly but with urgency.

"Not that way," said Valtteri. "Belowdecks, aft of the crew mess. There's a citadel room there."

He led them rearward along the vessel's port side, beyond where the RPG had impacted and detonated. They dodged burning debris on the way to the staircase, Alex tiptoeing to avoid having her bare feet shredded by fragments of jagged shrapnel. She felt a sharp stab in her right foot but pressed onward. Smoke billowed as Valtteri pulled open the door. A large man spilled out, hacking and coughing, a pistol extended. Alex grabbed his arm and deftly locked up his gun hand, then flipped him onto his stomach. Still in control of his wrist, she relieved him of his firearm. She was about to strike him in the back of the head with the butt of his SIG Sauer when Valtteri called out.

"Wait!" he shouted. Alex paused, her arm cocked in midair. "He's the head of my security team."

"You couldn't have mentioned that sooner?"

She climbed off him, straightening her dress. The man gave her a once-over as she covered her exposed thigh. He seemed perturbed that a woman in a tropical print halter dress could have bested him.

Valtteri added the requisite introductions. "Alex, this is Iain Street. Street, Alex."

Just then, two men wearing dark, unmarked military uniforms and carrying rifles appeared from behind a bulkhead twenty meters away. As they leveled their guns at the group, Alex dropped into a low crouch and fired two shots past Street, dropping the lead tango. The head of security pushed Celeste and Valtteri to cover as the second tango fired a burst that struck the door to the stairs behind them. Alex dove out of the way, coming out of her somersault behind a steel pillar and returning fire. Her first shot missed, but the next two found their mark, and the second tango dropped like a heavy sack next to his companion.

She covered left, right, then to her rear to ensure there were no more surprises.

"Street?"

"We're good," he said.

She glanced over her shoulder at him while keeping the gun trained to her front. "Give me more, Street. What's happening?"

He hacked again from the smoke he had taken in. "We counted four Zodiac RHIBs. Not sure where they came from." He spoke with a pronounced accent—Scottish, she thought. "By the time we picked them up on the ship's radar, it was too late to establish their origin before the fireworks began."

"These aren't your men, I take it?"

"That pair of numpty ballbags? No way."

Yup, Scottish for sure. "How many tangos?"

"Thermal showed four badgers in each boat—three assaulters and a driver."

"Badgers?" Alex asked.

"Badgers and doves, Alex. Old SAS terminology for bad guys and their hostages or victims."

So, out of sixteen men attacking the ship, there could be as many as twelve already onboard, minus these two.

"And then there were ten," she mumbled.

"Are these pirates?" asked Celeste.

"Once upon a time, maybe," she answered. "But here and now on the Mediterranean Sea, kitted out like that? These are no Barbary Coast privateers, ma'am." Then to Street, "What about your men?"

"Down to eight, including myself. They're engaging the ones that boarded." The sound of muted gunfire from somewhere else on the ship punctuated the air. "But I'm afraid we're outnumbered and probably outgunned."

She nodded, handing him back his pistol.

"I'll get these two to the panic room," he added. "You good for now?"

"I will be."

"Good."

"Go," she said.

Valtteri's arm was already around Celeste's shoulders, steering her toward the stairwell.

"Wait," Celeste said, pulling free. "Alex, what are you going to do?"

She shrugged.

"No, Alex. You don't even have any shoes, let alone your gun. And look, you're bleeding!"

Alex glanced at her feet, where a small puddle of blood had formed. She had kicked off her boat shoes earlier and been padding around barefoot since the ship came under attack.

"I'll be fine," she said. She tore a long strip of material off the bottom of her dress, wound it around her foot, and tied it off with a square knot. "Street, get them to safety. Do you have comms?"

He nodded. "Take this." He was about to throw her his radio.

"No, keep it. You'll need it to coordinate with your men."

"If you get to the bridge," he said, "there's a room at the back, behind the charting table. Grab a radio from there." He turned and herded the couple toward the stairs. "We declared a Mayday and activated our ship security alert system, including the multi-frequency EPIRB—the emergency position-indicating radio beacon," he called over his shoulder. "But out here, it could take twenty, thirty minutes at least for someone to get to us, if at all."

Guess we're going it alone, then.

She glanced at the Rolex Submariner on her wrist: 9:52 P.M.

The three disappeared down the stairs as Alex stepped to the corpses she had created, relieving the first of his rifle, an FN SCAR-L.

She rolled the fallen assailant onto his back with her knee and took two spare mags from the load-bearing vest he wore over his body armor, slipping one into a slash pocket in her dress. She'd have preferred to take the whole vest, but prying it off him would have left her defenseless and exposed for too long, validating her maxim that a dress without pockets was about as useful as retroreflective camo.

She stepped behind the bulkhead for cover while she inspected her new weapon. The firing selector was pointing to *A* for full auto. She ejected the magazine that was half full of ammunition and swapped it out for one of the full thirty-round mags.

Send me, she thought.

CHAPTER 3

When the first explosion hit, Caleb immediately recognized the moment for what it was: *Aurora* was under attack. Jocko had been slower to react, and his hesitation almost cost him his life.

"Get down!" yelled Caleb as the second RPG cut across their path and impacted the ship's superstructure twenty meters away. He tackled the younger man, and they fell together behind the cover of a center support wall.

"What the fuck is going on?" Jocko asked.

"Armory. Now!" yelled Caleb, pushing him forward.

Jocko snapped into battle mode. "Come on," he said, drawing his sidearm.

They ran up a flight of stairs, arriving at the back of the bridge at the same time as a pair of tangos appeared.

"Get down!" shouted Jocko.

Caleb ducked as Jocko fired half a dozen rounds at the two tangos, dropping one while the other took cover. It bought the men enough time to enter the ship's command center. The officer of the watch and the other men on the bridge had taken cover inside, behind the level 8 bullet-resistant ballistic glass. Two security officers appeared from a back room, their arms filled with rifles and ammo.

"Here!" said one, handing Jocko a carbine and extra magazines.

Jocko made sure it was ready to go before pointing Caleb into the room.

"Grab what you need. Make sure you take extra ammo."

Caleb emerged from the armory carrying an AR-style tactical rifle and extra mags.

"All good?" asked Jocko as he stepped out.

"I still have a pulse," he said. "So yeah, all good."

Knowing that the bridge would be defended by others from the ship's security detail, Caleb was antsy to get moving. The best defense was a strong offense, so he and Jocko needed to take the fight to *Aurora*'s attackers and link up with Alex, who would do what Alex does.

The two men hurried to the door on the port side of the pilothouse. Caleb took the lead and, flinging it open, immediately came under fire. He ducked down and fired back, permanently preventing those tangos from accessing the bridge.

* * *

Alex peered through the rifle's holographic sight as she moved out from behind the bulkhead. She paused, listening for sounds that might give away the location of other attackers. Two were down. That left maybe ten tangos unaccounted for somewhere aboard the ship, not including the four driving the RHIBs.

The music on the deck below had been cut off. Occasionally, screaming from the guests would punctuate the salty air. The revelers aboard *Aurora* were her canaries, signaling not the presence of carbon monoxide or other harmful gases but the ship's attackers. The sound of gunfire was sporadic, telling her that whoever they were, they were here for a defined objective and not just to rack up a body count.

The deck in front of her was clear, but not being familiar with the ship's layout was problematic. Forging on, she soon came to a TV-sized touchscreen panel on the wall next to another stairwell. A few taps later, her location on the front half of the fourth deck popped up on the display. The massive *Aurora* had seven decks in all.

The crew quarters and mess were shown below the beach club. While not marked, that was the most likely location of the panic room if she was interpreting Valtteri's description correctly. *Aft of the crew mess,* he had said. She hoped that would be where she'd find them or where she'd send rescue crews.

The bridge was on the ship's sixth level. Tactically, did she make her way there and maybe link up with some of Street's security team? And where was Caleb? Is that what he had done? The pull to find Caleb was formidable, but lone wolf had always been Alex's preferred operating style, as evidenced by her two previous Army occupations—combat medic and sniper—so her decision to pursue the badgers solo seemed preordained.

Find Celeste.

She pulled open the door to the stairwell and stepped in, sweeping her rifle left and up. The diamond-tread metal floor felt cold against the soles of her feet as she descended the stairs to the level below. She pushed the door open a crack and found three badgers standing in the middle of the Orient-themed room, their backs to her. Wedging the door open with her bare foot, she braced her rifle on the jamb.

"Howdy, fellas."

They turned her way in unison, the middle badger's gun coming up first. Alex pulled the trigger and shot him center mass, but her rifle jammed on her next shot.

Shit!

Bullets from the other badgers' weapons sprayed the doorway, sending metal shrapnel and sparks flying all around her as she ducked back into the stairwell, falling backward in the process. A flaming dagger of pain sliced through her cheek as something embedded into her skin.

"Fuck!" she yelled, pulling a thin metal shard from her cheek.

She ran her tongue along the inside of her mouth. *Clear.* Grateful the shrapnel hadn't penetrated through, she tossed it away and wiped blood from her face with the back of her hand.

She cleared the jam and slapped a new magazine into the magwell, hoping this was a one-off failure. She tapped the magazine, partly for good luck. Having lost the element of surprise, popping the door open again was a less-than-desirable option, but she needed to reengage.

She breached the room for a second time only to encounter one dead badger. Pushing his rifle out of reach, she helped herself to two more mags from his load-bearing vest—his LBV. Her dress was getting weighed down, pulling heavily at her neck. *Hell with this,* she thought. She pried the badger's vest off him and donned it, transferring the mags from her dress's pockets to the LBV. She picked up her rifle and moved forward.

Back to work.

CHAPTER 4

Three of the twelve badgers were down. Nine to go—assuming the ones driving the RHIBs hadn't boarded *Aurora*.

But why were they here? Valtteri Lehtonen was a wealthy man, sure, as evidenced by this enormous private yacht. Was this an attempted kidnapping for ransom? Clearly, there could be a hefty pot of gold at the end of that particular rainbow.

Or was it something else?

Alex crossed the room, peering through a window into a corridor that led toward the bar and disco. Seeing it was clear, she pulled open the door and advanced quickly down the hallway, her rifle up and ready.

She pushed open the door at the far end of the corridor and was met by gasps and shrieks from guests of the boat sheltering behind the bar and overturned tables in the disco. To her left, a woman about her age cowered beside a man, both their faces plastered with looks of sheer terror. She placed a finger to her lips to keep them quiet, then swept her rifle in a wide arc ahead and to her sides.

As she pressed onward, a pair of muffled pops accompanied by muted flashes of light pierced the darkness to her left. She wheeled that way, and her reticle filled with the shape of a man kitted out in black military gear like the others. His rifle was pointed toward her as he collapsed to the deck. He was on the opposite side of the dance floor and had been moving in the same direction she was when he lined her up in his sights. She hadn't seen him—he was in shadow, she was not.

She ducked low and trained her rifle in the direction from where the sound of the gunshots had come. A man wearing beige pants and a black fleece, carrying an integrally suppressed rifle in gloved hands, appeared under the dance floor lights. *Street.* Their sights locked on to each other. Then, as quickly as he'd engaged, he lowered the barrel of his weapon.

Thanks, Alex mouthed, scanning for other badgers. She had made an error and somehow missed seeing the bad guy. Street had saved her life. "Where's Clicquot and Valtteri?"

"Safe in the ship's fortress with two of my men," he called back. "Head on a swivel, Alex."

Worse than being bested by the badger was having to acknowledge a tactical error that had nearly gotten her killed. She had lost situational awareness while focusing on the civilians, and that had almost cost her her life. Was she losing her combat edge?

Street signaled that they should keep moving. Alex crossed the dance floor and scooped up the Soviet-made RPG-7 launcher and two grenades in a small ruck the badger had been carrying. Then she fell in behind him.

They stopped at a railing. Below them, three badgers were gathered around the shallow end of the pool. For the first time, she noticed they appeared Middle Eastern. They were speaking and gesturing animatedly. Two women and a man in deckhand uniforms knelt before them, hands atop their heads.

"Sounds Arabic," Street said, backing away from the railing.

Aurora's engines were steaming ahead, and the deep rumble coupled with the breeze made it difficult to hear what was being said.

"Not Arabic."

"What?"

"It's not Arabic, it's Persian," she whispered.

"Same thing."

"It totally isn't. They're speaking Dari. It's a dialect spoken across Afghanistan and a couple of other countries."

"How do you know?"

"I speak Dari."

His eyebrows shot up. "What are they saying?"

Below them, one of the invaders yelled in heavily accented English at the trio before them. "Where are they?" he shouted, but his hostages shook their heads, not having an answer to give.

"We have to get any VIPs off this boat," Alex said. "How many are there?"

"There's a plan in the works."

"Care to let me in on it?"

"Not now."

She was going to press him on that, but the badger was still shouting at the hostages.

"What's your assessment, Street? Valtteri is your client. What are we dealing with?"

"Maybe a kidnap and ransom scheme. Or an attempted assassination. Or a corporate coup."

That would give a whole new meaning to hostile takeover.

"Have you tried, you know, calling anyone?"

"No phones. We don't have contact with anyone beyond this ship right now. Our radios are operating more or less by line of sight. No encryption and no digital, just old-fashioned radio waves. Beyond that, it's dicey. Something must be blocking the signals."

"Like a jammer?"

He nodded. "I'm not even sure the EPIRB signal is getting out past it."

She thought about that. Not good. It meant they truly were going it alone. She glanced at her watch: 10:06 P.M. Fourteen minutes had elapsed since she dropped the first badgers, and still no sign of a maritime rescue by French authorities.

Dropping into a crouch, she headed for an open staircase that ran against the starboard side of the ship, down to the beach club.

"I'm going in for a closer look."

"What? No, wait. *Alex!*"

But she had already laid the grenade launcher at his feet and crept halfway down the stairs.

The man who had spoken English a moment ago held up his rifle, pointing it at the hostages. "I'm going to ask one last time, where are they?"

The woman pleaded with him. "I don't know who you're talking about. Please, let us go."

The man slapped the woman hard across the face, then pointed the rifle at her female companion's head. "One of you speak now or she dies."

"Please, I have no idea who you mean."

The man struck her again with the back of his hand, and she fell to the deck. As she did, her male companion lunged at him. It was the last heroic act he would ever attempt, as one of the other badgers shot him in mid-flight.

Fuck! Alex felt physically sick. Seeing soldiers maimed and killed was one thing—hard enough to get used to, but par for the course in combat. Seeing innocent civilians being brutalized and murdered was a whole other ball game, and it enraged and sickened her, awakening her guardian within.

She got Street's attention. He nodded, and she raised three fingers for him to see.

The man raised his weapon, more agitated than before, pointing it menacingly at the woman.

Three, two, one . . .

She stood and fired, taking out the man who had backhanded the woman. Street simultaneously shot the one who had killed the hostage, and he fell to the deck screaming, a through and through gunshot wound below his collarbone. Blood pumped from his wound, spraying objects twenty feet away.

The third man was quick to react and grabbed the other woman by the hair, using her like a human shield as he backed into the darkness. Alex finished descending the stairs, her gun trained on the attacker, a brightly glowing red dot hovering in her gunsight over his ugly face as she closed the space between them.

The man whose blood pumped from his shoulder wound didn't seem to recognize that his day was over. She might not have let him bleed out, might even have helped stanch the bleeding, but when he reached for his weapon with his good arm, he sealed his fate. Alex double-tapped him in the chest and continued advancing on the man holding the woman hostage, not giving a second thought to the life she had just ended.

Street raced to the bottom of the stairs and darted over to protect the woman who had been slapped. He used his body to shield her from the remaining badger, then directed her up the stairs, away from danger.

He moved in behind Alex, his rifle also trained on the badger with the cowardly face.

"Drop your gun or I'll kill her!" the badger shouted, jamming the muzzle of his rifle into her side.

"Okay, okay," said Alex, unslinging her rifle. "No one else needs to get hurt." She crouched low and placed her weapon on top of a patio table, her empty hands in front of her. "What do you want?"

"I'm going to find my men," he began, his rifle coming off the hostage and now pointing straight at Alex. "And then—"

He didn't finish his thought before Street's rifle spit a polymer-tipped 190-grain jacketed hollow-point into the man's cranium and he joined his friends in the afterlife, his limp body dropping onto the deck. The woman screamed as blood and brains splattered against the side of her face and head.

"And then there were five," Alex whispered.

CHAPTER 5

Street's shot with his suppressed carbine caught the badger just below his right eye. The result was immediate and gruesome. Two-thirds of his head was gone, its contents splattered across the deck. Fragments of skull embedded into the fiberglass wall surrounding the beach club area.

Alex reached her arms out to the hostage Street had just saved. The woman, barely out of her teens it seemed, fell into her arms, sobbing, her head against Alex's shoulder. She let her cry, feeling the tension in her own muscles melting away with her deep sobs, before settling her into a chair and handing her a beach towel to clean off with.

"When we leave, head up those stairs," Alex told her, pointing behind them.

"Where are you going? You can't leave," the woman sobbed.

"Keep low and make your way to the disco. There are others there. Can you do that?"

The woman stared at her wide-eyed, then nodded.

Alex picked up her rifle and rejoined Street as the woman ran up the stairs.

"We need to get Valtteri and Celeste off this boat."

"Come on. Follow me."

"One sec," she said, dashing up the stairs to retrieve what she'd left behind when they engaged the badgers.

* * *

Ahead of the kayaks and paddleboard racks was an unmarked door. Street punched a six-digit code into a keypad on the wall and yanked it open. Alex followed him down a flight of stairs, through the crew mess, and into another chamber where Street engaged with a panel on the wall. A steel door shifted outward revealing another room.

Alex turned to find Madame Clicquot and Valtteri Lehtonen standing in the concealed room along with two guards.

"You're bleeding," said Clicquot, lightly touching Alex's cheek.

She had already forgotten about her shrapnel wound and gently brushed Clicquot's hand away. "It's nothing. I'm fine, ma'am."

"And still barefoot."

"*I'm* not the focus here," Alex said, sounding perhaps more irritated than she'd intended. "We need to get you off this boat."

"Agreed," Street said. Turning to Valtteri, his boss, he added, "We're going to get you both ashore."

"You finally going to let me in on the plan, Street?" said Alex.

"My men are going to launch one of the tenders—a twenty-eight-foot speedboat."

"Okay . . ."

"Two of my security team will be on it. They'll head for Monaco, about four kilometers east."

"A decoy maneuver? Then what?"

"I'm hoping the badgers will fall for it. It should seem logical that Valtteri and company would head for the safety of the principality and give chase."

"Assuming he's their target," she said.

"Aye, assuming that. Meanwhile, I'll take them away in the thirty-seven-footer and head for the port at Saint-Jean-Cap-Ferrat, six klicks behind us."

"Doesn't sound very complex. That's the best you got?"

"Sometimes simple is better, Alex. There's no way any of their RHIBs can catch us. The Axopar BRABUS Shadow 900 Black Ops—the thirty-seven-footer—can do sixty knots. That's just shy of seventy miles an hour. And ours has a modified enclosed cabin that's hardened against small-arms fire. Think of the presidential limo, only ours floats."

Clicquot piped up. "We're not leaving without Mikko," she said.

"Who's Mikko?" asked Alex.

Just then, a commotion down the hall in the mess caught her attention. Alex pushed Clicquot back into the panic room and dropped to a knee, her gunsight focused on three subjects forty feet away.

Street stood over her, his rifle braced against the doorway.

"We're good. They're with me," he announced.

Alex lowered the muzzle of her rifle but remained in position, watching. A ship's security officer and two other guards walked toward them. The man in the lead turned to cover their flank, allowing the others to pass in the narrow corridor. Behind him was the man Alex had seen coming out of the room with Clicquot earlier—tall, handsome, older.

Behind him . . .

Caleb.

"Hey, Shooter," he said by way of greeting.

He's alive.

"Glad you could make it. I thought you missed the party—as usual," she said.

"We've been having our own little party on the upper decks. Did you need rescuing?"

"In your dreams. Who's this?" she asked, indicating toward the older gentleman.

"This is Mikko Selänne," said Valtteri.

Alex waited for more. Clicquot offered it up.

"A friend of Valtteri's. He is also Finland's permanent representative to NATO."

"A NATO ambassador?" asked Alex, sizing the man up.

Clicquot nodded.

How intriguing.

For now, she resisted her inclination to probe deeper, knowing full well that there was more to the story. This wasn't just a pleasure cruise for the high-ranking Finnish diplomat. Instead, she gave the other security man a cursory assessment. He wore body armor and carried the same sidearm and close-quarter combat rifle Street carried. For his part, he eyed her up and down as well.

CHAPTER 6

"Let's roll," Alex said, taking point for the group.

The sound of the engines from the boat being used by the security men to stage their mock escape could be heard in the distance, the high-pitched note carving through the thrumming resonance of the megayacht's propulsion system. The fleeing boat's engines revved loudly, hoping to draw the ship's assaulters away from *Aurora*.

Alex entered the tender garage and button-hooked through the doorway, sweeping her weapon through the space. A heavy, transparent curtain separated the starboard and port garages, and she could just make out the outline and trailing foam-crested wake of the fleeing tender. She also saw the shapes of two Zodiac RHIBs in pursuit. That was a good sign, but where were the other two?

An open slip in front of her held four personal watercraft, a pair of jet boards, and six Seabobs in a rack above the waterline. A fast-looking boat nestled in a harness over the pool of seawater. It was sleek and black and looked to be around forty feet long, with a modest beam and shallow draft. Street ran past her and punched a button on the wall that brought the port-side door down, closing them off from the outside world and ensuring the badgers wouldn't see them from their Zodiacs should they look closely.

"There's another entrance to this garage from the front," Street said, pointing to the opposite side of the docking area. "Caleb, cover that entry."

Street moved to the hoist that held the boat suspended and hit a button on the frame, lowering it. It had barely touched the water before

It seemed her floral-print summer dress with the mid-thigh side split, coupled with the load-bearing vest, rifle, RPG launcher, and grenades, were making quite an impression with Street's team. But then, if they knew her and her generally edgy fashion sense, they mightn't have been so surprised.

Street noticed, too. "Don't let the pretty dress fool you, Jocko," he said. "She's the real deal."

Caleb looked at Alex with his eyebrows raised. "Real deal?"

She flipped him the bird.

She turned to Street. "What do you need me to do?" asked Alex.

"Cover our escape. That's when we'll be most vulnerable."

"Agreed," she said.

He directed two of his men forward to the port-side tender garage.

"We'll give them a head start before we head to the garage on the other side," he said. "Once they've launched, we'll wait about a minute to see what the RHIBs do."

"If the badgers have any operational discipline at all, they'll leave at least one boat behind."

"We've accounted for that," Street replied. His eyes darted to the rocket launcher and grenades. "And I'm hoping you'll be able to help deal with that contingency before heading to the bridge to link up with my men."

"Understood," she said. Then looking to Caleb, she added, "We'll do what we can."

Jocko was leaping over the gunwales. He disappeared into the pilothouse while Street assisted Celeste aboard, followed by Valtteri and Ambassador Selänne.

A pair of 450-horsepower Mercury Marine Verado XL outboard engines roared to life as Street undid the mooring lines that secured the vessel to the hoist and dock. Alex took her cue and did the same, and Street jumped aboard.

"When we're clear of *Aurora,* close the door," he said, pointing to the blue button on the wall next to her. "We're going to head for the harbor on Cap Ferrat, back toward Nice. With any luck, I'll be able to raise the French authorities and send help."

Celeste stood along the side of the boat as Jocko piloted the vessel past the hull of the ship. Her eyes conveyed a message words couldn't have expressed as fully. Alex nodded back.

"I'll do what I can from here," Alex told Street, tapping her rifle.

"I know you will," he replied.

She punched the button, and the hydraulically operated tender bay door flipped down, sealing her off from the outside. Her world went quiet, except for the sound of the engines and the prodding of the sea against the doors, and she was filled with a sense of déjà vu. Being alone wasn't new, but the sense of isolation was an unfamiliar feeling to the former sniper who had once relished the individualism of her military designation.

She turned and was relieved to see Caleb. "Let's go," she said.

She ran back to the stairwell near the crew mess and, still shoeless, ascended to the next level, Caleb on her six. A scene from the movie *Die Hard* played out in her mind, where John McClane found himself in the same shoes, figuratively speaking—that is, barefoot and outnumbered against a heavily armed adversary. She hoped having to run across a floor covered in tiny shards of glass wasn't in her future.

She scanned the area of the beach club and beyond for badgers as she made her way to a railing overlooking the sea. Off to the right and about a thousand meters away, the decoy tender was heading at full throttle for Port Hercule at Monaco. Behind them by nearly a quarter mile, two

RHIBs trailed. Meanwhile, the thirty-seven-foot Axopar BRABUS Black Ops appeared from behind *Aurora*'s stern, steaming directly for the port at Saint-Jean-Cap-Ferrat, whose lights were visible on the distant shore.

She scoped the two Zodiacs chasing the decoy tender but estimated the odds of obtaining a clean hit without her sniper rifle and telescopic sight were no better than the random chance of a stray bullet skipping across the water and hitting a duck. In other words, they were pretty much zilch.

"You've got no shot, Alex," said Caleb, following her line of sight.

She nodded and turned her attention back to the boat with Celeste and company aboard. Without its running lights on, the Axopar was merely a sleek gray shadow moving against the slate-colored canvas of a dark sea. But then a sound caught her ear, and she turned her head.

A third Zodiac was rounding the bow of *Aurora,* making directly for the fleeing tender.

Shit!

She eyed the rocket launcher at her feet. The revered military strategist General Carl von Clausewitz had extolled the utility of the "fog, friction, and fear" produced by swift and overwhelming violence of action. And an exploding RPG was better at delivering the shock and awe Clausewitz had advocated than any NATO-compliant bullet. But it had been years since she had used the infamous and ubiquitous Russian RPG-7; the last one she'd fired had been provided by Uncle Sam during a training exercise while she was still with the 75th Ranger Regiment.

They were simple to operate, but it wasn't as if they weren't replete with inherent risks. This one looked older than the ones she had used, as did the grenades. The simple impact fuse at the tip might have corroded or could malfunction when loaded into the launcher, causing it to detonate prematurely, which would turn this into a very bad day for her and Caleb.

Just as she was weighing her options, the two Zodiacs that had been pursuing the decoy boat veered off and made a beeline for Celeste and Valtteri's escape launch.

Sometimes, decisions were foisted upon us amid our own vacillation.

She scooped up the rocket launcher and removed an olive-drab high-explosive anti-tank grenade from the rucksack, seating the three-foot munition into the weapon. She pulled the fuse cap off the tip of the grenade. To her relief, it didn't explode. She hoisted the rocket launcher to her shoulder and glanced behind her one last time to ensure that no one was standing in the backblast area of the weapon.

Caleb stared wide-eyed at her. "You've got to be kidding."

"Nope."

The truth was she wasn't so sure about this plan. Her chances of scoring a direct hit on the moving Zodiac were about zero. It was three hundred meters away and traveling at thirty knots or more across a rolling sea. Plus, with *Aurora* still underway, she'd have to factor in a right-to-left crosswind. She pointed the weapon toward the dark moving smudge of the Zodiac anyway and aimed considerably above it, beyond the five-hundred-meter marking on the rear sight, thumbed the hammer down, and pulled the trigger.

A loud *whoosh* and a kick at her shoulder propelled the grenade assembly out of the launcher. At eleven meters out, the sustainer rocket ignited in a puff of smoke and fire and boosted the rocket to its maximum velocity, equivalent to three football fields per second. It overshot the Zodiac, as Alex intended, and reached its maximum range of nine hundred meters, then self-detonated over the sea in a glorious blast of high explosive, the cracking report reaching her ears in under three seconds. And although the Zodiac was well outside the grenade's hundred-meter kill zone, its pilot steered the craft sharply to port. Too sharply. Alex couldn't be sure in the low light, but she hoped they had swamped their vessel. And while it was nearly impossible to sink a Zodiac, it might slow their ability to catch up to the speeding Axopar if they took on enough water.

She turned to Caleb and grinned.

"Nice shooting, Tex," he said, grinning back.

She looked to the east and saw the other two RHIBs still on an intercept course, but they were considerably beyond the nine-hundred-meter maximum range of the last RPG in her bag. They likely didn't have the speed to catch the Axopar, but they still could make the port on Cap Ferrat before Celeste and the others had a chance to get to safety.

Alex and Caleb considered their next move. They could stay aboard *Aurora* and try to meet up with the remaining members of Street's security team, maybe eliminate the fourth and final RHIB and the last of the badgers, or they could find a way to get to Celeste and back Street up in the small town where they would disembark.

Suddenly, more gunfire erupted somewhere on the decks above them.

"Shit," Caleb said. "They must still be trying to breach the bridge."

"We need to split up," she said. "You go help security up top. I'm going to try to catch up with Street."

Decision made. She grabbed the ruck containing the last grenade assembly and ran back to the stairs.

CHAPTER 7

Street had taken over the helm, piloting the thirty-seven-foot speedboat toward the glow of lights ahead. Saint-Jean-Cap-Ferrat was a sleepy little community on an appendage of land jutting out from the French coastline. Home to the fabulously wealthy and members of the European aristocracy, it had a year-round population of about fifteen hundred. Her port lay four kilometers across the sea to their west but appeared closer, the distance compressed by the darkness.

To their stern, *Aurora* grew smaller in their wake, still steaming in the opposite direction, on autopilot for Port Hercule in Monaco. A thin trail of smoke wafted behind her, evidence of the damage she had incurred in the attack. But she wasn't ablaze. The fire-suppression systems appeared to have largely mitigated that threat for now. Street hoped her captain had maintained command of the 485-foot vessel and that she wouldn't simply run aground when she encountered land in a few kilometers.

Valtteri, Celeste, and the Finnish ambassador sat tenuously on a luxurious leather settee in the enclosed cabin, rocking gently with the movement of the boat. The Axopar's sharp bow cut through the waves at full throttle.

"How long until we reach port?" Celeste shouted above the roar of the engines.

"Two and a half minutes," he replied. "If all goes well."

She looked over her shoulder again at the dark shape of the rigid-hulled inflatable boat speeding toward them. "Will we make it?"

"Yes, ma'am," he said with more certainty in his voice than his heart.

Valtteri rose from his seat beside her to sit next to Street at the helm.

"Where do we stand?" he asked.

Street nodded toward Jocko, who now stood braced in the port-side doorway, a hand gripping the railing over his head. "He managed to raise our colleagues on comms. They're on their way from Nice."

"But?"

"No *buts,* sir. It'll be close. The Maritime Gendarmerie is responding with two patrol vessels. One is coming from Menton, east of Monaco, and the other from somewhere between here and the port in Nice. Even at their top speed, it could take them ten to fifteen minutes or more."

"So, there is a *but.*"

Street shrugged.

"I ask again then, Street, where's that leave us?"

"Crossing our fingers that our backup doesn't hit any traffic snarls."

Just then, a fiery streak coming from *Aurora* appeared behind them. A cracking explosion lit the sky a brilliant orange, raining fire down onto the sea midway between the Axopar and her pursuers. The Zodiac veered off course, and in the short-lived light given off by the exploding rocket-propelled grenade, they watched as the boat nearly flipped over, corrected course, and reset. The RPG hadn't struck the Zodiac, but the RHIB had lost a lot of ground on the Axopar before resuming the chase.

Celeste smiled. "Alex," she said, almost to herself.

Street returned her smile. "That's one determined woman you have back there, ma'am."

Celeste beamed. "She's the most infuriating Interpol agent I've ever had the pleasure of hiring."

* * *

Four personal watercraft bobbed in the water inside *Aurora*'s tender garage. Alex hit the blue button on the wall and the garage bay door clamshelled open, the water inside becoming turbulent as the water outside rushed past relative to the megayacht's speed. She donned a life jacket—a personal flotation device or PFD—and hopped onto one of the brawny-looking Sea-Doos.

She fired it up, easing the throttle open. So far, so good. She attached the safety lanyard coming off the digital key to her life vest, just in case. If she got thrown from the machine, it wouldn't continue racing away from her, and she'd stand a shot of getting back on.

The engine made a gratifying burbling rumble that echoed in the enclosed space. She untied and aimed for the open sea.

It wasn't lost on her that she quite probably looked like a vengeful anime character in a third-person shooter game—rifle slung one way across her back, grenade launcher the other, a ruck with a rocket-propelled-grenade assembly squeezed under her calf, her tattered summer-patterned dress flapping in the forty . . . fifty . . . sixty . . . sixty-five-knot wind as she accelerated toward the speedboat Celeste was on. She could just make out the shape of the badgers' Zodiac in front of her, midway between her and the Axopar. There was no time to hatch a plan. She would have to wing it and hope things went her way, all the while quelling the *fail to plan, plan to fail* mantra playing on a loop in her brain.

Soon she was close enough to breathe the exhaust from the RHIB's big outboard motors. She kept to the calm water in the sailing line directly behind them, minimizing the chance of being upset by a wave and maximizing her odds of firing off a semi-accurate burst from her rifle. There were two badgers aboard, not just one as she had hoped. When she was within twenty-five meters of the Zodiac, she swung the rifle into her left hand and pulled the stock hard into her shoulder.

She reduced her speed and turned the handlebar to the left, angling the Sea-Doo so she would traverse the wake created by the Zodiac. Now she had the badgers lined up without the Axopar in the kill zone.

She was about to pull the trigger when her Sea-Doo struck a large wave and went airborne. Her legs flew into the air, and her rifle came out of her hand as she grabbed for the handlebar to keep from being launched off the Sea-Doo. She came down hard and found herself side-saddle and sideways to her target, dead in the water, the rifle dangling by its sling in the salty Mediterranean.

"Shit!"

Miraculously, the RPG was still at her right foot. At least she hadn't fallen off the machine into the sea.

Ten meters behind the RHIB, she traversed the wake again. She pulled the butt of the rifle into her shoulder and with one hand, fired a burst at the man driving the boat. Her rounds went wide-right, smashing into the center console and sending bits of plastic and sparks off the metal frame flying into the air. The man not driving swung toward her, his own rifle spitting leaden fury in her direction.

Alex tucked low and raced off in the opposite direction, zigzagging through the sea as the unmistakable buzzing of bullets whizzed past her. She turned to reengage as the man attempted to exchange his spent magazine for a fresh one, but he was fighting to keep his balance in the boat.

Releasing the handlebar and throttle, the Sea-Doo slowed to a crawl, and she took aim through the holographic sight, squeezing another full-auto burst from her rifle. She watched as her bullets zippered up the legs and back of the man at the helm. He fell against the console, then dropped dead to the deck, his arm catching in the steering wheel on his way down. The RHIB careened left, went airborne off the Axopar's wake, and splashed down hard on its side. Still carrying a load of speed, it cartwheeled twice before stopping suddenly, upside down in the water, the other gunman lost from her sight in the chaos of the crash.

Alex snapped the handlebar hard right to avoid hitting the out-of-control RHIB, and once again found herself launched over its wake, flying through the air, yelping in full voice as her heavy rifle swung on its sling into her knee.

CHAPTER 8

Street's portable radio crackled from atop the helm station.

"Go," he answered brusquely.

"They're not falling for it," a voice shouted above a backdrop of wind and engine noise. "They must have been called off by the Zodiac on your tail. They're heading your way now, boss. We're up their ass, but they might intercept you before we get there."

"Right," Street replied, looking out off his starboard side in the direction of the other Axopar. He tossed the portable radio onto the captain's seat behind the bolster he was leaning against. "Jocko," he said to his security man. Jocko straightened, and Street directed him to the starboard aft quarter of their boat with a nod.

He could make out the shapes of three vessels—two Zodiacs with the twenty-eight-foot Axopar BRABUS Shadow 500 Black Ops giving chase—against the dark horizon, still a couple of klicks away. Meanwhile, a drama continued to unfold behind them, with Alex on a Sea-Doo, engaging the Zodiac chasing them. Jocko trained his rifle on the approaching Zodiac but didn't dare engage with Alex hot on its tail, her Sea-Doo zigzagging and bouncing across the waves.

"Glad she's on our side," Jocko quipped. "But I wish she'd get on with it or get the hell out of the way."

Suddenly, the Zodiac lost control, shot sharply left, and cartwheeled to a stop, upside down in the sea.

"Fuckin' *A*," said Jocko with little fanfare. "That's more like it."

"Aye," said Street with a smile.

"That's my girl!" shouted Celeste.

"I could use a few more like her on my team, that's for sure," Street shouted to no one in particular over the cacophony. "No offense, Jocko."

"None taken, boss," said the burly ex-Marine, an admiring smile on his face as he peered through his scope.

Together they watched as her Sea-Doo emerged from behind the Zodiac, caught air, and settled back into the sea with Alex in control again. Twenty seconds later, she was abreast of their starboard side, and Street peeled off most of the Axopar's speed so they could hear each other without yelling over the racket of the engines. He saw blood running down her leg.

"We'll get you aboard and patch you up," he said, pointing his chin toward her wounded knee. "You can just drop your jet ski—"

"No way," she hollered. "I'm going back out after the other two RHIBs."

"No, Alex, you're not. You're injured. Besides, I need another gunner on board to fend them off."

"Negative, Street," she said as Jocko looked on, amused. "It'll be better if their attention is split between multiple targets anyway. This way, there's three of us against two of them."

She could be aggravating, but it was hard to argue her logic or results.

Street saluted her and pushed the throttle forward, once again ripping for port. Then, over his shoulder, he watched as Alex spun her Sea-Doo around, accelerating hard as she headed straight for the onrushing pair of Zodiacs.

* * *

Alex squeezed the seat of the Sea-Doo between her thighs and rode her machine over the waves like a restless mustang across the great rolling plains of Montana.

She was on a head-on collision course with the two Zodiacs, still a couple of hundred meters ahead. She turned her machine to the right, taking a wide arc she trusted would make the badgers think she had peeled off and disengaged. Her plan was to come in behind the smaller twenty-eight-foot Axopar, then confront the Zodiacs by popping out and ripping ahead, as she had done to the one chasing Street's vessel. Beyond that, she had no idea what her next step would be, but she was resolved that it might likely involve her remaining RPG.

Forty seconds later, she came astern of the shorter Axopar and the two maritime security officers aboard. She brought her Sea-Doo into the wake of a pair of 250-horsepower Mercury Marine racing engines. She hoped Street had given them a heads-up, and judging by the absence of gunfire coming her way, he had.

She came alongside the cross-cabin speedboat and could see that the Zodiac was putting more distance between them. She glanced at the speedometer. Even though she and the Axopar were both doing more than fifty knots, somehow, this Zodiac was outrunning them.

As she prepared to race ahead, one of the RHIBs broke formation and headed for shore. She had to assume it was a ruse of some sort, but there weren't a lot of options available to her, so she ignored it and went after the solo RHIB.

And then there was one.

Her hope was that the men on the speedboat behind her would continue monitoring the location of the Zodiac in case it circled around behind, while she focused her attention on the one in front of her.

She pushed the throttle all the way forward, the Zodiac growing larger by the second. The saltwater spray blurred her vision, but she had no problem discerning the little licks of flame emanating from the rifle being wielded by someone in the front of the RHIB. She dodged and weaved among the waves, hoping that between her actions and the pounding of the RHIB on the water, the shooter wouldn't get a bead on her.

Suddenly, a searing pain shot through the cap of her left shoulder.

Sonofabitch!

She reflexively dropped her arm off the handlebar and slowed to assess her injury—it stung like a bugger, and she was bleeding, but it was a minor graze; might not even need a stitch.

Assholes! You're going to pay for that . . .

She twisted the handlebars and aimed her watercraft for an imaginary intercept point along the path the Zodiac would take to attack the Axopar.

She took her thumb off the throttle, and as the machine slowed and settled into the sea, Alex reached down to retrieve the assembled RPG and launcher. Not having any idea if the water had ruined the grenade, she said a silent prayer to Saint Michael, pulled the fuse cap off the tip, and perched the launcher on her shoulder. She took the grip in her right hand, and after flipping up the iron sights, stabilized the launcher with her left hand, her shoulder protesting with stabs of pain. She located the black Zodiac against the black water—it was coming virtually straight at her.

A man stood in the bow, firing. Bullets zipped by her ear, angry bees racing in for the kill. She was determined to end this.

Two hundred meters.

Waves raised and lowered her Sea-Doo in their swell, the palpable pulse of the sea alive beneath her. The Zodiac danced in her sights.

One hundred meters.

The Zodiac turned ever so slightly toward her, seemingly intent on ramming her.

Fifty meters.

If she didn't fire now, the RPG wouldn't even have time to arm before she was run down.

She squeezed the trigger and was gratified to hear the crack of the gunpowder booster charge launching the grenade out of the tube. Even more gratified at the almost immediate ignition of the sustainer rocket, its bright flash blinding her.

A split second later, the grenade hit the Zodiac and exploded, but Alex was already ten feet deep in the Mediterranean and swimming deeper, having tossed her PFD after hitting the water. She had no desire to be in the kill zone when the thing detonated.

The concussive effect of the explosion rocked her under the waves. Small missiles of shrapnel coursed past her, dragging little iridescent tunnels of air through the water. She focused on exhaling slowly through her nose as she dove away, deep into the darkness. When she felt she was safe, she waited a beat, then swam for the surface.

All around her was fiery debris. Nothing resembling the original Zodiac remained, and there was no sign of its previous occupants.

Yippee-ki-yay, motherfuckers.

She had surfaced at the edge of the debris field. She surveyed the damage and thought it unlikely that anyone had survived. Scanning the horizon, she located a Zodiac heading in her direction.

The other Zodiac, she thought. *The one that had peeled off toward shore.*

It was fast approaching her location. She took a deep breath and dove underwater, out of sight. She saw the telltale white foam forming behind the engine as the boat weaved through the debris field above her.

She'd have given anything for an air tank. The urge to take a breath was beyond overwhelming. If she didn't breathe soon, the blackness that was descending on her would envelop her and carry her away forever.

As the boat moved off, she inched her way upward through the darkness, fighting every instinct to race for the surface like a whale intent on breaching. When she finally reached it, she took such a deep inhale that she was sure everyone on land must have heard.

The Zodiac weaved around the remains of the other RHIB; she presumed to look for surviving comrades or maybe to search for her waterlogged corpse. She spun in the water, looking for her Sea-Doo. It was ten meters behind her. She swam to it and gingerly climbed on from the rear, lying flat on the seat in the hopes she wouldn't be seen. Her rifle was gone, one more piece of treasure lying at the bottom of the Mediterranean Sea.

CHAPTER 9

She fired up her Sea-Doo and wasted no time spinning it around and heading toward the marina at Saint-Jean-Cap-Ferrat. Once again, the buzzing of bees in her ears left her no doubt the Zodiac had spotted her escape.

She weaved her machine as much as she dared, but she was spent. Her arm and knee ached, her chest hurt, she was exhausted and short of breath, her vision and hearing were not fully clear yet, and she felt nauseated. Ahead of her, she could make out the outline of the Axopar pulling into port.

She squeezed the throttle trying to put more distance between her and the Zodiac. She risked a backward glance in time to see one of the badgers aiming an RPG toward her and firing, the bright flash illuminating the sea.

Are you fucking kidding me?

Once more she dove into the sea, the cold from the repeated dunking combined with the chill of the night finally seeping deep into her bones.

A massive explosion erupted as her Sea-Doo was struck by the 85-millimeter grenade. She held her breath and turned to swim down and away from the flames. A deep rumble resonated through her body, and a large wake appeared above her.

Exhausted and unable to stay under any longer, she dared to rise up through the water column and finally broke the surface twenty-five meters away, gasping for air yet again, her lungs and brain on fire. A long, gray-hulled Navy ship ran through the burning debris, cutting off the path of the RHIB, the waves from the newcomer threatening to swamp her in her state of exhaustion. On its foredeck, a sailor aimed a deck-mounted machine gun at the Zodiac, while other crew members lined the railing armed with more portable but equally lethal automatic weapons. Bullets were fired across the Zodiac's deck and commands shouted over loudspeakers. The two men aboard dropped their weapons and raised their hands into the air, surrendering to the overwhelming show of force.

Barely able to think, she put her head down and swam for the lights demarcating the safe harbor at Saint-Jean-Cap-Ferret, still hundreds of meters away.

Just swim, she told herself. *Swim to the lights.*

The temptation to give up and let the water take her under was profound. If she let go, would her late husband's arms be there to wrap her in their warm embrace? Her stroke faltered and she choked on water. As she slipped under the surface, an unexpected image of Caleb floated across her consciousness, his eyes piercing her soul, giving her the strength to kick up and swim to the lights . . . to Caleb.

Alex . . . Alex . . . Alex, swim. She swam. *Alex! Alex!* "Alex, Alex, grab the line! Alex, Alex!" Through water-filled ears, she heard a voice breaking through the cold and the muffled sound of her strokes punching through the waves. Suddenly, she was blinded by a light and a man-overboard alarm blared as the searchlight continued to track her. The hulking ship swung toward her, like an orca suddenly aware of its prey.

A rescue diver plunged into the sea and swam to her, placing a floating hoist line and sling under her arms. Before she fully comprehended what was happening, she was lifted into the air, the diver clinging on to her, her legs wrapped around his hips as she held the line tight in her numb hands, shivering violently as she was raised by a davit aboard the vessel.

She was cold, weak, exhausted. She didn't care about any of it. She just wanted to lie down where she was and go to sleep, relieved that it was over but too spent to care if it wasn't.

A medic approached her with a foil blanket, throwing it around her shoulders. "*Venez avec moi, mademoiselle.*" *Come with me, miss.* Then, in heavily accented English, the medic said, "Let's go to our medical room to warm you up."

All she could do was nod and shiver as another man approached and draped a woolen blanket over the one made of foil.

"Hey, Shooter."

She recognized the voice but thought she must be dreaming. Until she looked up and saw him.

"A little late for a swim, isn't it?" Caleb asked, a broad grin stretched across his face.

CHAPTER 10

The *Thetis* lay at anchor in the outer harbor of the Saint-Jean-Cap-Ferrat marina. One deck below and down a narrow gray hallway, Alex lay on a gurney inside the medical bay. She wore a blue wraparound patient gown, a heavy blanket pulled up to her chin.

"You are very fortunate, mademoiselle," said the ship's physician. He pulled off his nitrile gloves as a nurse placed a bandage over the stitches he had just finished sewing into her left shoulder. The doctor turned to her and tucked his hands into the pockets of his lab coat. "It closed easily and will heal well. Someone should remove the sutures in about a week. I would do it, but alas, we will still be at sea, and you will be wherever you will be."

Caleb was standing in the corner and raised his hand to volunteer for the task.

"No," Alex said firmly.

She sat up on the stretcher, and an ice pack slid off her knee. The nurse watched it fall to the floor, then nudged it under the bed with her foot.

The doctor continued. "Lucky for you, the waters of the Mediterranean are at their warmest this time of year. Still, you had a mild case of hypothermia, Ms. Martel. But your body temperature is back to normal now. The fact you were able to keep down the warm fluids we gave you is a good sign." He indicated toward her arm. "We can remove that intravenous now, and you will be free to go."

"Can she have anything to eat, Doctor?" asked Caleb.

"I'm starving," she added.

"Of course, something high in carbohydrates would be good. If you're going to have anything to drink, avoid alcohol or caffeine for the time being."

"Thank you, Doctor," Alex said as he left the examination room.

The nurse removed the IV catheter, applying a Band-Aid over the site and bending Alex's arm up.

"Hold," she said.

"Hear that?" Caleb asked, his hand cupped around his ear.

"What?" Alex asked suspiciously. All she could hear was the drone of the ship's main engine.

"That's the sound of a hamburger calling my name."

"Good luck with that. Maybe a baguette with ham and brie."

"Not the same, but I'll take it," he said.

"You can relax your arm now," said the nurse, pulling the curtain closed around the cubicle. From a cupboard, she handed Alex a pair of flip-flops, along with dark blue sweat pants and a hooded fleece sweat-shirt emblazoned with the insignia of the French Navy.

"You can keep these as a souvenir of your time aboard," she said, smiling. "I'm sorry we had to throw your dress away. It must have been beautiful before . . ." Her voice trailed off.

"It's okay," said Alex, gently touching the woman's hand. "It was just a dress. I've always been more comfortable in these anyway."

The woman gave her a sympathetic smile. "*Vous êtes une* tough cookie, Alex," she said. Alex had the sense she was referring to more than just her injuries.

"*Merci.*"

When she finished pulling on the comfortable sweats, she opened the curtain. Caleb gave a low wolf whistle. Alex flipped him the bird.

"Let's go."

She led them up the stairs, her bruised knee and cut foot complain-ing with each step, her shoulder doing the same.

"You okay, Shooter?"

"Stop asking."

They reached the main deck. She took a deep breath of the night air as she gingerly touched the cut on her cheek and sighed. The salty air was cool and cleansing after the sensation of nearly drowning only a few short hours ago.

Caleb interrupted her thoughts. "I updated the deputy director," he said.

"Bet she's pissed."

"In a manner of speaking."

"Would she have preferred if we had all been killed and the ship sank?"

Off his look, she didn't pursue it further.

A ship's tender—in fact, it was a RHIB not unlike the ones they had battled earlier—took them from *Thetis* to the mainland, where several police vehicles waited. They were greeted by a uniformed officer as they reached the top of the steps along the boulevard lining the marina.

"Mademoiselle, *mon capitaine* wishes to have a word."

Alex nodded. It was unavoidable. The local constabulary would expect a full account of the incident.

"This way, please."

The policeman led her and Caleb across the street and into a bistro, its patio doors opened to the night. A slender man of medium height with wavy hair was standing at the bar, stirring a freshly prepared espresso. He glanced over his shoulder as they approached.

"Captain," Alex said.

"*Oui*," he replied, turning and eyeing her up and down. "Please, be seated."

Alex sat at the small café table he had indicated. She was getting a feeling this would be more *interrogation* than *interview*.

The man tilted his coffee back and swallowed it in one gulp.

What was the point? she thought.

"You must be hungry, yes?" he asked.

She nodded, and he called the barman over. Although it was 2 A.M., the proprietor delivered a tray with a hot bowl of onion soup, followed by a *croque monsieur*—a ham and Gruyère cheese sandwich grilled on white bread—and *frites.*

Caleb had ordered a hamburger.

Alex wolfed the offering down with a bottle of sparkling water like it was her first meal after returning to base following a drawn-out skirmish.

"Ms. Martel, what is your occupation?"

Her soup spoon stopped and hung suspended in the air, a strand of melted cheese sagging back into the bowl. *Shit,* she thought.

The question was to be expected, but in her state of hunger and exhaustion, she hadn't mentally prepared a suitable response that wouldn't pull the Central Intelligence Agency into the investigation.

"US government employee," Caleb said.

The police captain glanced over at Caleb and his hamburger, unamused.

"And you are?"

"A coworker."

Alex continued eating. Between bites, the police captain dutifully recorded her account of the evening's events in his notebook, interrupting her now and then to clarify a point, establishing a timeline of who shot whom, when and where, and so on.

"And what about the *Aurora*?" asked Alex.

At that moment, two cars pulled alongside the curb outside the restaurant. Celeste Clicquot emerged from the second sedan joined by Street.

Celeste ran into the shop and pulled Alex out of her chair to hug her.

"Alex," she said. "I'm so glad to see you." She stood back to assess her at arm's length. Alex winced at the pain from her shoulder. "Oh my dear, I'm so sorry—"

"It's nothing," Alex replied. "I'll be alright."

"We need to get you back to the villa to rest, Alex. Capitaine, how much longer?"

"Just a few more questions, madame."

Caleb lingered one table over. Alex could see him listening intently to every word she said, never interrupting to interject a note of concern or caution. As Alex's supervisor at CIA, he could have taken her away from here, relieved her of the official demand to deliver a statement regarding the events aboard *Aurora* and after. In the short time she had known him, and the even shorter time she had worked with him, Alex had learned that it would be a mistake to think of him as the affable character he appeared to be on the outside. She knew him to be inwardly calculating and severe in his dealings with those who made that kind of miscalculation.

Alex wrapped up her statement and was told she was free to go. A bone-deep exhaustion overcame her, and she wondered if she'd ever be able to get up out of her seat. The desire to place her head down on the table and go to sleep was overwhelming. Celeste looked at her and motioned for Street to come help her up.

"Alex, you are coming to the villa with Valtteri and I. You need to rest."

Lacking the energy to argue, Alex let Street help her up from the chair.

"Nice work out there, Alex," Street said as he guided her out the door.

She smiled at him and then caught Caleb's reflection in the window as he glared at Street.

If looks could kill.

CHAPTER 11

The senator strolled into his study, a warm, wood-paneled sanctuary with a coffered ceiling and four glass trophy cases mounted into the custom walnut cabinetry. One contained a signed Lionel Messi jersey. Another, Michael Jordan's iconic 1998 NBA Finals Last Dance jersey, which he'd picked up at auction for a cool $10.1 million. In the third, the Dunlop Maxply Fort tennis racket John McEnroe used to defeat Björn Borg to claim the 1981 Wimbledon Championship was cradled in its stand. A fourth contained the man's most prized and illicit sports memorabilia—Jack Nicklaus's first green jacket, size 43 regular, from the Masters. The Golden Bear had won six Masters tournaments at the Augusta National Golf Club in Georgia, but this first winning jacket had slipped into his possession courtesy of a mutual acquaintance who knew of the senator's admiration for the famous golfer and course architect. And all it had cost him was a series of curried political favors.

He slid the pocket doors of his study closed behind him, shutting out the sounds of ordinary life—if one could call his that—and the boisterous clamor of his five young grandchildren, visiting the country estate in Northern Virginia for the weekend. He padded in stockinged feet across the plush, madder-red silk Persian carpet he had acquired from a black marketeer in Isfahan during one of his clandestine visits there decades ago, a city two hundred miles south of the outskirts of Tehran where he had been touring as a political wannabe. The man's gang—*associates*—had liberated the priceless carpet from within the city's central mosque at an enormous price. The city's conservatives, who hailed from the more austere section of the metropolis, and therefore controlled access to the mosque north of the Zayandeh River, didn't sell their antiquities or history cheaply. The senator had paid a suitcase full of cash for the transaction, but it had additionally cost him the Rolex on his wrist to get the carpet smuggled out of Iran and to his home. His Rolex was a small price to pay for a logistical transaction that had been essentially an act of faith, as befitted a treasure stolen from a place of worship.

Such was the nature of alliances, frequently comprised of a mutual desire for guaranteed survival, supported by implied existential threats amid costly and nuanced transactions.

The man lowered himself into a chair and tapped a remote, switching on the large-screen television on the wall. While the anchorman read from his teleprompter, the scrolling chyron covered the latest global sports headlines: Canada defeated Australia in the finals of the Davis Cup. Max Verstappen won the Formula 1 Dutch Grand Prix. Bayer Leverkusen advanced over Atlético Madrid in the UEFA Champions League group stage. Finland and Denmark had been tied 1–1 at the Helsinki Olympic Stadium when their match was suspended during the first half of play following a nationwide power outage across Finland.

There it was.

The senator unmuted the TV, leaving the volume on low as he waited for the anchor to get around to the news report. While he waited, he removed a Cohiba Behike 56 from the wooden humidor lined with Spanish cedar that sat atop his desk and absent-mindedly rolled the body of the cigar between his thumb and fingers. He drew it under his nose and inhaled deeply, as if he were judging an ultra-scarce glass of Rémy Martin Louis XIII Rare Cask Grande Champagne Cognac.

He popped a hole in the cap and lit it, then swiveled his chair toward the glass door to the garden, opening it to allow the blue smoke to float weightlessly into the cool morning air.

Puffing, puffing, puffing, savoring the pungent chocolate and coffee flavors, feeling the spicy burn in his mouth, spitting the rogue flake of tobacco from the tip of his tongue.

He settled back in his leather chair, legs outstretched and ankles crossed, smoking the cigar that had been hand-rolled at the El Laguito factory in the tree-lined Miramar section of Havana, its importation to America circumventing the laws prohibiting such transactions. Unlike the Cuban workers who labored to make these, the man's life was blessed with riches beyond measure, and it would only keep getting better for him and his children's children, even if it meant leaving a little destruction in his wake to ensure that the destiny of his scions could be realized.

Sacrifices would have to be made in the short term, but doing so would yield dividends he could only have dreamed of a few short years ago.

His ears perked up when he heard the anchorman say, "And in Finland tonight . . ."

He spun his chair around and turned up the volume as the correspondent in Finland came on-screen, a pretty young woman holding a microphone emblazoned with the network's logo.

"Thanks, Chris." She was cast in a faint glow from light powered by generators in front of a row of dark buildings. "I'm standing near the waterfront in the Ullanlinna district in central Helsinki, Finland's capital. Tonight, this city's residents, along with almost five and a half million of their countrymen, were plunged into darkness just after 9 P.M. while many were still enjoying dinner and drinks in the restaurants, bars, and clubs behind me." Her English was flawless even though her accent revealed she was obviously a native Finnish speaker. The shot cut to shaky footage that looked as if it had been filmed with a mobile phone. "When it became apparent that the electricity would not come back on right away, people started flowing out into the streets with an almost party-like atmosphere.

"But while some found it entertaining, the impact on emergency services like the nation's hospitals could be more serious." The image on-screen cut to a scene inside a hospital. "Though backup power was

immediately and seamlessly provided by the hospital's inline generators, the administrator I spoke with expressed concerns over the scale
and possible longevity of the crisis. A spokesperson at FinnPower, the
country's energy regulator, said they do not yet know when the grid
will be back online, as they are still trying to determine the cause of the
computer glitch that disrupted the distribution system.

"They were quick to add that the five nuclear reactors that account
for fully one-third of Finland's power-generating capacity are all online
and functioning normally, thanks in part to the adoption over the past
several years of so-called smart grid technology designed to restore systems to full functionality quickly and safely. Chris, back to you in the
newsroom."

The man watching the news from his study took another puff of his
cigar.

Everyone seemed rather too cheerful, but that wouldn't last long.

CHAPTER 12

Alex awoke in a canopied bed surrounded by lemon-chiffon-colored walls. Daylight had set her room aglow. The blue skies outside her windows were dotted with puffy white clouds suspended low over glittering azure waters and rocky, green-flecked peaks in the near distance. She had slept like the dead. Her muscles protested, and she was quickly reminded of her various aches and pains as she got out of bed.

She padded barefoot across the wide-planked white oak floors and slid open the patio doors, letting in a temperate breeze that fluttered the sheer linen curtains. The view was magnificent as she cast her eyes to where the legs of the Alps dangled into the Mediterranean Sea. It was amazing how the dawn of a new day could expunge the horrors of the day before.

Below her, the verdant lawn joined with an infinity pool that stretched to the edge of the property. A granite deck accented by tall cedars overlooked the town beyond. Madame Clicquot and Valtteri Lehtonen already occupied their chairs around a large table, where a server was delivering a platter of fruit, pastries, and—most important—a pot of coffee.

Celeste caught sight of her on the balcony and waved.

"Be right down," Alex called.

She brushed her teeth, changed into a pair of light slacks and a blouse, and combed through her tangled hair. The cut on her cheek was a bit crusty but hadn't reopened as she slept. On the main floor, she bumped into Street, looking more casual than he had last night in cotton pants, a white linen shirt opened to the third button, and carrying a steaming mug of coffee.

He appeared taller today, too, six feet plus, with dark brown short-cropped hair that showed the first hints of gray around his temples. He had broad shoulders and a well-muscled chest and arms. She was surprised now that she had been able to take him down with such ease last night. But then, in fairness to Street, he *had* been suffering from smoke inhalation at the time. He had the kind of clean-cut, clean-shaven good looks that would definitely make the ladies swoon.

And, Alex thought, *under different circumstances, I might be one of them.*

"Everybody has one of those but me," she said, eyeing his coffee.

"*Aye,* we can fix that," he replied, his Scottish brogue full and thick. "Follow me." He led her into the kitchen toward a series of drip coffeemakers, percolators, and a monstrous, plumbed-in espresso machine. "Pick your poison."

She grabbed an American-sized mug and topped it up from one of the pots, then added three sugars.

"How you doing?" he asked, studying her. He had the tone of one of her former commanding officers from her Ranger unit. He had been a hard-ass, but he knew how to look after his soldiers—not mothering, not hovering, but caring.

"Fine," she said as she rolled her sore shoulder and winced.

"I see. Not the sharing type, eh?"

"Something like that."

"I get it."

She knew for a fact he didn't—*couldn't*—get it, but that didn't matter. She had never been one to complain about that, or anything else. Like her late husband had been fond of reminding her, she was too proud to gripe about anything. Oversharing of her personal feelings or aches and pains—in fact, *any* sharing of personal matters—could only serve to damage her reputation with the incumbent risk of being labeled weak, a tag that she and anyone who knew her would most emphatically reject.

Having moved between units, and even from one military occupational specialty to another, she found that she had to prove herself
to each new team; that the Ranger scroll, though it should have been
enough, often wasn't for some. So, admitting she was hurting from
being battered during last night's hostilities was something she would
never do.

She sipped from her mug and squeezed her eyes shut. The sensation
of that first hit of flavor from the dark-roasted arabica beans brought
back a distant memory. That had been after a long night, too. A highly
motivated group of al-Qaeda fighters had attacked their compound,
a forward operating base two miles east of Khost, Afghanistan. They
were determined to purge the American infidels from the region. Alex
had killed several of the aggressors, including two suicide bombers,
before they could penetrate the defensive line formed by the HESCO
barrier surrounding the base and detonate their deadly ordnance. But
others had made it inside, and the battle had raged on for hours, her
unit sustaining heavy casualties. Among them were several CIA officers attached to the mission. Eventually, her Ranger unit gained the
upper hand, and afterward, the coffee in the canteen, while not as
robust, had imparted comfort, not unlike the feeling she was experi-
encing now.

Today, just as then, morning had come, she had opened her eyes, the
coffee was hot, and she was still breathing. Any day that started out that
way was off to a great start.

"I know that look, Alex."

She snapped back to the present and sized him up. "Who dares
wins?" she guessed, citing the motto of the United Kingdom's Special
Air Service, a Special Forces unit of the British Army.

"Aye, SAS for sure," he said with a wink.

"You're Scottish."

"Aye, we're still part of the United Kingdom after all."

"Of course," she said. "I didn't mean anything by that."

"I'm pulling your leg, Alex. And you, I understand, were Army."

"Combat medic. 75th Ranger Regiment."

"And a sniper?" he asked, squinting, clearly not quite sure how to ask the obvious question about how a woman could have been deployed with that military occupational specialty.

She saw his confusion and filled in the blanks.

"Our unit was on an op, and I was asked to look after two wounded Special Forces soldiers performing overwatch from a grape hut on the side of a mountain." She left out the fact that one of them later became her husband. "While I was looking after them, my unit's convoy ran into an ambush—IEDs, technical vehicles, swarms of bad guys. Next thing we knew, the grape hut we were in came under RPG and small-arms fire. One of the operators was KIA, and the other was too badly wounded to manage the sniper rifle—the TAC-50—so he made me pick it up while he spotted for me and coached me through."

"And the rest, as they say, is history? Is that it?" Street asked.

"Something like that. Plus, I did a stint with a covert intelligence unit after Uncle Sam's Army didn't want a girl playing with them in a combat zone anymore."

Street was shaking his head. "Of course," he said. "You're clearly the fairer sex, lassie."

She shot him a look. He was needling her, but it was hard not to let a remark like that get under her Kevlar. Some wounds don't heal.

Street saw it but only smiled, clearly relishing the fact he had found a button to push.

"It's different now. The military's come around," she told him.

He raised an eyebrow.

Not wanting to get into a political discussion, Alex said, "From one soldier to another, big man, our greatest talent might be knowing where the chow line is, so . . ."

"Oh, right," he said, jostling his belly. "Let's get some grub."

They strolled across the lawn next to the pool and joined Clicquot and Valtteri at the table. Celeste was back in possession of her usual of-fice demeanor, which was to say subdued and deeply analytical. Given the previous night's events, the mood was understandably somber. In total, two guests, one deckhand, and two of Street's team had been killed aboard *Aurora*. As for the badgers, it was unclear. They presumed that at least sixteen had assaulted the ship, but it was less clear how many had perished in the fight. Authorities had found nine bodies aboard from among those who had attacked the yacht. Three corpses were fished out of the sea, but the search was ongoing. Three were in custody. And any others who survived had gotten away. The captain had retaken the helm prior to the yacht running aground on the shores of Cap Martin, on the far side of Monaco. Arguably, her computerized navigation wouldn't have allowed her to collide with land, but everyone was grateful the system hadn't been tested to that extent.

"The futility of the incident is staggering," Celeste said. "So many lives lost. And to what end?"

It was a rhetorical statement, but Street responded anyway.

"I'm afraid we don't know yet, Madame Clicquot. But we'll see where the evidence leads, insofar as we're able, given that it's an open investigation with French authorities. And, of course, we will cooperate fully with their efforts and help where we can. I hope to know something concrete soon. Meanwhile," he added, indicating toward the highly visible presence of guards around the property, "we have upped our complement of personnel on-site and will be implementing changes to our daily operations. At least temporarily."

She nodded. Valtteri wrapped his hand around hers.

"Where is Mikko?" Alex asked.

"Gone home," Valtteri replied, somewhat aloofly.

Alex looked over at Celeste. "Care to tell me what he was doing onboard?"

"Alex, dear, I told you, he is an old friend of Valtteri's."

She regarded her former boss skeptically. She was unconvinced. "Uh-huh."

"For heaven's sake, you have a suspicious mind."

She hadn't yet pieced things together. Ostensibly, and irrespective of his diplomatic credentials, Mikko Selänne was just another passenger aboard *Aurora*. But Selänne was Finland's permanent representative to NATO—a full NATO ambassador—and as such, the head of his country's diplomatic mission to the Alliance. Despite Celeste and Valtteri's insistence, the odds of him being merely a casual guest on the cruise were as good as Alex not being a CIA officer on a covert operations team.

In other words, none whatsoever.

"You know that if there's more to it, I'll find out, right?"

"What would we be hiding?" Celeste said, glancing at Valtteri and Street for support.

On cue, Street added, "After hearing of last night's events, Finland's president, Jarkko Ruusu, recalled Ambassador Selänne to Finland, as was entirely appropriate. A protection detail arrived early this morning to escort him home."

She let her suspicions slide for the time being. "Humor me with a theory, Street. Why'd this happen?"

"It's too early—"

"I said humor me, not bullshit me. What's your working theory?"

He paused. "Valtteri is one of the world's richest citizens. And some of his companies attract a lot of attention from competitors, business rivals, and even state actors interested in seeing him fail or wanting to steal corporate secrets. I'm sure you can appreciate that there have been frequent attempts at espionage, network penetrations, and the like. Kidnapping for ransom—"

"Or worse," added Celeste.

"Yes, ma'am, or worse. These things are not unheard of, even in this day and age."

"Attempted assassination?" Alex asked.

"Maybe."

"To what end? Eliminate a rival? Regime change?"

"It wouldn't be out of the realm of possibility," said Street. "Our working theory for the time being is that Valtteri is still a target for whoever set last night's deeds in motion. We'll continue to let the police investigation lead wherever it leads."

Valtteri jumped in. "But as to the question of regime change, Alex, I don't suspect that anyone inside my company would have been involved—"

"—but we're not ruling anything out," added Street.

She nodded as she tore into a warm croissant. Flakes of buttery pastry flew off like grenade shrapnel. She glanced again at Valtteri, who was gently caressing Celeste's hand in his own. He smiled warmly at her, but even so, a shiver ran up Alex's spine.

Was that the chilly morning breeze off the Med, or . . . ?

She considered *Aurora* and its sheer scale. The last few years had revealed just how many megayachts were owned by bad actors— transnational criminals, Saudi princes who liked having journalists cut up into more manageable chunks inside embassies, Russian oligarchs—any of whom could easily provide the funding to plan and execute an operation of the sort that had played out last night. The money required for such an undertaking, even if it stretched into the millions, was a pittance compared to the daily revenue from their quasi-legal enterprises. It might even be a tax-deductible business expense in Sergachev's Russia.

President Sergachev himself, despite topping the sanctions lists of every country in the West, still managed to surreptitiously own a fleet of megayachts. Alex was sure that if she looked closely enough at the twenty or thirty luxury ships dotting the large bay in front of her, she'd find more than a few that could be traced back to a Russian energy or petrochemical baron who had sworn fealty to the president-for-life Sergachev. And, while nominally the owners themselves, she would bet that the boat, in fact, belonged to the Russian president, arguably the wealthiest man in the world.

No, Alex had always considered megayachts the domain of dudes of the sketchiest kind. So, despite Celeste's apparent fondness for Valtteri and his pronounced Boy Scout credentials, she couldn't help but feel wary of their host.

She scanned the property and observed that Street's team had the place covered from top to bottom. She had to wonder, though, was everyone here as safe as Street believed or let on? And, among them, who was at greatest risk?

She found it hard to believe that, after last night's failed mission, there wouldn't be another attack.

But on who?

CHAPTER 13

The stately redbrick Victorian townhome needed work. It stood wedged between buildings of a similar provenance in the tony neighborhood of Logan Circle, trapped in flux between the White House and the less gentrified sections of the U Street Corridor.

But inside the home, Kadeisha Thomas, the first African American deputy director of the Central Intelligence Agency, slept soundly in the queen-sized bed she shared with her king-sized husband, a former pro linebacker. But her sleep was disturbed by something buzzing like a mosquito on steroids. She rolled onto her other side and brushed her hand past her ear as if swatting away the pesky insect. Then, after a beat and with the mosquito still buzzing, she opened one eye. The clock on the nightstand read 4:37. Next to it, the glowing display of her mobile phone cast shadows on the ceiling. She thrust her hand out and picked it up. The name Viking burned brightly into her consciousness.

"It's zero-dark-there-better-be-bodies-o'clock," she said. "How many?"

Caleb's muffled voice crackled through the tiny speaker. "Somewhere between a handful and a baker's dozen, ma'am. So far, they've found nine dead, but there could be more. Three are in custody."

"Sugar honey iced tea," she whispered.

"What?"

"It's an acronym; spell it out." She swung her legs off the side of the bed and did toe curls in the carpet fibers. "Okay, Viking, give me the bottom line up front."

He laid it out for her. As he spoke, she climbed out of bed so she wouldn't wake her husband and ambled to the bathroom, straightening her Alabama Crimson Tide V-neck nightshirt. She perched on the edge of the double sink, listening to his sitrep.

Christ, she thought. *What a shit show.* "That all of it?"

"More or less."

"Is it who we thought?"

"Fits the profile, ma'am. No positive IDs on any of the bodies yet, but they're males, most likely Central or South Asian origin. The three in custody are starting to sing—in Dari," he added. "We'll know more soon, ma'am."

"We better. The president doesn't like uncertainty." Then, not quite an afterthought, "How is she?"

"I haven't spoken to her yet this morning, but she nearly drowned last night. She's resilient, though. She'll live."

"Yes, she is. But need I remind you what *sheep-dipped* means?"

"No, ma'am, you did that last night."

"Well, as your superior, let me do it again. It implies a low-profile operator, usually someone separate from the military but actually given a covert assignment as a clandestine intelligence officer with CIA. In Alex's case, she was sheep-dipped from the FBI because of her military intelligence and operations background. Does that sound familiar, Viking?"

"Yes, ma'am, it rings a bell."

"That is, after all, how we brought her on board your cross-matrix team."

"I understand."

"So, I'll say it again, Viking, it's gonna be hard for her to maintain her cover if she keeps blowing shit up and calling attention to herself and the Agency."

"Yes, ma'am. I'll impress upon the local constabulary that their discretion would be appreciated."

"And while you're at it, tell Shooter to keep her head down."

"Of course, ma'am. But in her defense, there wasn't another option. Wrong place, wrong time."

Thomas grunted. "Then get her a compass and a watch. There's no room on the memorial wall for excuses or footnotes next to her star if she gets killed. Tell her to check herself. It's becoming a habit."

"Yes, ma'am."

"I want you both back at Langley. Vacation's over."

"Yes, ma'am."

"And Viking . . ."

"Yes, ma'am?"

"You asked for her, I got her for you. Don't make me regret it. Control your pet shark."

"'Night, ma'am."

"Too late for that. I have to go wake Director Avery now so he can brief POTUS," she said, ending the call.

And Director Avery hates being woken up early even more than I do, she thought as she punched his speed-dial button.

CHAPTER 14

Kadeisha Thomas placed the telephone handset back into its cradle with deliberate care. What she wanted to do was slam it down, but the CIA's deputy director was far too composed to allow herself such an outburst. Temper tantrums were expressions of entitlement, the purview of those raised without self-discipline and from whom she sought to distance herself.

Thomas was the granddaughter of a famed flying ace who had flown a red-tailed P-51 Mustang with the 332nd Fighter Group—the Tuskegee Airmen—during the Second World War. Through diligence and exceptional leadership acumen, she had risen to the level of deputy director of the CIA with an office on the seventh floor in the Original Headquarters Building at Langley. Having been appointed to one of the highest offices in the intelligence community, she would never permit herself to be reduced to the level of her subordinates. Or those to whom she reported.

Growing up in Alabama, her grandfather had taught her that the eyes of the world would always be on her: sizing her up, assessing her worthiness, ready to tell themselves they were right, that people like her didn't belong. She always had to do better, be better—not to prove she was right, but to prove they were wrong.

Vultures, the lot of them. And there were plenty at Langley, ready to swoop in and steal the prize she had rightfully earned and claimed for herself. *The vulture should be the state bird of Virginia,* she thought. *Or Fairfax County, at least.*

Director Avery was fired up, as she had correctly anticipated he would be. He questioned how it was that one of the newest members of one of her special Ground Branch teams—a contractor, no less—had managed to engage in a deadly gunfight at sea, taking the lives of several Afghan mercenaries. Not that he didn't have the right to demand answers, but Avery was a career bureaucrat and a political sycophant who relished making others feel small while stoking the egos of those who could make him feel superior. Like President Moore. But even the director of the CIA wouldn't make her feel small. No one had that power over her.

Intel had confirmed that the men who had attacked *Aurora* were part of a group of former Afghan National Defense and Security Forces soldiers known to farm themselves out to the highest bidder. What was worse was that they had received their training from ISAF, the International Security Assistance Force—a force established by a resolution of the United Nations Security Council after the 9/11 attacks—and by the United States.

The director was primarily annoyed that he was being assailed by other sections within the Agency. The Paris station chief was furious that an op had taken place in his jurisdiction without his knowledge. The South Asia desk was irate for not being informed about a planned op against these soldiers of fortune who had originated from within their zone of operations. And the director himself was exploring his options for how best to explain to the president that a cadre of Afghan mercs had eluded the Agency's detection.

Truth was, they hadn't. Instead, senior case officers and analysts—with her blessing—had chosen not to include this bucket of information in the president's daily brief until the Agency had actionable intelligence on the purpose of this particular Afghan cell. POTUS had other more pressing matters on his plate. It was her call to make, and it had been the right one; though that fact was a little harder to align with the current reality after the events on the Med last night.

It was the worst-kept secret in Washington and within the intelligence community that the director and the deputy director hadn't bonded yet. In fact, they were well into the second half of this president's first term with still no signs of a ceasefire, let alone a détente.

The question remained, did this group pose a threat to America, or its interests and citizens abroad? Or were they acting more akin to an Afghan or Pakistani version of Blackwater, a company of former soldiers available for overt and covert ops on a fee-for-service basis? However much or little it had mattered before last night, Martel's actions would force the administration to respond on multiple fronts. And no president in the history of the union liked to have his actions dictated by the misadventures of a rogue CIA employee. In this, President Taylor Moore was no exception.

"*Fix this!*" the director had ordered her.

CHAPTER 15

T he senator opened his browser to his personalized newsfeed. There
it was. The third story featured a photograph with the caption: OIL
SPILL THREATENS GULF.

Nice caption, he thought.

Emergency Declared After Ghost Ship Causes Phantom Spill, Environmental Disaster Looms

Russian president Dmitry Sergachev has backed a proposal to declare a state of emergency on a federal scale, days after a tanker leaked thirty million liters of light crude oil into the Gulf of Finland, 50 kilometers outside the port in St. Petersburg and 150 kilometers east of Finland's capital, Helsinki. The spilled crude threatens an ecological disaster along the entire length of the fragile Baltic Sea ecosystem.

Authorities in the Regional State Administrative Agency for Eastern Finland had already declared a state of emergency, a move immediately followed by the country's federal government after the oil spilled from a so-called ghost tanker, one of a class of ships generally poorly maintained and in a state of disrepair that skirt international registration and insurance requirements. It is unknown who would be accountable for the cleanup of such a spill, given the lack of insurance by the operators of these vessels.

Russian Federation emergencies minister Sergei Ovechkin called for the spill to be declared a federal emergency—a move that would allow the use of Russia's federal capabilities to tackle the situation at sea.

Russia's Investigative Committee announced it had launched three criminal investigations over environmental violations and detained an employee of the shipping company.

Both Greenpeace and the World Wildlife Fund (WWF) had previously warned about the dangers of such vessels operating in the Baltic region following Western sanctions on Russian oil exports. Both environmental groups issued a joint statement claiming that the spill had the capability of decimating sensitive commercial fishing stocks upon which the Finnish economy depends, and has called for other European and world governments to assist and launch a maritime cleanup operation to save the fisheries and avoid a catastrophic level of pollution washing up on land in both Estonia and Finland as currents spread the spill in several directions.

The senator was pleased that the media was framing the operation as an act of incompetence tied to greed, rather than the planned act of vandalism it was. It had cost a lot of money to stage an event to look so genuinely negligent, mirroring the dire warnings of environmental groups that had been raising the alarm for years.

But he had also heard that, in more political channels, there were rumblings that this was an intentional act bordering on state terrorism, with each side blaming the other. Behind closed doors, Finland and the Nordic Council were accusing Russia's internal security forces of plotting the spill. Russia, meanwhile, had fired back at Western intelligence agencies accusing them of staging the incident to look like Russia was the culprit, in the same way they blamed Russia for vandalizing the Nord Stream 1 and 2 pipelines, major conduits for Russian natural gas deliveries to Germany and points beyond in Europe.

Good. Another successful operation that would cause Finland and NATO to question Russian malfeasance, while Russia would once again feel ganged up on by Western alliances, further raising the tensions of political discourse at both the United Nations and NATO.

He was proud of himself and his team. And why shouldn't he be? Time, effort, and resources had been poured into this operation. And, while it was unlikely war would break out overnight, the kindling was getting drier, the temperature hotter. Going forward, the littlest spark could ignite a conflagration.

Doubts, distrust, whispered accusations. That's how this play would begin, and he was the puppet master.

CHAPTER 16

After a light lunch, Celeste had finally convinced Alex to retreat to her room for a short nap. It was clear that the physical effects of the previous night were still taking their toll on her, but true to form, Alex didn't go down without a fight.

Overlooking a tranquil garden in the corner of the villa, Celeste, Valtteri, and Street convened in Valtteri's office.

"She's finally gone to bed," said Celeste. "Poor thing. And you," she said, turning to Street. "You seem to have hit it off with her."

"You sound surprised."

"Perhaps a little. She's not exactly subtle, our Alex, is she?"

"As subtle as a charging bull," Street said.

Valtteri laughed. "Please, Street. Enlighten us with your professional assessment."

"Your Alex has a certain irresistible pull on people, that's all."

Celeste smiled. "Mr. Street," she said. "You've summed it up rather adeptly. I've never met anyone who didn't fall under her spell. She is a formidable woman."

"Aye, that she is."

She considered him for a moment. His response highlighted what she admired about Alex. Countries had fought wars over women of lesser beauty, that was true. But more than that, Alexandra Martel had a rare combination of intellect, charm, and self-confidence. There was a brightness about her that glowed from within.

Celeste thought about her own experiences as a young, attractive female police officer in France and understood many of the obstacles Alex must have faced throughout her career. Yet Alex had not shrunk away from her male-dominated vocation, her true calling. She had, in fact, embraced it, and excelled beyond anyone's wildest imaginings, against all odds. She was exceptional in every role she tackled.

"Are you going to tell her everything?" asked Valtteri, breaking into her thoughts as if he knew what she was thinking.

"I was prepared to," she said. "It's why I wanted to speak to her in private last night, why we sat down together on the boat just before you arrived. I had talked it over with Ambassador Selänne. He agreed that Alex's abilities as an investigator could be beneficial to us. But after the attack on *Aurora*, I'm not sure we should involve her."

"She's already involved," said Street.

"Perhaps. But first, let's examine why *Aurora* was attacked last night. To begin with, it occurred while Finland's ambassador to NATO was aboard. He and I were discussing what to do regarding what is known about the disruption operations targeting Finland that their intelligence service says can be linked to Russia."

"And is it Russia?" asked Valtteri.

"Let's just say it's easy to point your finger at the bully in the playground, but that doesn't mean they're always the ones that cut the chains on the swing set."

"I see. Interesting example. And who could have known Ambassador Selänne was even going to be aboard?" asked Valtteri.

"The better question," said Street, "is who *didn't* know he would be there. Anyone could have pieced that together from any number of open sources of information."

"So, Ambassador Selänne and Celeste were the targets," concluded Valtteri.

"Plausible," agreed Celeste. "Or, it could have been an attack on Interpol generally but directed against me specifically. We've been swamped the past few months with taking apart transnational criminal organizations. They don't react lightly to having their global influence and finances vaporized."

"True, Madame Clicquot," said Street. "Or maybe the Russians simply wanted to kill that other Interpol poster child."

She looked at him. "Alex?" She hadn't really considered that possibility, and it made her shudder. Alex was, in many ways, the child she never had. They had drawn close, as two women with shared experiences do. But it was more than that. Alex displayed loyalty to her and had risked her own life to save hers and Valtteri's. That was loyalty on another level entirely.

"You said it yourself—she's not exactly subtle," Street continued. "That tends to upset a lot of people. Especially if her actions interfered with their well-constructed plans, as they did not so long ago."

"Seems too heavy-handed, even with your sound reasoning, Mr. Street. Besides, I believe that the entire incident was resolved following the events in Paris. It's rumored that President Sergachev himself had a hand in cleaning house."

"It could have been an attack on me," said Valtteri. "I have many business rivals that would like to see me out of the way."

"That's cute, dear," she said, lightly touching his hand.

"I'm serious."

"I know you are, and I'm not trying to be dismissive, but it's a pretty strong tactic to use against a business rival, even when there is so much at stake. Attacking you at your home or at a public venue, perhaps. But a maritime assault as sophisticated as the one used last night to eliminate a rival would be farfetched, even with billions of dollars at stake."

"She's right," said Street. "Nevertheless, we'll need to keep an open mind, at least until the police have wrapped up their inquiries."

"Sooner or later," she agreed, "the French authorities will determine who was responsible for putting last night's events in motion, and they'll tell Interpol. So, as much as I had been hoping to bring Alex in on our suspicions unofficially, I don't think it would be fair to involve her now.

With the level of infamy the attack has generated, though, it will only be a matter of time before she finds out."

"She could use her considerable resources to get answers, couldn't she?" Valtteri said.

"Yes, she could. But at this point, that might not be wise. The United States has no official capacity in this investigation, so I hardly think involving a CIA officer—a clandestine one at that—would be prudent."

"I've updated Mikko with the information we have on the mercenaries," said Street. "The ambassador will take what he knows to his prime minister, and then he and Finnish intelligence can decide how best to interpret last night's incident. As for us, we will maintain our elevated security posture. We may not be out of the woods just yet."

CHAPTER 17

It was late afternoon when Alex awoke. She headed downstairs and through the rooms of the villa, searching for the others. Hearing the tinkle of a glass from the covered patio, she headed in that direction. Caleb stood alone, mixing himself a Manhattan.

"I'll take one of those," said Alex.

Caleb turned, smiling as he took her in. "Coming right up."

"Where is everyone?"

"Getting ready for dinner, I guess."

He handed her the drink and started fixing himself a new one. As she was reaching past him to snatch an orange slice from a tray, he turned toward her. Her face came so close to his that she could feel the heat of him. She breathed in his scent. Their lips almost touched. She stared at them for a moment too long and felt a warm glow spread down her neck and across her chest before it settled in her stomach. The gravity of his pull on her made her knees weak. Her cheeks flushed as their eyes locked. And then he smiled.

At that moment a member of the house staff appeared to replenish the drinks cart. Caleb abruptly stepped back, picking up his glass.

"Cheers," he said.

Alex was jolted from her trance. She awkwardly lifted her drink to her lips. They practically sizzled as they touched the ice-cold Manhattan. She downed half of it in one shot.

"Cheers," she stammered back.

What was I thinking?

Caleb didn't say anything. He just gave her one of his patented, goofy smiles.

Just as she was about to blurt something out before the thought and the words had fully formed, his mobile phone rang. He checked the display, then took his glass and walked out toward the pool.

Saved by the bell, she thought.

But she wasn't sure to whom the thought applied.

CHAPTER 18

Kadeisha Thomas fished her secure mobile phone from a desk drawer and tapped the speed-dial button for Caleb. He answered after the third ring.

"Ma'am," came the voice on the other end of the call.

"Not waking you, am I, Viking?"

"Hardly."

"Is Shooter with you?"

He gazed back up the lawn to where she was walking barefoot in the grass admiring Valtteri's well-tended gardens.

"She is."

"I expected a sitrep from you earlier."

"Yes, ma'am. There was nothing more to report since our last call." He paused. "Our local friends are still reviewing the game stats. I read the report you transmitted. Pretty much as we expected."

"Yes, their preliminary findings are consistent with what we expected. We know the *who*, but we're still missing the *why*."

"I assume we don't yet know who funded the op, either. Or do you?"

"No, Viking, I don't know." As soon as the words left her lips, she chastised herself for sounding defensive, like so many of the men around her frequently did. She modulated her tone and carried on. "You know what I know. But frankly, once you're back here, we'll be leaving the matter in the hands of French internal security at the DGSI to sort out."

"Shooter's not going to like that, ma'am."

"Shooter doesn't run the Directorate of Operations."

"No, ma'am, that's not how I meant it."

She understood his point. Almost getting killed had left Alex with skin in the game. Literally. It was personal. No one liked being shut out when things got personal. "At this point, it's a matter for our French allies until proven otherwise, so it'll remain solely in the hands of the DGSI. They'll keep our Paris station updated if appropriate. And Shooter better learn to separate her *personal* interests from the *actual* interests of the United States."

"I had a similar conversation with her not that long ago," he said.

"Good. We'll debrief when you get here in the morning."

Thomas ended the call and set her phone on the desk, swiveling her chair to gaze out over the forest of flowering dogwoods glowing brilliant scarlet beyond the Memorial Garden in the late-day September sunlight. The long shadow cast by the OHB at sunset seemed to stretch all the way to the Potomac.

There was a knock at the door.

"Come," she called.

She shouldn't have been surprised to see who was standing there. But she was.

Here's one of Virginia's state birds now.

Terry "Hacksaw" Gault was the associate deputy director for operations at the Defense Intelligence Agency, a sister agency to the CIA that specialized in defense and foreign military intelligence. Gault had commanded DIA's special operations forces within the agency's Defense Clandestine Service, or DCS, before becoming an interrogation expert at the tail end of the Global War on Terrorism. It was then that he earned his moniker, Hacksaw, but Thomas never cared enough to inquire exactly how. Most of the time, such matters were best left to the preserve of myth, rumor, and folklore.

Also, the less you know, she had often quipped, *the less you have to lie to the polygraph or under oath before the Senate Select Committee on Intelligence. Plausible denial.*

Now it was Hacksaw's job to oversee all of DCS.

"I hope I'm not bothering you, Deputy Director Thomas."

"Not at all, Associate Deputy Director Gault," she lied.

* * *

Caleb heard the click of Deputy Director Thomas's not-so-subtle sign-off in his ear and tucked his phone back into his pocket. Dealing with Mustang was one thing, but now he had to go back and face Shooter. If he had to choose who to piss off, he would pick his boss over Alex ninety-nine times out of a hundred.

She had been right there in front of him. *Right there.* How many times had he pictured that moment, imagined the outcome? Her breath had brushed his lips. Her skin radiated that sweet *woman* scent, inviting and alluring, hypnotic in its pull on him. It made his nostrils flare. Even without alcohol on his brain, her effect on him was intoxicating. Her eyes had locked on his, and what had he done? He had . . . smiled. Not kissed her, not taken her hand in his, not reached up to gently touch her hair or to whisper something profound, or at least intelligible. He froze. And then he smiled. Like an imbecile.

He took a long sip of his Manhattan as he walked around the pool. From the first time he'd laid eyes on Alex, she had bewitched him. He was intrigued by her service record and accomplishments. She held the world record for the longest kill shot from her time in Iraq—a sniper extraordinaire. He was fascinated by her fiercely independent personality and constantly amazed by her tactical prowess and her uncanny ability to not get killed. It took a certain kind of skill and not just luck to survive in one battle, let alone as many as she had been in. Beyond that, she was as pretty as any woman he had known in a long, long time.

He made his way back to her and found her lounging in one of the plush deck chairs. She looked up as he approached.

"Bad news?" she asked.

"That was Deputy Director Thomas on the phone. We fly out of Nice first thing in the morning," he said. "Mustang wants us back in DC."

"I thought we were going to stay longer."

"Vacation's over."

"But aren't we going to help with this investigation?"

His eyes bored into hers. "Who do you work for?"

"I know who I work for, Caleb, but between what happened on the *Aurora* last night and what Celeste was going to tell me, I think we should stay longer."

"If you think Madame Clicquot has something important to tell you, you should walk in there and ask her what it is. Either she'll tell you or she won't, but—"

"That's not how I would approach an obviously delicate matter with the secretary general of Interpol. Something had her rattled, and I know she was eager to talk to me about it."

"Not our problem, Alex."

"Give me another twenty-four hours. I'll be on an afternoon flight tomorrow—"

"You'll be on a morning flight with me." He took a beat and drew a breath. "Alex, your boss and your boss's boss have concerns over what happened last night, and none of them have to do with the *why* so much as the *who*—meaning *you,* and your involvement in yet another high-profile incident. Now, those are her words, not mine, but still, I'm heading to DC first thing in the morning, and in case there was any doubt in your mind, you're coming, too. That's an order, Martel."

CHAPTER 19

Dr. Nikolas Kapanen studied the computer monitor and read the chart, summarizing for himself with clinical dispassion the case before him. The twelve-year-old boy had fallen from his speeding electric scooter a few blocks from the hospital and struck his head on the interlocking brick roadway. EMS responded, and a paramedic had intubated the unresponsive child en route to the emergency department. On arrival, the child's airway was patent, and medics were assisting ventilations, but the boy remained unconscious. A respiratory therapist was in the room with him now, connecting him to a ventilator.

Kapanen rubbed his chin and sighed deeply. The X-ray and ancillary reports showed a depressed skull fracture, complex maxillofacial fractures, a subdural hematoma, lacerations, abrasions, contusions, and a closed fracture of his right humerus—broken bones and other injuries to go along with his severe TBI, a potentially life-altering traumatic brain injury.

He wished they'd outlaw those damn e-scooters. ER and hospital admissions had surged proportionately with the growth in their popularity. Everybody rode them like they were Kimi Räikkönen on too much Red Bull—no helmets and seemingly no common sense.

It wasn't looking good. Kapanen had a granddaughter the same age. The resemblance was uncanny and disturbing to the emergency medicine specialist, right down to their hair color and length. He had been a physician for the better part of four decades, and every few years, he had to take a step back from treating a patient who reminded him of his sister, brothers, mother, or father. It was an occupational hazard. Having empathy for one's patients was never a bad thing, but when he started seeing in them his close relatives, identifying with them on a personal level, he knew he'd crossed the line.

The telltale sound of the ventilator pulsing air through the patient circuit told him the respiratory therapist had completed hooking the boy up to it. The child's parents still weren't there, but the police officer had assured him they would be arriving soon. That was something else Kapanen wasn't looking forward to. He had spoken to the boy's father on the phone to provide an update and obtain consent, but it would be a whole different ball game once they arrived and saw their baby hooked up to life support.

He was standing outside the sliding glass doors to the boy's room when a nurse called him back to the station.

"What is it?" he asked.

"You have to see this," she said.

He walked back around the nursing station counter and stared at the computer monitor. The entire screen was red. At the top was a yellow hammer and sickle, like the one on the flag of the former Soviet Union. There were several lines of Cyrillic text in bold white font, followed by the translated text in the paragraph below it.

Этот компьютер и сеть были заблокированы и зашифрованы.

Ваша система и периферийные устройства больше не работают.

This computer and network have been locked and encrypted.

Your system and peripherals are no longer operational.

To fix this, deposit €100,000.00 in cryptocurrency to help-decryptme through this hyperlink (an interface window will open). Once the ransom is paid, enter the decryption code in the space below.

DO NOT:

-attempt to rename encrypted files.

-attempt to recover the system with third-party software.

-turn this computer off.

If you do, all system files and data will be

permanently deleted and unrecoverable!!!

Enter Decryption Code: _____

"One hundred thousand euros? What is this? Is this a joke?" He knew what it was. And he knew that it wasn't. "Call IT and security—" But just as the words left his lips, the lights went out.

CHAPTER 20

It was a little after 10 A.M. when Caleb turned off Dolley Madison Boulevard onto the campus of CIA headquarters in Langley, Virginia. The drive over from the family restaurant on Chain Bridge Road in McLean had taken only minutes.

Alex had skipped the meal offerings aboard the transatlantic flight, and by the time they landed at Dulles, she was famished. So when Caleb said he knew just the spot for breakfast, she was all in. Turned out the thick-cut French toast drenched in syrup with bacon and coffee had hit their mark perfectly. Caleb had opted for the Western skillet of home fries, diced ham, onions, green peppers, and melted cheese, topped with two eggs over easy. When the two of them got back into his Chevy Tahoe, neither was sure they'd be able to do their seat belts back up, but they managed.

At the main gate on the Langley campus, the security officer scanned their IDs and vehicle tag before allowing them through. Caleb gave a two-fingered salute and drove a short distance before making a left. Then he turned left again, away from both the Original and New Headquarters Buildings.

"Aren't we meeting Mustang in her office?"

Caleb said nothing. He wended his way through a forest of trees until an all-white, two-story home—*Cape Cod? Georgian Colonial?* Alex wasn't sure—loomed in front of them atop a grassy knoll.

"Where are we?"

"The doghouse," he replied.

He pulled into a curving driveway and drove up a rise to the front of the residence, parking in the shade of a tall conifer. Alex stepped out of the SUV and looked around. It was hard to imagine they were still on the grounds of the George Bush Center for Intelligence—CIA headquarters. Their view was all trees and grass, the sound around them a tranquil mix of birdsong and rustling leaves.

She followed him as he walked around to the back of the property.

"What is this place?" she asked again as they proceeded past an enclosed veranda toward a set of doors guarded by a pair of George Washington captain's chairs.

"Welcome to the Calvert Estate, or as it's called now, the Scattergood-Thorne Conference Center."

Three dormers protruded from the second story as if to accentuate the anachronism of an early-twentieth-century historical residence existing side by side with one of the most secure buildings on Earth.

They entered the walled-in veranda bathed in sunlight that streamed in through mullioned windows. It was decorated with heavily cushioned wicker chairs and patio tables topped with seasonal floral arrangements. Inside the house, the room was laid out with rows of folding chairs. Thirty or so people were listening to an unseen presenter.

Caleb silently opened the door that divided the two spaces, and the pair took up positions at the back of the room as Deputy Director Kadeisha Thomas addressed a class of men and women who directed their rapt attention on her.

"The intelligence community," she said, "indeed the very mission of the Central Intelligence Agency, is one that many at the so-called end of the Cold War thought would be obsolete." She paused to allow chuckles from the crowd to die down. "You're a bright group. I usually have to paint a more vivid picture when I do a version of this talk for members of Congress." More chuckles. "Like you, the Agency knew better than to believe the Cold War was over." She paced at the front of the room like a football coach giving her pregame speech. "We have constantly had to evolve, to absorb the mantle of new challenges that took shape before us. A rise in radical extremism and a man named Osama bin Laden, or OBL as we called him around here . . . among other things." More laughter. "He and others like him helped us redefine and reinvigorate the mission of the Agency." She became animated and her face took on an expression of raw gravitas as she spoke. "Iran, Libya, Syria, Somalia, the Horn of Africa, Central America, the Middle East, the Far East, Yemen, the Caucasus, Eastern Europe, and other republics of the former Soviet Union—the once supposedly great USSR—and now Russia, Ukraine, et cetera, et cetera, not to mention the dozens and hundreds of sub-state actors, cause us to constantly reevaluate what we do and how we achieve our ends. To misquote a misquote, 'Reports of my death are greatly exaggerated.' The Central Intelligence Agency is not dead and is every bit as vital to the security of these United States of America now as it was during the Second World War and in the days of the OSS Jedburgh teams your instructors at the Farm already talked to you about.

"And yet, in the past few years, we have faced even greater challenges, and not all of them from our enemies. Some in the highest offices of this land have questioned not only our mission but our values, our commitment, our ethos, our effectiveness." She paused to make eye contact with individuals around the room, men and women who seemingly hung on every word. "And yes. Even. Our. Integrity. There are those who have attempted to erode this nation's belief in our trustworthiness, the very currency that underpins everything we do, in order to sow discord and promote their personal agendas, and in a cynical attempt to heighten their own fame—or infamy—within the polarized audiences over which they hold sway and from every nook and cranny of the political spectrum.

"Without trust, without faith—ours and of those we serve—who are we? What good can we do this great nation without the confidence of our citizens, our partners, our allies, and our assets who entrust their very lives and the lives of their families into our care? But let me assure you, we have been systematically rebuilding all our disciplines at CIA with a focused strategy and with the utmost diligence. The future of this great agency will be based on achieving capabilities in providing the kind of intelligence our customers—that is, POTUS, Congress, the

American people, and our allies—deserve. The president has ensured that this will be the case. As an intelligence agency, and as the premier such agency in the world, we constantly learn and improve, adapt and overcome, and at no time will we ever allow our integrity or our willingness to make difficult decisions to be compromised. By anyone.

"I thank you for your attention . . . and your patience." Laughter from the group. "And I wish you all the very best when you receive your assignments in the coming weeks. There is no more noble purpose than to serve one's country and fellow citizens. The director and I are proud to have you aboard."

Thomas flashed one last smile to the group as they stood and applauded. Then she walked up the center aisle, straight for Caleb and Alex.

"On me," she said, the smile all but vanishing from her lips.

"See?" Caleb whispered. "Doghouse. You go ahead; I'll catch up."

* * *

CALVERT ESTATE, LANGLEY

While Caleb went off to god-knows-where, Thomas led Alex to a room on the second floor that she had commandeered for their meeting. While once upon a time it had likely been the bedroom of one of the building's previous occupants, now it functioned as an administrative hot desk for whoever required the space. And the CIA's deputy director needed it now.

A cabinet holding mementos of CIA tradecraft stood in a corner, and two metal filing cabinets lined the adjacent wall. The deputy director sat behind a large wooden desk. Behind her, in an alcove created for the window, hung an eight-by-ten framed photograph. Pictured was a squad of soldiers, their faces not hidden behind blurred pixels, lined up in front of an Abrams tank. The photographer's elevated position revealed a never-ending desert landscape beyond, littered with the smoldering corpses of Iraqi cars, trucks, tanks, and an assortment of other fighting vehicles.

Alex had seen many pictures of the infamous Highway 80 before. The six-lane road ran between Kuwait City, Kuwait, and Basra, Iraq.

But this image stood out starkly from others she remembered for its depiction of the grimness of the scene contrasted by the smiling faces of the soldiers in the foreground. The more appropriate designation for this highway was the Highway of Death. Alex wondered at the circumstances of this photograph: Had the pictured soldiers just disengaged from a battle? Of the thousands of vehicles destroyed along this section of road, how many had these soldiers accounted for? How many hundreds of lives had just ended, and how many more were slowly ebbing away in and around those vehicles, as unsalvageable as the machinery around them?

She crossed her arms and brought a fist to her lips, getting swept up in the emotional pull of the image frozen in time in the yellowing print behind the glass as if it were a memory of her own making. When she had been in the heat of battle, these sights hadn't disturbed her. But now, years later, images like these triggered something inside her, as if the armor surrounding her soul had been stripped away and the lid opened. Unprotected, she marched through daily life, and every once in a while, she felt the sting as she had never felt it before.

"Did you need me to repeat the question, Martel?"

Alex was tugged back to the here and now. "What? No, sorry, ma'am."

Thomas glanced over her shoulder at the photo. "Mesmerizing, isn't it?"

"Something like that."

"You ever see anything like that in all your days, Martel?"

"Yes. And no, ma'am." Thomas turned to regard her. Alex continued. "I've been on my fair share of battlefields, witnessed a lot of the devastation of war, devastation we made or were a part of making. But this"—she gestured to the photo—"the starkness of it is striking. The destruction goes on forever."

Thomas nodded. "I understand your father led troops during Desert Storm."

"He was a colonel during the first Gulf War, commanding the 1st Armored Division's 1st Brigade at Medina Ridge."

"Hell of a tank battle."

"One of the biggest in history, they say. Top two or three, for sure."

"You come by your battle skills the old-fashioned way, then."

"Ma'am?"

"It's in your blood, Alex."

"Like yours, I suppose."

Thomas gave a hint of a smile. "I was never a soldier. And my grand-father was a fighter pilot, not a ground-pounder."

"Yes, ma'am, but not just any fighter pilot. I heard he was a member of the Tuskegee Airmen. That means he must've kicked open a few doors during his lifetime that others couldn't or wouldn't."

"Yes, he did," she said proudly.

"And for you to be in that chair . . . well, I'm sure I'll never know the half of what it took you to get there."

"You won't." Thomas stood and walked over to a framed black-and-white photo on the opposite wall. "Do you know where we are?" she asked.

Despite the affable tone of their conversation, Alex felt like a high school student caught smoking in the gym. *The vice principal's office?*

"No, ma'am, I'm afraid I don't," she replied, joining the deputy director in examining the print.

The subjects of the grainy photo were two women in their thirties or early forties. They sat in rocking chairs on the porch of a house. Alex looked more closely. It was *this* house before the veranda had been enclosed.

"Any idea who these women are?" asked Thomas.

"Not a clue."

"The lady on the left is Florence Thorne. The other woman is Margaret Scattergood. Do you know what you have in common with them?"

"I don't, Deputy Director Thomas."

"They were activists in the labor movement. Very successful, by all accounts. They were able to buy this five-thousand-square-foot home and the surrounding thirty-two acres of land, so their success, to a certain extent, is an assumption, but I think it's safe to infer it from these facts. Isn't that what we do in intelligence, Martel?"

Alex wasn't sure if she was being baited. "More or less," she answered noncommittally.

"Well, which is it—*more* or *less*?"

"Intelligence work involves the collection of facts and information that is then sent to analysts. The analysts' role is to interpret the information, validate its accuracy, and determine its significance. They decide what is actionable and what can be disregarded."

"Long-winded, but accurate," replied Thomas. "Ten years after they bought the property, Miss Scattergood and Miss Thorne were approached by no less than the United States federal government, wanting to purchase it from them to build more office space. The women sold the property for a tidy sum and negotiated the right to remain living here until their deaths. How do you suppose they achieved that?"

Alex looked more closely at the photo, then turned to look out at the property through the window. "They were ground-breaking, no-holds-barred rebels."

"Hell, yeah. Wouldn't take shit from anybody. Held strong beliefs. Got paid for their knowledge, skills, and expertise in labor rights. Rumor has it many a director of the CIA dined here with them and sent them holiday hams and Christmas turkeys every year to boot. Even had our security teams watch over them. To protect them—not to spy on them."

"Impressive."

"But they continued to walk their own paths, right up to hosting activities of a questionable nature right here at the house. More than a few guerrillas showed up at the front gates of Langley looking for this place."

"Quite the rebels."

"Like I said, Alex, you have a lot in common."

CHAPTER 21

While the deputy director and Alex went off for a little confab, Caleb scanned the historic photographs in the main foyer, reminiscing over his time spent here as both student and guest lecturer to new CIA recruits. He stopped to admire a few photos of some of the handsome dogs that once lived here, being put through their paces on an obstacle course when the Calvert Estate was quite literally the CIA's doghouse. Before it became a conference center, the Scattergood-Thorne residence had housed K-9s. The building and its adjacent property were effectively a kennel and training ground for dog teams. It was a lot less fancy then—some would say downright run-down—but Caleb had enjoyed getting to know the dogs and their handlers back then.

He headed to the kitchen to wrestle a coffee from the fancy machine, a little confused by the steps involved.

"Still preferring the old ways, I see." The voice came at him from behind, and while he hadn't heard it in forever, it still conjured a sour taste in his mouth, like a bad oyster. "I thought cowboy coffee was your thing."

He finally got the pod oriented into the cuppy thing, closed the machine's lid, and hit the button. The coffeemaker made some noise and began spilling out a frothy rendering of rich, black coffee from the spout below.

"It still is. I heard you died in a Bangkok hooker den," Caleb said without looking up. He took his ceramic mug emblazoned with I'M NOT A CIA AGENT and added a hit of raw sugar.

"I think the PC term is *comfort women*."

"Charming. But in your case, I'm sure you meant comfort *girls*."

"I see you're still the asshole I remember from back in the sandbox, Viking."

"I tailor my approach to the audience, Hacksaw." Caleb didn't much appreciate that the man had used his CIA code name but felt no need to show his irritation beyond replying in kind. Instead, he sipped his java, which was hot, strong, and full of flavor. Even Terry Gault couldn't ruin that. He turned to face the associate deputy director for operations of the Defense Intelligence Agency head-on. The man still wore the scars from flaming shrapnel he had caught across his face and forehead in Iraq. Or it might have been Syria. Either way, it was an improvement to his looks and hadn't made his personality appreciably better or worse. "So, what are you doing here?" he asked. "You're a little outside your AO, aren't you? Last I checked, DIA was twenty miles downriver." He pointed over Gault's shoulder for effect.

"Nothing gets past you, Copeland. Let's just say Langley still fits snugly within my area of operations these days."

"Always the cunning linguist, Gault. And still nobody likes you."

"You know what they say: *keep your friends close and fuck everyone else*."

"And here I thought we might be on the same side."

"Then you're being naive, as always."

Caleb walked past and leaned in. "Well, Hacksaw, catching up was great. I gotta go, but let's do it again sometime."

"You can't still be harboring old grudges, can you?"

Caleb turned back, set his coffee down on the countertop, and squared himself to Gault. "Look, Terry," he said, tucking his hands into his pockets, in part to restrain himself from punching him in the face. "Maybe you fooled a bunch of career administrators into giving you a lofty promotion at DIA, but clearly no one asked your team. Or me. So, no old grudges here—I just don't like you."

He was about to retrieve his coffee and perform a retrograde when Gault said, "Still pretending to be the Goody Two-shoes—"

"I was never that and never claimed to be, but at least I wasn't a sick fuck who did what you and your team did."

"What we did helped serve up Bin Laden and others like him."

"You were never near OBL. You got good intel *once,* and even that was pure luck. If you take enough bad shots, sooner or later, you might hit something."

"My team was effective."

"Your team was out of control, and you, as its commander, single-handedly forced an administration into changing every US intel agency's SOPs."

"My techniques saved lives."

"Your techniques almost always delivered faulty information and people died—theirs and ours."

"Not always."

"That's a swell unit motto," Caleb scoffed. "How many stars on the Memorial Wall over in the main building can be directly attributed to you and your team's methods? Men and women lost their lives because of your ineptitude. Maybe we should just tack a note under the star of every hero you put into the ground acting on your bad intel: *Sometimes we kill our own, but don't worry . . . not always.* I'm sure that touching explanatory footnote will make all the difference in the world to their grieving loved ones."

"If only walls could talk, Viking . . . the things I've seen *you* do."

Caleb never claimed to be perfect, and he'd always acted within the boundaries of, if not the actual rulebook, then its fuzzy margins. Whatever he did in the name of his fellow soldiers, special operators, and country, he did with an absence of malice or cruelty toward the enemy. His conscience and his humanity were intact. Same couldn't be said of Hacksaw. The man had no boundaries. Zero.

"I asked why you're here," Caleb said.

"Yes, you did." Gault offered nothing more than his continued emotionless stare.

"Okay, nice chatting with you," said Caleb, walking away.

"See you around, Copeland—you and your ISA girlfriend." Bile crept into Caleb's throat. The muscles in his shoulders and arms strained within their confines. His palms itched as his fingers curled into a fist, nails biting flesh.

Caleb flipped him the bird as he headed for the stairs.

* * *

Knock, knock.

Alex listened as Kadeisha Thomas explained the genesis of ACCT, the Advance Counterterrorism and Counterproliferation Team headed by Caleb that fell within CIA Special Activities Center's domain. Deputy Director Thomas interrupted herself to shout at the door. "Come in."

Saved by the bell, thought Alex. She'd heard the ACCT spiel more times than she cared to count, but in deference to the deputy director, she had sat patiently throughout. All she really cared about were the missions, and since concluding the operation in Ukraine a few months back, there hadn't been any more of those.

Caleb walked in carrying a steaming mug. After their recent gorging, Alex couldn't imagine taking another bite or drink of anything for a week, but the smell of his fresh-brewed coffee set off her yearning, and she wiped drool from the corner of her mouth.

"Copeland," said Thomas. "I was just getting to the part where I bring Martel up to speed on our situation."

"How'd she take it?" he asked.

"I haven't told her yet. That's your job, Branch Chief."

"Well, ma'am, you're the deputy director of this agency, so why don't *you* tell her?"

Alex looked at Thomas, who had stopped smiling.

"Come again?" she said.

The two women watched as Caleb closed the door behind him and walked to the window, letting out a deep sigh.

"If I didn't know better, Mr. Copeland, I'd say you ran into our friend from DIA."

"Yes, ma'am."

"And can I assume that this is the reason for your sour disposition and lack of good judgment when addressing your superior?"

Caleb turned to her, his eyes narrow, his lips frozen in a pained expression. At last, he spoke. "I'm sorry, ma'am." He looked at Alex. "We've been assigned to a joint task force."

"What kind of task force?" asked Alex.

"One with the State Department and FBI," he said.

Alex sensed their apprehension as they awaited her reaction. Not long ago, she had been one of the Bureau's most promising special agents—until they had terminated her employment for the very thing for which she was awarded the Presidential Medal of Freedom from President Moore as well as the highest decoration awarded by France.

"If you're waiting for me to throw a hissy fit like he did," she said, thrusting her chin in Caleb's direction, "it's never going to happen."

"Good," said Thomas.

"What's this task force about, and why are we joining it?" Alex asked.

"Well, we're not exactly *joining it*," Caleb said.

Thomas chimed in. "Oh, good Lord, Copeland. Get your head out of your ass and get to the point."

Whatever demons Caleb was wrestling, he shook them off. "Yes, ma'am." Straightening up, he put his mug down on the desk. "For a few months now, not just CIA but several other US and foreign intelligence agencies have been hearing a lot of the same rumblings that Russia is poised to move against NATO and that they're behind major incidents of sabotage in Finland."

"Why would they do that? It would be suicide," said Alex.

Thomas nodded. "It would be, and yet it seems they are."

"They would have a hard enough time against Finland even by itself, let alone if the rest of NATO came in under Article 5. Russian infantry and armor are heavily committed to Eastern Europe, to say nothing of their air force. Do they actually think they have the needed capacity for that?"

"Well, here we are, so you tell me," Thomas replied.

"I wouldn't have said this back when I was in Syria and elsewhere, but Russia's military is not the powerhouse we thought it was," she added.

"Suspicious events in Finland over the past twelve months all point to Russian involvement," Caleb said. "Widespread blackouts, an uptick in targeted malware, chemical and oil spills at sea, hospitals and other infrastructure targeted with widespread denial-of-service and ransomware attacks. There's also been organized unrest like what we saw before in the Baltic capitals—anti-government, mass skinhead-type violence, riots, that kind of thing—but in the past those events were isolated to Estonia, Latvia, and Lithuania. Now they're happening across the Baltic Sea in Helsinki and throughout Finland."

"Moscow denies involvement in any of it, of course," said Thomas. "But as you know, denial is their modus operandi."

"When you say it points back to Russia, do you mean Directorate 13 is behind it?"

"Either D13 or their parent GRU unit, Unit 29155," said Caleb. "They're still active. It might even be one of the other federal security services, like the SVR."

She paused a moment to consider what he was saying. "I don't buy it."

"Why not? You're the one who was all over D13 being the bad guys when we dealt with them the last time, even when no one else believed you."

"But does it make sense that they would be working a major disruption op at the same time as the events in Paris were unfolding a few months back? Wouldn't that risk exposing both operations in such a way that neither succeeded?"

"It would," agreed Thomas. "But I don't think I have to remind you that they're specialists in that sort of nonsense, Alex. And by that, I mean they're accustomed to being obvious and incompetent and bold enough not to care who knows it."

Caleb added, "We also learned *ex post facto* that Paris was off the books. So arguably, it was the Paris op that was unauthorized and occurring behind D13's officially sanctioned disruption game."

"If that's how it went down," said Alex, "all the more reason a rogue colonel would have trouble pulling off something of that magnitude while working other high-risk ops. And he's gone now. Directorate 13's been decapitated. Neither the general who established it nor the colonel in charge are even alive anymore."

"The latter thanks to you," Thomas said.

She ignored the compliment. Or the statement of fact. Alex had a way of compartmentalizing her missions. The elimination of Colonel Gerasimov had been all in a day's work, and General Tikhonov's execution in Lubyanka was merely a data point that logically flowed after the others. Other than the satisfaction she felt at having successfully completed her assignment, she had no feelings one way or the other about the task she had performed.

None that she consciously acknowledged anyway.

"Don't be so sure," cautioned Caleb. "The GRU is the most highly funded of the security services. Now that Yevgeny Prigozhin has been eliminated, it's even more critical that a new leader rise to fill the void left by the Wagner Group in Europe and Africa. Someone has to fill that void. The GRU and its generals are that *somebody*."

"What about the attack on the megayacht the other night?"

"What about it?" asked Thomas.

"Are we any closer to figuring out who did it and why?"

"Alex, it's not our business."

"Until it is."

"And right now, it isn't," Thomas said sternly. "The attack was carried out by a band of Afghan mercenaries."

"Which means somebody paid them."

"That's what *mercenaries* means," said Thomas.

"So there's no nexus between them and the Russians?"

"That's for the French police and Interpol to find out, and you are neither the French police nor Interpol. Other than being an involved party, you're not involved at all, if you catch my meaning, Martel. You are a contract employee. More precisely, a global response staff special agent and subject-matter expert with the Central Intelligence Agency, not the French police or Interpol."

"But what if there *is* a connection to whatever is happening in Finland? Maybe it was the Russians, but maybe it wasn't. Is that something the CIA is looking into, ma'am? Finland's NATO ambassador was aboard *Aurora,* so isn't that enough of a reason for us to, if not suspect, then at least not rule out the possibility the target was the ambassador? Or even Madame Clicquot herself, who had arranged the meeting for a reason we don't yet understand?"

"That's a lot of *don't knows* and *what-ifs,* Alex."

"I'm just exploring theories, ma'am. That's what we do, isn't it—collect and disseminate?"

"And analyze, yes. And right now, the analysis is thin."

Thomas studied her. Alex shifted uncomfortably in her seat, again feeling like she was waiting for some adjudication from her high school vice principal.

"Request permission to speak freely, ma'am—"

"Oh, Alex, you're not in the fucking Army anymore. Speak your mind, girl."

"The attack on *Aurora* failed. Celeste and Valtteri are still alive. The wrong people died. Lots of them. That means somebody must be seriously pissed off that a shitload of money went down the drain on a failed op." She paused to size Thomas up before she went on. Thomas studied her with a grim expression as Alex continued her appeal. "I owe a debt to Madame Clicquot to protect her. She and her boyfriend are in danger. I need to go back to liaise with French police while the investigation is ongoing. Then, when we know more—"

"And when exactly will that be?"

"Maybe a couple of days . . ."

Thomas waited a beat before responding. "Martel, let me make this as simple and as plain as I can." Her Alabama accent was now in full flower. "There is no way on God's green earth that the C-I-A"—she deliberately enunciated each letter of the acronym—"will permit one of its own, contract or otherwise, to assume the role of an investigator from one of our other myriad agencies, F-B-fucking-I included, 'cause that's what you're asking me to approve. You feel me, Special Agent?"

"Yes, ma'am." She didn't.

"So, you're going to have to suck on the bitter pill of a joint task force while Caleb here deals with his old friend."

"What?" Caleb had been leaning against a radiator on the wall but flew to attention. "We have to work with that prick?"

"Not work *with,* work *for.* The Defense Intelligence Agency has been brought into this, and as the senior member of the task force, Deputy Director Gault is in charge."

"Whose cockamamie idea was that? How is this a DIA-led task force? Show me the military component that suggests DIA is in charge. Shouldn't Homeland or State be taking point?"

She cut him off with a raised hand before he could protest further. "Not another word, Copeland, or I'll post you to mucking out kennels on the other side of the compound, seeing how much you love dogs."

He sunk back against the radiator.

"Back to this task force then," Alex said, still seething a little inside but content to let her frustration simmer until she came up with a better plan. The deputy director didn't seem receptive to alternative work strategies at this point. "What's its purpose again?"

"The chatter we were hearing had always only involved Finland, never the United States directly—except in the context of a NATO ally being threatened, bringing the possibility of an Article 5 intervention into play, as you noted earlier. And for the past several months, these issues, which we and several of our allies have tied to Russian adventurism, have been raised quietly at the United Nations, only recently being elevated to the attention of the Security Council. Technically, we had only a peripheral involvement." She paused.

Alex filled in the silence. "What changed?"

"It seems the Russian bear isn't content to rattle its saber at our friends the Finns. Now we're hearing about threats to high-ranking US officials. CIA and FBI are on it, as is just about every Washington agency with a three-letter acronym. But it's this small task force, compartmentalized and limited to its present membership, that is tasked with diving deeper and acting as a clearinghouse for information collected and analyzed by the other teams. Personal feelings aside, Alex, it's a feather in your cap. Take that shit seriously."

Just then, Thomas's phone rang. She answered it and listened intently to the caller.

"Is the director aware?" she asked. Then, "Yes, I'll take care of it. We'll be right there." She stood from the desk.

"What is it?" Caleb asked.

"It seems the Russians are making a move. Follow me."

"Where we going?" asked Alex.

"The West Wing."

CHAPTER 22

Deputy Director Thomas stepped out of the up-armored Suburban she was required to travel in and eyed her surroundings. Her close protection detail had parked in the zone adjacent to the staging area for the vice presidential motorcade. VPOTUS's car was in its spot, and Thomas paused to take in a cleansing breath, knowing she might have to speak with Vice President Barbara Garcia if she were there in the West Wing.

Maybe if I walk fast . . . , she thought.

Babs wasn't the most convivial conversationalist, and Thomas frequently eye-rolled when walking away from the often strange conversations she'd had with the VP in the past.

Inside the double doors, Secret Service officers from the Uniformed Division manned the checkpoint in the reception lobby. The two officers gave her a nod as she hurried past and entered the Situation Room complex that occupied much of the floor space of the lower West Wing.

"Deputy Director," called a voice from behind her.

Shit. Not fast enough.

She turned to find Vice President Garcia striding toward her, her long triple-strand necklace in full bounce and sway. The VP was youthful and energetic and full of herself in the way young people are, except she was in her mid-forties and should have jettisoned that shit by now. She generally took a harder line on policy issues than President Moore, which satisfied the fringes of the party but could also be disconcerting to the moderates in the administration, as it frequently put her and the president at odds with each other in public statements.

"Madam Vice President, nice to see you," Thomas fibbed.

"Oh, you can cut the bullshit, Kadeisha. I know what you think of me."

The VP wasn't wrong. Thomas wasn't fond of the vice president using her first name like they had been sorority sisters, but she was the veep, after all. She folded her hands in front of herself, smiling patiently, waiting for her to get to the point.

"But despite that," Garcia continued, "I know that, like me, you want what's best for our nation."

As always, the patriot card. "As does President Moore," Thomas reminded her.

"Of course, but . . . how should I put this? The president is rightfully concerned with his polling numbers and reelection. As his vice president, I like to think of myself as the conscience of the Office of the President."

"And a potential successor."

"The way I see it, *Deputy Director,*"—Garcia added emphasis to her job title—"that could work in your favor."

"With respect, Madam Vice President, I know President Moore to be an honorable man and a committed public servant. Why would he need an extra conscience?"

"Maybe that was a poor word choice on my part." Garcia clammed up as Martel and Copeland walked past. When they were clear, the VP continued. "There are events unfolding as we speak. You'll hear more of it in your meeting in a moment."

"You're not coming in?" asked Kadeisha.

The VP shook her head, then continued. "I'm concerned about the safety and security of our country, and sometimes my views and the president's opinion on how to achieve those objectives diverge. Our enemies are watching, and I'm not just referring to the ones who sit across the aisle in the House. I don't have to remind you that there are bad actors around the world with an interest in seeing these United States become . . ." She searched for the right word. "Unstable," she added at last.

No, Babs, you don't have to remind me, thought Thomas, who didn't take kindly to being told by the VP what her nonpartisan role at CIA was. *Dammit, girl. It's my job to know.*

Though that was what she thought, she instead said, "How can I be of service, ma'am?"

"I'd like you to keep an ear open, along with an open mind. The Russian bear, I'm afraid, is stirring from its sleep. We can't continue to back down from the bear. *We* are the bear. The bigger, stronger motherfucking bear." Thomas was taken aback by the language from the vice president. "Oh, don't be so shocked, Director Thomas."

"I don't entirely disagree with you, Madam Vice President, but—"

"Good. All I ask is that should the president be leaning more toward the doves in our administration, and you are presented with an opportunity to play devil's advocate, well, then, I hope you might seize on that moment. For the good of the nation."

"For the good of the nation," Thomas repeated.

"Yes. And I would like you to feel comfortable calling me directly should you have any concerns or think there is anything I should know."

Thomas nodded noncommittally. "I will keep your request in mind, ma'am."

"Thank you, Kadeisha. That's all I ask. Alliances are usually at their most advantageous when both parties work together. Well, I must go. Enjoy the briefing."

"Yes, ma'am."

Garcia disappeared down the hallway in the direction of the exit, her protection detail forming up around her as they stepped outside. Thomas stood for a moment digesting the VP's request.

Did the vice president just ask me to spy on the president of the United States and report back to her? WTF?

CHAPTER 23

Caleb and Alex pulled into the White House compound behind Deputy Director Thomas and watched as she entered the Situation Room complex. They eventually fell in behind her, but when they caught up, she was engaged in a tense conversation with the vice president, so they carried on ahead.

The John F. Kennedy Conference Room was a modern version of the intelligence management center initially conceived and built following the bombing of Pearl Harbor on December 7, 1941. But that first iteration had been outgrown by the demands and technological needs of its updated counterpart that, in today's White House, hosted up to twenty-five meetings a day. Despite the generous volume of space, it always seemed crowded.

Kadeisha Thomas caught up to them and led them inside Conference Room 1.

"Grab yourselves a coffee," she said, pointing to a small kitchen area off to the side as she stepped away to speak with some familiar faces. Alex watched while people came and went from the conference room. Small groups formed and dispersed, their conversations stilted and clipped in anticipation of the briefing that would get underway when the president arrived.

Alex grabbed a bottle of water as Caleb helped himself to a coffee.

President Taylor Moore entered the room, his chief of staff, Titus Pelletier, and Secretary of State Katherine Hayward at his hip. Immediately, everyone took their seats. Caleb touched Alex lightly on the elbow, and the two grabbed chairs along the side wall.

President Moore was from the Texas Panhandle, and like pretty much everyone else from Amarillo—and West Texas in general—he wasn't much for small talk or preamble. He dove right in.

"Everybody here knows everyone else, so let's get started. Give me what you got, General," he said, firing his steely gaze up the conference table at his national security advisor, General Lucas Hughes.

Alex looked on as a man in a US Army uniform rose and opened a leather portfolio, the four stars on his epaulets catching the overhead lights. Next to him, a lieutenant controlled a large display system at the front of the room. She turned her head along with everyone else to watch the screens.

"Mr. President," General Hughes began, "as you know, we've been monitoring increased activity along the border of Finland and across the gulf in the Baltic states."

The video revealed satellite imagery of . . . something. It looked like a long column of ants marching two by two: dark dots on a gray surface next to curving black lines. It wasn't monochrome, but the image wasn't blazing with color, either.

"What are we looking at, General?" President Moore asked, squinting.

The lieutenant made some adjustments on his computer and the magnification increased exponentially.

"Over the past eighteen hours," said Hughes, "the Russian 6th Army in Agalatovo, Leningrad Oblast, north of St. Petersburg, has shifted resources and fortified their troop positions at the top end of the Gulf of Finland. Multiple mechanized brigades, missile brigades, and other resources have been repositioned just in the past twelve hours alone. Mobile missile sites in Kaliningrad have also been readied for operations." The video shifted to a different sequence. "There has also been increased movement at the Levashovo Air Base near St. Petersburg. Levashovo ordinarily is a base for small Antonov transport aircraft, as well as squadrons of Mi-6 and Mi-8 helicopters, used primarily for supply and transport." Time-lapse imagery showed an airfield at two-hour increments filling with staged aircraft and activity. "What you're seeing on-screen, sir, is an armored battalion on the move and a generalized mobilization of Russian armed forces and equipment unlike anything we've seen since the buildup to the war in Ukraine."

He pointed to the screen. "These are mostly Su-27 fighters," he said. "And this cluster over here"—he used a laser pointer to draw circles— "are Tupolev Tu-160s. We call them Blackjacks, sir. They're a supersonic, variable-sweep wing, heavy strategic bomber and airborne missile platform."

"That doesn't look good," said Katherine Hayward, the secretary of state.

"No, it doesn't," agreed Moore, leaning forward on his arms.

"No, sir," said General Hughes. "Not good."

"How many troops, General?" asked Moore.

"Roughly sixty thousand, sir. Plus, coastal missile units have been put on alert. Additionally, to the south in Kaliningrad, the Russian Federation's 11th Army Corps Headquarters has deployed resources from other regions. Twenty thousand or so troops plus equipment."

The images shifted again to patterns of trains and transport vehicles off-loading personnel and equipment at various staging locations around St. Petersburg.

"Well, Jesus H. Christ, where do they find the resources?" Moore asked. "I mean, considering their losses in Eastern Europe, how do they have anyone left alive for this?"

"Well, sir, the prisons continue to be emptied to support the numbers. And there's no end to the stream of mandatory conscripts since they raised the maximum age of citizen soldiers now to forty-five."

Moore shook his head. "Ships?"

"Those as well." Lucas's aide fiddled with the keyboard some more and put up additional imagery. "Their Baltic fleet has sixty ships at sea." Some colorful pictures filled the screen with groups of battleships steaming across blue waters. "They say they're holding naval drills, sir, to test the readiness of defenses at Kaliningrad and St. Petersburg in the event of Western aggression."

"Of course they are. Naval drills, my ass."

"Yes, Mr. President."

"What about their nuclear arsenal, General?" asked SecState Hayward.

"Madam Secretary, as near as we can tell, there has been no change in the readiness of their nukes. But to be clear, ma'am, their Kaliningrad missile assets are capable of carrying nuclear armaments and are most likely already loaded out that way."

President Moore turned to Deputy Director Thomas. "Can Central Intelligence confirm this?"

"Yes, Mr. President," she replied. "Our analysis supports the general's report in all respects, including the likelihood that the battery of missiles in Kaliningrad are nuclear-tipped."

"What's Finland's troop strength, Lucas?"

"Twenty-four thousand active personnel, sir," answered the general. "But they can boost that number in wartime to two hundred and eighty thousand, with an additional eight hundred thousand reservists, or thereabouts."

"Have you spoken to them?"

"Yes, sir. I've been in touch directly with both President Jarkko Ruusu and Prime Minister Sanna Rantala."

"And? What did they have to say?"

"They're none too happy about these developments, sir."

"I can't imagine why," Secretary of State Hayward said sarcastically.

"So, Deputy Director Thomas, what's President Sergachev up to?" asked Moore.

Alex watched Kadeisha adjust in her seat. But, true to form, she had a response. "Mr. President, we haven't completed a full analysis yet, but the buildup is similar to what we witnessed leading up to Russia's incursion into Ukraine."

"Their *special military operation*."

"Yes, sir. A rose by any other name."

"Indeed. So, do we think the Russians are going to invade Finland? Or any of the Baltic states, for that matter? General?"

"I'm not sure we can afford to ignore that risk, Mr. President," replied Hughes. "We were caught with our pants down before."

"What would you recommend?"

President Moore's chief of staff chimed in. "If I may," he said.

Alex disliked Titus Pelletier. He was a hawkish peacetime former Marine who, after America was attacked on 9/11, discovered he had more of an aptitude for politics and self-preservation than combat or leadership. In her mind, by his actions and generally unlikable disposition, he had forfeited his right to bear the Marine Corps' Devil Dog moniker.

"Speak, Titus," said Moore.

Alex suppressed a grin. *On the other hand,* she thought, *maybe he was more cut out to be a lapdog anyway.*

"Sir, we have no idea what the Ruskies are up to. In light of the general's assessment, I would recommend we bolster our Sixth Fleet's presence in the Baltic Sea and the Gulf of Finland and initiate a troop buildup in Western Europe. We should also raise our defense readiness condition from DEFCON 5 to DEFCON 4."

"Oh, poppycock," said Hayward.

The president leaned back in his chair, his jaw clenched, his hands gripping the armrests of his chair like he was riding the Space Mountain roller coaster.

"Sir," said Thomas.

"Go ahead, Kadeisha."

"I would strongly recommend against that course of action at this time."

"I agree with the deputy director, Mr. President," said Hayward.

"Why's that?" asked Moore. "It seems prudent to counter President Sergachev move for move at this point, doesn't it, in light of past events in Eastern Europe?"

"I would disagree, sir," she said. "The Russian president is already on record saying that the conversations being had at the United Nations regarding alleged Russian aggression against Finland are simply a prelude to war; that America is spoiling for a fight to save face after it failed to prevent Ukraine from being, to use his words, reabsorbed into Russia."

Pelletier jumped back in. "Mr. President, the deputy director makes my point for me. President Sergachev watched us literally do nothing as he amassed troops and resources along the Ukraine border. For months he assured us that the troop and equipment movements were merely part of a large-scale domestic exercise, the same rhetoric he is using now. I'm afraid if we wait, it will be too late—he'll swallow up Finland, and while he's at it, he might just seize Lithuania, Latvia, and Estonia for good measure, giving him a complete and utter stranglehold on that region, and a broader foothold from which to attack Western Europe."

The president was nodding.

Thomas waded back in. "Ukraine wasn't a member of NATO the way Finland is now," she argued. "With the invasion of Ukraine, Russia had no need to fear an Article 5 response from NATO allies. President Sergachev would certainly have to consider the ramifications of one now, sir, even without us threatening all-out war by boosting our presence in the area. Respectfully, sir, I believe the best way to project a unified front is through diplomacy at this point."

"Mr. President," said Pelletier. "Nuclear weapons only deter the sane. If we're counting on Sergachev backing down under the threat of an Article 5 response—wherein his attacking Finland would trigger retaliation by the whole of the NATO alliance—I'm afraid that won't work. He's demonstrated he can blackmail us into sitting on our hands doing nothing but complaining. His next step would be to threaten the use of his nuclear weapons, as he has threatened to do in Ukraine, betting that the US and her allies will stand down and that we have no appetite to trigger a mutually assured destruction scenario. And, of course, he's right, we don't." He sneered, then started in on Thomas with a newly condescending tone. "With respect, Madam Deputy Director . . ." Alex saw Thomas's skin turn a deep shade of *murderous intent* at the condescension, but then Alex saw her take an almost imperceptible deep breath as she kept a pin in it.

She'd make a great sniper, Alex thought.

Titus Pelletier blathered on. ". . . the United States has already demonstrated its weakness against Russian aggression by backing down every time Sergachev has waved the nuclear rattle in our faces. We would back down again, and I fear we would not come to the aid of a fellow NATO member under such circumstances as I have outlined. This administration has proven that we and the American people have no appetite for nuclear brinksmanship. We've become too soft for hard realities."

"Is that what you think, Titus?" Moore's infamous temper was threatening to ignite. "That America is weak? You think we wouldn't respond with force to defend a NATO ally, as is our obligation under the Washington Treaty?" he asked, invoking the common name of the North Atlantic Treaty that constituted the basis for the establishment of NATO.

Instead of backpedaling, Pelletier doubled down. He was nodding.

Read the room, Titus, thought Alex.

But he kept stumbling forward, like a man who had laced on skates for the first time and was headed for open water. "I do," he replied feebly.

President Moore squinted at his chief of staff, trying to discern if he had understood him correctly.

Pelletier went on. "There are too many doves in Washington and at the UN as well as in NATO that could get in the way of swift, decisive action."

"Alright. I've heard enough. Titus, Kadeisha, I'm glad you're both on our side," he said, striving for a modicum of levity. "I'm not looking to turn this into a cage match, so—"

"Mr. President," began Pelletier.

President Moore's patience was legendary, but his temper, when challenged, was equally so. One look from him and his chief of staff fell silent and slouched in his chair.

"General," Moore said to his national security advisor, "you've heard these impassioned arguments here. What say you?"

"There may be another option, Mr. President."

"I'm all ears, Lucas."

"It's a bit of a hybrid solution, sir, somewhere between the status quo and an active military response." The president nodded, leaning in to listen more intently as General Hughes continued. "US Naval Forces Europe-Africa and the Sixth Fleet wrapped up this year's BALTOPS exercise less than seventy-two hours ago. It's an annual operational exercise in the Baltic Sea that we coordinate, and this year it was run from Tallinn, Estonia, right across the gulf from Finland."

"I know where Estonia is, General."

"Of course, sir. This year, Finland participated for the first time as a full NATO member, along with nineteen additional NATO allies. Material resources and personnel included sixty ships, more than fifty aircraft, and approximately eight thousand personnel." He glanced down at papers in his portfolio before continuing. "NATO members exercised a myriad of capabilities, demonstrating the inherent flexibility of their combined maritime forces. Including Finland, there were seven allied nations bordering the Baltic Sea participating in this year's BALTOPS."

The president could see where this was headed and smiled. "Go on."

"It wouldn't take much to recall most of those resources to the region— since many of them call the region their home anyway—ostensibly to extend the exercise, ensuring a combined response capability to preserve freedom of navigation and security in the Baltic Sea, sir."

"Won't the Russian president see that as a further instigation of hostilities?" asked the secretary of state.

"It's a tempered response, Madam Secretary. And I think our allies will be onside."

Thomas waded in. "I'm cautiously optimistic about the general's idea, sir," she said. "President Sergachev might be angry, but it would be difficult for him to argue that this wasn't merely an extension of the exercise or that those resources didn't belong there. Instead of a new offensive buildup, these are regional assets conducting drills in local waters as they make their way back to their home ports. It's a bold move, but I think it's a good option."

Moore nodded in agreement. His chief of staff appeared to be smoldering under the cool white LED lighting.

"Deputy Director Thomas," said Moore. "What about these rumblings that Russia's behind all the events we've been hearing about for the past year? How far has CIA gotten in determining the veracity of those claims? Is Sergachev's security apparatus up to no good again, as they were in Paris, or is something or somebody else behind it all?"

"I'd be lying if I said I know yet, sir." Beside the president, Pelletier scoffed. She ignored him and continued. "But we have a task force looking into it. Unfortunately, it might be some time before I have a definitive answer for you."

President Moore was nodding. "Not too much time, I hope. The gravity of this situation demands a timely resolution to the question."

"Yes, sir."

"If Sergachev is responsible, we need to know soon. And if he's not, we need to find out who's making it look like he is. Right now, we're being forced into a game of Russian roulette, and that seldom ends well for somebody." He cast his eyes around the room and settled on Alex.

"Speaking of Paris, Special Agent Martel," he began. "I almost didn't see you back there in the shadows."

"It's where I like to hide, Mr. President."

President Moore looked at Thomas and then back to Alex, moving his finger from one to the other, making the connection and smiling. "Yes, I see," he said. "The Agency snagged you up, did they? Nice move, Kadeisha. So, Deputy Director, is Alex on this joint task force of yours?"

"Yes, sir. Along with Mr. Copeland beside her," she said. "And a select group of others. The team is being headed by Defense Intelligence under Associate Deputy Director Gault."

"Hacksaw?" he said. "Better you than me, Alex. And Mr. Copeland. But don't tell Gault I said so."

Caleb grunted audibly but Alex ignored him. "Yes, sir. Your secret's safe with me, Mr. President."

"I know it is, Martel. Okay, General, back to you for a recap."

When General Hughes finished, Moore stood. "Issue the requisite orders, General," he said. "And, Katherine, you'll do a presser denouncing Russian aggression and so on, saying the United States and her allies won't tolerate it, et cetera, et cetera. Then we'll sit back and watch what that distempered old bull does."

Caleb leaned over and whispered to Alex, "I don't think that word means what he thinks it means."

"He knows what it means," she whispered back.

"But," Moore announced to the room, "one more stumbling move out of Sergachev, and we'll rain fire and brimstone down on his ass."

Titus Pelletier beamed.

* * *

"Deputy Director Thomas."

As Kadeisha Thomas stopped in the foyer of the Situation Room to collect her phone from its Faraday lockbox, General Lucas Hughes walked up on her.

The entire lower level of the White House below the West Wing was classified as a SCIF, a sensitive compartmented information facility. Mobile phones inside Twilight—the Secret Service's code name for the Situation Room under President Moore's administration—were strictly prohibited.

"General, interesting developments. I appreciate your sitrep," she said, pocketing her phone.

"Not at all, Deputy Director. And I appreciate your support with the president and his chief of staff."

"Titus is a windbag," she said. "Well-meaning and always looking out for the president, but a class-A windbag."

Hughes chuckled. "He is that. I worry about his ulterior motives. He's more political than the president, who I find always has the country's best interests at heart."

"What can I do for you, General?"

"You're a straight shooter, Director Thomas, so I'm hoping you can fill me in on this task force of yours."

"And you're the national security advisor, so I'd've thought someone would have brought you up to speed." It was a friendly poke, not said with malice.

"I'm like a mushroom most days—always kept in the dark and fed a load of shit."

Thomas laughed. "I highly doubt that, General. President Moore seems to rely heavily on your expertise and guidance, or he wouldn't have asked you to weigh in on strategy. But there's not much to tell. And anyway, it's not my task force. Terry Gault from Defense Intelligence is leading it. If there is any more you should know, it would be something he's privy to, not me."

"I understand. So, nothing for me to concern myself over, from your point of view?"

Thomas was by nature a suspicious person. At CIA, one had better be. So the questioning, even in the friendliest of tones, raised her hackles. General Hughes knew what he needed to know. And he had never attempted to pry additional intel from her on an active task force before.

Alarm bells rang in her brain. Small ones, but alarms just the same.

"Nothing at all to be concerned about, General. There's a good team on it."

"Well, if you hear anything more that might affect how I advise the president, perhaps you'll pick up the phone and let me know."

"No promises, General."

"Of course. But as a courtesy, please keep me in mind."

"As a courtesy," she echoed.

Courtesy, my ass. What the hell is in the water around here?

CHAPTER 24

Alex threw her bag onto the bed and unpacked, separating her clothes into an *A* pile, a *B* pile, and a *C* pile. Everything in the latter went straight into the hamper for the laundry she'd do first thing in the morning. The *A* items went into drawers or onto hangers and were promptly put away. The *B*s were left folded neatly on a chair in the corner for further sorting tomorrow.

All told, it had been a tiring few days, topped off by the unexpected meeting with the president. The cruise on the Med from Antibes to Monaco should have been the highlight. And maybe having survived the assault on *Aurora*, in an odd way, it was. But she had endured and survived an event that should have killed her. Again.

When she finished her laundry triage, she flopped onto the bed. Even before her eyelids fluttered closed, she was fast asleep.

* * *

PARIS, FRANCE

"Cover me," she called to Caleb, but he was already diving for cover as more shots emanated from the tunnel.

Hugo screamed out in pain. "Je suis touché!" he called. I'm hit!

Alex turned to see him crumple to the ground. Caleb raced over and dragged him deeper into the tunnel. Alex fired a half-dozen shots into the other tunnel to suppress any return fire. Then she emptied the rest of her Glock's magazine into the front of the B61–12.

Sparks flew, and smoke curled out from the tip of the bomb. Five short beeps emanated from the bomb in rapid succession, followed by a loud buzz. Alex looked at the display on the B61's control panel as Caleb fired more shots toward the tunnel in which Malkin and Kane had taken cover. It flashed 00:00:10 and began counting down.

"Shit!" she yelled. "Caleb, run! We're out of time!"

She bolted for the tunnel where Caleb had dragged Hugo. She grabbed him by the belt, and together they backpedaled as fast as they could as far into the tunnel as they could get.

"Cover!" she yelled, and they both dropped down on top of Hugo, pressing themselves as flat and as close to the ground as possible.

Alex had felt the concussive force of blast waves many times before. She prepared for this one as best she could—she pressed her body onto Hugo's, low to the ground, in line with the expected shock wave, facing away: mouth open, eyes closed, arms above her head, hands covering her neck. But when the explosion came, it was like nothing she had ever seen, heard, or felt before. While the power of the blast was exponentially less than almost any she had been exposed to downrange, the difference was they were in a confined space and within fifty or sixty feet of the explosion.

The ceiling, walls, and tunnel reflected the blast wave, magnifying it as it traveled away from the site of the explosion. Fortunately, the angle at the entrance to the tunnel had shielded them from most of the shrapnel, but not all. They were enveloped by a tornado-force gust of wind lasting just a few seconds that lifted them momentarily off the ground before dropping them back to Earth again several meters down the tunnel.

After it had passed, Alex felt her lungs fighting against her efforts to breathe, spasming inside her chest like an empty water balloon whose sides were stuck together. She tried to inhale, but there was just no air. Her clothes were torn and she was covered in cuts and abrasions.

The loudest sound she could hear, in fact the only sound, was the ringing in her ears. She opened and closed her mouth like a guppy, rolled off whomever she was lying on, and prayed that soon some air would find its way into her lungs.

Please, God, let me breathe.

The tunnel was filled with smoke and dust and the acrid post-blast smell of a polymer-bonded high explosive. On top of the smoke and the haze, her brain was in a fog, and she had the worst case of hypoxia-induced bed spins imaginable. Finally, a second gust brought with it cool, breathable air. She sucked it in, gasping, hungry, swallowing big gulps of it. The oxygen it carried fed her starving brain, and slowly her focus returned.

Caleb. Hugo. The bomb.

She got to her knees and crawled through her pain to the first body she found. It was facedown. She rocked its shoulder. "Hey! Hey, can you hear me?"

A groan, and then a face turned up toward her. It was Hugo. Alive. He had taken a bullet in his ballistic vest, but he was alive. He was conscious and breathing and could focus on her. All were good signs. She propped him up against the wall and moved on.

Another body. Caleb. He was supine, eyes closed, head lolled to the side. Only a few of the lights in the tunnel had survived the blast, and she had a tough time seeing him clearly, but his chest was rising and falling in a regular pattern, albeit too quickly. Her medic brain kicked in and she detected the coppery, sweet scent of blood in the air. She ran her hands over him and stopped when they got warm and sticky over his abdomen. She searched for her phone and turned the light on. Lifting his shirt, she found a shrapnel injury to his lower abdomen with a partial evisceration. An eight-inch section of bowel protruded through his skin. She had no dressings, no abdominal pads, so she pulled his shirt back down and placed his hands over the area, but they slid off.

"Caleb! Can you hear me?"

He wasn't responding. His pulse was thready. He was bleeding internally *and was going into hypovolemic shock. He needed surgery—if he survived that long.*

"Caleb," she whispered. "Please don't die on me."

* * *

She woke with a start and bolted upright in bed. Sweat poured off her, her heart raced. Her throat pounded as if someone were squeezing and releasing their grip around it. She threw off the covers and leaped out of bed, wobbling unsteadily into the en suite bathroom. Bending over the sink, she scooped cold water from the faucet onto her face. She toweled off and stared at her image in the mirror. The person staring back at her was not the person she knew.

At one point in the dream, Caleb's face had taken on the appearance of her late husband, Kyle, who had been killed in combat years before.

What the actual fuck?

She sat on the toilet seat, remaining there for several minutes until the memory of the dream receded and the sense of imminent danger lifted. Finally, her pulse slowed, and she no longer felt like a marching band on steroids was living in her throat.

Jesus, what kind of messed-up shit is this?

She did an exercise called box breathing to clear her mind and shake out the cobwebs. Slowly, she recomposed herself. She must have been hyperventilating, as only now was she becoming aware of the tingling in her fingers.

Get a grip, Alex.

She forced herself to get up and move around to get her blood circulating; to do anything that would put time and distance between her and her nightmare. She set herself to the mundane task of opening the bathroom cupboards and drawers to take stock of the items provisioned by the Agency's housing and logistics team, determining what items she still needed to shop for if she was going to be remaining in DC for a while.

It didn't take a shrink to figure out what had happened. While she typically didn't experience nightmares, they came often enough—as they did to so many combat veterans. She knew not to dwell on them and considered herself lucky. She had seen what combat stress could do to soldiers, both in the field and back home after they returned from deployment. Post-traumatic stress disorder—PTSD—could take a heavy toll on a person. Her answer was to avoid thinking about it; to immerse herself in exercise or work when she felt the effects of her past experiences weighing her down.

So, she looked around her surroundings and ignored what had just happened.

The house loaned to her by the CIA was a two-story Colonial located less than five minutes from Langley, in a little hamlet of homes sandwiched between George Washington Memorial Parkway and Chain Bridge Road in McLean. It had been recently renovated and updated in sections, with new flooring in the hallways, while the bedrooms were left with what was likely the original hardwood, the kind of square parquet flooring favored by a previous generation.

She headed downstairs to the kitchen and fetched a drinking glass from a cupboard. Through the window above the sink, the incoming rays split into streaks of shadow and light, the sun hovering behind trees in the backyard, their leaves a mix of fading greens and yellows, the brilliant reds of fall maples still days or even weeks away. The fenced property terminated at what appeared to be parkland on the other side. A small wooden gate looked worn but functional, and she made a mental note to inspect it later to see where it led, hopeful it might lead to a good walking or cycling path.

She ran the water for a minute or so, then filled the glass and took a long drink.

The meeting with Deputy Director Thomas had produced a twist in the expected direction her contract time with CIA would take. After she was unceremoniously released by the FBI, Caleb had been quick to snatch her up for his hastily assembled op, one designated as being of the highest national security interest. And with that first op on the Ukraine border completed months ago, Alex had expected others to soon follow. But none had.

Instead, they would be engaging with a task force headed by someone from outside the Agency. That its leader riled Caleb so much was an inauspicious start. While the Bureau had curtailed her options when they terminated her employment, she had joined Caleb's team and mission voluntarily and with a renewed sense of purpose.

That was then. Now, Deputy Director Thomas's plan for Alex was to have her assist in the gathering of intel on the ongoing destabilization incidents targeting Finland, NATO's thirty-first member state. It seemed an unlikely global flashpoint, but then much of the world hadn't expected Russia to launch a full-on offensive into Ukraine, either.

Is this going to be the best utilization of my skills? she thought, setting down her glass.

Her concern wasn't that she disagreed with the objective, but she wasn't much of a desk jockey. Analysis of raw intelligence was best left to the experts. Her skill set was more . . . kinetic.

She rummaged through the cupboards and fridge, sniffing jars. Before she knew it, her nightmare was forgotten, and she was making herself a tuna melt on a toasted English muffin. Setting herself at the island that divided her kitchen from the dining room of her new digs, she took a bite.

Everything tasted sweeter than what she had grown accustomed to in Europe. Maybe it was the taste of home. Or maybe it was the realization that after all she had been through—ambushes in Afghanistan, fatal missteps in Iraq, the dark underground of Paris—she was still alive while so many of her friends and brothers- and sisters-in-arms were not.

CHAPTER 25

Dinner had been splendid—the service was efficient, the food good, the wine excellent, and the company superb.

How Celeste Clicquot had managed to meet and fall for this man at this stage in her life was still a mystery to her. Her friends—those few close ones that she had—were not quite as puzzled. Celeste had the vigor of a woman twenty years her junior, and while she was burdened with an exhausting schedule as the head of Interpol, she possessed an inexhaustible reserve of energy that kept her moving at a frenetic pace that her younger colleagues and underlings had difficulty matching.

But not Valtteri.

He had flown into her life—quite literally—one evening after a plenary session she'd attended with the European Parliament in Strasbourg, France. She had been a distinguished visitor called upon to discuss Interpol's efforts to combat the rise of transnational crime, in particular via the banking sector, and to implore member countries to work more cohesively.

Valtteri had also been a distinguished visitor, speaking on the topic of energy conservation and power generation strategies within the European Union. While Celeste had missed most of his speech, he hadn't missed hers. Afterward, she noticed him loitering in the lobby while she spoke at a presser, expounding on the bullet points of her speech for the gathered members of the media. He had hovered within her sight lines and made eye contact often enough that, following the scrum, she'd approached him and invited him for coffee. Coffee had turned to cocktails and cocktails to dinner. After dinner, Valtteri had them flown in his ultra-luxurious helicopter for a weekend at his ten-thousand-square-foot chalet in the resort community of Courchevel, and the two had remained a committed and passionate couple ever since.

That memory was as fresh as the smile on her face as she gazed at him across the table throughout their evening.

"What are you staring at?" he asked, sipping from a glass of cognac he warmed in his large hands.

"You," was her uncomplicated reply, and they continued to gaze into each other's eyes until the check arrived, the comfort of silence more intimate than any dialogue.

Street met them at the front door, where he had posted himself throughout their meal. Even after the events aboard *Aurora* the previous night, Valtteri had insisted on a small security footprint, a detail that caused Street some discomfort, but he had agreed, mostly to appease the man who would have preferred no security at all. He went through the door first to ensure Jocko was parked outside and behind the wheel of the INEOS Grenadier, the large SUV's engine running. Then he signaled to Valtteri and Celeste to follow and ushered them into the back seat of the formidable vehicle.

Street gave a one-word command to Jocko: "Home."

Jocko merged the bulky off-roader into traffic in The Hague's city center, heading toward the waterfront and the five-star Grand Hotel where Valtteri held the presidential suite.

As they approached their turn, a roadworks crew barred their path, so Jocko steered them to their alternate route.

Celeste noticed Street's shift in demeanor at the changed plans. Valtteri took note as well.

"Everything's fine," he told her. "Just a little detour."

That the mega-billionaire inventor and eco-entrepreneur was attempting to allay her fears was charming. She had spent her career on the streets of France as a police officer. First, in the rough-and-tumble northern neighborhoods of Marseille, then in the Barbès, Pigalle, and Red Castle areas of the eighteenth arrondissement in Paris, as well as its protest-rich central districts.

"I'm not worried," she said. "I'm confident that Street and his trusty sidekick are skillful centurions who will see to our safety."

"Aye, Madame Clicquot, but you make us sound like Don Quixote and Sancho Panza, and I'm not sure that's the comparison I'm striving for," said Street, scanning the road around them. "We'll have you home in under five minutes."

Suddenly, two Mercedes G-Class SUVs appeared behind them.

"See what I'm seeing?" Jocko asked Street.

"I do."

"What's happening?" asked Valtteri, glancing over his shoulder.

"I don't know," came the reply. "Sit tight and snug up your seat belts. This might get bumpy."

Jocko kept the vehicle moving along at a steady forty kilometers an hour to see what the Mercs would do. They were close and closing in, in staggered formation, but held ten meters back. To their right, a steel pedestrian barrier ran the length of the roadway. To their left, a concrete abutment protected a set of tram tracks along the side of the road.

A set of headlights from what appeared to be another G-Wagen came toward them from ahead.

"What are they up to?" asked Valtteri.

They didn't have to wait long for an answer. The oncoming Mercedes hit the brakes and fishtailed so that it came to a stop diagonally across the narrow roadway, blocking both lanes of travel.

Jocko slowed the Grenadier on approach. "Any thoughts, boss?" he asked.

"You're the driver. Your call," said Street.

Jocko was now crawling along, the two Mercs behind them moving closer, preparing to flank the Grenadier. As they drew to within twenty-five meters of the newcomer in front, Jocko instructed everyone, "Brace yourselves."

"For what?" asked Valtteri.

Without answering, Jocko stomped the gas pedal to the floor, and the Grenadier lurched ahead just as a man in the front seat of the Mercedes SUV swung the muzzle of a submachine gun out the window toward them and began to fire. Jocko lined the Grenadier up with the passenger door. Celeste watched as the man dove away from the window where the impact would come, his bullets missing wildly. At the last second, Jocko gave a slight pull on the wheel and moved the Grenadier to the left, lining it up with the rear axle of the G-Wagen.

The force of the impact lifted the back end of the Grenadier off the ground while the Merc was sent careening in a double three-sixty down the road, its rear end popping off the axle. The two twin-turbo-powered G-Wagens that had been trailing now began the chase, and as they caught up to the Grenadier, which had been slowed by the impact, their occupants thrust carbines out the window toward them.

The sound of gunfire filled the night, flames spit from muzzles, and the rear window of the Grenadier exploded.

Street yelled out, "Get down!"

Jocko weaved the car from side to side, while Street reached under the glove box and popped open a hidden compartment, producing an even more compact version of the rifle Clicquot had seen his team use the other night aboard *Aurora*. Both men in the front seat hit the power window buttons to allow them to engage.

Crouched in the back, Madame Clicquot reached into her black lambskin Bottega Veneta clutch and pulled out a micro-compact 9-millimeter Glock.

Street stared at her.

"What?" she asked. "Do you honestly think that the head of Interpol runs around unarmed? Where do you think I live—Canada?" She press-checked her pistol like a pro and assumed a good grip, keeping her muzzle pointed at the floor.

A Mercedes G-Wagen came up alongside Jocko's window, and as one of the badgers stretched his carbine out the window, Jocko swerved into them, banging them off their line.

"Push back into your seat!" shouted Street, and as Jocko obeyed, Street fired a burst of .300 Blackout into the Merc. The passenger's head exploded with the impact of the subsonic rounds, and the Merc fell back. But a second later, it resumed the chase. "Assholes," he cursed.

Clicquot could see they would soon exit the forested section of roadway and enter a more congested area, close to the beach in the Scheveningen district of The Hague. Jocko knew it, too, and cranked the wheel, forcing the Grenadier to veer left. They clipped the front of a passing tram and jumped the rails, momentarily catching air before landing on the high-profile tires.

"Everyone okay?" he asked, but there was no time to wait for an answer.

The third AMG-powered G-Wagen tried to follow, but as it gave chase, it slammed into the side of the tram, sending both vehicles careening off the rails through the grass.

"*Yah fuckin' dobber!*" shouted Street in a heavy brogue. "Duck down," he implored in less-accented English as he swung his weapon to the rear, aiming it out the back window at the last of the Mercedes SUVs. Celeste and Valtteri did as directed, and Street let loose with a burst of gunfire that peppered the badgers' windshield. The driver swerved sharply to the right, and the passenger-side wheels lifted off the ground. The driver corrected to the left, bringing the wheels back in contact with solid ground. Their pace had been slowed, though, and Jocko opened up some distance between them. Only now he found himself running off-road into the tall grass of the park.

"Those bastards won't be able to keep up with us through here," he said, smiling. His glee was short-lived, however, as a fourth G-Wagen appeared through the trees ahead of them. The area was poorly lit, but Celeste could see its headlights bouncing up and down fifty meters away as it ran parallel to them on the other side of a long pond. Bursts of light and the crack of a pistol-caliber carbine helped confirm her observation.

"Looks like we've got more company," Jocko said.

Street leaned his own rifle out the window and let off multiple bursts of fire toward the newest arrival. Celeste spotted sparks coming off the metal of the badgers' SUV, and Street doubled down.

Behind them, the other Merc bounced along. It wasn't gaining on them, but they weren't exactly losing it, either, the occasional round making contact with the Grenadier.

"Find me some solid ground to shoot from, Jocko," said Street.

"Right, boss."

The paths of the vehicles converged, and Celeste saw little by way of escape routes. But then the Mercedes on the other side of the pond plowed through a flock of geese and ducks and, amid the ensuing carnage, skidded sideways and down the bank, rolling onto its side into the shallow water of the pond.

Jocko swerved and struck a small rut that sent them airborne. The other Merc was nearly beside them, but the driver offered ineffective fire from a large-caliber pistol.

Celeste rolled her window down and stretched her arms toward the G-Wagen, letting loose a three-round burst. The Merc swerved but came back at them. She fired more bullets toward it, and at least one found its mark, the driver's head thrown backward against the headrest. The Merc swerved sideways, flipped, and barrel-rolled down the embankment into the pond, crash-landing with a huge splash that sent more resting birds into the night.

Jocko slowed the Grenadier. They could see the flashing blue lights of approaching police vehicles as he reentered the roadway.

"Anybody hurt?" asked Street. Celeste and Valtteri shook their heads. "Good."

Just as the word left his lips, their SUV was struck with a devastating impact in the right rear. The Grenadier spun sideways into the path of the SUV that hit them, which continued forward, its engine revving. They flipped onto their side, and as the SUV kept pushing against them, their momentum sent them barrel-rolling down the road.

Celeste's head banged against the steel frame of the door, blood running down her dress. At last, they came to a stop on their side. Dazed, she tried to unfasten her seat belt, but suspended as she was, there was too much tension on the mechanism, and she couldn't release its hold on her. Jocko moaned from the front seat. Street lay still beside him.

Next to her, Valtteri groaned, but his eyes remained closed.

"Valtteri," she called. "*Valtteri!*"

Through the deformed windshield, she watched as two sets of boots approached the car. Shots rang out, and Jocko's body shuddered under the impact of lead. She searched for her gun, which had been ripped from her grasp in the crash. She spotted it lying against Valtteri's foot and tried to pick it up, but it was just beyond her reach. She struggled against her seat belt as the men outside moved silently around the vehicle. At last she was able to wriggle enough to relieve some of the tension and the buckle released, dropping her onto Valtteri. She grabbed her pistol from beneath him.

As several police cars began to arrive on the scene, a man looked down through the rear passenger window and thrust a gun into the space. Celeste fired until the magazine of her compact pistol was empty. The man's face burst open, filled with multiple rounds of 9-millimeter hollow-point ammunition. His blood rained down on her and her dying lover.

There was more commotion outside, and commands were shouted in Dutch and English.

"Valtteri," she whispered as consciousness ebbed away from her. She whispered his name again.

As more gunshots rang out and blackness engulfed her, one more name crossed her mind.

Alex.

CHAPTER 26

MCLEAN, VIRGINIA

O n the counter, Alex's iPhone lit up with a text. The display read *Jonathan Burgess*. She swiped to her messaging app.

Jonathan: 911

What the . . . ?

Jonathan was a good friend. An information systems security analyst with Interpol, he was also an MIT-educated computer science wizard and, before that, was a rising star with the Communications Security Establishment, Canada's foreign signals intelligence agency. He had been with CSE's cryptology division prior to his secondment to Interpol headquarters in Lyon, France, and Alex had told everyone that he was the primary reason she had been able to solve her last major case working for Interpol.

She punched the call button. He answered on the first ring.

"I wanted you to hear this from me first," he said without so much as a hello.

"What's going on? What time—"

"Secretary General Clicquot is in the hospital. She's in critical condition. Alex, it's not looking good."

What? "What happened?"

"They were returning to Valtteri's suite in The Hague after dinner when their car was ambushed."

"But I just left them in France. She was staying at his estate, near Nice."

"She was scheduled to meet with Chief Bressard in the morning, so they flew back to The Hague late in the day."

Her mind reeled. *What did this say about the events from the other night? Had Celeste been the target of the attack on* Aurora *after all?*

"What about Valtteri?" she asked.

There was silence on the line.

"Jonathan, how's Valtteri?"

"Alex, Valtteri is dead. He died shortly after the ambush."

Her chest tightened. *Oh my god. Celeste.*

She brought her hand to her mouth as she tried to process what she had just heard. The man she had met two nights ago aboard his mega-yacht, the billionaire whose intentions and ambitions she had questioned just yesterday morning at breakfast, the love of her friend and former boss's life, was dead.

"Alex, you still there?"

Street. What about Street? He must have been with them.

"And their bodyguard, was he there, too?"

"I don't know the names of the two protection agents in the car, but one died at the scene and the other is in the hospital. I don't know how bad it is."

"What kind of ambush was it? I mean, one attacker? Multiple? Were they in vehicles?"

"I don't have all of the details, but I was told there were multiple bogeys that chased them down and ran them off the road. There was a gunfight, too. It was a real shit show straight out of a movie, but that's as much as I know, Alex."

Shit, she thought. *I should have been there. Fuck, fuck, fuck!*

"Where's Bressard?" she asked, referring to her former supervisor at Interpol.

"I just got off the phone with him. The chief's on his way to the hospital now."

"Okay. Let Chief Bressard know I'm coming, just as soon as I can catch a flight out."

"Can you do that?" he asked, concern leaking through. "I thought you're with . . ." He stopped himself before mentioning the Agency over the unsecured line. "I thought you had a different assignment now."

"Never mind that. This is a priority." *Madame Clicquot is a priority.* "I'll text you when I have my details squared away."

* * *

"Absolutely not."

Caleb's voice rang crystal clear through her cell phone.

"What are you talking about? I *have* to go."

"Alex, I'm sorry about your former boss and her boyfriend, but you have responsibilities here . . . in the States."

"Caleb, I'm not asking for your permission."

"Well, you *were* in fact asking for my permission, and I just said no."

She was fuming. She was already furious with herself for not standing up to the deputy director after being denied her request to assist with the investigation into the attack on the *Aurora*. Now, her friend was lying in a hospital bed and might die, and all because she hadn't been there to prevent it.

"Alex, did you hear me?"

"I'm going, Caleb."

"Alex, you're going to torch your career. Again. I can't let you do that."

"Then give me permission to go see her."

There was a pause on the other end of the line. She was sure he'd changed his mind.

"I'll call the deputy director—"

"Hell with that, Caleb! When you talk to her, tell her she can find me in The Hague at Secretary General Clicquot's bedside."

He sounded exasperated. "I'll call Deputy Director Thomas and *request* personal leave for you for a few days. You might not think highly of the task you've been assigned, but that's not your call. Orders are orders, and you've been given a lawful order by your boss, the deputy director of CIA. Given the elevated stakes at play initiated by an enemy of the United States, your employer deems the task force mission to be of the highest national security interest, which means *you* should also believe that the nation's security is under threat."

"With respect, Caleb, I heard nothing in our meeting to indicate a clear and present danger to the United States."

"With respect, Alex, that's not your call. Why are you always so stubborn? Even POTUS is eager for you and the task force to get to work. Again, I'm so sorry to hear that Valtteri is dead and Madame Clicquot is in the hospital. Honestly, I am."

"Then approve my leave."

"Alex, you know I have always had your back."

"Do I? Like you had it in Paris?"

"That's not fair, Martel. I showed up and was there for you."

"Yeah, after I left you with no other choice. Just like I'm leaving you now."

"Damn it, Alex!"

"Please, Caleb, I just need a day or two."

"Look, I'll call the deputy director and get back to you, but I'm pretty sure you already know her answer."

"One way or another, I'm going. Tell that to the DD when you talk to her."

CHAPTER 27

More than an hour had passed, and still, Alex hadn't received a call back from Caleb. *Whatever.* Her go bag was packed, and she was ready to head out the door. It felt lighter without her FBI service pistol and loaded magazines, but as a contract operations officer with the CIA, she wasn't permitted to carry a firearm on Company business without a well-defined reason beyond *because I always carried one before.*

As she grabbed a light leather jacket, the doorbell rang, followed by a gentle knock.

Who the hell is that?

She retrieved her everyday carry—every day, that is, except when she was on Company time—a Kimber R7 Mako subcompact pistol with an attached Crimson Trace reflex sight, and tucked it into the back of her jeans, the cold frame sending goose bumps up her spine.

Ding-dong, ding-dong.

"Coming," she called. "Keep your shorts on," she added, swinging the door open.

An older man stood on her doorstep.

"Dad?"

"Hi, Alex."

"What are you doing here?" She stared at her father in disbelief.

"You going to invite me in?"

"Sorry," she said, stepping aside for him to pass. She waved him in, the cool Virginia autumn air following him through the door.

David Martel was tall, lean, and just as fit as she remembered him as a young Army officer when she was growing up. But the retired general was showing his age in other ways. All the morning runs and hours at the gym couldn't hide the worry lines, forehead furrow, or the crow's feet around his eyes that had become more prominent since she'd last seen him. But her dad had earned every mark, every scar, and he wore them as a senior combat leader of distinction, as Deputy Director Thomas had pointed out when she had asked Alex about his service during Desert Storm.

She closed the door behind him, and when she turned back around, his arms were outstretched. She stepped in for a hug, and as he squeezed her tightly, she was convinced that her battle-hardened father was the best hugger on the planet.

"So, what are you doing here?" she asked again. She led him to the kitchen, where they sat at the island on faux-leather barstools. "Can I get you a drink? I don't think there's any beer, but I can get you a Coke or milk—"

"No, I'm good."

She popped open a can of Coke for herself and sat across from him. Then, remembering, she pulled out her gun and tucked it into a drawer.

He eyed the pistol and looked around. "Nice digs."

"I only just got in this afternoon . . ." Then it dawned on her. How had he found her? The number of people who knew where she was or even who she was at CIA could be counted on one hand. Yet, here he was. And so soon after her conversation with Caleb. Her smile faded, and she rose out of her chair.

"Okay, Dad, spill it. Who sent you?"

"Now, Alex, it's not what you think."

"Whenever anyone leads with *it's not what you think,* it's almost always exactly what I think."

"I just wanted to see you—"

"Bullshit, Dad. How did you find me? Why are you even in town? I thought you were on some government project in Africa."

"I was—I am. I had to come back to DC on business—"

She crossed her arms and tilted her head, unsmiling.

"No, seriously, it's true," he said. "And I thought it would be nice to catch up. We haven't seen each other except on Zoom calls and Face-Time in, what, a couple of years now?"

"Something like that. But you aren't answering my question. Who sent you? Caleb or Deputy Director Thomas?"

Her dad drew a deep breath and stared into her eyes. And then directly into her soul. It was his voodoo power over her and almost everyone else. He had the ability to see the disquiet within and to calm her troubled mind almost at will. As a child at moments like these, she would grow calm and wait for some wisdom or life lesson to be bestowed on her. But she wasn't a child anymore, just a suspicious daughter wondering what her father was up to.

"It's not going to work," she said.

"What's not?"

"Your voodoo sorcery. Your shaman ways."

"Alex, look—"

"Dad? Why are you really here?"

"Okay, fine. Caleb called me, but it was Kadeisha—"

"*Kadeisha?* You're on a first-name basis with the deputy director of CIA—my boss?"

"She's looking out for you. She knew I was in town and she told your partner to call me."

"He's not my partner."

"You work together."

"Not the same."

"Tomato, tomahto. I'm sorry about your old boss. Caleb asked for a temporary leave on your behalf."

"A three- or four-day leave of absence. That's all. To look into who attacked Madame Clicquot—the head of Interpol, no less—and her boyfriend, who's dead by the way, along with at least one of their bodyguards."

General Martel took a sharp breath in and held it a beat before letting it out. "Got any bourbon?" he asked.

"What? I don't know. I haven't had a lot of time to recce the premises."

"It's a CIA safe house, Allie. It's gotta have whiskey."

"What do you mean it's a safe house? No, it's not." The general looked at her with pity, as if she had just declared the earth was flat. "You really think it's a safe house?" she asked.

"In this neighborhood, this place would sell for, what, three or four million, easy. And you're on a short-duration contract with the Agency. Does that compute, Einstein?"

She hated when he called her that, but he was right. "Why would they put me up in a safe house?"

He shrugged. "It was either this," he said, "or the Staybridge Suites in McLean, so I think you got the better end of the bargain." He followed her into the living room, where a teak cabinet lined one whole wall. "Nice seventies vibe. Look," he said, pointing. "It even has a Pioneer component stereo system and tower speakers. This is definitely a safe house. Russian expats love this shit. I bet you'll find Barry Manilow on vinyl in a cupboard."

She ignored him, sliding cupboards open. Then, "Bingo!"

"Bourbon?"

"A half a bottle of Four Branches."

"Ah, the good stuff!"

They went back into the kitchen where she grabbed a couple of glasses, wiping them with a tea towel before giving them each a two-finger pour.

"*Salut*," he said.

"Cheers. You're not off the hook."

"I never thought I was."

They both took a gulp.

"People are worried about you, Allie."

"People are worried about themselves."

"Maybe, but in this town, that's the same thing. What you don't want is for them to worry about *you* affecting *them*. That's dangerous."

"All I'm asking for is time to go see my old boss. She's my friend, and in a way became my mentor and greatest ally. Without her faith in me, I never would have found the bomb in Paris. And if I hadn't done that, think where we might be today."

"I'd rather not," he said. "But it's not *what* you asked for, it's *how* you asked for it. I'm told it was more like an ultimatum. That's not the soldier I raised. Or the daughter."

It didn't matter that she was a grown woman who had served her country through multiple tours of duty and saved the world at least once. Getting lectured by her dad was never easy—not when the high school vice principal had ratted her out for smoking in the quad, not when the general had caught her with a boy and a bottle of vodka in the back seat of his vintage Mustang in the garage, and sure as shit not here and now. She was angry that he was in her home, safe house or not, scolding her. And she was pissed off with Caleb for calling him, and Kadeisha Thomas for putting him up to it. And dismayed that Thomas didn't understand the sense of duty she felt toward Madame Clicquot.

"Look," he continued, "I didn't tell you before, but your boss and I— Deputy Director Thomas, I mean—we go back a ways."

"So, have you been keeping tabs on me this whole time?"

"What? No," he said. "In fact, the opposite. What you do is your business and I respect that and intentionally stay out of it."

"So I see," she said sarcastically.

He ignored her. "You've always called me and asked my opinion when you needed a sounding board. But—"

She didn't let him finish. "But this time, you thought you'd butt into my business when I never asked for your help or opinion."

"Allie, you're being unreasonable."

"Am I?"

"This is different. DC is its own planet. People here are easily threatened after spending their whole careers building up their little fiefdoms. They want to know they're protected and not exposed."

"Exposed to what?"

"Everything, Allie. They're fearful of anything that could knock them out of power, or down a peg, or off a committee, or off of some list they thought they were on for that next director's job at a military contractor or lobby group or whatever. See what I'm getting at?"

She did. It was why she hated Washington and the career bureaucrats who wore their uniforms covered in shiny baubles they'd earned off the blood of the frontline bullet catchers, the infantrymen who laid their lives on the line every day.

She took another sip of bourbon.

"I *need* to go," she said. "For me, it's not an option."

"I get that. It's who you are. But in every strategy, there's an inherent compromise."

"Meaning?"

"Meaning, by choosing one path, you consciously or subconsciously reject another. By default, in every decision, there's a winning and a losing proposition. The world really is binary—on or off, yes or no, true or false, hold 'em or fold 'em. The trick is to make it so that the other side doesn't feel like they've lost or been disrespected in the process. You have to know what you want, but you need to understand what the other side wants, too. And if there's a way to give them something in exchange for your plan winning out, do it, and they won't feel like you've picked up all the marbles and run."

"Compromise."

"Compromise, cooperate, accommodate, whatever you want to call it. In the end, Allie, you're an employee of the CIA now, contract or otherwise. Your world is nothing but unrealized potential. If your boss gives you an order or tells you that you can't do something, then you'll need to put on your big-girl pants and do what you're told. Or you'll have to find a way to live with the consequences of ignoring it and going down your own path."

Her dad was a true leader of warriors, famous for not beating around the bush. It was the secret to his success.

Just then, her phone rang.

"About time," she said on seeing the display.

"Who is it?"

She spun the phone so he could read it.

Caleb, it read.

CHAPTER 28

"I'm sorry, I tried."

Alex thought Caleb would have had her back with the deputy director, but instead, he caved. There was nothing she could say in response that wouldn't make her sound like a petulant child, so she remained silent.

"You still there?" he asked.

She couldn't shake the image she'd painted for herself of Celeste in the intensive care unit of a hospital in The Hague, wires and tubes protruding out of her. As a combat medic, she'd seen it hundreds of times. Likely more. She had initiated some of the same invasive treatments on the battlefield, performed them in Black Hawks during casualty evacuations, and aided the medical teams in the operating rooms at combat support hospitals. She was intimately familiar with the sights, sounds, and smells of trauma units and ICUs.

Celeste.

"I'm going to see her," she said matter-of-factly.

"Alex, I don't know what more to say. Deputy Director Thomas listened. She's sympathetic to your situation."

"And when you knew my request for compassionate leave was denied, you went running to my dad to tell on me, knowing I might not take it well?"

"I didn't, Alex. Thomas called me and—"

"All I'm asking for is a few days to make sure Madame Clicquot will be alright."

"Alex, don't go AWOL on me again. One day you'll need friends, and going rogue will just leave you dangling out in the cold."

She looked at her father, who sat there staring back at her, silently sipping his bourbon.

"I don't know what more to say. I'm used to being by myself."

"Alex—"

She ended the call and drained her glass.

Out in the cold was fine with her.

CHAPTER 29

Despite her years as a medic—or perhaps because of them—Alex hated hospitals. They smelled like death, and she'd grown weary of that.

As her Uber pulled up to the Den Haag Centraal Hospital, she saw it featured a modern glass-and-steel façade bolted onto the old building, forming a sunlit extension. That renovation added a sense of modernity to a tired old building. Inside, the lobby was expansive and flooded with natural light from its southwest exposure. Someone had used a vibrant color palette to revitalize this wing, making it resemble a modern shopping center—that ultimate comparator of lively civic spaces—rather than a place of illness, mortality, and death.

A waterfall and a reflecting pool added to the tranquil ambiance. Overhead, a complex system of polished wooden arches reached skyward to the top of an enclosed glass arboretum populated with trees, ferns, and tropical plants, giving the impression one was center stage in a rainforest. A young woman sat at a baby grand piano on the other side of the pool, playing a lively tune that might have been Scott Joplin. Alex hummed along to the melody, and as she did, she was struck not with the whiff of illness and death she had feared but with something else altogether—toasted bagels. A modern food court extended off the main lobby.

She resisted the urge to get one and instead walked past the security desk, where a guard gave her a once-over as she strode from the main lobby toward the elevators.

Stepping off the elevator on the sixth floor, she was relieved to find the signs were written in both English and Dutch. She hurried down the hallway, passing into the locked ICU as a porter wheeled a patient out through the door.

Once inside, she found herself in a hallway lined with single-patient rooms running down both sides. The step-down portion of the unit was for patients requiring somewhat less care. She kept going until she came to a ninety-degree bend that led her around the front of the nursing station. Doctors and nurses hovered over keyboards and banks of monitors that beeped with the vital data of the patients in the unit. Opposite the desk, the beds were separated by curtains, not walls, allowing for a more fluid response and dynamic approach to care that any given patient might need.

It took her back to her early days as a 68W—an Army combat medic specialist—and her training at the US Army Medical Center of Excellence at Fort Sam Houston in San Antonio. The smell of an ICU was the same the world over. Whether in Texas or Baghdad, Bagram or The Hague, a mix of cleaning agents, soaps, and medical-grade plastics, as well as more human odors, hung in the air.

So focused were the staff in performing their tasks that not a single person even lifted their eyes to her as she continued her quest. But as she rounded another corner of the horseshoe-shaped ICU, two heavily armed, uniformed police officers barred her further progress. Beyond them stood Jonathan Burgess, IT security specialist extraordinaire, in the doorway of a large room, his arms folded, chin resting on a closed fist, hovering at the foot of a bed.

Madame Celeste Clicquot lay comatose on the bed. Intravenous lines ran into her arm from a multitude of IV medication pumps. A ventilator moved highly oxygenated air into a hose connected to an endotracheal tube, the inside of which fogged up and then dissipated on the other side of the breathing cycle. Monitors displayed her ECG, breathing patterns, and other vital signs.

Alex gasped at the sight of her friend, tears welling up in her eyes until one burst free and ran down her cheek, dampening the corner of her mouth. She wiped it as much as wished it away. The quote about time being fleeting was only a half-truth. It was not *time* so much as *life* that flies past while we cling to it as tenuously as a dying rose holds on to the last of its wilting petals.

Mom.

The involuntary association came to her, and suddenly Alex could barely contain her grief, feeling more overwhelmed than she had since her mother's funeral and, more recently, the one for her late husband, Kyle.

Jonathan turned toward her at the sound of her sniffle.

"Alex," he said as he hugged her. "I'm glad you're here."

She realized then that they had never met in person. All their work together had been over the phone and computer. He was handsome and as young-looking in person as he was over a video chat. Goateed and dressed in a light-colored casual dress shirt and black pants, he fit the image of a capable IT security specialist with Interpol.

"I'm glad we finally get to meet."

"Shitty that it has to be like this," he said, waving toward Madame Clicquot's bed, "but it's great to finally meet you, too."

She felt a hand placed on her shoulder from behind. At first, she thought it was a staff member or a police officer coming to escort her away for being there without permission from the nurses. She was braced to resist, but when she spun around, there stood Martin Bres-sard, her former boss at Interpol, an expression of compassion on his face like she had seldom seen before. She leaned into his arms, and he wrapped her tightly in an embrace.

"Chief," she sobbed.

"I'm glad you're here," he said.

She stood back, and he stared at her, an uncle assessing a favorite niece not seen in years, although, in this case, it had only been a few short months.

"I'm so sorry, Alexandra."

He was dressed in a dapper double-breasted suit, as always. Ever stylish, Chief Bressard was of medium height and build, with wavy salt-and-pepper hair and a short, nicely groomed beard. His royal-blue silk tie lent him a more cheerful than formal appearance.

"Has she been unconscious the whole time?" she replied, composing herself.

Bressard nodded his head. "I'm afraid so," he said, his baritone voice and Belgian French accent on full display. "There has been no change since the paramedics brought her in. In fact, the doctor said they're intentionally keeping her in a coma."

She understood this. A medically induced coma allowed the brain and vital organs to rest, better equipping the body to heal from damage suffered during a traumatic event. In this case, the event had been another attack that Alex might have been able to prevent had she been there.

She straightened up. "I'm going to find out who did this, Chief."

"God help them when you do."

* * *

Bressard told her everything that Interpol and Dutch police knew as they sat in the family room off the hallway outside the intensive care unit. Multiple vehicles, multiple bogeys. Same MO—right down to the hired Afghan mercs—as the attack at sea, only this time on the streets of the Netherlands' de facto capital.

"I shouldn't have left her."

"It's not your fault or your responsibility, Alexandra," Bressard said. "Valtteri had a security team—"

"About that," she said. "Where were they? I understand there were only two of them there when the attack happened. How could that be? Any protection detail worth their salt would have had triple that number assigned to these two."

"I am told Valtteri declined a heavy security detail. He, and quite honestly Madame Clicquot as well, found it too ostentatious."

"Security isn't a fur coat, Chief. Protection should always be right-sized to the threat and circumstances. Street knew this. He had at least twelve men on board the *Aurora* when it came under attack, and look at all the casualties. This was a determined adversary. Why would he have scaled the protection detail back like that?" Bressard said nothing. "What? He's in this hospital, isn't he?"

"He is, Alexandra. He took two bullets in his vest, and one grazed his shoulder. I'm told he'll be okay in due time—"

"Not when I get through with him," she said.

"Go easy on him. According to Street, Valtteri said it was to be him and one other bodyguard or none at all. And remember, he lost men in the raid on the *Aurora,* and now one who was with him last night. That must be a powerful blow. He's only human, Alexandra."

"Is he going to be okay?"

"The doctor said he had bruised lungs and a myo-something something."

"A myocardial contusion. Bruising of the heart muscle."

"Yes, that's it."

"And what about the other man? Do we know who that was?"

Jonathan piped up. "The second man's name was Jocko. I don't have a last name. He was driving. He didn't make it."

The ocean of white noise in her ears sounded like a gale-tossed sea. Every other sound around her faded into a hollow, distant din. How many times had she lost friends and comrades? Too many to count.

The concept behind the Secret Service and other agencies charged with dignitary protection and the guarding of VVIPs—very, very important persons—was to apply layers upon layers of defense. From the gathering of protective intelligence to the analysis of threats, to advance teams that liaised with boots on the ground, to proactive and dynamic close protection of their principles, to responding to threats with an overwhelming show of force and violence of action. Street should have applied a scaled-down version of this model, but he didn't. He had taken a minimalistic approach to his duties, and now two more were dead, and another was at death's door.

Isaiah 6:8. Send me.

"I should have been there, Chief."

Bressard was shaking his head. "It's not your job, Alexandra. You have your own responsibilities."

"But I would have pushed Street for more security." She nodded in the direction of the ICU. "I would have forced her and Valtteri to up their protection. Or at least convinced Street to stand fast and not let his client dictate the protection *they* wanted like they were at some security buffet when it was *his* job to spec out the details. Or, as a last resort, to lock things down. They shouldn't have gone out to dinner. That was cavalier."

Like a patient father, Bressard listened before speaking. "Neither Valtteri nor Madame Clicquot could be confined for very long," he said when her rant was over. "Besides, she was still piecing things together herself. She was considering a request that had been made of Interpol."

Bressard was a good cop, the polar opposite of those portrayed by the news and entertainment media. Or the ones who discredit their uniform and colleagues by doing stupid and abhorrent things. Criminal things.

"What request?"

"She had been speaking with a Finnish official—"

"Their NATO ambassador, Mikko Selänne."

"Yes," he said. "Ambassador Selänne. He had met with Madame Clicquot aboard *Aurora* before the attack and told her that he had been approached by Finnish intelligence. They wanted him to ask Interpol to quietly investigate any connection between events that had transpired across their country over the past year or so."

"Why the back channels?"

"Obviously, she felt other avenues of approach were compromised."

"Government channels?" she asked.

Bressard shrugged. "Diplomatic channels."

"Okay, but surely Selänne had specific objectives. What were they?"

"The Finns wanted to know if the events were linked to Russia or if they represented something else."

"That's not new information. I knew that already."

"But did you know that Madame Clicquot may already have turned up evidence linking it to another group, and possibly not the Russians at all?"

She didn't know that, but it would make sense. She was still angry with herself, though. And angry with Street. And mad at whoever was orchestrating this.

What was this all about? Who was behind it?

Whatever it was, whoever was responsible, she vowed to find out.

* * *

Alex stood beside the hospital bed, warming Celeste's cold hands in hers as if warming the hands of a small child who had lost their mittens in the snow.

A nurse stepped into the cubicle and hung a new medication bag from the overhanging IV pole suspended from a track in the ceiling that circled the bed. Then she punched a series of buttons on the medication infusion pump and gave Alex a reassuring smile.

To the uninitiated, the frenetic activity and cacophony of sounds in the ICU could be overwhelming, but Alex took comfort in watching the nurse perform her routine. An ICU nurse was a highly educated professional with the knowledge, skills, and expertise to hold a frail life in their hands, as this young woman did. The nurse's environment was different from the one in which Alex had practiced her combat medic trade, her work environment more controlled, but it was no less consequential.

"Thank you," Alex whispered as the woman stepped away.

She gathered her thoughts and gripped Celeste's hand more tightly, gazing into a face disfigured by the breathing tube that entered her mouth and descended her windpipe. The tube was attached to a machine that performed the most basic act of living for her. It *breathed* for her. Meanwhile, other medications held her cradled deep in sleep and free from pain, causing the muscles of her face to go slack.

"I'm sorry, Celeste," she began. "I don't know who did this, but I will find out. And when I do, I'll make them pay." Her Saint Michael medallion hung from a box chain around her neck. She pulled it free of the confines of her blouse and wrapped a hand around it. "I can't bring Valtteri back, but I can do what I do best. Your suffering and your loss will be avenged. This I swear."

CHAPTER 30

It was early evening when Alex left Chief Bressard and Jonathan at the hospital, but she had changed time zones so many times over the past few days that she no longer had any idea what day it was. She wouldn't step away from Clicquot's bedside until she could barely stay awake. In fact, Bressard had caught her sleeping and half out of the chair, her head on the mattress next to Celeste's unmoving hand, and ordered her to leave and to get some rest.

She would have protested, but by then, she was so far gone that she hadn't bothered to put up a fight.

"I'll call you if there is any change," he had promised as she finally walked away.

She'd summoned an Uber, and moments later, she was strolling through the entrance to her hotel, walking past subdued aqua and beige leather armchairs and small tables in the bar off a colorfully carpeted lobby. It was modern and elegant, similar in design and finishings to almost every other member of the hotel chain worldwide. But being situated in the heart of The Hague made this property distinct and highly desirable.

A pleasant young woman greeted her at the reception counter. "We were expecting you earlier," she said cheerfully.

"I had to stop"—Alex hesitated before continuing—"at the office to get some work done."

"Of course. It's not a problem." The woman smiled, handing her a key card. "The Greatroom Bar & Restaurant is open until midnight. You can also call down and order from the menu in your room around the clock if you're hungry."

A bellman stood waiting to take her suitcase, but Alex politely waved him off. Walking to the elevators, she heard music pouring out of the bar. Room service would be the better way to go tonight.

Stepping into her suite, she was met by an unobstructed view of the ocean. In fact, off to the right, she could see the apartment building where she'd lived until just months ago. The sheer drapes fluttered in the breeze coming in through the partly open window. She pushed the curtains aside and stood there, drinking in the sight. These moments were to be savored because she knew better than most that they could end without notice or fanfare.

Just ask Jocko or Valtteri.

She picked up the room service menu, spotted a ham and brie with strips of sweet red peppers and sliced tomatoes on a baguette, paired it with a white wine from the Loire Valley, and phoned down her order. It would arrive in forty-five minutes, which, although she was famished, suited her just fine since what she really needed was a good soak in the tub anyway. She started the bath, the steam curling up and clinging to the walls. As it filled, she stripped off her clothes, grabbed a small bottle of red wine from the minibar, and strolled back into the bathroom.

She lowered herself into the tub, her body sore and tired. The hot water soothed her aches and stung the wounds on her shoulder and foot. Lying back, she turned off the faucet with her toes and pushed the water in waves up her arms and over her shoulders. It was soothing and sensual, and she closed her eyes and fell into the moment, wholly immersed in both the water and her mood.

She took hearty sips of the red wine she'd liberated from the minibar and gently swished it around her mouth. Notes of raspberry and black currant excited her palate as she drank. Before long, she was totally relaxed, sunk down in the tub with her chin below the surface.

Thoughts of guns and bullets and evil men drained from her subconscious at the coaxing of the hot water and alcohol. She drifted into a gentle slumber, and before long, she felt the sensation of big, strong hands caressing her, evoking feelings she hadn't experienced in a long time. The blurred image of a man appeared like an apparition. It loomed over her, speaking softly, and leaned over the bathtub to kiss her.

Kyle, she whispered. As she relaxed into the sensations, the image of the man came into sharper focus. Her body rose to his.

Caleb.

An insistent noise brought her back to the present. She opened her eyes and looked around at her surroundings.

Knock, knock, knock!

Fully alert now, she called out from the tub.

"Just a minute!"

She leaped out of the water and grabbed a bath towel, wrapping it around herself as she hurried to the door, trying not to slip on the marble floor in the foyer.

"Room service," announced the voice on the other side.

She opened the door, remaining half-hidden behind it. A young man wheeled the cart into the entranceway, and she bid him onward into the living room of the junior suite.

"Um, thank you," she muttered.

She quick-stepped into the bedroom and fetched some euros from her purse, handing them to him when she came back.

"Thank you very much, madam," he said.

She closed the door gently behind him and threw on the deadbolt, then turned and leaned back against it, sighing deeply. She stepped back into the bathroom and dropped her towel to the floor, swapping it for a much more appropriate terrycloth robe from a hook.

Better.

She hadn't realized how truly ravenous she was until she took the first bite of her sandwich. It more than hit the spot. She wolfed down her food, savoring the pure pleasure of the act.

Don't think about the dream. Don't think about the dream.

* * *

It was eleven o'clock when Alex finally slipped off the terry robe and slid partway under the covers of the king bed. She set the alarm on her phone for 6:30 A.M., left the radio playing on the bedside table, and clicked off the light. A refreshing lick of cool air drifted across her skin through the open window.

She stared out the window at the moon, three-quarters full and casting silver shadows of the mullions across the bed. Its subdued light was hypnotic. Tranquility washed over her, aided by the wine, and she closed her eyes.

Another song came on the radio. The intro was a piano playing two bars of four pairs of eighth notes, and her subconscious promptly recognized the song. It had been years since she had last heard "Talking to the Moon" by Bruno Mars, but the lyrics came to her quickly, as fresh in her mind as if she had heard them only yesterday. By the time the chorus arrived, her tears were flowing down her cheeks.

Memories engulfed her. Painful memories. How many years had it been—five, six? More? She knew the exact date Kyle was killed, but that wasn't the same as remembering how long ago. But the song remembered and drew her back in time until she felt a familiar ache in her soul as fresh as a new wound, raw and sore. Back to a time before the pain had turned the memory into an ugly scar. Suddenly, she was transported back to the small apartment she had shared with her late husband outside DC. She looked out over the Potomac River, the moon shining overhead, and the song playing as they spoke.

"Can you see it?" he asked.

"I'm looking at it now," she told him.

"Me, too. Reminds me of you."

"You're a dork. How does it remind you of me?"

"I mean, when I look up at the moon, and I know you're far away, but looking at it too, I feel like we're connected, and I'm not so alone anymore."

"You're not alone there, Kyle. You have all the men in your unit with you and more than a few women, too."

"You know what I mean."

She knew what he meant.

And then came the other memories: a flag-draped coffin, a motorcade with black limos, dignitaries spewing platitudes about war and the meaning of the ultimate sacrifice.

Sorry for your loss. You have the respect of a grateful nation.

Words soothing to no one but those who spoke them.

Strangers hugged her. Gold Star Mothers and widows of fallen soldiers embraced her. These gestures meant something to her, lessened her burden, her loss, and her pain by exposing their own, like intermingling blood.

But the truth of war for Alex, a warrior from a family of warriors, was that it was ugly, anonymous, and unmindful of the duty, valor, and sacrifice of the men and women who fought and died.

Or lived while others died.

Kyle.

Her eyes closed and sleep came. She dreamed she was running through a vast forest with tall trees—evergreens and hardwoods mixed together, growing out of bare rock exposed by the scraping of colossal sheets of ice many millennia before. The forest opened onto a cliff above a raging river, and she came to the edge, naked and exposed. She hesitated, then leaped into the air, striking the water and being taken by the current.

Away.

Away.

Away.

CHAPTER 31

When her alarm went off, Alex climbed out of bed, pulled on her running clothes and shoes, and headed out on a run through her old neighborhood—the beaches and the pier at Scheveningen. Before she left her life in The Hague and Interpol behind, this had been her old stomping grounds. It was a lively, fun area right next to miles of wide, sandy beaches—a perfect spot for morning runs, dinners out, and moonlit strolls.

She wandered along the esplanade past the Grand Hotel. The sky over the North Sea was beginning to come alive with the first light of dawn, and her eyes were greeted by the incredible canvas painted by the sun rising in the east. She stood, arms folded, allowing a sense of tranquility to wash over her, bathed in the gentle sound of the surf. At this moment, there wasn't a better sound in all the world for her troubled soul than the sound of the sea and silence around her. She permitted herself to appreciate the view of another day arriving.

From the faint glow of the beach, the ocean stretched to the horizon like a dark cape, the crests of waves catching the early light.

One of the cafés along the esplanade was open, so she popped in to pick up a double espresso and an apple strudel. The young barista recognized her from the many times she had come in before, and they chatted for a few minutes before Alex strolled to the pier, settling on a bench between the giant Ferris wheel and the bungee-jumping tower. There she sat, enjoying the pastry, rich with cinnamon and coated in chunky sugar crystals. Quiet times like these were few and far between. And, while she preferred to experience life at a more hectic pace, she knew enough to be grateful when the quiet moments arrived, even for a short while.

She checked her phone for the umpteenth time to see if she'd missed a message from Jonathan or Bressard updating her on Celeste's condition. Nothing. It was more likely that they were still at home at this early hour getting ready to head into the office, in which case maybe one of the nurses would call. But she had no new notifications—a blessing, she supposed. Her plan was to head over to the hospital, but after that, she wasn't sure.

Her thoughts drifted to Caleb and her father. Caleb had had no right to call the general, and her dad had had no right to meddle in her affairs. David Martel had always been protective of her, but he knew where the boundaries were between parenting and intruding. This time, he had ripped right across that line. She sipped her coffee, already too cold to enjoy. She shot down what remained, its bitterness not unlike how she still felt about the events of the past few days.

Sometimes, a problem could be thrown at her, and she'd instantly see how everything fit together. Other times, she could be staring a solution in the face and not come up with it. That's when she felt truly lost. That's how she felt now.

Her run back to the hotel took her through the park and past the scene of the ambush. The area had been reopened, but there were still remnants of crime scene tape tied around trees, their torn ends flapping in the breeze. She surveyed the area, taking in the tire tracks in the grass, skid marks on the pavement, bits of metal and broken glass along the side of the road and next to a duck pond. She played out the facts of the scene before her, comparing what she saw to what she knew. Evidence of a violent encounter formed into moving images in her mind's eye: the finality of Valtteri's Grenadier being flipped by one of the badgers' vehicles; Jocko being summarily executed as he sat trapped in the SUV; Street injured; Valtteri succumbing to his wounds; and Celeste facing off against and ultimately killing one of the assailants before another badger, approaching the vehicle to finish her off, was shot dead by police.

But it still begged the question: *Why had someone targeted Valtteri and Celeste?*

She wasn't seeing all the pieces of the puzzle yet, let alone its solution.

It was like a keystone was missing from the peak of an archway. Without that big chunk of rock to lock it all together, the entire structure and everything it supported would collapse.

* * *

Half a block away, a dark-haired woman in a light green jacket leaned against a wall, pretending to check her phone. She watched as Alex entered the hotel.

Good to see you again, Alexandra.

* * *

Back in her suite, Alex stripped off her running clothes and stepped into the glass shower stall, allowing the hot water to drench her hair and body. She winced at the throbbing pain under the bandage that covered the wound on her shoulder. Her foot hadn't ached much during the run, but it complained bitterly now from the immersion.

She washed and conditioned her long hair, then rinsed off with a bracing burst of cold water, her skin erupting in goosebumps, feeling instantly refreshed. She stepped out of the shower and towel-dried her hair, then wrapped herself in a fresh one and strolled into the bedroom. Standing beside the bed, she was about to drop her towel when a reflection in the window caught her eye.

She spun around. "Who the hell are you?" she demanded, facing an attractive stranger sitting on the sofa in the living room.

The woman was elegantly dressed in beige slacks and a camel-colored, mid-length coat over a navy blouse. Her hair was blond and, judging by how much of it Alex could see, at least as long as her own.

"A friend," she replied with a pronounced Nordic accent. *Swedish? Finnish?*

"My friends don't usually let themselves into my hotel room while I'm in the shower."

"I knocked, but no one answered," the woman said.

"Right. Like I said, I was in the shower." She didn't bother asking how she'd gotten in.

"So I see." The woman smiled reassuringly, but Alex wasn't quite so encouraged under the circumstances. "Let me modify my answer. I'm a friend of Valtteri. And Celeste."

Alex sat on the edge of an easy chair adjacent to the sofa, still wrapped in her towel. "Let's pretend for now that I believe you. What do you want?"

The woman shifted on the couch so as to face Alex directly. Without her gun, Alex felt even more naked and exposed than she already was.

"We believe our mutual friends were targeted because Madame Clicquot had discovered evidence in a serious matter she had been looking into, unofficially."

Her accent was very distinctive and as pronounced as Valtteri's.

Finnish for sure, thought Alex. *So, Finnish intelligence, then.*

Which was starting to make sense.

"Is that she had been looking into it unofficially, or you're telling me this unofficially?" asked Alex.

"Both, but more the former. And I'm not sure the distinction is important."

"I suppose not."

"Now, let me ask you," said the visitor. "Why are *you* here?"

Alex considered how much she should share with the woman. "Celeste is my friend. And although I had only just met Valtteri, he was her special friend, so that made him a friend of mine."

"They were lovers. Just call it what it was."

"We aren't usually so blunt," Alex replied.

"You are joking, right?"

Alex repositioned in her chair. "I'm sorry, I didn't catch your name."

There was a pause before the woman replied. "Emmi."

"Emmi . . . ?"

"Just Emmi. Alexandra—"

"Alex is fine."

"I'm sure it is. So, Alexandra, why are you *really* here? You no longer work for Interpol. And, of course, you are no longer a special agent with the Federal Bureau of Investigation. So . . ."

"No, I'm not with the FBI anymore. Like I said, even though Celeste was my boss at Interpol—"

"She was not your boss at Interpol. Chief Inspector Martin Bressard was your boss. Madame Clicquot is the secretary general of Interpol. That puts her well above the pay grade of your friend and former boss, Martin Bressard."

"Anyone ever tell you you're too literal?"

"I'm Finnish. It comes with the territory."

"Like I said, Celeste is my friend."

"Of course. And I suppose it is just a coincidence that an officer with the Central Intelligence Agency finds herself in The Hague investigating an incident tied to a Finnish security and intelligence probe."

"I'm not with the CIA."

"Please don't insult me. Do you think that because I work for an agency that's a mere speck on a speck in comparison to the whale-sized one you work for that we are poorly informed?"

That confirmed it. Emmi was with Supo, the Finnish Security and Intelligence Service.

"I didn't mean to imply that."

"But you did, so humor me. We are colleagues, Alexandra. Let's start off by being honest with each other. Then I will feel comfortable sharing what I'm about to tell you."

Alex didn't really see a downside. Unless, of course, the woman was lying. But at this point, it was worth the gamble. "Fine, you're right. So what evidence did Celeste discover that got Valtteri killed and put her in an ICU?"

"Get dressed. Let's go for a walk."

* * *

They crossed the wide boulevard in front of the hotel, skirting the grounds of the official residence of the prime minister of the Netherlands directly across the street. The women walked in silence before setting out onto a walking trail in the sixty-acre Sorghvliet Park. A tall, redbrick wall surrounded the park on land that formerly comprised part of the official estate.

Very few people were out and about for a stroll. And as this was a location of Emmi's choosing, Alex felt vulnerable to surveillance or anything else that Emmi might have set up in advance. So she knew better than to let her guard down, and kept a watchful eye on her surroundings.

"You have heard there have been incidents in my country for more than a year, yes?" Alex nodded, and Emmi continued. "Incidents targeting important installations, threatening our power supply, our fishing and maritime industries. Putting tens of thousands of lives at risk. Many in government and at my agency believe these events originated with the Russians."

"And what do you believe?" asked Alex.

"I am not so sure."

Ahead of them on the trail, a woman approached wearing a light green jacket, its hood pulled low over her eyes. They walked in silence until she passed.

"So, if it's not the Russians, who do you think is doing these things? And what would their motive be?"

"It would not be a stretch to imagine others who wish to make Russia seem like the culprit of these deeds. First of all, blaming them is easy. Once upon a time, a wall came down and everyone believed the Cold War had ended. But the people of Finland didn't believe the fairy tale. We have lived with the threat of the insatiable bear's appetite for more than a century and we were not fooled. That was about the same time my country started to construct nuclear fall-out shelters. Did you know that there is enough space carved out of the rock underneath Helsinki to house a million people in the event of a war with Russia?"

"I had no idea," said Alex truthfully.

"Thirty years ago, America was hoodwinked into dismantling much of their espionage and counterespionage apparatus, but the Finns never believed the fairy tale that the Russians had suddenly turned into *peaceniks*. Instead, Finns believed the bear had only entered a brief hibernation but that it would be back."

Alex zipped her coat up against the chill. Her hair was still damp from her shower and wasn't getting any drier as they ambled slowly through the park.

"How so?" she asked.

"Russia has always suffered from its own tragic sense of inferiority." She pointed across the park at a group of people using an off-lead area with their dogs, some big, some small, all playing together rambunctiously. "The dog most likely to bite," she continued, "is not the biggest or the smallest but the one least confident in its ability to protect itself. When threatened, as such animals easily are, they lash out at anyone—man, woman, or child. In English, you call such a dog a *fear-biter,* meaning it attacks out of fear, not aggression. The Russian bear is a fear-biter."

Alex had known plenty of fear-biters in her day: officers—men *and* women—who lacked confidence in their leadership skills or possessed none; men who couldn't stand that a woman was in the same Army that they were; soldiers who hated being bested at the firing range or in the battlespace by someone who was a better operator or a better shot, as if it were even some kind of competition to begin with.

And of everything Emmi had said, Alex knew what she said about the Russians to be true, if her last mission was anything to go by.

"How does this theory of yours take them off the hook?"

"Because when a police officer—or an FBI agent, for example—is looking for a fall guy—what's the word for it in American English? A *patsy*? There is no one easier to indict than the one who is most likely to be guilty. Occam's razor—you know what this is, yes?"

Alex nodded. "It's often oversimplified as stating that the simplest answer is usually correct."

"But?"

"But it's not so simple. A better explanation is that if you have two competing ideas to explain the same phenomenon, you should prefer the simpler one."

"Exactly. The world is ready to believe that Russia could be guilty of anything—"

"Because they have proven just that, time and time again," said Alex. "Ergo, Occam's razor."

"Yes. But using a razor can be dangerous. It's very easy to get cut."

"Cute."

"In this case," said Emmi, "Russia's past behavior makes us want to believe they will always be the guilty party, but such assumptions can be used against us, too, by those who wish to manipulate our responses. The Russians, in fact, might not be guilty of everything of which they are accused, all the time."

Alex had made this very point just the other day with Caleb and Director Thomas.

Emmi continued. "Your friend, Madame Clicquot, wasn't convinced, either. That's why she contacted me specifically."

"You? No offense, Emmi, but I assumed you were an operations officer, just another worker bee like me. Why would Celeste reach out to you as opposed to the director or a deputy director, someone more at her level? Someone more able to initiate the right kind of collaborative intelligence probe with Finland's allies?"

Emmi stopped walking and turned to her. "Because, Alex, she thought there was a mole inside Supo. And because Valtteri Lehtonen was my uncle."

CHAPTER 32

After Alex's initial shock wore off, Emmi told her that she and a handful of other officers within Suojelupoliisi—better known as Supo—had been investigating the incidents that initially seemed unrelated. But after further analysis, it seemed more like the series of events going back a year or so were, in fact, connected.

The heir apparent for blame in all such matters was the security services of the Russian Federation—the SVR, GRU, and FSB. But over the past few months, their investigations had uncovered signals intelligence that had shifted suspicions toward a different party altogether.

"And who else knew of these findings?" Alex asked.

"Naturally, the interior minister was made aware. He has ultimate accountability for Supo investigations. Then he briefed the prime minister, Sanna Rantala, and she briefed President Jarkko Ruusu."

Alex considered this. How many others knew? Such secrets were hard to keep, even where secrets were the name of the game.

"Anybody else?" she asked.

"No, but we transmitted a packet to US intelligence."

"What kind of packet?"

"An intelligence summary from the analyst assigned."

That was news to Alex. Maybe Caleb or Kadeisha Thomas knew something about it.

"And the prime minister was supposed to brief her cabinet," continued Emmi. "But she and President Ruusu elected to keep the circle small, so they excluded them."

"Probably a good call."

Three can keep a secret if two of them are dead, Alex thought. So said Benjamin Franklin.

She stopped walking and touched Emmi's arm lightly. "Hey, I'm sorry about your uncle. Valtteri seemed like a very good man."

"Not just *seemed like.* He *was* a good man." Alex acknowledged the statement with a warm smile. Emmi went on. "He took very good care of his family. His whole family. And I don't just mean financially. When I was growing up, life wasn't always carefree and easy. I didn't get along with my parents. I mean, even by Finnish standards, they were very stoic about life and living. I wasn't like that, and as I'm sure you could see, neither was my uncle, who believed a life should be well-lived and fun. That often put me at cross-purposes with my parents, and Valtteri was always there if I needed someone to talk to."

Emmi stopped talking and looked across the park. The wind rustled the leaves along the narrow trail they were following, but they were otherwise alone.

"What is it?" asked Alex.

"Nothing." Emmi didn't sound convincing.

Alex followed her line of sight. The woman who had passed them minutes before was disappearing around a bend in the trail a couple of hundred feet away.

"Did you recognize her?"

"I don't think so."

"But you're not sure."

"We are in a business that requires us to be suspicious, Alexandra. But no, I am not sure."

"I noticed her earlier. Outside my hotel. When I saw her again just now, I thought she might be with you, one of your team."

"She is not."

They watched as she slipped out of sight. She and Emmi hadn't exactly been meeting *in obscura.*

"I'm sorry," said Emmi.

"For what?"

"I thought it would be better to go for a walk. That hotel is a known hangout for agents and spies. I was afraid the walls might have ears."

They resumed walking.

"What was the nature of the intelligence you uncovered?" asked Alex.

"There was a series of phone calls intercepted, but their origins had been masked behind various technical tricks."

"Such as?"

"Simple things, really. Using commercial messaging apps to make encrypted voice calls over the internet, and hiding connections behind daisy-chained VPN strings."

"What did the phone calls reveal?"

"The conversations were mostly in English. The voices and accents were multinational—some American, some European, some Middle Eastern. A real hodgepodge of subjects. Veiled references to the incidents. And we found a lot of money being moved around. Some was through standardized financial procedures, but much of it utilized the *hawala* system."

Hawala was less a system and more an informal way of transferring money across borders. It was one of the methods preferred by transnational criminal and terrorist groups because of the trust established within those networks and because it avoided banking fees and the systemic tracking and reporting of large transactions. And because it was suitable for transfers to remote parts of the world.

A brick wall loomed ahead, an iron gate obstructing their path forward. Emmi tugged it open and they strolled through, out onto Scheveningseweg, a long, straight road constructed in the mid-seventeenth century that joined the old Hague to Scheveningen.

"I shouldn't be saying any more at this moment," said Emmi.

"Then why exactly are we here?"

Just then, an SUV pulled alongside them. Two beefy men dressed casually in low-profile paramilitary garb emerged. But there was nothing casual about their demeanor.

Alex looked at Emmi. "What's going on?"

"These men are going to take you to the airport, where a plane is waiting."

"What are you talking about?"

"Your bag is in the car."

"Emmi, where am I going?"

Emmi checked the watch on her wrist. "You have a meeting scheduled in three hours. You better get going."

One of the men opened the rear door of the SUV for her.

"A meeting with who? Where?"

"It was nice meeting you, Alexandra. I hope we meet again. Enjoy your flight."

* * *

DEFENSE INTELLIGENCE AGENCY HEADQUARTERS,
JOINT BASE ANACOSTIA-BOLLING, WASHINGTON, DC

Caleb hated going to DIA—it was such a pain in the ass to get to.

As usual, the Anacostia Freeway was backed up as far as the Navy Yard Bridge with a car-versus-transport collision, adding ten minutes to his already late start. The headquarters for the Defense Intelligence Agency was located on Joint Base Anacostia-Bolling, where the Potomac and Anacostia Rivers met in southwest DC.

He rolled up to the Arnold Gates at the base entrance, where security personnel checked his ID against a printed list of names, then directed him to the main building.

"Pick up your visitor's pass at the security desk inside the front door, sir," the polite young guard had instructed him.

Visitor's pass, my ass. He might as well have sent me to the South Gate with the tour group.

He parked the Tahoe and hurried inside.

The operations center for the joint task force was a windowless conference room on the second floor. Associate Deputy Director Gault was already addressing the small group of team leaders but interrupted his briefing when Caleb walked in.

"Good of you to join us, Copeland," said Gault.

He quietly took a seat at the table. It was his own fault that he was late, but he still hated eating crow for anyone, let alone Hacksaw.

Gault handed the briefing over to Special Agent Willie Tam from the Diplomatic Security Service—the DSS. Happily, there was no accompanying PowerPoint presentation, and Tam updated the group on what Caleb had discussed with Deputy Director Thomas and Alex the day before, which had also been reinforced during the White House briefing.

The special agent summarized a subset of incidents that had taken place over the past twelve months or so, the kind that pointed directly back to the Russians in the apparently careless way in which GRU missions always seemed to go off.

"In your estimation, Tam? Is the guilty party Russia or other?" asked Gault.

"Too soon to call categorically, sir, but if it walks like a duck and quacks like one . . . Our signals intelligence has been hampered by the sophisticated procedures employed by whoever's responsible. But we're getting closer."

"Oh?"

"Nothing definitive yet, but I deployed a new signal-tracking algorithm. I'd say we'll be better able to make a clearer determination in a day or two."

Gault shook his head. "Not good enough. I'll connect you with additional resources down the hall. It's a step above what you've been authorized for at DSS. Alright, next," he said.

There was some additional conversation around the meaning and purpose of these disruptive events, with the consensus being that they could be a way for Russia to soften up its target and to put the populace, the media, and the government of Finland off balance ahead of any military incursion.

"Keep working that angle. And let me know the second you have anything. Obviously, there's a lot riding on this."

FBI Special Agent Clare Duffries spoke next. "And while a determination that Russia might be to blame seems a foregone conclusion, we have to consider the misdirection angle carefully, as Special Agent Tam alluded."

"Is there any evidence to support that someone other than the Russians is responsible?" asked Caleb.

Duffries looked at Gault, who nodded.

"We're all on the same team here, Agent Duffries. Even Mr. Copeland."

Asshole, thought Caleb.

"Yes, sir," she said. Then addressing Caleb directly, she continued. "We received information from Finnish intelligence strongly suggesting that another entity could be setting the Russian Federation up to take the blame."

"But why?" asked Caleb. "Why would anyone want to lead the world to the brink of another world war? I mean, Eastern Europe is a powder keg already again. It won't take much of a spark for everything to blow up, and we know what that would look like."

"It would be Armageddon," said Tam.

Caleb was nodding. The thought of how close they had come in Paris still haunted him.

Gault chimed back in. "I don't have to tell you this, Agent Duffries, but the key here is motive. Why would someone want to make Russia the patsy?"

"That's obviously the reason this task force was struck, sir," Duffries said.

"It is," said Gault. "But I'm going to have to agree with Copeland." Hearing those words, Caleb could have fallen out of his chair. "Our mission is straightforward. First, defend America's interests at home and abroad. Second, find out who's behind these disruption operations and what their motive is. Tam, continue to work with State to ensure our Foreign Service employees and facilities are not on anyone's target lists. For my part, I'll set you up here at DIA with resources beyond your everyday. Copeland, you're the primary liaison with our allies' intelligence people—the Five Eyes, NATO, German, French, Dutch, and Finnish intelligence, as well as the EU Intelligence and Situation Centre. And in the event it's necessary, you'll be tasked with spearheading any direct action, of course, as authorized by Joint Special Operations Command. Duffries, Copeland's going to need help with intelligence." Duffries snickered. "You two dovetail your resources however you see fit. Copeland, your deputy director has approved the use of your team, minus one, I understand."

"Martel's on another assignment," Caleb replied.

"Still can't keep your ISA pet on a leash, huh, Copeland?"

Caleb envisioned his fist connecting with Gault's face and the satisfying feeling of bones splintering beneath knuckles. With that image in mind, he turned to Duffries. "We might all be on the same team here, but the coach is a fucking asshole."

CHAPTER 33

Alex deplaned from the private jet in Helsinki and was shuttled over to a sleek executive helicopter. Lehtonen Enterprises was stenciled across its sea-blue and white livery colors, conjuring the visual impression of the flag of Finland.

The rotor-wing aircraft was a level up from the helicopter she had flown in during an operation in Arnhem seemingly a lifetime ago. The rear door was open, revealing a luxurious six-seat cabin of finely stitched leather.

"Afternoon, ma'am," said the pilot from the front seat.

"Where are we going?" she asked.

"You haven't been told?"

She shook her head.

"If it's all the same to you, I'd just as soon not say. We'll be there in ten minutes."

"We waiting for anybody else?"

"You're it," he said.

"Mind if I ride up front?"

He smiled and waved at the vacant seat to his left. "Be my guest."

She climbed into the front as a member of the ground crew stowed her bag into a compartment behind the cabin and closed the door.

"Buckle up, Agent Martel."

"I'm not—" she began to say, but the engine was revving up and the rotors already spinning. The noise wasn't nearly as loud as that time in Arnhem, nor when she had been in-country back in her days with Intelligence Support Activity and the Army, but it was loud enough. The pilot pointed to the headset hanging above her seat. She fitted it over her ears and swung the mic down. "It's Alex."

"Markus," came the reply.

"I'm sorry about Valtteri," she said. "He was a nice man."

"He was the best, Alex."

She couldn't tear herself away from the view as they flew south toward the city center. The deep blue of the Gulf of Finland lay ahead of them. Below, exposed granite jutted from the ground, ancient bedrock left bare by the passing of mile-thick sheets of ice thousands of years ago. Long seams of exposed rock gave her the impression of flying over parts of upper New York State and other places in the rural northeast. Only here, the Finns had built their capital city over it.

Thousands of feet below them, as everywhere, the city grew denser the closer they got to its center. Even from the air, the hustle and bustle was apparent.

Markus flew out past the shoreline and circled a series of connected islands, then straightened out. Judging by the position of the sun, they were heading west. A minute later, he banked again and rounded a small reach of land jutting into the sea. The property had several residential buildings—a large house with a viewing tower, outbuildings, and a red tennis court.

"We're here," he said, pointing down. "That's Kesäranta."

"*Kesäranta*?"

He nodded. "The official residence of the prime minister of Finland."

Markus set the helicopter down gently onto the roadway next to the residence. Men in suits who had been standing off a safe distance to avoid the downwash from the helicopter's blades approached as the rotors slowed.

The air felt crisp as she climbed down out of the chopper. A light breeze blew in off the Baltic Sea, and she hunched her shoulders against the chill.

"Ms. Martel," said the lead agent. "Follow me, please."

* * *

ACCT OFFICE, FALLS CHURCH, VIRGINIA

Caleb and Special Agent Clare Duffries pulled into the nondescript strip mall that housed his team. The storefront was wedged between a barbecue restaurant and a tanning salon on Leesburg Pike. He parked the dark gray RST-edition Chevy Tahoe in the row of unassigned spaces, blending in surprisingly well with the Range Rovers, Escalades, and Navigators endemic to the community of Falls Church, Virginia.

His teammates all drove variations on the theme—domestic pickup trucks and SUVs that didn't scream *CIA paramilitary operations team* to members of the general public or, more important, to those with a vested interest in noticing the comings and goings of Caleb's specialized unit, ACCT. Falls Church was, on the one hand, a sleepy little bedroom community. But on the other, it was a hotbed of spies and roving eyes— some friendly, some not. Equally important, it was often impossible to distinguish between friend and foe.

Two of ACCT's members were already present when he walked inside. In the front room, the tables were arranged in a square, with a gap to pass through into the middle. At its center was another table laid out with take-out trays from the barbecue restaurant next door—beef brisket, ribs, pulled pork, smoked brisket chili, mini cornbread muffins, chopped coleslaw, red quinoa salad, and a hefty dose of baked macaroni and cheese.

"What the hell?" said Caleb, smiling as he came through the doors. His nose filled with the scent of American barbecue.

"Hey, boss. Thought you'd be hungry." Rocky was a former boxer. He was short, compact, and densely muscled. As a secret squirrel—that is, a classified operative with CIA's Special Activities Center—he had earned his nom de guerre, Rocky, from his resemblance in physical stature to the famous cartoon character, Rocky J. Squirrel. In fact, sometimes they just called him Squirrel.

"I *am* hungry, but—" Caleb gestured at the vastness of the spread.

"No worries, boss," said Moose, his voice lower than a Louisiana swamp. "We used your corporate card." At six-four and weighing two-sixty, he seemed every bit the size of his namesake.

"Clare," Caleb said. "Meet Rocky and Moose. But don't be fooled. They're smarter than they look."

"It's not true," said Rocky.

"Yeah," said Moose. "First impressions count."

"In that case," said Clare. "Pass me a plate."

"Right," said Caleb. "Eat, but make it fast."

"What's going on?" asked Moose.

"Get your kits sorted. I have a feeling we'll be going wheels up soon. And pack a jacket—it could get cold."

CHAPTER 34

"I thought you might be hungry after your journey, so I took the liberty of having some food set out."

Prime Minister Sanna Rantala led them into a sitting room with wide mullioned windows overlooking the sea.

"Thank you," said Alex. "That was very thoughtful." Now that she was being reminded of it, she was starving.

Plates of salmon, cured meats, and what the prime minister called Karelian pies were laid out in the center of a side table next to a large bowl of fruit. Alex eyed the oranges and was transported back to a terrible event she had been the center of in the Diyala region of Iraq, northeast of Baghdad near the Iranian border, years before.

"Or would you prefer an orange?" asked Sanna, following Alex's gaze. "I'll have someone bring a knife—"

"No, thank you," said Alex, shaking off the memory.

"You'll love the salmon then—it's amazing. And our chef bakes sautéed reindeer into a delicate puff pastry like nobody's business. It's to die for if that's your sort of thing. Tangy, like wild game should be."

Finland's prime minister was a beautiful woman in her early thirties and not at all what Alex had expected. She was fit and slim with long dark hair, hazel eyes, and a killer smile.

"Thank you. That's very thoughtful . . . Your Eminence."

Rantala laughed. "First of all, the proper address would be *Your Excellency*. I think *Your Eminence* is what you would say to the Pope. But to be honest, I'm a lapsed Lutheran, so I have no actual firsthand experience with the Roman Catholic papacy. Is that redundant?"

"The papacy? Or saying *Roman Catholic papacy*?"

She laughed again, wagging her finger at Alex. "No, no, no. I just know we would get into a lot of trouble together. Let's skip formal titles and go with first names, then, if that's okay with you, shall we?"

"Fine by me."

"I'm so very pleased to meet you, Alex," she said, extending a hand that Alex graciously accepted.

A server arrived bearing a silver tray with two stemmed glasses of white wine, the frost line evident on the sides of the glasses.

"I can get you a soft drink if you'd prefer," Sanna offered.

Alex lifted a glass off the tray. "Why waste an open bottle? This looks wonderful."

Sanna smiled and retrieved her own glass. "I thought it might be. What I know of you—and rest assured, our intelligence agency might be small, but it is mighty—I was convinced a nicely chilled white would please you. Sancerre, right?"

Alex pulled back and regarded her host with curiosity. "Yes, but—"

"Don't panic. Your preference for wine was noted in a magazine article. *Newsweek,* I think. Or maybe it was *People.*"

"That was very thoughtful." She swirled her glass expertly and took a sip. Cold and dry, it was comfort on her tongue. "Oh, this is a good one," she declared.

Sanna looked pleased. "You know your wine."

"Some more than others. But don't be too impressed, I'm a sucker for a good Loire Valley white."

Sanna said something in Finnish to one of her house staff who stepped forward and handed Alex a plate.

"Try this. My household chef is amazing." The server lifted a slice of grilled fish off a platter and placed it on Alex's plate, then put a thin wedge of lemon next to it. "This is the finest salmon you will ever taste. It's been lightly seasoned, then grilled over an open fire and drizzled with a maple-syrup-brandy mix."

The server put some more food on Alex's plate and then served the prime minister. Together, they strolled to a small table next to the window and watched as waves rolled onto shore, lapping at the footings of the dock.

"Or would you prefer a walk by the sea?"

Alex smiled. "I'd like that."

"Follow me," said Sanna. "Leave the plate. Bring your wine." *Leave the gun, take the cannoli* echoed through Alex's mind. "Someone will bring those for us. There's a bistro table in the gazebo."

The two women strolled through a side door out to the rear of the house.

"I'm sure you would like to know why you are here." Alex nodded and Sanna continued. "Valtteri was an interesting man, was he not?"

Alex considered the question. Prime Minister Rantala prided herself in being well-informed, so surely she would know that Alex had only just met the man.

"He was Celeste Clicquot's boyfriend," she replied, "so that should have been enough for me."

"But?"

"So, I'm embarrassed to say that a part of me wondered if he could be involved somehow."

"Really?" Sanna asked. "And do you wonder still?" Alex took a moment too long to reply. "I see," said Sanna. "My father and he were friends. They grew up together. Played hockey on the same teams. And even though they grew apart over time and distance, their friendship continued. Valtteri was very supportive when I entered politics. He even provided some important campaign financing and opened doors that might otherwise have remained closed.

"So, you see, Alex, Valtteri Lehtonen wasn't related to me by blood, but he was very much like an uncle. And to Finns, family is very important. We are a reserved and forthright people, and we are also very protective of our kin."

Alex listened as they ambled along a path that led them down to the dock. Two of Finland's top executive protection agents followed behind.

"Can I ask a question?" asked Alex.

"Of course."

"Why was Finland's NATO ambassador aboard the yacht the other night?"

Now it was the prime minister's turn to stall. She took another sip of wine. Two large sips, in fact. It occurred then to Alex that Sanna might still be sizing her up, trying to decide how much to reveal.

* * *

HELSINKI, FINLAND

The woman drove past the hospital compound on her left and the prime minister's residential compound on her right. Her view of Kesäranta was blocked by the foliage on the trees that hadn't yet fallen victim to the cool air of early autumn. Veering onto Merikannontie, she continued for a hundred meters before making a right. She found a vacant parking spot in the spaces adjacent to the small marina and slipped her Volvo into an empty one overlooking the bay that was nestled between her and the prime minister's official residence.

She fished out a pair of Zeiss 8x25 binoculars from her pack on the seat beside her. They were indispensable at moments like these. Being able to watch Finland's prime minster walking beside Special Agent Martel as they enjoyed the fresh air and sipped wine—*how bougie was that*—made up for the risk of detection she faced holding the binoculars above the steering wheel of the late-vintage Swedish automobile.

CHAPTER 35

Willie Tam's office was little more than a cordoned-off space behind a locked door in a windowless room. It wasn't a closet, but it wasn't exactly a room at The Ritz, either.

Special Agent Tam worked the keyboard in front of a series of screens. He was targeting a variety of intercept stations that were tied into the Five Eyes' ECHELON system version 4.0. Five Eyes was an alliance composed of the intelligence agencies of Australia, Canada, New Zealand, the United Kingdom, and the United States that cooperated on sharing signals and other intelligence. Tam had also inserted himself into Frenchelon and Onyx, the French and Swiss versions of ECHELON, respectively.

The computer code he had written functioned to mine and aggregate information that could identify threats to the United States' foreign service and other American assets abroad. His understanding of his mission, in this case, was that events tied to the aggressive actions of the Russian Federation against Finland threatened American interests abroad as well as global peace and security in general. And in so doing, the NATO alliance was being directly challenged. To prevent an escalation of hostilities between the major superpowers, Tam needed to get to the bottom of the mystery. And fast.

Tam's normal duties at DSS focused on threat analysis, protective intelligence, and cybersecurity, which is why he assumed he had been tapped for this joint task force in the first place. He was an information systems expert and a closet coder who had been designing online security systems for the Diplomatic Security Service and American embassy computer systems worldwide for years. As Director Gault had explained it, someone was trying to draw the US into a war. Consequently, his task was to identify targets, intercept mission orders, and expose the conspirators. In essence, stop the next global conflagration before it began.

The way Tam saw it, a war was already underway, and it was just a matter of time before it blew up in everyone's faces. It was up to him and the other members of the joint task force to prevent that from happening.

Since he arrived, he had been exposing threads, tugging at them, processing them, and trying to assemble them into a cohesive fabric that he could share with the team. But the task was difficult. Technology today was such that it made it simpler for disciplined players to hide behind masks of electronic deception. Using a TOR browser, routers, gateways, networks, and logless VPNs, malign actors could hide their identities and plans from prying eyes, including those of lower-level intelligence monitoring systems.

But Tam had been given access to tools available only at the highest levels of American signals intelligence. His latest stroke of luck had come when ECHELON spat out a report based on a query algorithm he had written—so, in that sense, not just luck, but his brilliance. In the report, he saw a framework. The problem was that it was incomplete. It was akin to discovering a roadmap that bore no names or physical features, just lines connecting dots.

Where others could only see the zeroes and ones of the digital world, he saw form and color. There were people with synesthesia, those on the spectrum who experienced words or sounds as colors or tastes. Tam couldn't see sounds or taste colors, but he had a rare gift for the digital realm. When the gibberish of lines of code, numbers, or seemingly random words scrolled past his eyes, his brain translated the mess into meaningful forms and shapes, revealing ideas, objects, and people.

When ECHELON spat out its semi-comprehensible and dissonant report, Tam found what no one else would have seen. *Could* have seen.

"You have to see this," he said into the phone, barely containing his excitement.

"What is it?" Gault asked on the other end of the line.

"I found something."

"I'll be right down."

The deeper he dug, the more he recognized that what he was looking at had its origins in the States, not abroad. The communications patterns represented a group with a common purpose, but he couldn't yet see the players. What he could see was, in his mind, glaringly obvious.

Money transfers, matériel support like in a combat zone.

He dared not speak aloud the word his brain saw. *Conspiracy.*

Gault arrived a few minutes later. As best he could, Tam walked him through the process he had used to get the system to reveal its secrets to him. Partway through, Gault cut him off.

"Tam, I never cared much for magic tricks. Get to the point."

Tam offered a blank stare. "Right. Okay," he said, pushing his glasses back up the bridge of his nose. "I know who did it. Or rather, who didn't do it."

"Could you be a little more specific? Are we talking about the JFK assassination?"

"What? No, sir. I know who perpetrated the attack on the Finnish guy's megayacht and the assault on him and the Interpol secretary general in The Hague."

"Old news, Tam. We already know they were soldiers of fortune—hired Afghan mercenaries."

"Yes, but I know who is conducting the disruption operations in Finland, too. Well, not exactly who, but what."

Gault's face lit up as Tam explained the spiderweb he saw in front of him, and the connections he'd made to get there.

"It's not complete, but it's an evolving model," said Gault. "There's no actionable intelligence here, but it's an excellent development. Nice work. Have you told anyone else?"

"No, sir."

"Nobody?"

"Not a soul."

"Keep it that way. This goes deeper than I was willing to guess. And higher. I'll feed it up the chain, but as far as you're concerned, not a word to anyone—not to Copeland or Special Agent Duffries. Not to Martel. No one."

"Yes, sir."

* * *

Gault walked quickly to his office deep inside the Defense Intelligence Analysis Center. Once behind his closed door, he placed a call.

"We have a problem."

* * *

WEST SPRINGFIELD, VIRGINIA

Tam lived in a cozy, tree-lined subdivision forty minutes from DIA headquarters. His wife had asked him to stop at the grocery store three miles away for milk and eggs. There were closer grocers, but tonight was date night, since his mother-in-law liked to babysit for them one night a week so she could have her grandkids all to herself for a few hours, and Kelly wanted Ben's Chili Bowl for dinner, her favorite chili, finally available from the supermarket.

He took the Capital Beltway and eventually found himself on Old Keene Mill Road in Springfield. He continued straight where he would normally have turned at Rolling Road, oblivious to the team of vehicles shadowing his drive.

On a curve approaching Lynch Pond, Tam heard a loud pop, and his pickup truck suddenly veered right.

What the—?

He overcorrected for the front-tire blowout and struck the curb guarding the grassy center median, then plowed over it, scattering damp sod in all directions. Then he bounced across the lanes of traffic going in the opposite direction. As he hit the other side of the parkway, a second small explosion detonated in the opposite front tire, and the truck flipped. He found himself barrel-rolling through the trees and bushes, then cartwheeling into the pond, his vehicle on its side in the water.

When the debris and water had stopped raining down around him, two men appeared beside his truck.

One called out to him. "Hey, buddy, you okay?"

Tam was stunned breathless by the impact of the crash and feeling dizzy as he dangled sideways in his seat belt, but he popped his head out of his shattered driver's-side window to tell the Good Samaritans he was okay. As he did, he saw a flash of light and felt something impact the front of his throat as the subsonic small-caliber round entered through his Adam's apple and pierced his cervical spine before lodging in his brain.

The last thing that went through Tam's mind as he sank into the water filling his truck cab was that Kelly was going to be upset about missing her chili and the spicy half-smokes he had picked up just for her.

CHAPTER 36

KESÄRANTA, HELSINKI, FINLAND

Alex and the prime minister sat in the gazebo of the prime minister's official residence, gazing out at the sparkling waters of the Baltic Sea. A pair of servers had carried their plates and platters of food to them and topped up their wine as they continued their conversation. Prime Minister Rantala seemed to be avoiding answering the question Alex had asked about why Finland's NATO ambassador had been aboard *Aurora*.

Instead, she deflected, and posed one of her own. "What did you think of Emmi?" she asked.

"The Supo officer who kidnapped me? She seemed nice. Intelligent." Then, "Young."

"Yes, don't take this the wrong way, Alex, but all women in their twenties appear young compared to us. But we were once that age, too, and only a few short years ago," she added, taking a sip of wine.

"I liked her. She seemed self-assured."

"Very," Sanna agreed. "And do you know why I asked that it be her to go see you in The Hague?"

"I presume because she is related to Valtteri and that she knew both him and Celeste."

"Yes, and while there are others I could trust to deliver the same message and get you to come here, I thought you might relate better to someone so much like yourself and be less threatened by the request that you come to Finland to speak with me."

"It wasn't a request. In fact, quite the opposite."

"I suppose it wasn't. Still, you could have declined."

Could I have? "None of this answers my original question, Madam Prime Minister," she said.

"Mikko Selänne is a trusted emissary of my government. I wanted to convey important information to the head of Interpol, and I was afraid that doing so via electronic means or intermediaries would not be secure. Such is the nature of eavesdropping measures these days, as you know. A few years ago, an Israeli company created powerful spyware that can be placed in one's phone without you ever being aware it's there. Then the user can simply listen in or track your location for whatever illicit means they choose."

"I'm aware," said Alex, recalling her brush with such software not so long ago that had been traced to Russian hackers. She bit into a piece of flaky puff pastry. *Reindeer?* She couldn't remember what Sanna had said it was.

The prime minister continued. "Finland has a complicated history with Russia. So, although we might have preferred to stay not so much neutral as unaligned, we have been forced to choose to join NATO. We knew in doing so there might be trouble, but with Russia's unprovoked and illegal war of aggression and genocide against Ukraine, how could we not? Sergachev is worse than a tyrant—he is an animal. There is a revanchist movement underway in Russia, a rebirth of Sovietism, irrespective of what they call it. He strives to reunite the former members of the Soviet Union into a grandiose New Russian Empire, but he and the Russian Federal Assembly do not take into account that none of the former republics—save for perhaps his puppet state Belarus—is agreeable to this in any way. All the others have evolved systems of government that at least pretend at some form of democratic process."

"But take me back to Mikko Selänne," Alex cut in. "With respect, Sanna, you haven't answered my question: Why was he specifically sent to see Celeste and Valtteri?"

"I'm sure you are aware of the many incidents in Finland that have disrupted our electrical grid, threatened our nuclear plants, sank ships in our coastal waters that contaminated our land and sea. We have had civil unrest in our streets like none we have experienced in our history before, much of it precipitated by agitators from outside our country that come in, stir things up, and then leave. All this within the last twelve months or so."

"And you believe Russia is to blame—that their security forces have set these events in motion, hacked your infrastructure, vandalized ships and equipment?"

"That's just it, Alex. I don't."

"What?" A flaky piece of reindeer fell off her fork on the way to her mouth.

"Are you telling me that the CIA has heard nothing about alternate theories regarding the cause of these disruptions?"

Alex wasn't sure how much to let on that she knew. She bought some time by setting her plate aside and taking a sip of wine. "To be honest, until the other day, I wasn't aware of these events at all. As you probably know, Sanna, I've only been with the Agency for a short while. Before that, of course, I was with Interpol on a secondment from the FBI."

Sanna continued. "Mikko was sent to meet with Madame Clicquot to share our concerns—mine and our intelligence service's—that a third party might be responsible. But the citizens of my country are demanding action against Russia, and the media continues to pressure my government into delivering on this blood lust, this thirst for justice or revenge—"

"A fine line for sure," said Alex.

"So while everyone is out for the head of the Russian autocrat, some of us believe that it might not be him and his minions at all who were responsible for the attacks. And make no mistake—these *were* attacks. Lives have been lost."

"Then who *is* responsible?"

"That's why I sent Ambassador Selänne—to ask Interpol to open an investigation. Quietly, if necessary. On the surface, we and our allies would continue to raise the matter at the United Nations and with NATO, including at the summit that will take place here in Helsinki in a few days. Supo was gathering information to share with its sister intelligence and security agencies as well as Interpol. But the attack on the ship you were aboard happened before an official investigation—or any, really—could begin. I believe this was intentionally done to prevent any such thing from happening. You were just as much a target as Madame Clicquot or Valtteri Lehtonen."

"Me?" Alex's eyes grew wide at the revelation. The notion of being someone's target was frightening, but it wasn't the first time she had been singled out this way. Still, it was unsettling, and she reached for her glass of wine.

"Your reputation precedes you, Alex. Merely by being aboard that ship at the same time as Celeste and Valtteri, when an emissary of my government was requesting assistance from Interpol, was cause enough to paint a target on your back, too. Lucky for you, and much less so for the attackers, they underestimated you, as I understand many have done before."

"Story of my life. And judging by the office you hold, Excellency," said Alex, "perhaps yours as well."

"You have impressed a great many people and angered more than a few, I imagine."

"Comes with the territory." Alex put aside her plate and took a sip of wine before continuing. "Madam Prime Minister—"

"Sanna."

"Sanna, I'm not sure why you brought me here. I flew to The Hague to see Madame Clicquot. And if I'm to be one hundred percent honest, my only objective is to track down those responsible for putting her in the hospital and for killing Valtteri. I'm already guilty of abandoning my responsibilities back home to visit my friend, so I'm not sure I can also be of service to you."

"Alex, I know more about you than you might think. I spoke with your deputy director before you arrived. I'm quite sure she wasn't very happy about my perceived interference, and she made it very clear that she wants you back on your assignment. By the way, she wouldn't elaborate on what that was."

"Of course not."

"But you have been provided with some degree of latitude to assist me—to help Finland—as a fellow member of the NATO family. You are in a unique position to do so, having worked with Interpol, the FBI, CIA, and I'm told in other covert, undisclosed assignments as well. That provides you with unique insights and abilities."

"What can I do to help?"

Alex's phone vibrated in her pocket. Sanna noticed her flinch and smiled.

"It's alright. You should get that. It could be important."

Alex apologized and reached for her phone, worried it could be bad news. In fact, it was a text from Caleb.

> Caleb: Just checking in. How is Clicquot?
>
> Alex: Not good.
>
> Caleb: I'm so sorry. Where are you now? Anything I can do?

Alex thought for a moment about how to respond. She wanted to say he should get on a plane and join her, but she didn't dare signal that she needed his help.

> Alex: I'm having lunch with a friend. I'm okay. I'll fill you in soon.

She tucked her phone back into her pocket.

"Everything okay?" asked the prime minister.

"Everything's fine. Just someone checking up on me."

"Where were we?" asked Sanna. "Oh, yes. I was about to tell you how you can help."

* * *

ACCT OFFICE, FALLS CHURCH, VIRGINIA

Caleb tossed his phone down on the table next to his plate and shoveled some more mac and cheese into his mouth.

I'm having lunch with a friend.

Street? he wondered.

It could have been anyone, and it shouldn't have mattered, but it gnawed at him. He told himself it was because she was a teammate, because she should be there with him and the rest of the team. He was concerned about what she did because she was his subordinate, and he was responsible for her, at least from an operational perspective.

But he knew it was more than that. He thought about her more than he should. How could he not? He had lobbied to get her on his team, and in the end, Kadeisha Thomas had cajoled the FBI into releasing her so she could join the Agency. Okay, cajoled them into firing her.

But it was more than that and he knew it, and that scared the crap out of him.

But Street? Seriously? Then he remembered that Street was injured in the attack the other night and was still in the hospital. *Good.*

He picked up his phone to make another call.

* * *

HELSINKI, FINLAND

She'd have given anything to hear what the two women were discussing while they sat at the bistro table, still sipping their wine, looking neither distressed nor excited.

So bourgeois.

This meeting should have been anticipated. Her colleagues should already have planted listening devices on the prime minister's property. Or, at the very least, a team could have been deployed on the waters in front of the estate, armed with boom microphones capable of picking up the words being spoken.

Sometimes it was as if the Great Surveillance State forgot that the enemy often lay outside of Russia and not necessarily within the confines of her borders, where they wore the disguise of the ordinary working class, people whose employment and income were insecure and who committed the unforgivable sin of wanting to have more—to *be* more—than the state allowed them to be.

Special Agent Alex Martel, she thought. *I knew one day our paths would cross again, and now here we are.*

* * *

ACCT OFFICE, FALLS CHURCH, VIRGINIA

Caleb dialed Deputy Director Thomas's number. She answered and, without even a hello, said, "Your protégée has had an interesting twenty-four hours. But then, I suspect that's just her normal every day."

Caleb replied, "I wouldn't know, ma'am. I haven't spoken to her." Technically, he wasn't lying. *Text messages don't count.*

"Maybe you should change that, Copeland. She's still on your team."

"I'm aware. I texted her a few minutes ago. I'll give her a call."

"Do that. I've authorized her to assist the Finnish prime minister with an inquiry."

"You what?"

"Is your phone secure?"

He checked for the small indicator at the top of his phone's display. "It's in secure mode, ma'am."

"The Finns were chasing down an angle you should be aware of. The PM doesn't buy the whole Russia-as-bad-guy story."

"Oh?"

"And some other developments came to light. Copeland?"

"Yes, ma'am?"

"Alex is hanging out there with no cover. She has no official Agency protection. She's not on official government business in Finland. So we can't afford to get tangled up in any diplomatic wrangling, and we can't make her official right now, either. There are too many eyes on this. The Russians get access to our embassy staff rosters all the time to screen Agency assets in-country, just as we do their SVR and GRU staff. So she's by herself, Copeland. Understand?"

"Understood, ma'am."

Alex was a big girl and she'd made her own bed by choosing to go on her own to see her old boss in The Hague. And now she was in Finland, a country most Americans couldn't find on a map without a lot of help. Being an intelligence officer with nonofficial cover was about the most dangerous role she could have in a foreign country, and it could land her in some serious jeopardy.

"Don't get me wrong, though," she continued. "As much as I wouldn't mind seeing your girl suffer the consequences of her choices, now's not the time."

Your girl.

"Yes, ma'am."

CHAPTER 37

Alex had plunged face-first into the puffy pillows on the king-sized bed, and there she remained as sleep took hold. But a rhythmic, almost pulsating, buzz woke her out of a deep slumber. It was still early evening and she could see light peeking through a crack between the heavy drapes, but the room itself was dark. The glow of her phone gave her a target to shoot for, though, and she scooped it up on the third ring.

"Alexandra." Chief Bressard's baritone voice.

Oh, no. Celeste. "Is everything okay? Madame Clicquot? How—"

"She's fine. Well, not fine, of course, but there has been considerable improvement since yesterday. If all goes well, they will move her out of intensive care in a few days."

If all goes well. The curse of wishful thinking.

"That's good news, Chief." When she spoke, she managed to make herself sound more optimistic than she felt. "And Street?"

"Street checked himself out this afternoon. He's apparently much improved."

"What? That's great news, of course, but I had no idea."

"I was expecting to hear from you by now. I didn't know where you were. When you didn't come to the hospital, I began to worry."

"Sorry about that. I should have at least called."

"Where are you?"

"Helsinki."

"What? How is that possible?" The tone of his voice lay somewhere between surprise and irritation. "What's going on, Alexandra?"

"It's a long story."

"I'm sure it's an interesting one. But still . . . tell me at least that you are there in an official capacity and you haven't gone rogue?" he asked.

"Do you mean gone rogue *again*?"

"I didn't say that."

"Well, the truth is, I don't really know."

"It's a simple question, Alexandra."

"Not as simple as you might think, Chief."

"You know," he began, "hearing you're in Finland does not exactly alleviate my anxiety for your well-being. Ignoring the counsel of friends and the orders of superiors is a dangerous game, Alexandra. I know there have been times throughout your career that this independent streak of yours, this *ronin* mindset, has served you well, including while you worked for Interpol. But . . ."

There it was again, the *dot, dot, dot* in his conversational tone. Bressard clearly had many questions and maybe more than a few concerns. He had compared her to a ronin—a samurai who had no lord or master and, in some cases, had severed all ties with his family or clan. One who traveled in search of a purpose, or in search of none but who was compelled to assist those in need of his martial talents. Like Denzel Washington in *The Equalizer* franchise.

Normally, she would have accepted the comparison as a compliment, but she wasn't convinced that was his intention in this instance. There was a pejorative connotation that could also be taken. The movies *M3GAN* and *Ex Machina* ran through her mind—not exactly the finest illustrations of the independent spirit.

Okay, those last two weren't great examples, she thought.

"Are you still there?" he asked.

"Yes, Chief."

"Sometimes, Alexandra, pride tricks us into believing that we know more than we do, that we have all the information, all the answers, and that we can see the big picture. But that's not always the case. In fact, as often as not, pride is a smoke screen that blinds us from the truth."

He was beginning to sound like her late husband, Kyle.

"The job of a leader is not to burden those who work under them with extraneous information. A leader often must keep the cards close to their chest. In other words, Alexandra, there are times that you are not given all the information, not because of someone's nefarious intent but to allow you to focus on one job, to have but one priority."

This wasn't the first time Bressard had lectured her on the chain of command, or on professionalism.

"But Chief—"

"No, Alexandra. I'm telling you what Madame Clicquot would tell you herself if she could—that you owe your allegiance now to the CIA. You know this. If you've been tasked with a mission, see it through." His words cradled within them the sting of accusation. She was torn between her loyalty to Celeste and her responsibility to Caleb and the Agency. He continued, "Reconcile the demands being made of you, Alexandra, and make a choice. You can only serve one master."

He was right, of course. Her conversation with Prime Minister Rantala had been fruitful. Sanna had said she had spoken to Alex's boss at CIA, and that the deputy director now wanted her to aid the Finns in their investigations—to determine once and for all if the Russians were up to no good or if someone else was shaping the future for their own purposes.

There was a lot at stake. She was more convinced now that the attack on *Aurora* and the ambush that killed Valtteri and Jocko and put Celeste and Street in the hospital were all part of an elaborate plan, all of which was linked to the events in Finland and the mobilization of forces in the Baltic Sea that was occurring in response to perceived aggression by Russian president Sergachev.

There was too much at stake for her to continue wandering aimlessly down a directionless path. Her best option, the only option whereby she could serve the bigger picture and not just her own desires, was to insert herself back into the game. Everything else was distraction.

She saw it clearly. Caleb was her boss now. He would be her guide-post.

"Thanks, Chief."

"And stay out of trouble. I will let you know if there are any changes to Madame Clicquot's condition. She is in good hands here. Go do what you do."

She said her goodbyes and clicked off, then grabbed her coat and headed out to find some grub. Checking the Rolex Submariner on her wrist, she did the math and decided she would have dinner first, then call Caleb and bring him up to speed on everything she had found out and everything she suspected.

As much as she wanted to satisfy her hunger, her need to stretch her legs was paramount. She felt cooped up after a day of traveling and talking, her muscles needed exercise, and the exercise would bring her greater mental clarity.

She opened the map app on her phone, and while the street names were near impossible to pronounce, she spotted one word that looked promising enough: Esplanadi. It was a shopping district practically out-side the hotel's doors, and zooming in, she saw that there were plenty of food options.

A cool breeze blew from behind as she walked along the wide boule-vard. She wanted to let her mind go blank and tried willing herself not to think of Madame Clicquot lying in the ICU. She tried to push away thoughts of Russia gunning for another senseless war. Or some other group manipulating everyone into believing it was Russia. For what purpose, she couldn't imagine. She could, but she tried not to.

She couldn't shake the feeling that she was being followed and con-sidered doing a full surveillance detection run. But she was in a strange city and feeling hungry.

Maybe I'm just being paranoid.

She began searching in shop windows for the reflection of anyone who might be following her. Checking menus in front of restaurants and bars was both functional and an innocuous countersurveillance technique. Periodically, she popped her head into one, but nothing on offer seemed to suit her cravings. Nor was she successful at detecting a tail.

What she was genuinely craving was a hot dog off a street vendor's cart. Or better yet, a ShackBurger from the Shake Shack in DC, the one on the corner of F Street and 9th, a block away from FBI headquarters. She could taste that cast-iron sear, the slight char, and the caramelized beef and animal fat flavor.

She crossed to the wide grassy esplanade and continued her trek with her stomach on full rumble. She stopped at a fancy-looking restaurant halfway to Kauppatori, the outdoor market by the harbor, and read through the first few items on the menu board: fish roe and horseradish with toasted malt bread. Roast reindeer and cranberry sauce. Fried whitefish with a white wine and clam sauce.

All of it sounded delightful and might make for a great night out sometime when she was in the mood for some gastronomic adventure—like if she ever dined with the prime minister again—but it just wasn't the quick bite she craved tonight.

And then she saw her. A reflection in the glass. Forty feet behind her.

A woman wearing an all-weather jacket, gray this time, the hood pulled low over her eyes, was trying not to be noticed. The jacket was a different color, but there was no mistaking the lines of her body, her posture, height, and gait. It was the same woman she had seen before. *Twice.* Once as she and Emmi had strolled through the park in The Hague, and before that, leaning on the wall of a building next to her hotel. The woman had been pretending to look down at her phone, but Alex had suspected she had been watching her surreptitiously, filing away a mental image of her just in case.

She recalled the Moscow Rules she had memorized years before, borrowed from the CIA during her training with Intelligence Support Activity, the Army's own secret army of which Alex was an alumnus.

Specifically, she recalled the rule about noticing people during surveillance detection runs: *Once is an accident, twice is a coincidence, but three times is an enemy action.* Taught to officers within CIA and other agencies that deployed officers into hostile foreign environments, they had saved Alex's life on more than one occasion in the past.

Dinner was going to have to wait.

CHAPTER 38

The phone in his coat pocket started to buzz as he walked out of the meeting. He wasn't happy when he read the call display and, for a moment, considered letting it go to voicemail. But instead, the president's chief of staff hurried to his cubbyhole down the hall from the Oval Office and picked up on the sixth ring.

"Why are you calling me?" asked Titus Pelletier, closing his door.

The voice on the other end sounded cocky. "It's not exactly the development we anticipated, is it?"

"It's perfect. The president is sailing a virtual allied armada into the Gulf of Finland like it's the D-Day landings at Normandy all over again. President Sergachev will blow a gasket. How is that a problem?"

"I'm not sure D-Day is the best metaphor, but that's not what I'm concerned about."

"Then what *are* you concerned about?" asked Pelletier.

"Special Agent Martel. She's in Finland."

Pelletier spun around and looked up at the ceiling as if searching for divine guidance. "I'll admit it, she's a bit of a loose cannon, that one. But I was already aware and it's being handled. You have to trust me. Besides, she's just one little agent, bouncing from one agency to another quicker than a flea changes dogs. How much damage can she do to our op?"

"Get your head out of your ass and read her file, Titus. Underestimate her, and we'll all pay a heavy price."

"No need to get your panties in a twist, Senator. I hear Helsinki isn't as safe as it used to be. Random acts of violence against tourists seem to be on the rise."

There was a pause. "I understand. Good. We're too far along to let a woman fuck things up for us now."

"It's under control, Senator. The former Little Miss Interpol is about to meet the same fate as her nosy late boss."

"But Clicquot's still alive."

Pelletier's voice took on an authoritarian edge. "Not for much longer. Messages have to be both sent *and* delivered. Otherwise, what's the point?"

* * *

DEN HAAG CENTRAAL HOSPITAL, THE HAGUE, THE NETHERLANDS

The man in scrubs stepped off the elevator onto the sixth floor. Nobody noticed him or cared about his forged ID. In fact, no one ever noticed or cared about anyone's ID except the guards, and he had already gotten past them in the lobby, pretending to be a visitor carrying flowers.

He waved a stolen prox card at the reader and was grateful when the magnetic lock released and the door swung open into the unit. Inside the ICU, a mobile patient charting station had been wheeled up to one of the rooms that ran down both sides of the hallway. The nurse it belonged to was at the patient's bedside, jamming something into the wall behind the bed. He scooped up a plastic clipboard from the station's desktop.

"*He*," the nurse called in Dutch, glancing over her shoulder. He stopped and, for a moment, considered how he could kill her quietly. "*Kun je me dat geven?*" *Can you pass me that?* She nodded over to a three-foot coil of ribbed plastic tubing on a nearby table. "Hurry, please. My back is breaking."

She was sandwiched between a ventilator and an IV pump, tangled in cables and wires.

"Of course," he mumbled in moderately coherent Dutch, stepping forward to hand it to her.

"Thanks."

He backed out of the room and reached into his pocket, touching the two syringes there as he strode deeper into the unit. One contained twenty milligrams of vecuronium, a drug classed as a paralytic agent used to keep your body still during surgery. It worked by paralyzing all muscles, including the respiratory muscles, effectively stopping someone's breathing. Since the secretary general of Interpol was on a ventilator, this was technically redundant, but he would do as he had been directed. The real work would be performed by the second syringe, loaded with a lethal dose—in fact, triple the required amount—of potassium chloride, which would induce cardiac arrest. Once injected, even when the alarms started ringing on the cardiac monitors, no amount of resuscitation would bring her back.

He rounded the bend past the nursing station and saw two police officers posted in front of her room, each with a hand resting on the grip of their H&K tactical rifles. He recognized their shoulder flashes as belonging to the Koninklijke Marechaussee. The KMar, as it was more commonly known, was the national gendarmerie force of the Kingdom of the Netherlands that performed both military and civilian police duties, including VIP and dignitary close protection.

He considered turning around and backing out of the assignment. His intel had said there would only be one police officer, not two highly specialized tactical officers. The presence of the KMar increased the dangers of this assignment exponentially, and he wasn't a gambler.

On the other hand, he was a professional.

He paused outside one of the draped rooms to pretend to read the chart in his hands while he devised a plan.

* * *

HELSINKI, FINLAND

Kauppatori, the year-round harborside market with its tented stalls, was all around her as Alex reached the east end of Esplanadi. Wading deeper into the market, she was met with the sweet smell of burning maple firewood and huge sides of salmon being prepared over a fiery grill.

But despite her appetite, she crossed the street to a shop window displaying high-end housewares, dishes, pots, and pans. It carried crafts from local artisans and was the kind of place tourists strolled into, but she doubted many local Helsinkians shopped here for tableware. More important, she saw in the window's reflection that the woman was still lingering thirty feet behind as she pretended to read a restaurant menu.

Maybe I should invite her for dinner and just talk out whatever it is that's on her mind.

Alex stayed calm and considered her options. She needed to work out the motive behind the surveillance. If this woman wanted Alex dead, she could have done it already or made an attempt while they were in The Hague. But she hadn't. Instead, she had followed her from the Netherlands to Finland; no simple feat when the logistics of Alex's travels had involved an unplanned ride in an SUV, a trip by private plane, a private helicopter ride to the official residence of the Finnish prime minister, then to her hotel, and now on a dinner run through central Helsinki. This had all the earmarks of a high-level, state-sponsored operation that may or may not have involved some form of tracking device.

Alex thought back to her last dealings with the Russians, when they had exploited spyware illegally planted on her Interpol work phone.

Is that what is going on here again? The Russians are tracking me?

She thought of Jonathan. Would he know what was going on?

She quickly fired off a text.

Alex: 911

In Helsinki. Being followed. Is my phone ok?

She didn't wait for a response. Instead, she tucked her phone into her pocket and walked into the store. Strolling to the back, she kept an eye on the big window beside the entrance, hoping to catch sight of her pursuer again.

See one, think two, she thought, recalling the mantra of her friend and mentor, Deputy US Marshal Marc Cameron, a frequent guest instructor at Quantico.

Or, in this case, it's likely more than two. In fact, it's highly probable that I'm being followed by a whole team of surveillants.

She considered other reasons she might be tailed. Someone could be hoping to make contact but might be under surveillance themselves. Someone could be tailing her to observe and report to her superiors. Or, maybe they were following her in the hopes of passing along information, evidence, or something else.

Her phone buzzed. It was Jonathan.

CHAPTER 39

The man in scrubs stood in the hall outside Madame Clicquot's hospital room, pretending to read the chart he had lifted from another patient.

Suddenly, alarms started ringing inside the cubicle next to him. Electronic beeps and double beeps, long tones, and raised voices signaled something was going terribly wrong for someone, meaning things were about to go terribly right for him.

"Call a code blue!" he heard someone shout as nurses ran toward the cubicle, and the overhead speakers blared the code as staff poured in through the ICU's doors. In the growing commotion, he squeezed past unnoticed, still reading his chart, approaching Madame Clicquot's room.

The two KMar officers who had been eyeing the frenetic activity now turned their attention briefly to him, and he casually flipped his ID over for them to see and smiled. They gave it a cursory glance and nodded, then went back to watching the chaos down the hall as he stepped into the room. He flipped the plastic cover over on the chart as if to read it while assessing his patient.

He had been told she was on a ventilator, but now realized she had been removed from it. Good thing he brought the vecuronium. Once he administered it, every muscle in her body would become paralyzed, including those that performed the basic act of breathing. She would already be suffocating before he administered the potassium chloride that would eventually stop her heart. Even if she became conscious while he was killing her with the lethal cocktail, the paralysis would prevent her from calling for help or fending off his assault.

He looked at Clicquot's face. He didn't know her, didn't even recall seeing her on the news or the internet. She was a stranger to him, which somewhat dulled the thrill, but he was feeling pretty good despite that.

He put the chart down on her chest and removed the two syringes from his pocket, laying them on the blanket. He picked up the first one, uncapped it, and lightly depressed the plunger with the syringe inverted and the needle pointing at the ceiling, bleeding air out of it. A droplet of liquid emerged from its tip and slid down onto his hand. A ridiculous gesture, to be sure, but it made him feel like a bona fide Dr. McDreamy. There were two IV ports in the tubing, so he performed the same preparation with the second syringe and then inserted the needles into the two adjacent ports.

Two birds with one stone, he thought.

He slowly depressed the plunger of each syringe. With his eyes closed, he injected the deadly cocktail into her vein, pushing it deliberately, savoring the moment, the macabre thrill.

"Hey, what are you doing?"

The voice came from behind him. It was the nurse he'd encountered when he first entered the ICU—the one who had been adjusting medical equipment.

Nosy bitch.

"I said, what are you doing? Stop!"

She grabbed him by the shoulders and tugged him backward. She was surprisingly strong. As he stumbled, the syringes were pulled from the IV injection port in Clicquot's arm. The man swung to face the nurse, and as he did he jabbed one of the needles into her neck. He relished the sight of her terror and surprise as he squeezed the rest of its contents into her just before he was struck in the head by the butt end of a tactical rifle.

* * *

Lying on the floor, the nurse managed to raise herself onto her el-bows after her attacker had been knocked unconscious by one of the KMar officers standing outside Secretary General Clicquot's room. She watched, semi-dazed, as he and his partner flipped the man she had seen earlier onto his belly and cuffed his hands behind his back while blood flowed freely from the large gash on his head.

Serves you right for touching my patient, she thought.

As she continued to watch, she felt a strange clinical detachment, as if she were an observer not just of what was happening to *him* but of what was happening to *her*. A warm sensation spread through her arms and legs and throughout her body. Then she grew hot. Her hands went numb first, along with the muscles in her face, preceded by an odd tingling sensation. Then her arms became weak, and she felt sud-denly shrouded in cold as if she had been wrapped in a wet blanket and thrown into a snowbank.

She fell flat onto her back and felt a flash of pain as her head struck the floor. She was unable to call out and couldn't move her limbs. It was an odd feeling, and she was almost completely unaware of the paralysis setting in. It came over her like an insidious wave of emptiness. She could *feel* but she couldn't *move*. Panic set in as she became aware that she had stopped breathing. She wanted to gulp in great lungfuls of air, but she couldn't take a breath no matter how hard she tried.

The vecuronium rendered her body immobile, but her mind stayed sharp, focused, and it raced.

A paralytic agent, she deduced. *He's injected me—and Madame Clicquot—with a neuromuscular blocking agent—the kind we use in sur-gery. A drug used for euthanasia. Oh my god! Am I going to die?*

Her friend Lize ducked around the commotion and came to her side.

"Vera, are you okay?" she asked.

No, she tried to say, but no words came out. Not even a whimper.

Oh, God, I need to breathe! she thought, but she couldn't draw a breath.

"Vera!" Lize was looking down at her, directly into her eyes.

Help me, Lize! she wanted to scream. *I can't breathe!* But no words left her lips.

"Doctor!" called Lize. "Something's wrong with Vera."

He turned and knelt beside her, grabbing her hands.

"Vera, can you hear me? Squeeze," he said. She could feel him touching her, but she couldn't close her hand around his. "Vera, squeeze my hand," he repeated more emphatically.

She couldn't squeeze his hand. What's more, she knew she couldn't squeeze his hand. Worse than the paralysis that had overtaken her was the complete awareness that there was nothing she could do about it. Her senses functioned, but any voluntary control of her muscles had completely abandoned her.

Her vision took in the faces of her friend and the doctor, both looking professional, but both gravely concerned by her sudden condition. And behind them, Madame Clicquot's coworker, the nice man with a beard, stood at her bedside.

How strange to suddenly find oneself the patient.

"Doctor, this patient, too. She's not breathing," called another nurse.

Neither am I! thought Vera as her vision began to blur.

"Vera's not breathing, either," said Lize.

Finally! You get it!

"They must have both been given a paralytic agent," Lize said.

Yes! thought Vera. *Hurry, I'm suffocating!*

There was an immediate flurry of activity around her as someone brought a resuscitation bag valve mask—an Ambu bag—and placed it over her nose and mouth. They squeezed air into her lungs, over and over.

Don't stop! she thought. The sensation was euphoric as her blood filled with oxygen and her vision began to clear.

"Get me two vials of Bridion!" shouted the doctor. "Stat!"

More! she thought as the nurse squeezed air into her lungs. *Faster! Give me more!*

As if hearing her thoughts, Lize increased the rate at which she was providing ventilations. Someone else started an IV, and the doctor administered something into her arm. Slowly she began to feel warmer, less air-hungry, as the reversal agent she was injected with took hold.

Then the cardiac monitor attached to Madame Clicquot began to emit a steady tone.

CHAPTER 40

Alex headed for a door marked EMPLOYEES ONLY and pushed through, hoping to find an exit that would take her away from the main street and the team of surveillants out front. She squeezed between rows of boxes marked PENTIK POSIO PLATES and bags of something labeled MOOMIN PLUSH TOYS.

At the rear of the space there was a door, and she hurried toward it, reading Jonathan's text as she went:

> Jonathan: Sorry it took so long. Getting into your phone is harder than you think when you don't work for us anymore! Phone's clean. Are you safe?

She pushed through the door and found herself in an enclosed courtyard surrounded by four-story walls. She fired off a quick reply:

> Alex: I don't know yet.

Dashing across the quadrangle, she tried a door into the building on the other side. Locked. She walked to another door and tried it. It yielded to her pull, and she found herself in a hallway next to a pair of unisex toilets. She walked toward the sound of voices, the *whir* of a grinder, and the aroma of coffee, into a café full of people. She stared longingly at the food in the refrigerated cabinet but forced herself through the front doors, finding herself smack dab in the middle of Senate Square. One of the most iconic images of the city, Helsinki Cathedral, loomed atop a long flight of steps directly in front of her.

She took a moment to get her bearings. Her hotel would be to her left, a kilometer away—maybe less. A side street to her right was the most likely place for the woman following her to show up, so she headed left. Just then, a man wearing a determined expression rounded the corner behind her. He had a military bearing: tall, fit, lacking humor.

Shit. I only saw the woman. There must be a whole team on me.

Another man of similar comportment to the one behind appeared ahead of her.

Now things are getting interesting.

She wasn't carrying a firearm, making her feel particularly vulnerable. Back home and on her own time, she could carry whatever she liked as long as it was legal. But the CIA had strict rules about such things. Since she wasn't technically on a covert operation or deemed to be in a hostile country—despite mounting evidence to the contrary—a firearm would have been entirely illegal. Yet despite that, she'd have given anything to have her Kimber R7 Mako tucked into an appendix holster with two spare mags on her belt.

She made a hard right, aiming for the center of the square, and picked up her pace. A young man and a woman stood in front of her beside a pair of electric scooters. Apologizing, she bumped the man out of the way and hopped aboard, propelling herself forward with a kick and hitting the thumb accelerator, jamming it all the way to the handlebar.

"Whoa!"

The exclamation left her lips involuntarily as the e-scooter took off faster than she had anticipated, like a Tesla Plaid on steroids. She bounced along the interlocking brick roadway, bumped into the side of a car parked diagonally along the square—*oof, sorry!*—then soared over the curb like she was astride a bucking bronc. She peered over her shoulder at the two men running after her.

If they don't kill me, this scooter will!

In front of her, a parade of Ukrainian flags snaked through the square. The tail of the group ran all the way back to where it disgorged

from a side street. The head of the pack walked in tight formation, filing between the statue of Alexander II and the steps to the cathedral
before marching midway up the stairs to where the group clustered at
its center.

"What do we want? No war! When do we want it? Right now!"

Within seconds, she had arrived at the steps and bailed off the
e-scooter, running partway up the stairs and inserting herself into the
crowd. She slung her arm around the shoulders of a placard-waving
young woman and began to chant with her. The woman looked at her
and smiled, her rosy cheeks adorned with a flag of Finland on one side
and two parallel horizontal stripes of blue and yellow on the other:
sunny skies and wheat fields.

Alex turned to see the two men stalking along the foot of the forty-
three steps that led to the cathedral at the summit of the hill. Besides the
antiwar protesters, the stairs were dotted with small groups of young
people taking in the night air, enjoying a malted beverage or two. It
brought back a bittersweet memory of nights like this spent with her
friend Krysten on the steps of Sacré Coeur Basilica in Montmartre, the
skyline of Paris laid out before them, not so many years ago.

Alex pushed the memory aside and reached for a large Finnish flag
being brandished by a twenty-something, athletic-looking man. She
flashed him her biggest smile and he relinquished it, so she joyfully
held it aloft, hoping it would obscure her from view.

She glanced back toward the roadway, and there was the woman,
circling the periphery: clearly the more seasoned shark waiting for the
little ones to flush their prey in her direction.

The men made their move and started to push their way through
the crowd, jostling people as they focused on her. Alex hesitated long
enough to snap a photo of them, then began chanting loudly, stirring
up the crowd anew. For a moment, she considered bolting toward the
promise of sanctuary inside the cathedral.

But then she was struck by a bolt of inspiration. The crowd had become aware of the two interlopers, and Alex seized the moment.

She pointed to the men and began shouting, "KGB! KGB! KGB!"

The men froze in their tracks, clearly unsure how to respond to this anachronistic taunt. And they weren't afforded much of a chance to respond. The crowd took up the clarion call, joining her in a loud and boisterous chorus that stirred even her emotions.

"KGB! KGB! KGB!" they shouted. "KGB! KGB! KGB!"

The wave of people ceased its forward momentum and began to surge downward, a serpent undulating in a menacing sideways wave at the two men, two frogs at a snake buffet.

As they extricated themselves from the hostile encounter and retreated down the steps, Alex ran to the top of the stairs and the cathedral doors. She would hide inside while she contacted Jonathan to see if he could guide her on a safe path home.

Alex looked around for the woman, expecting to see her in the same spot or moving to join the men now that their cover had been broken. But as she searched the square, the woman was nowhere in sight.

She suspected it wasn't the last she'd see of her.

* * *

DEN HAAG CENTRAAL HOSPITAL, THE HAGUE, THE NETHERLANDS

The ICU was in chaos when Bressard walked through the door.

A commotion outside Celeste's cubicle was the first thing that met his eyes. A nurse—he was sure it was Celeste's nurse—lay on the floor on her back, another nurse and a doctor beside her trying to help her. A few feet away, heavily armed KMar officers were restraining a man wearing scrubs. He appeared dazed but was still offering up a struggle. A large pool of blood had gathered on the floor around his head. His hands were cuffed behind his back. A few cubicles away, a cardiac arrest team was frantically working on a patient. Five or six staff were performing CPR and attempting to resuscitate a young man Bressard didn't know but whose family he had spoken with in the quiet room often enough in the past two days.

Good Lord, what the hell is going on? he asked before crossing himself.

He hurried to Celeste's bedside.

"Madame Clicquot—*Celeste!*—can you hear me?" he asked, taking her hand. "Of course you can't," he admonished himself.

He looked around the bed—everything appeared in order, but what did he know? He was a career cop and an administrator, not a doctor. While Celeste looked the same as she had a few minutes ago, the nurse lying on the floor was going from bad to worse. That was one thing a cop's instincts were good for—observing the growing shit storm before anyone else picked up that something was awry. While other people went merrily about their business, he could spot *un merdier* developing a mile away.

Suddenly, Celeste's monitor began to alarm. Beeps and rows of waveforms flashing different colors.

"Nurse?" he said weakly. "Doctor." All those present were focused on the nurse on the floor. "Somebody help—now!" he demanded loudly.

A nurse came right away to clear the alarms.

"Oh, shit. Out!" she said to Bressard. "Doctor, this patient, too. She's not breathing."

He stepped back but didn't leave the unit, watching as the team worked on Celeste. The nurse started to breathe for her using an Ambu bag. The doctor called for medications and then looked at her cardiac monitor.

"Look at that waveform," the doctor said to the nurse. "She's severely hyperkalemic."

"There was a second needle stuck into her IV line when I got here," she told him. "He must have injected her with potassium."

"Get me ten mils of calcium gluconate and ten units of insulin. And initiate an IV of ten percent glucose. Let's get her ready for hemodialysis, just in case."

Just then the cardiac monitor attached to Madame Clicquot began to emit a steady tone.

"Call a code blue!" shouted the doctor. "She's in cardiac arrest!"

CHAPTER 41

Randolph Kennington III, the senior senator from Virginia, looked out across Constitution Avenue to the Supreme Court of the United States. But from his window on the third floor of the Hart Senate Office Building, his view wasn't of the spectacular colonnaded front entrance of the distinguished edifice. Instead, he stared at a long row of granite blocks that made up the north wall of the building. The boring façade was as much a reflection of the building's sober occupants as it was a statement of the strength and permanency of the institution.

Senator Kennington was ranked eighth by seniority among his peers but number one in the chamber by wealth, surpassing even the wealthiest senators in the Centimillion Dollar Club. He had earned his fortune the old-fashioned way. That is, it had been handed to him merely for being the firstborn male of the family. Consequently, he had received the entire family fortune when his father passed, leaving his older sister and two younger brothers dependent on a monthly stipend that he generously provided for them.

His father had been a peculiar man, descended from a long line of them. All wealthy. All eccentric. All possessed of a worldview dominated by a vision of a crushing American hegemony. None with the ability to achieve it. Until now.

He didn't need the financial support of his state's largest defense contractor, Grumfeld-Northing, but he did appreciate their patronage anyway when they came calling. In return, he was able to smooth out various obstacles at the Appropriations Committee on the company's behalf in order to ensure these United States were always prepared for war. And make no mistake, war was coming. Rules, he believed, shouldn't have to apply equally to all.

On his desk sat his teleconferencing line, and on the line was the edgy board of directors of Grumfeld-Northing. Kennington enjoyed being seen as the fixer, even though he was more aptly known as the one who set things in motion. Calming jittery nerves was his gift.

"Don't worry, Bill. I told you it will happen, and it will. This is the long game we're playing, but we're edging ever closer to a first-and-goal scenario late in the fourth quarter, and we're already three touchdowns ahead. The end is in sight. You saw how easily President Sergachev was goaded into his Eastern European odyssey. Did you think he came up with that idea by himself? And now he's intent on spreading the war farther, which should prove to be very much to your stockholders' delight. Go ahead and put me on mute. I'll wait while you all have a little powwow."

Kennington lit up one of his favorite cigars—a Cohiba Behike 52—as he waited while the CEO of Grumfeld-Northing discussed the revised strategy with the board. He pictured them sitting around the teleconferencing unit at the center of their gaudy walnut and epoxy resin conference table down in Roanoke, jawing away with other members of the company's ancient board of directors, each vetted individually by Kennington's security team to ensure information flow was contained and limited to only a few.

Finally, they took him off mute.

"Senator, we're generally a conservative company," said Bill, "but you've won us over with your strategy and, quite frankly, with your wildly successful achievements."

"The duck isn't quite in the bag yet, gentlemen, but we're close. I'm glad you see it my way at last. As I said, give it a week at the most, and you'll see your stock increase tenfold practically overnight."

There was a knock at the door. His staff assistant entered before he had invited her in. She lifted the remote from his desk and aimed it at the big-screen TV on the wall.

"Hold on a second, Bill," he said, muting the line. "What is it, Katey?"

"You'll want to see this, sir," said the pretty twentysomething woman. Frankly, her keen intellect wasn't exactly a trait he was expecting when he had hired her, but he was now glad for it.

The SNN banner came up on-screen with a BREAKING NEWS chyron scrolling beneath it. The newscaster mentioned *escalating tensions* between Russia and Finland over the past several months. On one half of the screen, a collection of battleships steamed against a blue ocean, their wakes indicating they were moving with haste. On the other half, the newscaster read from a fresh script just handed to him.

"Bill," the senator said. "Turn on Satellite News Network and we'll regroup later."

"Turn that up, would you?" he said to Katey, ending the teleconference.

Katey thumbed up the volume as a talking head joined the newscaster.

"Admiral, talk us through these developments," said the journeyman newscaster for SNN.

"Sure," said the other talking head. The retired US Navy admiral looked earnestly into the camera. "Russia has been playing cat and mouse with Finland for months now, but as we've talked about on your show before, Colten, it's ultimately been a game of brinksmanship with the West, and in particular, with the NATO alliance. Finland has really just been a proxy dalliance. Russia has been repeatedly upping the ante in this gambit of increasing risk. Today's developments are consequential in that the US has worked hard on the diplomacy angle. So, while Russia is suspected of being up to no good, American diplomats have been keeping the tone and rhetoric measured, choosing to pursue action only after consulting with our allies and by seeking a broader consensus at the United Nations and other bodies. Today, though, Russia has upped the ante by deploying some serious assets into positions that make it appear they're poised for an invasion of Finland's sovereign territory. This can only be characterized as a move to instigate a response from the West."

"And, Admiral, could you tell us how NATO has decided to respond to this provocation?"

"Well, Colten, in a rather uncharacteristic move for this administration, President Moore has ordered the Atlantic fleet back into the waters of the Gulf of Finland in the eastern reaches of the Baltic Sea in what can only be viewed as a direct challenge to Sergachev's troop and asset movements. NATO members had just wrapped up a large-scale maritime exercise and were heading home, but now everyone has been directed to return to their positions, ostensibly to resume the BALTOPS exercise."

"Is this likely to calm tensions in the gulf, Admiral, or inflame them?"

"President Sergachev is a man who operates with a simmering flame beneath his temperamental exterior. If you're asking me what his response will likely be, my answer is another question: What happens when you throw gasoline onto a fire?"

"I don't think we need to put it into words, Admiral. We get the picture. As always, thanks for bringing some context to this breaking news story."

"My pleasure."

The newscaster turned back to the second camera. "Stay tuned as we unpack this later tonight with our panel—"

Senator Kennington had heard enough. "Thanks, Katey. You can shut it off."

"Yes, sir. Will you be needing anything else, Senator?" she asked, placing the remote back on his desk.

"No, you can go."

The news was what he had been waiting for. It had only been a matter of time before President Sergachev would give in to his paranoia and push troops to the edge of the Russian frontier as he had just done. And in issuing such a challenge, the Russian neo-czar was inviting a response from the West that President Moore would have no choice but to provide. Two giant barrels of gunpowder rolling up against each other.

All that was needed now was a final spark.

He dialed his phone and waited for the familiar voice to pick up.

"Everything in place for the NATO summit in Helsinki?" he asked.

"We're good to go. Some obstacles have been eliminated; others are being smoothed over as we speak."

"Good," Kennington said. "We need this. Despite what our tender-footed president and Congress think, Russia needs to be put in its place. America needs to rise again to be the unquestioned and dominant force in the world. Make it happen, General, and you'll be richer than you ever dared to dream."

"With pleasure, Senator. It's being done."

CHAPTER 42

Alex pulled open the heavy door and stepped into the cathedral. Small groups of tourists filed along beside her in the nave as she walked up the center aisle toward the altar. The vaulted ceilings arched upward to the large central dome, seemingly miles above her head. It was plain and unadorned, fanciful only in its construction and grandeur.

She scanned the faces of the other visitors for signs of anyone paying her too much attention, but there was no sign of her pursuers in the crowd. She paused at the transept halfway up the center aisle, and stepped aside to text Jonathan.

Alex: Not out of the woods. Need eyes.

She attached the photo of the two men and hit send.

Jonathan: Call you?

Alex: Sure.

A second later, her phone buzzed in her hand. "I'm in a cathedral in Helsinki. A big basilica," she said in lieu of a greeting.

"Alex Martel found religion? I don't believe it."

"Okay, smart aleck."

"Helsinki Cathedral," said Jonathan.

"I think."

She heard keys clicking on a keyboard. "Big white building? Lots of stairs out front?"

"That's the one."

"Okay, you're still sharing your location with me. I got you." More clicking. "I'm running the photo you sent. That was the best you could do?"

"I left my tripod at home, so yes."

"You're hilarious. There's not enough there for facial rec, but I can try to pick them up on traffic or surveillance cameras. They're distinctive enough without facial details."

"*Try?*"

"Not every city has a camera for every ten people like London does."

He was right. She hadn't spotted many surveillance cameras during her brief walk.

"What about private businesses, that sort of thing?"

"Alex, this is Interpol. We're not exactly authorized for that level of intrusion without a warrant. I'm skirting several well-documented Interpol guidelines as it is."

"Well, as long as they're not actual laws or anything, we're good, right?"

The speakerphone picked up the sound of his grunt.

"Okay, you're not that far from your hotel—the Marski, right? It's only about seven hundred meters from where you are."

"How'd you know where I'm staying?"

"I'm in your phone, remember? Do you think you're safe to go back there?"

"I suppose there's only one way to find out."

She took another look around. There was no sign of either the men or the woman. They might have abandoned whatever plan they had. Or maybe they were waiting to ambush her as soon as she stepped back outside.

"There aren't a lot of traffic cameras near you. Will you be okay while I try a few things and call you back?"

Her phone buzzed with another incoming call. She looked at the call display—it was Bressard.

"Why is Chief Bressard calling me?"

"No idea."

"Okay, call me back. I better take this." She switched to the call from Bressard. "Chief," she said. "Everything okay?"

Bressard's voice was tinged with worry. "There was an incident at the hospital."

"What do you mean *an incident*?" she asked. "Is Celeste okay? What happened?"

"Someone tried to . . . ," he trailed off.

"To what? What did someone try to do?"

"Alexandra, someone tried to kill her again."

"Oh my god! What the hell, Chief!" she blurted out.

A priest at the altar preparing to celebrate evening Mass admonished her with a demonic look.

"Sorry," she whispered, turning away from the sanctuary of the church. "Is she okay?"

"I think so. No, I don't really know. They asked me to step out while they worked on her."

"*Worked on her* suggests she's not okay, Chief."

"Someone posing as a member of the hospital staff injected something into her intravenous line. She stopped breathing. But they're taking care of her now, Alexandra."

"How could that happen?" She was legitimately dumbfounded. And angry. "Aren't there guards posted? Why weren't *you* there?" There was more than a hint of accusation in her tone.

"The man was dressed like a doctor. He was wearing hospital ID. And staff were dealing with another emergency. Hold on," he said. "I'm going back inside."

Alex walked back toward the altar. A large painting hung behind it, a depiction of Jesus draped in a white shroud being held in the arms of his disciples after the crucifixion. It should have eased her mind, but she took no comfort from it while Celeste dangled near death's door.

Through her phone, she could make out the clamor of an ICU. It was the sound of organized chaos. Bressard asked someone what was going on but Alex couldn't hear their response clearly.

"What is it, Chief? What's happening?"

"Just a minute. The nurse is explaining. Hold on."

The explanation seemed to be taking forever. Alex had moved back up the center aisle of the cathedral, scanning the doors off to the side and at the rear of the church at the narthex for any signs of her pursuers. Could it be they recognized the church as a sanctuary? Alex thought that unlikely, so she stayed vigilant as she waited for Bressard to update her.

Finally, he came back on the line.

"Did you hear all that?" he asked.

"Not a thing, Chief."

She listened as he explained that Celeste had been administered a drug to cause paralysis that had stopped her breathing and another drug that caused her to go into cardiac arrest—

"*What?*" She looked up reflexively to see if the priest had heard her. He had, and she waved an apology. Again.

"But the doctor gave her medication to reverse the effects of the drugs and they've stopped CPR—"

"They've stopped CPR? Chief, is she—"

"What? No, Alexandra, she is breathing on her own now and whatever other drugs they have given her have stabilized her heart and rhythm."

She barely heard anything that followed until she heard the magic words *she's stable now* pass from Bressard's lips.

"Oh, Jesus." She looked around. This time the priest hadn't heard her outburst. "Okay, I get it," she said. "If they say she's stable, I'll take them at their word. But, Chief, you have to do something about those guards."

"I'll speak with the KMar supervisor when he arrives and insist that they implement tighter security protocols. They can't let just anyone into her room again willy-nilly."

No, certainly not willy-nilly. She managed a smile, despite the gravity of the moment.

"I have to go," she said. "I've got a bit of a situation of my own I'm dealing with right now."

"That's the other reason I called you—to warn you. If they came after Celeste again, why wouldn't they come after you, too?"

"Funny you should mention that . . ."

"Is everything okay?"

She was about to answer him when the two men who pursued her through Senate Square came in through the back of the church. In an instant, she decided Bressard had enough to worry about with Celeste.

"I'll call you when I can. In the meantime, take care of the boss, Chief."

She hung up and walked along the transept to the north side of Helsinki Cathedral. The men followed, one of them talking into a wrist mic. No doubt he was alerting the woman, who seemed to be the one in charge.

She found a roped-off staircase and slipped past the barrier, then hurried down into the darkness to a small wooden door. An underground passageway led her to an iron gate and the street beyond.

The footfalls of her pursuers echoed along the stone steps behind her. She tried the gate, but it only rattled against an ancient latch. The gate was surrounded by a stone archway. She turned and saw the men advancing quickly through the passageway she had just come through. She squeezed a finger into the space between the gate and the stone and worked away at the latch arm until it lifted from the catch. Finally, the gate swung open and she passed through to the sidewalk. As she did, a black van screeched to a halt on the cobblestone in front of her. A man leaped out of the passenger side, coming around the front of the van and grabbing for her.

The only rule in a street fight was survival, and Alex had always felt marvelously uninhibited in these situations, free to step outside the boundaries set by the rules of a competition ring. No Marquess of Queensberry rules here. She fended off his clumsy attack with a front snap kick to the groin, crumpling him to the pavement.

The van's driver hopped out, drawing a gun from his waistband. Alex expected to see him brandishing a Russian Makarov or GSh-18, both of which she had encountered when facing Russian agents in the past. Instead, it was a Walther PDP—one more typically fielded by American law enforcement—that he held at his side, its saber-toothed serrations prominently visible on the slide and fitted with what she knew would be an Aimpoint ACRO red-dot sight. But holding it at his side rendered him unprepared to use it, a situation she took full advantage of. She ran straight at him, her extended forearm catching him square across the throat as she stepped past, her follow-through snapping his lower jaw against his upper. He crashed to the ground, the back of his head cracking like a melon against the roadway.

Her two original pursuers were on her instantly. She took up a defensive stance as they tried to encircle her, but she pressed her back to the stone wall next to the gate. They hesitated, no doubt reassessing her after seeing their colleagues splayed out on the ground.

The woman in the hooded coat rounded the corner, and as Alex made eye contact with her, recognition dawned at last. There was no mistaking that fire in her eyes.

Tatiana.

The last time Alex had seen Captain Tatiana Burina was on a London street. Alex had been fighting for her life then, too, and it was Captain Burina from Directorate 13 of the Russian GRU who had been a hair's breadth away from taking it, her steely eyes focused, her Makarov leveled. But at the last possible moment and with the sound of police sirens bearing down on them, Tatiana had chosen to save herself. As she fled, she'd vowed they would meet again.

It appeared she was a woman of her word.

That previous meeting had seen the two women engage in a near-fatal encounter. Tatiana had been assigned to monitor Alex's investigation into the death of her friend and a missing nuke. But unbeknownst to Tatiana, her superiors were working off the books on an unauthorized mission. She had promised to kill Alex if she interfered, and it might have happened if not for the heroic actions of a chivalrous London cab driver named Gareth.

She had a decision to make. She could turn and run or stand her ground and fight. She might still be able to run fast, but she couldn't outrun a bullet, and she was sure everyone except her was strapped. If she fought, she stood a chance of disarming one of them. Or, better yet, maybe she could get to that 9 millimeter Walther lying on the ground only a couple of meters away next to the body she'd put there.

Decision made. She lunged at the man closest to her as he reached out to grab her. She batted his arms to the side and spun in like an F5 funnel cloud, followed by a stomp to the top of his foot and an elbow strike aimed at his chin. It missed its mark and glanced off his ear, which staggered but didn't incapacitate him. He fell to the side as she turned to meet the advance of his partner.

She parried his attempted punch and spun on her planted front foot, using a double-arm thrust to propel him into the wall. The first man had gotten back up and landed a punch that caught her on the back of the head. She staggered forward. The man she'd hurled into the wall had recovered enough that he was able to grab one of her arms, and as she lined up a punch to free herself, the other man grabbed her cocked arm. She side-kicked him behind the knee and he stumbled, still holding her arm. Tatiana approached them.

Well, this isn't going well.

Instead of coming at her as Alex expected, Tatiana surprised her by punching the man who controlled Alex's arm, catching him flush in the temple. Then she delivered a textbook front-thrust kick worthy of the Octagon that caught her other attacker square in the face, propelling him back into the wall with a satisfying thud.

What the hell?

Newly freed, Alex squared herself to Tatiana, prepared to fight but even more confused and feeling wobbly after being punched in the head.

"I told you I would see you again," Tatiana said. She seemed to take in Alex's mental state. "That's the trouble with you Americans. You are so sure of your superiority that you don't recognize a rescue when it stares at you in your face."

Her English wasn't perfect, but the words slowly crept into Alex's zone of comprehension.

"When it stares you in the face," Alex corrected.

"What?"

"Never mind." *Rescue?* "Aren't they with you?" she asked, splaying her arms out at the crumpled mass of attackers littering the road.

"They are not. They are American."

While she had already deduced this by their choice of firearms, it still shocked her to hear Tatiana confirm it. She had been so sure they were together.

What am I missing? Why am I being attacked by Americans in Finland? Or anywhere?

In the distance, the sound of sirens could be heard piercing the twilight. It was coupled with a sense of déjà vu that Alex was sure Tatiana must have felt as much as she did.

Meanwhile, the war protesters had come around to the back of the church, attracted no doubt by the sound of squealing tires and shouting, and arranged themselves into a viewing gallery as two of her attackers gathered themselves up and ran.

One man vaulted a low metal fence and disappeared across a grassy lawn, running away between the buildings, but the other headed straight for the van.

Oh no, you don't! Alex thought.

She gave chase and caught up with him as he threw the van into gear and stomped on the gas, the rear wheels struggling for purchase on the cold cobblestone. She jumped onto the running board and reached through the window, grabbing his arm. The van raced down the street, out of control as he punched her with his other arm while trying to steer with the one she held firmly in her grasp.

This could end badly, she thought.

Her legs were perilously close to striking cars parked along the street. Both her feet came off the sideboard, one of them kicking the sideview mirror off a Volkswagen.

She regained her footing, and with all her strength, twisted at her hips and thrust the man's face repeatedly against the steering wheel. The van spun sideways on the narrow street and struck several parked cars before coming to a stop. Alex was flung onto the engine hood of a Volvo, sliding up the windshield onto the roof, rolling off the other side into a pile of dirt from an excavated hole.

She lay there for a moment, taking stock of her condition. The wind was knocked out of her and she struggled to breathe, not quite able to draw a breath. But as she pondered that, she was aware that she had full sensation in her extremities—she could feel her arms and legs. She could see and hear. She was conscious. And, as the spasming inside her midsection subsided, she finally drew in a deep breath.

I'm alive, she thought.

She rose up out of the dirt and shakily approached the van on rubbery legs. The driver, a man maybe in his late thirties, was dazed and barely conscious, bleeding heavily from the face. She yanked open the banged-up driver's door and reached inside, thrusting his head back against the seat.

"Who sent you?" she demanded. "Who do you work for?" She grabbed him by his blood-soaked shirt and cocked her arm. "I said, who do you work for?" He smiled but said nothing.

A phone lay on the floor between the seats. She picked it up and aimed it at his face. Nothing happened.

"Open your eyes," she said. He didn't. "Open your fucking eyes!" She placed her hand atop his head and pulled open his eyelids, then put the phone in front of his face again. To her relief, the phone unlocked, and she pushed him over sideways so that he fell between the seats.

"Thanks for your cooperation."

She opened the settings on his phone and changed the unlock code, then tucked the phone into her pocket and walked back up the street to where Tatiana was waiting.

"We must get out of here quickly," she said when Alex arrived.

"Tell me first what's going on. Why are you here?"

"It is not what you think. I was too late to meet you at your hotel, but I watched you leave and followed you."

"Why are you following me? Why were you in The Hague and

now here? If you had anything to do with what happened to Madame Clicquot—"

A police car rounded the corner, lights flashing, siren wailing, followed by several more.

"I did not, but I don't have time to explain. I will meet you later."

"Where? Is this some kind of a joke?"

"No, Alex. No joke. Now you must trust me." She took off at a sprint. "I will find you later."

Police officers hastily exited their cars and surveyed the scene, looking at the crowd suspiciously. The protesters, including the young woman and man she had stood side by side with earlier on the steps of the cathedral, pointed to Alex in a coordinated gesture, and she found herself staring down the barrels of multiple police sidearms.

"So much for solidarity," she muttered.

CHAPTER 43

KRUUNUNHAKA, HELSINKI, FINLAND

Aside from her FBI training at Quantico—and maybe the odd foray on the wild side with her late husband Kyle when she was younger—Alex had never been placed in handcuffs before. She wasn't a fan.

Helsinki Cathedral, a Finnish Evangelical Lutheran church, was situated in the neighborhood of Kruununhaka in the center of the city. As the blue lights flashed atop the sedans and minivans of the city's police, many of her residents came out for a look to see what all the fuss was about.

Paramedics treated the injured men and placed them into ambulances, where they were handcuffed to their stretchers by police officers who accompanied them as they were transported to local hospitals. Alex, on the other hand, was detained at the scene by a constable on the order of his sergeant until he could arrive and assess her status. She held a chemical ice pack to the goose egg on the back of her head with her cuffed hands. The locals, meanwhile, continued to look on, no doubt speculating on the identity of the single white female who bested four men with a considerable advantage of size and numbers over her.

Alex said nothing to the constable beyond giving him her name. She was nauseated and had a headache, and the flashing emergency lights only added to her restlessness and agitation.

She wasn't thrilled about being detained, but she dared not play the CIA card, given that she was in-country unofficially and without diplomatic cover. She wasn't above calling her former chief at Interpol, though, and asked if she could make a call.

"No telephone," said the constable. "You can make a call from the station."

A short time later, his sergeant arrived. "Who was the other woman?" he asked.

"What other woman?" replied Alex.

"Look, you're in a lot of trouble, Miss Martel," he said. "Some of the injuries inflicted on these men are quite severe. I don't know who you are, but I'm sure you are more than you seem. If you cooperate, I might be able to help you. But if you deliberately obstruct this investigation, you will likely find yourself in the best-case scenario of being an overnight guest in our cells. Your choice."

She remained silent, so the sergeant explained the situation some more as he transferred her over to his car.

"You are not currently under arrest, but we are detaining you for further questioning at the station. You have the right to an attorney and to not incriminate yourself. But you will have an opportunity to plead your case before a prosecutor who will consider what charges will be laid based on the evidence. Do you understand?"

Alex nodded, her head throbbing. None of what he said alleviated her annoyance, but it at least gave her a process to anticipate.

As the sergeant was about to drive off with her, a gray Audi A8 sedan pulled up rather forcefully, boxing them in. The sergeant muttered something in Finnish that sounded like it might have been the equivalent of an f-bomb and stepped out of the car.

Emmi Rakkolainen, the Finnish Security and Intelligence Service officer she had met in The Hague, stepped out of the Audi and squared off with the sergeant. Alex couldn't make out what was being said, but when Emmi flashed her ID, he settled down as quickly as if somebody had used a shock collar on him. Alex was able to hit the electric window button with her elbow and it receded into the door.

"Do I need to remind you that Supo has preeminence in these situations?" Emmi asked in English.

"This is a matter of disturbing the peace and multiple instances of aggravated assault," the sergeant said.

"You are as misguided as you are foolish, and I'm not sure which is worse," she said, pulling her phone out of her pocket. "Do you think the woman in that car instigated all this, or might she have been defending herself?"

"*Defending herself?* She caused these men serious injury."

"I understand there were at least four attackers. Is that what's bothering you—she beat up some men? Would you have preferred she let them kill her?"

"Who are you calling?"

She ignored his question and spoke into the phone. "Prime Minister Rantala, thank you for taking my call, ma'am." The conversation switched to Finnish until Alex heard her say, "Yes, Madam Prime Minister. I will put the sergeant on the line." Even in the twilight glow of evening, Alex saw the man's face blanch. Emmi thrust the phone at him. "Prime Minister Rantala said that although she is currently meeting with the interior minister—the minister who oversees policing in Finland, as you know—she will gladly take a few minutes to educate you about the investigative powers of a Supo officer in matters pertaining to national security. At least I believe this is how she phrased it. But, please, by all means, talk to her."

The sergeant took the phone gingerly as if it were on fire. "Hello?" he said sheepishly.

There was a brief pause, then, "Yes, Your Excellency." Another pause, then, "Yes, Prime Minister. I understand, Prime Minister." Finally, "Yes, thank you. And I sincerely apologize for the misunderstanding and for interrupting your meeting, Madam Prime Minister."

He handed the phone back to Emmi, and she spoke into it. "*Kiitos, Pääministeri.*" *Thank you, Prime Minister.*

The sergeant opened the back door of the Volvo and helped Alex step out.

"You're not making many new friends here in Finland, I see," Emmi said as the young constable came over and freed her from the handcuffs.

"No one is taking the time to get to know me," Alex replied. "I'm told it takes a while for me to grow on some people."

"I, for one, don't believe it," Emmi said. The sergeant gave her a sideways glance as she said it. "Smile," she said to him. "This woman is one of the good guys."

"Right?" said Alex.

"If you say so," he said.

"Come on," said Emmi. "I'll take you back to your hotel."

"Thanks, really, but I'm starving."

"Then we'll stop somewhere first. How do you feel about pizza?"

CHAPTER 44

Thirty minutes later, Alex sat in front of her hotel inside Emmi's car, a pizza box on her lap.

"Are you sure you don't want me to drive you somewhere else?" Emmi asked. "I can't guarantee you'll be safe here."

"No, I suspect they won't try anything again right away." Whoever *they* were. "Hopefully, that was the end of them."

Emmi nodded, then reached over her shoulder and retrieved a package from the back seat. It was the size of a box of chocolates and gift-wrapped with a bow. "I was asked to give you this. From friends in town. Came in a diplomatic pouch."

"I have friends in town?"

"Who knew?" Emmi said sarcastically. "Let's regroup tomorrow morning to sort this out, yes?"

"Sure. It's time to find out what's really going on."

* * *

Alex sat on the sofa in her hotel room, working on her second slice of Margherita pizza, a pizza that was made with the colors of the Italian flag—red (tomatoes), white (mozzarella cheese), and green (basil leaves).

She fetched a Coca-Cola from the fridge and pulled open the tab, then took a long swig. Some liked beer with their pizza, but Alex preferred an ice-cold Coke. She was lifting a third slice out of the box when there was a knock at the door.

What the fuck?

She tugged the ribbon and bow off the box Emmi had given her and lifted the lid. From its weight, she had already deduced its contents. Inside was a note:

> *Shooter,*
> *Handle with care.*
> —*Caleb*

Beneath the note, wrapped in a microfiber cloth and bubble wrap, was her Kimber R7 Mako with a loaded magazine in the well, two fully loaded spare mags in belt pouches, and a box of 9-millimeter ammunition, along with her appendix-carry Kydex holster.

Aw, Caleb. She smiled. *You sure know how to please a girl.* She might have dwelt a little longer on the thought, but whoever was at the door knocked again, this time more insistently.

"I'll be right there," she called.

She press-checked the pistol, then fully racked the slide to chamber a round and slid the Kimber into its holster, which she tucked into the front of her jeans. She dropped the front of her shirt to cover it and walked to the door.

If it was still possible to surprise her, now was one of those occasions.

"Are you going to invite me in?" asked the woman standing outside her door.

Tatiana had changed her coat and now wore a pink fleece jacket and a gray knit beanie.

"Well, well, if it isn't Barbie of Siberia," said Alex.

Tatiana brushed past her as she stepped into the foyer. When she turned to face her again, she was holding a gun.

"And you must be Second Amendment Barbie, yes?" Tatiana said, stretching out the hand that held the pistol.

Fuck, thought Alex. *I should have known better.*

Alex patted herself down and realized Tatiana had stripped her of her own gun. If she wasn't so pissed off, she would have been impressed.

But then Tatiana did the unexpected. She dropped out the magazine, cleared the round from the chamber, and popped the slide off the top of the Kimber, executing the fieldstripping procedure in scant seconds. When she had finished, she deposited the disassembled weapon onto a side cabinet next to the coffeemaker.

Turning away from Alex, she walked deeper into the hotel room, glancing into the luxurious bathroom with its separate shower stall and whirlpool tub. She strode into the sitting room and helped herself to a slice of pizza, crossing her long legs casually as she leaned into the sofa.

"Nice digs," she said.

"I used a lot of my air miles for the upgrade."

She took a bite. "And good pizza."

"Are we going to stand around talking about my accommodations and choice of takeout, or is there something on your mind?"

Alex was tempted to reassemble her gun, but decided that since Tatiana hadn't shot her, the implied threat might be in bad form.

"You're very impatient, Alex. Saving your life worked up an appetite for me." Her English wasn't perfect, but her accent was diminishing. Or maybe Alex was just getting used to it. The Russian GRU captain strode to the fridge and plucked out a Coke.

"I suppose I should thank you," said Alex. "But it seems to me you were just making up for being a bitch in London."

"That is such a harsh word—*bitch*. I prefer *assassin*. And I am not making up for anything. It is my job, Alexandra."

"Yes, but you did it with such passion."

"Well, if one cannot love one's work, one should find a new job, yes?"

She had a point. "Who were those men at the church? I thought they were with you."

"They were Americans."

"Yes, I get that now. Forgive me if I seem a little confused, but what the hell's going on? Americans attacking me. *You* helping me. We're on different sides of this. We're enemies—"

"Our *countries* are enemies," she corrected. "You and I are patriots, which makes us like-minded adversaries, but not necessarily enemies."

"I think we're splitting hairs. You almost killed me—shot me to death, more specifically—in London not very long ago. And if I could have retrieved my gun or relieved you of yours, I surely would have killed *you*."

"That was then; this is now." Tatiana had made quick work of the slice and helped herself to another. "It's a difficult business," she said through a mouthful of pizza. "Decisions must be made in the heat of the moment. I made mine while I was performing my authorized duties for my country. You put two of my men in the hospital during that same encounter. Business is business. It's a funny game."

Alex didn't see the point of debating it further. "Why are you here?"

"It's true."

"What is?"

"I came here to kill you." Alex stiffened up. "Relax, that is my job. Americans take these things so personally." She finished her slice and chased it with a long gulp of Coke, then set the can down on the table and wiped her hands on her jeans. "But a good officer questions orders that are nonsense. Americans are better at this than Russians. I am only learning it now, thanks to you. This is one reason we are losing the war our president started—not enough creative thinking and initiative among mid-level officers. And faraway commanders have no grasp of the dynamics of the battlefield or proper tactics to adapt and fight effectively."

"I'm not complaining, but assuming you've decided not to kill me, why not?" asked Alex.

"Because if I did, it would reinforce what everyone already thinks, and no one would believe that Russia has no interest in starting a war with America."

"Playing devil's advocate for a moment, why then did President Sergachev just move all those troops closer to the Finnish border?"

"That is in response to a speech made by your Secretary of State Hayward that Russian aggression will not be tolerated. And now she is on her way with your president here to reaffirm NATO's determination to stop Russia, no matter the cost. This will lead to war for sure.

President Sergachev will feel he must answer such provocation with greater aggression. This is how men think, Alexandra. With their . . ." She grabbed her crotch to illustrate.

"Wait, go back. My country believes your country tampered with the Finnish power grid and nuclear stations; made ships collide with the coast; launched cyberattacks on hospitals and major infrastructure—"

"Alexandra, it is easier to believe a lie rooted in a logical conclusion based on prior beliefs than to believe the truth when it goes against one's strongly held opinions."

"Confirmation bias."

"*Da,*" Tatiana said.

"But those incidents had all the hallmarks of a GRU or Directorate 13 operation. And we have trails of intel pointing to Russia being behind it all."

"I'm sure you do, but if any such evidence exists, it is fake news, as you Americans like to say. Which seems now very convenient since you believe it to be true." Tatiana added, "There are forces at play making it appear it is Russia."

"Why would we believe anything your country—or you for that matter—says?"

Tatiana lowered her voice as if the room had ears. She leaned forward to speak. "You are right, Alex. My president is a megalomaniac, and there is no reason anyone should trust him. But I am here to tell you that it is not Russia doing this. A faction in America's own government wants this to happen; it wants to create tension between our two countries that leads to war.

"President Sergachev is a vain and egotistical man who likes to pose semi-naked on horseback, but he is not prepared for a global war that would escalate to Armageddon—something that would most definitely happen if the United States and Russia fought a war directly and not through proxies as is normally the case. Neither side could afford to let the other win, so everyone will, in fact, lose."

Her conviction gave Alex pause. She walked over to the side counter and fetched two crystal glasses, then opened the refrigerator and removed two mini bottles of Stoli. She emptied them into the tumblers and carried them to the sitting area.

Tatiana took a glass from her hand.

"You have a beautiful name," mused Tatiana. "Alexandra is Greek for *defender of men*." She stood, holding her glass aloft. "It seems our job, Alexandra, is to defend the men who would bring us to war. Or perhaps to protect the world from those men, yes?"

Tatiana hadn't really told her much she didn't already know or suspect. But it carried a greater ring of truth coming from the horse's mouth.

"So, am I to believe you're here speaking on behalf of Russia in the hopes of convincing me that your country is not to blame for any of this?"

"No."

"*No?*"

"I did not say I am speaking on behalf of anyone. I am here for myself, and I am here for my country, but not on behalf of anyone but the people of Mother Russia, who have suffered so much already as a mad president throws young men to their deaths in Eastern Europe fighting a war no one wanted. But even he isn't crazy enough to simultaneously open a Western front against all of NATO. He wishes to scare off the American people by threatening nuclear war, but even I know that this is not what he wants. He is a romantic who wishes to reunite the former Soviet Union, not destroy the world. Do you understand what I am telling you?"

"*Da,*" said Alex.

"And do you trust me?"

"We'll see," she said as they clinked glasses.

"To not eating bullets," said Tatiana as they shot back the icy-cold vodka. "Or falling to our deaths out of windows." Off of Alex's puzzled look, she explained, "Old Russian proverb."

"Sure it is."

"You cannot stay here," said Tatiana.

"Why not?"

"Because I know for a fact that there are men who know where you are. American men, like those at the cathedral. And Russians who do not think the way I think. And if my own people find out I've spoken to you about this, they will come for us both."

"Where would I go?"

"We have some places here that very few know about."

"Russian safe houses?" Alex asked. Tatiana nodded. "What sense does that make—me staying in a Russian safe house?"

"It is the last place either the Russians or the Americans would look for you."

Again, she was making sense. But the idea of staying in a safe house of an enemy of America was absurd.

"Thanks, Tatiana, but for reasons I probably don't have to explain to you, I'd rather shoot myself in the head."

"If you stay in this hotel, someone might do it for you."

Alex smiled and shook her head firmly.

Tatiana tried a new tack. "I could stay here with you tonight for our mutual safety."

Again, Alex shook her head. "I'm a big girl, I can look after myself."

"Okay, I can take a hint." She reached into her pocket. "Take out your phone."

Alex's phone buzzed. Tatiana had AirDropped her a link to a website. "Alex, accept the transfer."

"And just give you access to my phone?"

"Don't be stupid. I know this is not your CIA phone. I don't care about your sexy text messages with your boyfriend, Caleb."

Alex almost regretted not having any of those. "Then what did you send me?"

"It is a link to a Proton Drive account. I have transferred information there—documents, names. It will help in case you still don't believe me."

"I don't understand why you're helping me like this."

"I have explained it, Alexandra. We are more alike than you know. I want better for my country, not worse for yours. If you can make sense of the data trail, you'll see I am not lying. If anyone found out I gave this to you, I would be shot."

"Or you could fall out a window."

"In Russia, there is always that."

The implications of whatever evidence might be on that drive could prove world changing. Alex hit accept.

Tatiana stood to leave, then paused. "Password is *Girlfriend123!* Capital G, exclamation point at the end."

"Are we going to follow each other on Instagram now, too?"

Tatiana raised an eyebrow and left the room.

Didn't think so.

CHAPTER 45

That was weird, thought Alex.

The spy game truly made for strange bedfellows, but perhaps none stranger than an American and a Russian spy—two women—collaborating to create global peace in our time. Peace or not, she might still need her gun, so she reassembled it and tucked it back into its holster with a round in the chamber.

How'd this happen? she wondered. One minute, she was merrily sailing aboard a luxury megayacht on the Mediterranean, hoping to finally snag some downtime with Caleb away from the job, and the next, she was being chased by fellow Americans through the streets of Helsinki and conspiring with a Russian agent. *This ought to make for quite the contact report back at the Agency.*

As for whether she believed Tatiana's impassioned statements, it was still up to the jury of her subconscious to decide, but she was left with the impression she was telling the truth. A voice in her head, though, still told her to tread carefully. Only a few months ago, Directorate 13, of which Tatiana was a member, ran an op that came close to setting off another kind of global conflagration that Alex had barely survived. So, while she didn't know for sure whether Tatiana had known all the details then, arguably, she was guilty by association.

The idea that powerful people in America were trying to tease out a war between the world's two dominant nuclear superpowers seemed like some strange dystopian fantasy. It was a scenario fit for a postapocalyptic movie. Or, it could simply be another deception. But Tatiana had seemed stone-cold serious.

Some would say that Alex would be crazy to trust her. And *some* meant pretty much everyone. Caleb, for one.

It was much more likely she was lying, but to what end? Would she hope Alex would tell the American government it wasn't Russia but a group of Americans doing this? And, in so doing, hand the advantage to Russia?

Excuse me, Mr. President, might I have a word?

Sure, Alex, President Moore would say. Then, after hearing her argument, *Let's stand down our forces and tell all of NATO to do the same. A round of "Kumbaya," everyone?*

Not likely.

So, against all odds, and like many misguided patriots before her, Alex chose to believe her adversary's word, to trust the information handed to her by a sworn enemy of the United States. The fact that Tatiana had told her what she already suspected tilted the field heavily in her favor. Confirmation bias? Sure, but Alex had something others did not—a cell phone belonging to the enemy.

Trust, but verify.

She walked to the closet and punched her code into the room safe, then reached inside and removed the phone she had taken from the man in the van. Hoping that neither he nor anyone else had a chance to wipe it remotely yet, she entered the unlock code she had given it. To her relief, the phone came to life in her hands.

Great. Now what?

She resisted the urge to call Jonathan Burgess, her former colleague at Interpol. He'd dissect the phone in a matter of seconds, but she wanted to see firsthand what secrets the phone might reveal to her before handing it off, even to JB.

She thumbed through the pages of screens, looking at all the app icons, seeing if anything jumped out at her. All the usual messaging suspects were present: Messages, Messenger, WhatsApp, Signal, GroupMe, IronWhisper, Telegram. They were all there. And there were more than a few social media apps, any of which could reveal information about what was going on.

If the folks at Bellingcat could find a person based on a selfie posted to Instagram of someone leaning against a nondescript brick wall on a cloudy day, she should at least be able to find a loose thread in one of the phone owner's SMS conversations.

Who was she kidding? She could barely spell *geolocate* without a dictionary.

She opened his text messages app and thumbed through his conversations. *Boring.* Then she opened WhatsApp. Aside from a few spicy messages from a woman named Abby, there was nothing there either. She opened Telegram next.

This looks more promising.

But after scrolling through several Telegram newsgroups, her excitement petered out. Nothing there but some tame—and not so tame— nontraditional news source channels.

Signal was the same. *Why have all these secure messaging apps if you're not going to use them?* Then it dawned on her—maybe he was using them but had turned on a feature in each that makes messages disappear after a set period of time.

She found the messaging app IronWhisper buried on the fourth page of his phone. According to the notification icon, he had several unread messages. Opening the app, she noticed that the most recent were from only an hour or so ago. She scrolled through the thread. For some reason, the administrator hadn't turned on disappearing messages. Or maybe the time hadn't yet elapsed. Maybe they were just being cocky, or maybe they wanted to ensure a lasting trail for easy reference, but either way it seemed careless.

She was able to scroll back through a time period of several hours. There were references to an *op* tonight and multiple mentions of the *subject* of the op. All that was missing was her name. References to *intercept* and *interview*. It gave her a creepy feeling like the ones she had known in high school and even at times in the Army when she knew she was the topic of discussion but had no way to change or even monitor the conversation.

It had always been the price she'd paid for being the outsider, the different one—a woman on a field of play where only men were expected to engage and participate. It should have felt worse here with an enemy trying to kill her—even a domestic one—but oddly, it didn't feel as bad. These people were *supposed* to be her enemies.

Each participant in this thread had been assigned a code name. The dude who owned this phone went by AlphaWolf. Alex was pretty sure that anyone who referred to themselves as *Alpha*-anything surely wasn't.

She kept scrolling back through the thread.

Shadow Guard. What the hell is that?

It sounded like a basketball position. Over and over, though, the term *Shadow Guard* appeared in connection with the operation. In fact, she determined, it wasn't the operation but a key player in it. And besides Shadow Guard, two other code names cropped up repeatedly seemingly in connection to mission command—Eagle and Talon. It was almost too on the nose, but there it was.

But who were they?

The messages didn't mention a specific target or even the name or names of individuals, so a smoking gun this wasn't. It *was* suggestive of some form of a conspiracy, though. But it *wasn't* actionable intelligence at this point.

The job of the task force to which she had been assigned was to investigate the events in question—the disruption operations in Finland—to see who was behind them. But having gone to be by Celeste's side, she hadn't met the team and so had no clear direction regarding to whom she should take this new intel. Caleb, of course, but maybe not yet.

Instead, she dialed Jonathan's phone.

"Are you crazy?" were the first words out of his mouth after she filled him in. "I'll assume for now you're not, but let's review these new facts. You call me in the middle of the night. The last I heard from you—more than an hour ago—you were being chased through the streets by crazy Russians."

"Turns out they weren't Russian."

"Who were they?"

"I'm getting to that."

"Okay. Earlier, you asked me to make sure your phone was clean and that it hadn't been compromised by anyone. By Russians, specifically. Now you tell me you're practicing unsafe, unprotected AirDropping with a Russian spy who had previously tried to kill you—on more than one occasion, I might add—after your phone was hacked during a previous assignment by the same group of Russians for whom that Russian spy—your new best friend, apparently—worked. That about cover it all?"

"Well, it sounds worse when you put it like that."

"I think it would sound bad no matter how you say it."

"Now you're being judgy."

"Text me what she gave you." She sent it. "Did she give you a password for this Proton Drive account?" Alex gave it to him. "Seriously?" he asked.

"All I can do is tell it like it is, Jonathan. I have no choice but to trust her. For now."

"Okay, leave it with me. But delete it off your phone. Or, at least, don't log into that site until you hear back from me."

* * *

She needed to call Caleb.

"I got the package you sent," she said when he answered. "Thanks."

"Mustang filled me in and told me things were happening. She wanted me to look out for you."

"Aw, you sure know how to please a girl."

"It's the only way I know to make sure you're okay."

Clearly, he misunderstood his effect on her.

"I am. A lot's gone on since I got here."

"Oh?"

She told him everything she could remember, from seeing Celeste in the hospital to the meeting with Prime Minister Rantala, to the foot chase and fight at the cathedral, to seeing their nemesis Tatiana again and explaining how she had saved her butt. And then she told him of Tatiana's visit to her hotel room with the explanation of all that had been going on, and that Tatiana claimed it was forces back home in the States orchestrating all this and not the Russians, and that she had provided intel that Jonathan was now looking at.

"Jesus, Alex."

"Caleb, I believe her."

"Well, that's great. Why don't we go and tell the president."

He was being dramatic—she had already considered that and ruled it out.

"Why would she lie?" Alex asked rhetorically.

"Really? And not to put too fine a point on it, but is there a reason you handed over our intel to Interpol and not the task force that you're on?"

"Caleb, there's evidence of a conspiracy originating from back home. Who was I supposed to trust with this?"

"Well, for starters, me."

He was probably right—maybe she should have dropped this in his lap first before she went running back to Interpol. But she couldn't be sure who to trust. Sure, she could and did trust Caleb, but she already knew how he felt about the task force leader, Terry "Hacksaw" Gault. Could he somehow be involved in all this? She couldn't be sure he wasn't. But she was 100 percent sure that Jonathan Burgess and Chief Bressard at Interpol were completely above suspicion.

"I'm sorry," she said. She wasn't sure she needed to apologize, but she thought Caleb might need to hear it anyway.

"It's okay, Alex. I'll brief the deputy director. I'm sure she'll be thrilled."

CHAPTER 46

President Taylor R. W. Moore sat in a high-back chair in front of the fireplace and gazed at the *Resolute* desk across the room. It was made with oak timbers from the ill-fated British Royal Navy ship HMS *Resolute,* whose fate had been sealed when it became trapped in Arctic ice and abandoned in 1854.

He wondered if his presidency would suffer a similar fate. He hadn't expected to face the challenge of a looming world war midway through his first term. But then, no president expects to be beset by global calamity. His legacy would be determined by how his administration responded to the threat the revanchist Russian Federation posed.

Such were the consequences of a misstep in today's world of political brinksmanship. To heed the threats of a madman meant that nuclear deterrence worked, but not in the way it had been intended. America and its NATO allies now continually backed down to the very form of nuclear terrorism that the concept of an even distribution of such weapons was designed to prevent. Moore didn't like it, but to do anything else was too great a gamble.

It was the biggest criticism his political opponents could muster against him. Even his own party was at times inflamed by the rhetoric of his more hawkish vice president, Barbara Garcia. But to meet the threat head on—in essence, to call the bluff—was to risk bringing about an end-of-the-world scenario. Something Brash Babs didn't need to concern herself with in the number-two seat of this fast-flying jet fighter called America.

Would Moore's legacy be a new world order, defined by earnest measures aimed at true counterproliferation and eventual decommissioning of all nuclear weapons? Or would it simply end in an apocalyptic flash of light and a mushroom cloud reaching up to the heavens?

The iconic sculpture *The Bronco Buster,* by Frederic Remington, sat on a plinth next to his desk. Moore searched for some wisdom in the chaos of that one moment frozen forever in bronze. Had the rider survived that encounter with his mount? Had he remained in the saddle? Did the bronco settle and accept the inevitability of being encumbered by saddle, stirrup, and bridle?

Times had been simpler back home in Amarillo. Ranching was what he was born to do. Being the president was more like herding cats. He was a people person, for sure. But politicians weren't really people, and statesmanship wasn't like being the head of the Circle M Ranch in the Texas Panhandle, where everyone knew him and took him at his word.

His executive assistant's gentle knock at the door heralded the arrival of tonight's visitors. The door swung open, and Titus Pelletier, the president's chief of staff, led the small group into the Oval.

Trailing Pelletier were the president's national security advisor, General Lucas Hughes, and Secretary of State Katherine Hayward. Behind her were Kadeisha Thomas and Terry Gault, two unlikely allies if ever there were any.

"Thanks for coming," Moore said, rising to greet his guests and gesturing to the couches across from his chair.

"Of course, Mr. President," General Hughes said with a courteous smile.

"Thank you for seeing us, Mr. President," said Hayward, a tall, strongly built woman in her fifties with close-cropped hair that was transitioning from blond to gray.

An aide trailed in and placed a tray of coffee and tea on the table between the couches. General Hughes poured himself a cup and sat back.

"Troubling times," began Moore. "Secretary Hayward, I'm so glad you're joining me on our mission in Helsinki. These talks at the NATO summit call for just the kind of level-headed and thoughtful measures you were known for in your Army days."

"Thank you, Mr. President," she replied. "I know our allies are on side with your Baltic Sea strategy. Having you there in person, frankly, will smooth out any bumps that our partners might have been feeling. Honestly, sir, extending BALTOPS to bolster assets in the region was a bold, simple, and effective plan."

"Well, truth be told, that was General Hughes's idea," Moore said.

"I know, sir. Lucas mentions that every chance he gets," said Hayward. "And despite that, it looks as if it's working, Mr. President."

Moore let out a loud chuckle and looked over at his national security advisor, a painful smile stretched across his lips. It was the first time the president recalled his affable colleague's demeanor showing visible strain.

"Lucas, you look like you need a hit of bourbon in your cup."

"No, thank you, Mr. President. I recognize friendly teasing when I hear it."

Moore wasn't so sure.

"Tell me, Lucas. Are we ready for this? I know our allies are on side. The secretary of state has done a wonderful job shaping an alliance of the apprehensive into a coalition of the consenting, but what are you hearing?"

"Sir, the National Security Council is satisfied our actions are having the desired effect keeping the Russians at bay. President Sergachev is still adamant that he's not responsible for the actions of which his nation is being accused."

"And what of this DIA-led joint task force, Director Gault? Are you any closer to finding out if there's truth to these conspiracy theories I've been hearing?"

"Yes and no, sir. We've been accumulating scattered bits of intel. One theory that refuses to die is that there is a cabal of conspirators here at home that is involved."

"To what end?" asked Moore.

"It's all a little murky, sir. A little deep state–ish, even too much for my liking. But one of our team members was killed in a mysterious traffic accident after uncovering some as-yet-unverified intel that supports that theory. The FBI is now involved in that investigation."

"Fine, Terry. Keep Lucas apprised and he'll fill me in as needed. I'm generally of the mind that conspiracy theories are for the intellectually feeble, those looking to find structure in chaos, and the world's a chaotic place. But I don't want history to judge us as being the wrongful aggressor, so I will remain open-minded to this hoo-ha."

Gault nodded.

"Director Thomas?"

"I'm with Director Gault, sir. We're on top of changing circumstances here and overseas. The Finnish prime minister asked to use one of our assets to continue digging. A report on her progress is pending. Meanwhile, we've learned that Interpol had intended to launch an unofficial inquiry into some of these matters at Finland's request, but events of the past several days have ensnared them in some other lethal activities, including the death of the Finnish billionaire Valtteri Lehtonen, a personal acquaintance and friend of the prime minister."

"I see. And how is Secretary General Clicquot?"

"Still in the ICU."

"That's a shame. Anything else, Deputy Director Thomas?"

"Nothing concrete, Mr. President. The Agency asset is active in Helsinki, and we have others here in Washington trying to get to the bottom of it all."

"I'm assuming I would be able to guess who your asset in Finland is?"

"I'm sure you could, Mr. President. She continues to make friends, and even a few enemies, in high places."

"Indeed. Any chance I'll bump into her while I'm there?"

"I wouldn't rule it out. Sir, if I may . . ."

"Go ahead. This is—what do they call it on university campuses these days? Oh, yes—this is a *safe space*."

"Yes, Mr. President. With all the subterfuge going on, sir, I wonder if you might consider removing yourself from the agenda."

Both Pelletier and Hughes visually stiffened in their seats.

She continued. "It seems superfluous for the President of the United States to immerse himself neck-deep in a barrel of rattlesnakes. With the US and Russia this close to an armed confrontation, maybe discretion would be the better part of valor here."

"While I appreciate that you tailored that metaphor for my benefit, Kadeisha, you're not telling me anything my Secret Service detail hasn't told me ten times a day since I announced this trip. It'll be fine. But, if not, someone will need to rein in Vice President Garcia. When Babs thinks of Ruskies, it's not all sunshine and butterflies. So, y'all best keep me alive, and I'll do my best to attain that goal as well. Other than that, it's in the Lord's hands." He stood. "That's it," he said as everyone else rose out of their seats. "Tomorrow, the sun will rise in a faraway land, and we shall know the truth. Break a leg, everyone."

* * *

HAY-ADAMS HOTEL, WASHINGTON, DC

It wasn't often that Caleb frequented the same bars where the politicos and journos hung out around DC. Unlike most Washington insiders—and Caleb didn't count himself among them—he preferred to meet in the shadows out around Arlington, McLean, or Tysons Corner at appropriate dive bars like the ones he would visit in and around Fayetteville, North Carolina, back in the day.

Off the Record was the exact opposite of those bars. Located in the upscale Hay-Adams Hotel behind the White House, the glamorous speakeasy-style underground bar was centrally located on the other side of Lafayette Square. It made a convenient watering hole for those working in the West Wing or Capitol Hill. Of concern to Caleb was that it was also a good spot for those who inhabited the Washington bureaus of the newspapers, magazines, websites, networks, and, increasingly, the blogosphere. In short, if you weren't keen to have your business dealings and associations outed, it was an excellent place to avoid.

But, as he had learned in the past, the bartenders here mixed a great Manhattan, so that was a plus.

He descended the staircase off the lobby and arrived at the appointed time wearing a dark gray sports jacket over a white button-down collared shirt and dark chinos. He surveyed the room and spotted Director Gault against the wall in a corner nook, two frosty crystal glasses already on the table.

"I ordered you a Manhattan, if memory serves," he said as Caleb sank into a plush chair.

"Why are we here?" asked Caleb without foreplay.

"Look, Copeland, we're on the same side. So, why don't we leave the past to the dust heap of history and try to work together like professionals."

Caleb seized his drink. "To old friends and fallen comrades."

"To fallen comrades."

The Manhattan was as good as he remembered it. Contrary to common mythology, it wasn't the choice of whiskey alone that made the cocktail so good but the choice of sweet vermouth. Off the Record mixed Carpano Antica Formula with Bulleit rye, bitters, and a proper vintage maraschino cherry to create theirs.

"Does the term *Shadow Guard* mean anything to you?" asked Gault.

Caleb shook his head. "What is it?"

"Something Tam found. He unearthed information—banking records, records of payments, but nothing too specific. It all points to a conspiracy that was meant to implicate Russia in that mess that's been going on for the past year."

"Jesus," Caleb whispered, glancing over his shoulder for signs of anyone paying them too much attention. "That's what we've been looking for, isn't it?"

Gault nodded solemnly.

"What's the matter?"

"Tam's dead," said Gault, flatly.

"*What?*"

"Wrecked his car on his way home. Supposedly drowned in a pond in his pickup. But witnesses saw two men walking from the area. And that's not all." Caleb waited. "Coroner says the cause of death was small-caliber lead poisoning. Shot in the throat. Found a bullet lodged in his brain stem."

"*Sonofabitch,*" said Caleb through gritted teeth. "Why wasn't I told?"

"I couldn't before. I had a meeting with the president. I wanted to tell you in person."

Caleb sized up his task force leader. It was hard to get a bead on him, but this was the kind of thing Caleb worried about—that Terry Gault could do anything, at any time, to anyone, if it served his purpose. So, what was his purpose? "Hacksaw, if you had anything to do with this, so help me God, I'll—"

"Cool it, Viking. I had nothing to do with it. Why would I bring you here to tell you this if I was the one behind it?"

Caleb didn't have an answer to that. "Besides you, who knew what he found?"

"First call I made was to your boss."

"You told Deputy Director Thomas? Bullshit."

"Ask her yourself. And then ask her why you didn't know until now. Why would Mustang not tell you straightaway?"

That was a million-dollar question.

"I'm assuming," said Caleb, "that someone else is now examining the evidence Tam collected, verifying what he found?"

"That's just it. After he was killed, I brought in a forensic team to try to transfer the data to the NSA's computers, but they couldn't track it down. It looks like someone went in and killed the trail."

"Did you go back to Thomas and ask her if she knew what happened?"

"Are you kidding me? I called you instead."

It wasn't like Gault to shy away from asking hard questions. Or doing whatever needed to be done—legal or extrajudicial—to accomplish a task. Caleb had seen him outright fabricate evidence in Afghanistan and

Iraq to secure orders for a mission if the mission might bring him closer to his own objectives. And in doing so, Gault had steamrolled more than a few operators and gotten others into jackpots by inserting them into needless combat. Caleb knew he'd even gotten a few of them killed. He could be reckless and ambitious. So, what was the true story now?

"This has your heat signature all over it, Gault. Why didn't you take it to my boss?"

"Copeland, Deputy Director Thomas and I met with the president not more than an hour ago, and before I linked up with her, she was deep in discussion with the vice president. The two of them clammed up pretty fast when I approached."

"So?"

Gault looked around the room before speaking again. "Vice President Garcia has made a reputation for herself for opposing the actions of the president. The president wants my task force to figure out what's going on. How can I be sure old Babs Garcia isn't working against that objective and hasn't drawn your ambitious boss with her?"

Fucking Washington, Caleb thought.

"I've known Mustang a long time. There's no way she could be complicit in anything like this."

"Would you bet your life on it?"

Caleb didn't answer.

"Look, Viking, normally I wouldn't care what you think, but I'm dead serious when I say we're on the same side. We are edging closer to an all-out war with Russia, so I'm not fucking with you. I did not have Tam killed."

"So why didn't you go to her?"

"Because I didn't want to be the next spook to end up with a bullet through my brain."

"You're an asshole, Hacksaw. Thomas could never be behind this."

"No? Tam finds evidence. I tell Director Thomas. Tam ends up dead. So you tell me, super spy, who did this?"

Hacksaw would ordinarily be at the top of Caleb's list of suspects based on past experience. But, as rare as it was, sometimes people *do* change. Maybe he wasn't behind it. What Caleb knew for sure, though, was that there was no way Mustang was.

How best to flush out those responsible still eluded him. What he did know was that his team wasn't of much use sitting on their asses eating barbecue.

It was time for them to go wheels up.

CHAPTER 47

As Alex slept, she was overwhelmed by the sensation of being beneath the waves again, bullets and fire streaking through the sea, unable to discern which direction would take her back to safety at the surface of the Mediterranean. Bullets punched through the water with loud *bangs*.

Alex, the voice said. *Swim to the sound of my voice. I'll bring you in, I swear it!*

Caleb?

She opened her eyes and stared into the darkness, her disorientation amplified by her exhaustion and the strangeness of her surroundings. She searched for something familiar but couldn't right her mind.

Knock, knock.

There it was again—the same sound she was sure had awakened her, lifting her into a world of confusion.

Knock, knock, knock.

This time, the sound was louder, more insistent.

Shit. The door.

Finally, it dawned on her. She was in a hotel in Finland, finally sleeping after what had been one hell of a day.

"Alex?" She heard the muffled sound of her name spoken through the door.

She sat up, then fumbled around to turn on the bedside light. She got out of bed and strode to the door, her baby toe glancing off the tubular metal leg of one of the sitting room chairs.

"Shit! Shit, shit, shit," she cursed, hopping through the room. She turned back to the couch and threw on an oversized T-shirt, just barely covering up her nakedness, then limped the rest of the way to the door.

"Alex, you in there?"

You've got to be kidding me. She knew that voice.

She opened the door and there stood Street.

"I thought you must be dead," he said, his Scottish brogue tingeing his words with lament. "I've been out here knocking for five minutes."

"It's . . ." She looked to her wrist for her watch, but it wasn't there. ". . . late," she said. "I was asleep."

"Very deeply, I'd say. Are you going to let me in?"

She stepped aside so he could pass, and as he did, he gently brushed against her as Tatiana had. She instinctively checked for her pistol, which of course, given her state of dress, wasn't there.

She flicked on the lights.

"Nice digs," Street said.

"Everyone seems to like it." He gave her a quizzical glance. "Long story," she added.

His eyes roved over her briefly.

"Check yourself, Street. I didn't have time to get dressed."

"I'm not doing anything," he protested. "Just making an observation."

"Well, turn around and observe the wall while I put on some clothes."

He did as instructed as Alex searched for a pair of jeans.

"I heard you'd been discharged from the hospital," she said. He was about to turn and answer, but she stopped him. "Not finished dressing yet."

"Sorry," he said over his shoulder. "I let myself out."

"It's not a house party. I don't think it's supposed to work like that."

"Well, I insisted, and they finally let me go. It's just a bit of bruising."

"A myocardial contusion is not the same as *just a bit of bruising.* Your heart's been injured."

"That's a load of crap and you know it."

"It's not."

"I feel fine. If it will make you feel any better, I won't go running any marathons for a wee bit then."

"Done. You can turn around now," she said, straightening her T-shirt. He appraised her. "What?" she asked.

"I think just the T-shirt was a better look on you."

"Don't be an ass. You could still end up back in the hospital."

Street grinned. "I heard you were having some excitement here in Helsinki, so I thought I'd jet up and lend you a hand. Lehtonen Enterprises has given me free rein to help you in any way I can."

She sat on the couch with one leg crossed under her. "At this moment, I'm not up to much. I was enjoying my sleep, though." She leaned her elbow on the arm of the couch and tried to tussle her hair into obedience.

He sat in the chair and caught sight of the pizza box and glasses.

"You had company," he said suspiciously. "Anybody I should be aware of?"

"As a matter of fact, an old acquaintance from London dropped by." She proceeded to summarize for him the events of the past twenty-four hours as best she could.

"You have had a very busy day," he said, opening the pizza box and picking up the last cold slice.

"I'm really sorry about Jocko," Alex said.

Street slumped back in the chair and took a bite. "He was a good soldier. Not all are cut out for it like he was. I'm going to miss him."

In Alex's experience, that was as close as soldiers got to declaring their affection for another operator.

"Why are you really here, Street? How did you know where I was?"

He was down to the crust already and made quick work of it before answering.

"After the second attempt on Celeste's life, your Chief Bressard came to find me. He filled me in a bit and expressed concern for your safety."

"So, he sent you to babysit?"

"Not at all. He thinks you're a one-woman wrecking crew."

She nodded.

"I've lost too many good men these last few days, Alex. If I can help you even in the slightest, you have to let me. I have almost unlimited resources, both financial and matériel, that I can loan you for whatever the mission turns out to be. Payback's a bitch, and I want to be here for the show."

She thought about it. She had gone ronin, as far as Kadeisha and the Agency were concerned. A samurai without a master. And even though Caleb had indicated there was now tacit approval of her involvement on behalf of the US government to assist Finland, she was alone here—not counting Tatiana—with nothing but her wits and a pistol to take the next steps, whatever they were going to be.

"Where will you spend the night?" she asked.

He looked at her sheepishly. "I came here straight from the airport. The hotel is full, and any digs I might have access to are a long ways away. So, if you don't mind . . ." His eyes drifted to the couch where she sat.

"Seriously?"

"If it's not too much of a bother."

"Fine, but Street, so help me God . . ."

"No need to say a thing," he said, his hazel eyes twinkling. "Mum raised a gentleman, not a brute."

* * *

WASHINGTON, DC

The rear of the Lincoln Black Label Navigator L was a silent oasis where Senator Kennington could enjoy the serenity of the twenty-eight-speaker sound system in all its glory. Even traveling through the streets of DC, the back of his head nestled in the plush leather of the vehicle's upscale interior, the pitch-perfect meanderings of the Boston Pops Orchestra playing the theme from *The Patriot* helped drown out the voices in his head, the ones saying his plan would fail, that he couldn't stand up to the expectations of his father, who must surely be disappointed by his failings to date.

If only you could see the promise of what's to come, Dad. Months—

years—of preparation have gone into what lies ahead—just a few more hours.

His phone rang.

"General Hughes, it's late. To what do I owe this pleasure?"

"Senator, it *is* late," replied the president's national security advisor. "In fact, it's so late, it's almost sunrise in that Nordic capital where the world's fate will be decided. Is everything ready?"

"It is. But you sound like a pretentious ass. No need to get your parachute strings tied up in knots. Everything is in place, both here and at the NATO summit."

"By everything, you do mean both scenarios?"

"General, my team is made up of professionals. All will go according to Hoyle. You just concern yourself with your end of the bargain."

"Oh, not to worry, Senator. I've got my end covered. I'll execute my objectives as planned."

The senator let out a chuckle. "Indeed, General. Emphasis on the word *execute*. I'm on my way to the country estate. I'll have a chance to watch events unfold from there in real time."

"Very good, Senator. Good luck to you. When I see you next, America will be back on track to being the great superpower we know it is. The nation that the world should fear."

The senator hung up. General Hughes was a true believer. Hughes had really bought into the whole superpower legend. Admirable, to be sure, but the senator didn't trust anyone who wasn't in it at least a little for themselves. He would have to watch out for Hughes in the future.

Now, Chief of Staff Pelletier was someone he could understand. He didn't trust the little shit as far as he could throw him, but he understood him. Pelletier was in this completely for himself. He was ambitious, and he saw himself in a position of even more power once this was done and dusted. And, of course, there was the money accumulating in his bank account.

Never underestimate the value and utility of the almighty dollar.

CHAPTER 48

The pale light of dawn seeping through the gap in the heavy drapes gave her hotel room a faint glow. Alex awoke to find herself lying on her stomach, a bare leg outside the covers. The sound of running water caught her ear, and she turned her head toward the wall of smoked glass that divided the sleeping area from the bathroom. The privacy curtains covering the glass wall hadn't been fully closed, and through a veil of steam, she caught sight of Street showering. He was turned away from her, washing his hair. His back, arms, and shoulder muscles rippled while shimmering wet in the light.

Oh my, she thought.

Apparently, Street was an early riser.

Her heart rate did a little dance. She closed her eyes. It had been a long time since Alex had been with a man. Getting close to anybody after Kyle was killed wasn't a risk she was willing to take. She wouldn't allow it. Besides, nobody piqued her interest in that way. That is, until recently.

There was one man who had come into her life with whom she had imagined being intimate, but he was off-limits. Her feelings for Caleb from as far back as their mission together in Arnhem were impossible to ignore. It was those very feelings that meant that she could never allow herself to get close to him. People she got close to died.

She opened her eyes and looked again at Street standing in the shower, and desire stirred inside her.

Lord, it's getting hot in here.

She knew it was wrong to be watching, but the curtains *were* open after all. And then he turned toward her, seemingly unaware that he was being observed. She saw the bruising on his chest where the bullets had struck his ballistic vest. One looked like a giant target painted over his heart, the discoloration stretching from his collarbone to his belly. The other was not quite as large but covered much of the right side of his rib cage, overlapping the first like a gruesome Venn diagram.

She let her eyes drink in the rest of his body.

Her breaths came quickly, and she closed her eyes again.

Nope, nope, nope.

She heard the water stop. She got out of bed wearing pajama shorts and a T-shirt and strode over to look out the window. It was still early, but the wide boulevard in front of the hotel was already bustling with people, cars, and trams. She grabbed her phone and skimmed through an email from Caleb, something about meeting up with the team for an assignment at the NATO summit later today. She read it and then tossed her phone onto the sofa.

The bathroom door opened.

"Morning, sunshine!" His cheerful tone made his Scottish accent sound even better.

"Morning," she stammered, only now turning to face him. A towel was wrapped around his waist.

"Did you sleep well?" he asked, heading back into the bathroom.

"Good, thanks. You?"

"Aye, I was out like a wee lamb. Thanks again for letting me spend the night on your settee."

Awkward!

She ambled toward the bathroom, careful to avoid the chair she'd stubbed her toe on last night. The two came face to face in the hallway. Her mind spun. He smelled so good.

She tilted her face up to look at him, and his hazel eyes met hers.

The pull she felt from him was hypnotic. Magnetic. Gravitational. She imagined the feel of his lips on hers.

"Steady," he said. "I think you're still sleeping."

Dreaming would be more accurate.

She pulled herself together enough to comment, "You shaved."

Did his towel just fall to the floor?

She checked. It hadn't.

"And showered," he added, leaning toward her.

I know, I watched.

"Water pressure is great. And it's good and hot."

You don't have to tell me.

"That's great," she breathed and took a step closer.

Their lips touched. She wasn't sure who struck first, but it didn't matter. He felt and tasted so good. His lips caressed hers, and her mouth responded. At first, she held back, but when he gently bit her lower lip, she lost all her inhibition. She wrapped her arms around him and pulled his body against her own.

They kissed passionately, deeply, like two people just set free from prisons of their own making. He pulled her T-shirt off over her head and dropped his head to kiss her neck. Then his mouth moved lower. When she caught sight of the reflection in the hallway mirror of their bodies pressed together, she sacrificed her self-control for something more primal.

She slid her hand down and his towel fell to the floor.

* * *

HELSINKI, FINLAND

The overnight flight had taken a little more than seven hours from Joint Base Andrews. Caleb had slept well enough on the Gulfstream jet, so after the team had deposited themselves and their gear into a safe house on the northern edge of Helsinki, he took a Range Rover and ventured into town.

Waze led him down the highway and onto the streets of central Helsinki. Traffic was moderate, not nearly as bad as rush hour heading into DC. By 7:30, he was parked outside the Hotel Marski. Clare had done some digging over the secure network aboard the Air Force's C-37B and found Alex's hotel and room number. So, with two McDonald's Bacon and Egg McMuffins and two Americanos in hand, he strode through the entrance trying to compose a greeting, if not an apology.

Nice digs, he thought, looking around at the stylish décor of the lobby. As he got on the elevator, he chuckled aloud at a sign that read: YES, THIS IS A FINNISH ELEVATOR. So TRY TO KEEP QUIET LIKE A FINN, PLEASE.

It had only been two days since he had last seen her, but he was already feeling those familiar pangs of separation. Their bond was complicated. There was no denying his attraction to her, and he was compelled to believe that she felt the same. But he wasn't a teenager anymore and wasn't looking for a fling. That would risk screwing up his team dynamics or, more important, any chance for a real relationship he and Alex might have down the road.

Over the past couple of days, the level of friction between them had risen considerably. She was a strong woman by any measure, and Caleb liked that. But it meant that, as her direct supervisor, they were bound to find themselves butting heads occasionally. A breakfast meal from McDonald's wasn't exactly the epitome of romantic gestures, but, hey, it's the thought that counts. Right?

He got off the elevator on the sixth floor and knocked on her door. As it swung open, he was greeted by the sight of Iain Street, head of security for Lehtonen Enterprises, holding a croissant, dressed only in a towel, a surprised look on his face.

"Street?"

From the bathroom, he heard a hair dryer running. Then the noise stopped, and Alex stepped out wearing a terry cloth bathrobe, her hair still damp.

"Caleb," she said.

Caleb looked from her to Street and back again, then slugged Street square in the jaw.

* * *

SOUTH HARBOUR, PORT OF HELSINKI

The man walked with a pronounced limp, pulling his tool cart behind him along the interlocking brick pathway that led to the 220-meter cruise ferry, MS *Esmerelda*. A deckhand gave only the slightest of glances at his identification as a matter of routine since he had been a primary service technician for Suomo Marine cruise line for the past twenty years and was known to everyone.

The deckhand even helped when the wheels of the cart jammed in a small gap in the loading ramp where it met the vessel that ferried passengers and vehicles the eighty kilometers across the Gulf of Finland to Tallinn, the capital of Estonia. The ship was one of several that made multiple daily crossings, each taking less than two and a half hours to complete the one-way leg of the journey in fair or foul seas.

Once aboard, the going was smoother. It was a fact he was grateful for since his leg hadn't been the same since being broken two winters ago after he slipped on an icy gangway while disembarking from the ship. The company had been good to him in accommodating his rehab, and his workers' compensation benefits had kept him and his wife afloat. Still, he'd been forced to dip into his retirement fund to bridge the gap between his benefits and lost wages. His doctor had told him he would need to find new work, given that his leg wouldn't tolerate the strain of fifteen more years of moderately heavy labor until retirement. And any other job he could get in his condition would pay about half of what he earned now, and neither he nor his union could alter that fact.

So when he was approached by a beautiful woman offering him the equivalent of a year's wages, tax-free, to do her employer's bidding by placing a small explosive device aboard the *Esmerelda,* it was difficult to say no. Especially since her bosses, she said, merely wanted to cause enough damage to *Esmerelda* to allow them to cash in on a sizable maritime insurance policy, that no one would be hurt, and that any evidence of his actions would sink to the bottom of the sea along with bits of the ship's massive main engine.

He wanted to believe her. Visions of his accumulated debt had evaporated, and he was eager to see his depleted life's savings restored. And so he agreed.

He took the elevator from the embarkation deck to the primary engine room, three decks down. He removed the bulky cylindrical device from his cart and wedged it in behind the primary gas turbine engine, next to the fuel pump and filter assembly.

Above him, 2,400 passengers and three hundred cars, buses, and transport trucks would soon complete boarding. In less than an hour, *Esmerelda* would depart for Tallinn. One hour into its journey across the gulf, the device would detonate.

It was as simple as flipping the switch.

* * *

MARSKI HOTEL, HELSINKI, FINLAND

Unbelievable. That was the only word for it. Alex stepped back into the bathroom while Street got dressed. Then she ordered both men out of her room to work out whatever testosterone-enhanced angst was still floating around their bloodstreams and primitive brains. To be fair, Street had shown remarkable restraint by not striking Caleb back, but she could see his self-control was being tested.

It was more than a little awkward seeing Caleb standing outside her door. The look on his face was . . . sad. To be honest, she was embarrassed at having nearly been caught in flagrante delicto. As for Street, he was really just an innocent bystander caught in the middle.

She sighed deeply.

Of all the gin joints in all the towns in all the world, he walks into mine . . .

Okay, so maybe the famous line from *Casablanca* wasn't exactly on the mark, but it was the first thought that jumped into her head.

With the two men out of her hair, she got dressed and called Jonathan.

"I was wondering when you were going to call," he said.

"I was dealing with a crisis."

"What crisis?"

"Just two global superpowers who don't understand their limitations."

"Are you speaking geopolitically or more metaphorically?"

"Yes," she replied.

"Okay, I'm not even going to ask."

"It's better you don't."

"Fine. So, the intel is legit."

"Which intel?"

"I was asked to backtrack on a trail that one of the members of your task force uncovered. Honestly, Alex, I've lost track of who I'm even working for these days."

"I know how you feel," she said.

"Yes, but yours is self-inflicted."

Touché.

"According to what I found out," he continued, "a Diplomatic Security Service information security specialist, one Special Agent Tam—"

"Who?" she asked.

"Alex, he's a member of the task force you're supposed to be on."

"Oh."

"Special Agent Tam uncovered a trove of information linked to classified code words."

"Let me guess—Shadow Guard."

"How did you know?"

"You might say it came up in conversation."

She didn't mention that the conversation in question was a message thread on a stolen cell phone.

"And there are others. Did you ever meet Agent Tam?" asked Jonathan.

"Never."

"Then you don't know?"

"Know what?" she asked.

"Tam is dead."

"What? How?" she asked.

"Car accident."

"Bullshit."

"Got that right. After his pickup landed in a pond, someone shot him. Virginia State Police and the FBI are looking into how he could have been so conveniently murdered after uncovering the info. Whoever did it didn't even try very hard to hide it."

A member of the task force was killed and this was the first she was hearing about it—from a member of Interpol and not Caleb or someone else closer to home? She supposed she was as much to blame for that omission as anybody.

"Someone's sending a message?" she asked.

"It appears so."

"Jesus."

Her mind grappled with the realization that the ambush she'd been subjected to last night could have been much worse. It might be true that the men had only wanted to abduct her to find out what she knew, but it was equally apparent now that they might as easily have killed her to silence her and to put an end to her interference.

The events aboard *Aurora* and later in The Hague should have taught her that, but she had always considered herself somewhat invincible, even when that belief flew in the face of available evidence to the contrary. But that was just the nature of cops and soldiers—they always ran *toward* the sound of the gunfire.

If it wasn't personal before, it was quickly getting that way.

"What about the name *Eagle*?" she asked. "Did you find any mention of that in Tam's intel?"

"No, nothing like that. What does it mean?"

"I'm not sure, but I think it's a *who*, not a *what*. Keep digging and see if you can come up with anything on it," she said.

"Okay, Alex, and most of the intel we have now indicates that the Russians aren't behind all these disruption operations in Finland. But intel isn't evidence, and you can fake a paper trail. A code word isn't DNA, so it's not like we can drop the blame into anyone's lap just yet. And shy of a smoking gun, the American president is on record saying he'll continue to push back against President Sergachev and Russia's aggression toward the West. That's what everyone is expecting to hear from him at the NATO summit in Helsinki today."

"So, we're not off the hook yet, is that what you're telling me?" asked Alex.

"No, we—*you*—are not. One more thing."

"Of course there is . . ."

"We're still picking up a lot of chatter, Alex. There could be more in the works. Keep your head on a swivel."

CHAPTER 49

MARSKI HOTEL, HELSINKI, FINLAND

Caleb and Street sat side by side in armchairs in the hotel lobby. A raven made of resin holding a light in its beak sat on the table between them. Caleb was sure it was mocking them.

Well, this is awkward.

"Look, Caleb—" said Street.

"It's none of my business," replied Caleb.

"Maybe you should have considered that before punching me in the face."

Valid point.

"It was an instinct, Street. I'm just looking out for her."

"For *her* or for yourself? She's not yours to protect, Copeland."

"She's on my team, I'm responsible for her."

"Aye, in the field. But not in her private life. Whatever may have happened between us, go back to what you said a minute ago—it's none of your business."

The elevator door opened, and Alex stepped out wearing desert-colored khakis and a black golf shirt.

At least she read my email, he thought. She looked all business.

But though he was good at reading signals, he wasn't always great at heeding advice—even his own. "Alex—" he began.

She cut him off. "Not a word," she said. "Let's go."

* * *

In front of the hotel, two Range Rovers sat idling in the taxi lane, clearly annoying the taxi and Uber drivers standing on the curb smoking. Alex was out the door first, with the men sheepishly falling in behind. A woman whom Alex didn't recognize was behind the wheel of the first SUV.

Without breaking stride, she climbed in. Once inside, she hit the power door locks. The men wisely took the hint. Caleb climbed into the second Range Rover and blocked Street from doing the same, leaving him standing on the sidewalk. Alex glanced into the sideview mirror and saw Street standing there alone, looking for all the world like a fourth grader who had missed his school bus.

"Let's go," Alex said to the woman.

Without saying a word, the driver pulled away from the curb.

* * *

PARLIAMENT HOUSE, HELSINKI

"Sorry about that back there," Alex said, blowing at a loose strand of hair that she then secured into a ponytail.

"No need to apologize," said the woman driving. "Did you at least get the mission briefing?"

"I know where, but I don't know why."

Clare introduced herself and gave Alex the mission-briefing highlights on the way over to Finland's House of Parliament. The US Secret Service and a dozen other agencies would be onsite to secure the president and other dignitaries, the building, and today's proceedings. Caleb's team would be there ostensibly as an added element of security, but their primary function would be to respond quickly to any new and actionable intelligence that either the task force or the team's leadership directly assigned. FBI special agent Clare Duffries, it seemed, had been drafted from the task force to Caleb's operational team to assist with issues of jurisdiction.

"In the car behind us with Caleb is Rocky and Moose, our other two team members," Clare explained.

"Rocky and Moose?"

"Don't ask me, I don't get all this nickname stuff, but they're solid guys."

The imposing structure of the country's parliament building sat atop Arkadianmäki, a hill beside Mannerheimintie, the main thoroughfare through central Helsinki. From the outside, the stripped-down, classical architecture of the building lent it an air of understated power, like a muscular Acropolis adorned with flourishes of early twentieth-century modernism. The exterior walls were constructed from red granite that was more a pale salmon than a deep ocher, the façade lined by a row of fourteen five-story-tall columns.

Alex stared at it as they rounded the building and pulled into the underground parking garage.

"Something else, isn't it?" Clare asked.

"Sure is," answered Alex, who had quickly cooled down over the course of their four-minute drive. "My mind was elsewhere back there, but I'm back in the game now."

"I'm sure those two are a handful."

"You can say that again."

The underground parking complex was a whitewashed labyrinth carved out of the bedrock. It was part of an underground network—essentially, a giant bomb shelter—built by the Finns to cope with being geographically situated next to what amounted to be the world's most unruly and unpredictable neighbor; a neighbor with whom Finland enjoyed a fragile peace marked by compromise—cooperation that was necessary for the self-preservation of a nation.

A policeman directed Alex and Clare into a parking space where they unloaded Pelican cases from their vehicle. The men pulled in beside them and did the same, and together they wheeled the cases into an empty meeting room guarded by a uniformed police officer on the lower level of the building.

"This will be our temporary command post. Listen up, people," Caleb began as the last of the cases were moved into the room. "We're authorized for sidearms in the building and carbines if we're on the perimeter or if we go mobile. POTUS is above us in the Session Hall, about to address the delegates."

Alex strapped on her sidearm along with everyone else. They walked over to a bank of monitors where a small team of Secret Service agents were viewing the live feed and peered over their shoulders.

"Operations Center Actual is down the corridor," one of them chirped.

"I'm aware, thanks," Caleb said. "This feed only covers the main hall?"

"We have perimeter feeds as well. But, like I said, the main show is down the hall."

Caleb stepped away. Clare, Rocky, Moose, and Alex followed.

"Are we going into the Session Hall?" asked Alex.

He nodded. "There's a spot designated for us off to the side of the main dais. Alex, you're with me. We'll go to the primary location next to POTUS. Rocky, Clare, you take the main entry point. Moose, you're here with keys in hand in case we need to go mobile. And you'll be our lead on comms and liaise with the Secret Service's Counter Assault Team. President Moore's CAT team is out circulating within the building doing a final sweep."

"Right, boss," said Moose.

"Okay, team, comms up."

* * *

PARLIAMENT HOUSE, HELSINKI

Alex, Caleb, Clare, and Rocky made their way through the marble State Hall to the Session Hall. The hall was not unlike the House chamber in the US Capitol. The large wooden dais at the front was where President Moore would stand to deliver his historic address. The NATO chiefs of defense and other representatives would be seated in the hall, watched over by a tight blanket of security operating under a unified command structure from the operations center one level below.

Clare and Rocky took their positions beside the entryway, hidden inside an alcove along the curved wall. As Alex and Caleb found their positions, the Secret Service Counter Assault Team leader approached.

"You're Copeland?" asked the agent. Caleb nodded. "I know why you're here. Frankly, politics is not my area of expertise."

"Mine, either, Agent, but we're not exactly here to cast ballots," said Caleb. "It's politics that could make this summit go sideways. So, like you, we're here to make sure that doesn't happen."

The agent nodded. "If anything happens, keep your team out of our way so we can take care of POTUS and we'll be good."

He didn't say it with malice. The agent was just laying down the hierarchy of response under the circumstances. President Moore's code name was Longhorn, and his protective detail would secure Longhorn in the event of an incident. But if there was a direct assault on the president, it was the CAT team's job to actively engage the threat. And that meant that, to a certain extent, they didn't care who got caught up in the crossfire as long as their protectee escaped harm. POTUS was this team's first and final objective.

Alex watched as the hall filled up. General Lucas Hughes and Secretary of State Katherine Hayward were seated in the front row. As Prime Minister Sanna Rantala led her gaggle of cabinet ministers up the center aisle, she spotted Alex and gave a friendly smile. Following their group came Finland's president, Jarkko Ruusu, walking next to President Moore. The pair was led by NATO secretary general Lars Jensen. Together, the trio took their seats on the tall dais.

Caleb's voice popped into Alex's earpiece as he ran a final comms check with the members of the team. When all units had confirmed their status, he handed comms control back to Moose.

Secretary General Jensen stood and approached the mic, and the murmuring within the chamber subsided.

"Thank you," he began. "As you know, this extraordinary summit was to have taken place at NATO headquarters in Brussels. But, following the developments of the past several weeks, it was decided that our NATO Alliance would be best served hosting it here, in Finland, one of our most recent admissions to the NATO family." He turned toward

President Ruusu and smiled. "On behalf of the Alliance, Mr. President, I wish to extend my profound gratitude to your country for accommodating this change of venue."

Ruusu gently nodded, and the secretary general continued.

"NATO is first and foremost a political alliance. While we have repeatedly heard claims by certain nations that we are an offensive tool striving to hem them into their borders, this is not true. The Alliance strives to achieve security of all members by providing for a collective defense. And member countries always aim for peaceful resolutions—both here and at our sister organization, the United Nations—to any disputes. The use of military solutions is contrary to the objectives of the Alliance. Our aims can best be met by demonstrating a commonality of purpose and a steadfast resolve to resist aggression from other nation-states.

"It is perhaps superfluous to state that by avoiding war, we ensure a lasting peace. But if war cannot be avoided, then NATO member countries are resolved that no one country should stand alone. By coming together and by the lawful implementation of the terms of the Washington Treaty, a treaty originally signed and put into effect on the fourth of April, 1949, we, the members of NATO, solemnly swore to come to the aid of another member so threatened. This is the condition of Article 5, and it is nonnegotiable. An armed attack on one member of the Alliance is an attack against all members. The remaining members will take the actions the Alliance deems necessary to assist the ally who has been attacked.

"Article 5 has been invoked but once, after the September 11, 2001, terrorist attacks on the United States. But insofar as our newest member, our friend and host for this summit, Finland, is facing a dire threat from a belligerent neighbor, NATO must and will respond."

The chamber erupted in applause.

Alex had listened intently to the secretary general's speech. His words hadn't left much room for diplomatic compromise. In fact, none. Not that there should be any. But diplomacy is often built upon the shaky pedestal of fragile egos. Despite being aware that the inciting incidents leading the world to this decisive moment might not have been perpetrated by the *belligerent neighbor*, i.e., Russia, that didn't seem to matter much to the gathered representatives.

Both sides of the burgeoning conflict were moving pieces on the board that were already in positions from which to strike out at one another over the slightest provocation or misinterpretation of intentions. And that was a recipe for catastrophe.

Large conflicts and world wars had started over lesser crises countless times throughout history. Once put into motion, egos often faltered under the momentum of their own pride and arrogance to pull back from the brink.

As Alex scanned the room, she noticed Emmi off to the side. The Supo agent had her eyes fixed on Prime Minister Rantala in the audience. And not far from Emmi, Alex caught sight of someone she had never expected to see in the chamber of Finland's supreme legislature.

Although she had traded in her Barbie fleece for something befitting this grave moment in history, it was hard not to recognize Tatiana Burina even in a stylish fall overcoat.

CHAPTER 50

GULF OF FINLAND

The man usually spent the voyage from Helsinki to Tallinn either in the crew room, wandering around the ship performing minor repairs to pipes, faucets, heating and ventilation systems, and the like, or chatting with a small number of the six million travelers that made this crossing annually.

Although he had worked on various other ships, the MS *Esmerelda* was his favorite. Built in the late seventies, she wasn't the prettiest, but she had been refitted ten years ago with a newer combined diesel-electric and gas—or CODLAG—system, and she now ran more efficiently than most ships of similar size.

If he was feeling any pangs of guilt, they weren't showing. Instead, he felt buoyed up by the thought of what lay ahead. He was helping his employer, helping himself, and oddly, he thought he might be contributing to efforts to enhance maritime safety and security. Although he was sure he would escape undetected as the perpetrator of this vandalism, this crime-to-be, there would likely be an extensive inquiry into the explosion that resulted from the device he had planted that would no doubt lead to changes in practice and legislation to ensure this kind of event never happened again.

He considered shedding his uniform and taking a sauna in the spas located in the bow but headed instead for the passenger bar and lounge. He ordered a Coke and bought a bag of chips, then took a window seat along the port side. He sipped his drink and ate his chips and otherwise felt completely at ease with what would transpire in a short while aboard the *Esmerelda.*

When he finished, he went for a walk throughout the ship. As he strolled along the outer corridors, he double-checked the deployable life rafts and survival gear, just in case. He had been told the explosion would be relatively small, that the device was composed of a *shaped charge,* as she had called it, and would accomplish its desired effect with minimal risk to passengers and crew. And he was beguiled enough by her that he believed her.

He checked his watch. They were an hour into the crossing. It wouldn't be long now. His portable radio had been silent. That was a good sign. That meant the propulsion systems were running smoothly, as usual, so no engineers had been required to go into the engine room to service them. Good.

He walked along the restaurant deck and through the lounge. Maybe this weekend, he would host a large dinner for his children and grand-children. It had been a few weeks since—

BOOM!

The *Esmerelda* shuddered from the violent explosion. It was much larger than he had been expecting, maybe—

BOOM!

A second explosion, greater than the first, rocked the ship, and he felt her list to her port side. An enormous plume of fire and smoke was cast outward toward the icy sea. Fire alarms sounded and strobe lights flashed. People screamed. Surely no one was hurt, he hoped, but those two blasts—

BOOM!

The man had no comprehension that while the shaped charge had blown a two-meter-wide hole straight through the hull into the sea, the explosion had also ruptured the primary fuel line and tank. Fuel and fumes filled the engine room until the concentration of vapors set off a series of explosions that tore the metal skin of the noble *Esmerelda's* hull like overripe fruit. Belowdecks, she filled rapidly with water, and while that helped extinguish much of the blaze, it caused the weight distribution of the vessel to shift. Bulkheads meant to contain in-flowing water failed after being misshapen by the multiple blasts, and the more she listed, the more the spiraling effects of the explosion took *Esmerelda* along a path from which she could not recover.

There were no fuel tankers or dangerous cargo aboard, but cars and trucks slid into each other, and gasoline and diesel fuel spilled from their tanks. Electrical systems and cables were stretched to the max, and before the power from the diesel-electric generators could be cut, a spark ignited a blaze in the vehicle hold.

One blast followed the next until it sounded like a cacophony of pyrotechnic percussion in the middle of the sea.

BOOM, BOOM, BOOM!

No! he screamed inside his head as the ship heeled over farther than he thought possible, and he tumbled into one of the restaurant lounges. He clung to a table as passengers around him fell, tumbling across the floor, or rather down it, as its attitude shifted. The screams and shouts were deafening, but another roar seemed even louder. He listened to sort out the sound: it was the groaning of the steel and superstructure of the massive 721-foot vessel buckling under her own mass, plus the added weight of the sea.

What have I done?

Realization dawned on him that the ship was not only in peril but doomed. Below him—what should have been beside him—a woman clung to a table with one arm while clutching a toddler in the other. She reminded him of his beloved Kaarina, whom he had married when they were both so young.

There was six feet of space between their two tables. He was sure he could get to her, and together they could still find their way to a lifeboat. He stretched down, his hands grasping the top of the table, his legs just reaching the post that secured it to the floor. He wrestled his weaker leg into position against the post. Her eyes implored him to be careful, and he was. He let go and was about to grasp her table. Then they would be together, side by side, helping each other and her baby to safety.

BOOM!

The explosion caused his bum leg to give out. The woman tried to offer a hand, but that would have meant sacrificing her baby to save him, and she pulled it back. Maybe it didn't matter. Their eyes met. He did not blame her for the choice she made. He tumbled toward a gap where a window used to be, then struck the side railing and cartwheeled off *Esmerelda* into the brilliant sunshine above the cold, dark water.

As he plummeted to his death, he wondered—had this woman known that this was all his fault, would she have forgiven him? He thought she would not, and he forgave her that, too.

CHAPTER 51

President Jarkko Ruusu was wrapping up his speech in front of a solemn audience of representatives from NATO member states and the Finnish parliament. But Alex's attention was focused not on any of them or even on her president, who would soon take the microphone to deliver his speech, but on the face of Captain Tatiana Burina, a Russian GRU agent.

What are you doing here?

She nudged Caleb.

"Not now," he whispered.

She kept her eyes on Tatiana and tried to gauge whether it might be possible to approach her but decided against it. She tried to will Emmi to look her way, but that wasn't working either.

She nudged Caleb again.

"What is it?" he barked quietly—more snarl than bark.

She tried to point her out to him silently, but he wasn't getting it.

"Tatiana," she whispered.

"What?"

"*Tatiana!*" she yell-whispered.

Off his uncomprehending expression, she keyed her mic. "Alpha Two to Alpha One." He gave her an exasperated look. "GRU captain Tatiana Burina at ten o'clock."

He oriented himself in the direction she had indicated and searched the crowd. Finally, she heard his reply, which came as two short clicks over her earpiece.

A universal *10–4, message received* signal.

The audience rose to their feet and applauded President Ruusu's speech as he returned to his chair. President Moore stood and shook Ruusu's hand, and as he took his seat, Moore stepped to the podium.

Caleb spoke softly into his mic. "All units be advised, possible bogey in the crowd. Charlie One?"

"Go for Charlie One."

"Are you next to the CAT tech element?"

"I can be in two seconds."

"Advise them we have a known GRU operative in the crowd."

"But we don't know if she's hostile," added Alex over the radio. "Last night, she saved my ass and handed me critical intel."

"Isn't that pretty much what a Russian operative would do and say to make you see her as a non-threat actor?" It was Special Agent Clare Duffries's voice.

"Yes, it is," agreed Alex. "But I'm not convinced she's here to harm anyone."

"We can't take that chance," said Caleb. "Charlie One, advise the CAT comms team that we have a sighting of Russian GRU captain Tatiana Burina in the audience."

"Roger. Stand by."

"Caleb," Alex said directly to him. "I don't think she's a threat."

"Are you willing to risk the life of your president, Martel?"

She was not, and it took her all of a second to say so. He nodded.

"Charlie One, Alpha will hold here and maintain eyes on the target."

"Charlie One to Alpha One, CAT's coming to you. They said if she moves, take her out."

"Copy."

* * *

KENNINGTON RANCH, LOUDOUN COUNTY, NORTHERN VIRGINIA

Senator Kennington was awake early. He stood in a belted silk robe, staring out a floor-to-ceiling window in the study, his oasis within the ranch house perched on a low hill. Beyond the horse paddocks and the forest, the sun was beginning to come over the horizon and would soon burn through the low cloud layer hovering over a bend in the Potomac where it hemmed in his property. It held all the promise of a new day. A historic day. One that would live in infamy and elevate these United States to new heights, once and for all.

Kennington was a partisan but believed that even partisanship should be in service to the greater good. Red, blue, whatever. In the end, it didn't much matter. *America first. Country before party.* He was a patriot above all and took great pride in the fact that he had built his co-alition with the help of men and women from both sides of the aisle—patriots themselves whose only desire was to see America one day reach its natural and most deserved zenith in the world order.

And today, that day had come.

He glanced at the bank of monitors on a desk off to the side of the room and watched his security detail—more like a small platoon—in the low predawn light, getting ready for what might come. He had no illusions that his plan wasn't without risk, and as they drew closer to its outcome, he had instructed his team to elevate their readiness posture as a precaution.

He heard the breaking news tune from the TV on the wall and grabbed the remote to turn up the volume. The overnight coverage usually ran on a loop, but now the station cut to a night anchor, whose slightly messy hair indicated something big was breaking.

Video footage, probably provided by citizen journalists, was shaky as they zoomed in with their smartphones to record the events unfolding before them. But what was clear was the image of a large ship lying on its side, half submerged in the sea. Pleasure craft and military ships appeared to be racing to assist, but it seemed the ship would be lost, the fate of her passengers and crew uncertain.

A reporter was already conducting an interview, standing in one boat while talking to a woman on another.

"There were many explosions," she told him in accented English.

"What is known at this time," the reporter said, speaking toward his camera operator, "is that the Gulf of Finland is chockablock full of warships"—the studio cut to footage to illustrate what he was saying—"with American, European, and, of course, many Russian warships in the region. This follows an escalation of tensions between NATO countries and Russian forces, who earlier this week shifted more resources to the region after being accused of conducting destabilizing operations in Finland."

Another man rafted up alongside in his forty-foot cabin cruiser, and the reporter began interviewing him. He, too, had a strong accent when he spoke.

"I saw a trail of white foam in the water," he said.

"Do you mean behind the ship . . . its wake?" prompted the reporter.

"No, no, from the side. A trail of white foam in the water going out to the ship from over there." He gestured toward the open sea to the east as if pointing his finger directly at St. Petersburg. "It was a torpedo, I think."

The reporter practically fell off his boat in excitement. "You're saying you believe you saw a torpedo come from somewhere and strike the ship?"

"No, no," he said.

The reporter took a breath. "What are you saying, sir? What did you see?"

"I am not saying I *believe* I saw a torpedo. I say I *did* see a torpedo. Like in a movie. It must have come from far away, from a submarine or something."

The reporter turned to the camera. "Chip, we have no way to authenticate this eyewitness account, but you just heard him state he is certain he saw a torpedo strike the ship before she went down."

Reports of a torpedo? Oh, this couldn't get any better. Kennington let a self-satisfied grin spread across his face. *Who would have thought that the dreaded man-on-the-street interview would give such a boost to our plan?*

The sinking of the cruise ferry *Esmerelda* was nothing more than his confederates striking a match next to the powder keg. But, if the world wanted to believe that a Russian Borei or Typhoon-class boomer had fired a torpedo at a civilian vessel, so much the better.

The camera zoomed in on the rescue operations. Battleships and various-sized military vessels flanked the zone, while others pulled survivors from the sea. Sea Hawk helicopters dangled men and baskets beneath them, searching for survivors, recovering bodies.

It looked like a war zone. It *was* a war zone.

Or soon would be.

CHAPTER 52

PARLIAMENT HOUSE, HELSINKI

President Taylor Moore stood at the microphone before the assembled dignitaries, his Texas drawl reverberating off the ceiling. But Alex hadn't heard much of what he was saying. The CAT element's team leader was standing beside her and wanted an on-the-spot risk assessment.

They had stepped back farther out of view, but there was a buzz around the dais now that the Presidential Protective Detail had been alerted to a developing incident. Both CAT and the PPD wanted to know if it was time to evacuate the president. It would have been a tough call under any circumstance, but it was particularly so at this moment in history with a president eager to show the world the United States wouldn't be corralled into a fight nor back away from one. No one was eager for him to be seen running from the stage.

But dead presidents were also not a great harbinger of world peace.

"It's a yes-or-no question, Martel. Is that woman a threat to Longhorn?"

Alex was more than a little pissed that the CAT team leader was breathing down her neck as he spoke. He was a hair away from a right jab to the face, but she decided to be the bigger person and took a half step backward.

"Ordinarily, I'd say yes. But she gave me valuable intel and helped me out of a major jam last night. But I can't guarantee that she or her comrades don't have other intentions here."

"So much for a yes or no."

The team leader went silent for a second while listening to an incoming message over his radio. Then he turned to the leader of the president's protection detail standing next to him, and the two men had a brief discussion. When they finished, he turned back to Alex.

"Seems it's all academic now, Martel. We're going kinetic. We're evacuating Longhorn."

"What?" said Caleb. "What's going on? Is this because of Burina?"

He ignored the question as he spoke into his radio. "Longhorn on the move." He turned to Caleb. "Bigger fish to fry. We'll have him in the air in a few minutes. I suggest you might want to assist here if things get squirrelly. No time to talk. Figure it out."

And with that, the PPD in business suits were up on stage while the CAT element, clad in full tactical gear, fanned out into the Assembly Hall. One agent walked directly up to Tatiana and brought the muzzle of his carbine up to her cheek. It was a sound and practical method to suggest she sit still while they moved POTUS. She didn't move. She was a fast learner.

The Secret Service detail surrounded Moore. At first, the president was stunned, and it looked as if he was resisting their efforts to extract him, but within seconds, he allowed them to escort him backstage, presumably back to Air Force One for an expedited trip back to the States.

CAT remained in situ briefly, but, within moments, followed POTUS's detail out the door. Stunned by the turn of events, the president's national security advisor and the secretary of state rose from their seats. Alex advanced toward them with Caleb on her heels. The remaining three hundred or so dignitaries and other individuals rose simultaneously and headed for the doors. In the ensuing chaos and with her CAT minder gone with the rest of his team, Tatiana slipped out of Alex's sight.

"I can't see her anymore."

"Leave her for now," said Caleb.

"What exactly is going on?" asked Secretary Hayward as the four reunited in the aisle.

"I'm afraid we don't know yet, Madam Secretary," Caleb said. "We were assessing a separate threat. Next thing we knew, the Secret Service went full kinetic to evacuate the president, ma'am."

"Well, now what will we do?" she asked.

Alex wasn't sure if she was lost for a ride or worried about the state of the nation.

Emmi appeared next to Alex. "There are suddenly a great number of things going on," she said. "Let's try to catch up after, and you can tell me what you know."

"I'm sure I'll see you again."

Emmi dissolved into the crowd, soon reappearing next to Prime Minister Rantala.

"Where is your detail?" Caleb asked Secretary Hayward and General Hughes.

Just as he voiced the question, a lone Secret Service agent arrived.

"Sorry, ma'am. I'll need you to come with me," said the young female agent.

"What's happening?" asked Secretary of State Hayward.

The crowd of dignitaries was agitated, like cattle being funneled through a single-file chute, not knowing for certain but reasonably sure something terrible was about to happen. No one had stepped forward to explain what was going on, and in the absence of information, people—like cattle—began to imagine the worst.

"Madam Secretary, please follow me," said the lone agent.

"Where's your backup?" asked Alex.

The agent looked Alex over and eyed her photo ID before answering. "Look around. Everyone's tied up with something. My partner's assisting POTUS's detail. There's a bit of a hiccup, but all is well." She turned back to Hayward. "Ma'am?" she said. "This way, please."

"Can General Hughes join me?"

"It's not ideal, ma'am."

"It's okay, Kathy," said the general.

"No, it's not okay, Lucas. He's coming with us," she told the agent. "He can keep me company. He might even be useful until your partner gets back if it comes to that."

"Yes, ma'am. This way." When Alex and Caleb followed, the agent turned to them. "You're free to go. I'll take them from here."

"If it's all the same to you," said Alex, "we'll watch your six until you have them secured and we find out what's going on."

"Fine," she said. "I'm Agent Harris. Follow me. We have several rooms set aside for situations like this one."

Agent Harris led them to a side door barricaded by a pair of retractable belt barrier stanchions, the kind you'd find in a theater lineup. She opened the belt and closed it once they were through, then led them up a flight of marble stairs.

Caleb ordered Rocky and Clare to rejoin Moose in the command post downstairs and to make themselves available to the CAT team if needed while he and Alex helped escort the president's national security advisor and the secretary of state to safety.

"What's the plan, boss?" Alex asked.

"We'll make sure these two are squared away," said Caleb. "Then we'll head to the primary command post and get an updated sitrep. This isn't just about Tatiana being in the peanut gallery anymore."

Agent Harris led them to a lounge for Members of Parliament and other government staff. She stepped inside ahead of them, and once she was satisfied the room was clear, she brought them in. It was a nicely appointed space, with plush furniture, Persian rugs, and a refreshment table complete with a coffee machine and pastry tray.

A television in the corner was tuned to a local news station.

"Holy crap!" said Alex.

"Oh my god." Secretary of State Hayward came to stand next to Alex in front of the TV. The others gathered around them as the footage of the sinking *Esmerelda* filled the screen.

Alex found the remote and turned up the volume so they could hear what was being said, but the scrolling chyron carried all the info they needed: HUNDREDS RESCUED, HUNDREDS FEARED DEAD, DOZENS OF BODIES RECOVERED IN SINKING OF FERRY.

Agent Harris piped up. "This is what I was going to tell you, Madam Secretary. With this incident happening so close to us out in the Gulf, the head of the Presidential Protective Detail determined we needed to increase the number of agents on the president until we could get him clear of Finland."

"I understand," said the secretary of state.

When the anchor mentioned reports of a torpedo striking the ship, General Hughes reached for his phone.

"I need an immediate conference with the president," he said to whomever answered. "Yes, of course. I'll hold." A minute later: "Mr. President, are you safely aloft? . . . Yes, sir. I'm with Secretary Hayward now . . . Agreed, Mr. President, and I advise we move to DEFCON 2, at least until your plane is safely back at Andrews. These events are unprecedented, and if the Russians really did take out a passenger ship in the middle of the Baltic Sea with a torpedo launched from a nuclear submarine, that is tantamount to an incitement of war. We cannot leave such an act unchallenged, sir . . . Yes, sir. I understand, Mr. President . . . Thank you, sir."

"Well?" asked Hayward once he'd hung up.

"The president is meeting with the US secretary of defense and the chairman of the joint chiefs of staff to set the nation to Defense Readiness Condition 2."

"Have we ever reached DEFCON 2 before?" asked Hayward.

"Twice, ma'am," said Alex. "Once during the Cuban Missile Crisis, and then again at the outset of the Persian Gulf War in 1991."

Alex's stomach knotted up as they continued to watch the news coverage. Just offshore, a true maritime disaster of catastrophic proportions was unfolding.

"Could the Russians have torpedoed that ship?" she asked.

"They're capable of doing anything," said Hughes, sinking onto a sofa. "They're animals."

While she agreed, in part, with the first sentence, Alex was surprised he had gone that far with the second. She didn't much care for the Russian leadership, but to label *all* the people of Russia as animals was taking it one bridge too far—even for her, let alone hearing those words from the president's chief advisor on matters of national security, a man who had held high-level command roles for decades.

"I refuse to believe they could have done something so callous," said Hayward. "Surely, it must have been a terrible accident."

"I'm sure it wasn't that," he replied.

"Do you know something you're not telling us, General?" Alex asked.

He looked up at her, weariness creasing his forehead.

Just then, the door opened, and another Secret Service agent entered.

"We good?" he asked Agent Harris.

Harris nodded, then turned to Hayward. "Madam Secretary, let's get you out of here. General Hughes, could you please remain here? We'll have a separate team escort you out shortly."

"No problem," he said, waving her off.

Then to Caleb, Agent Harris said, "Would you two remain here with the general? Things are a little dynamic right now. We'll send a team for the general once we get the rest of the Presidential Protective Detail back from the airport."

Caleb nodded, and they were gone.

"General, everything okay?" Caleb asked.

"It's all a giant clusterfuck," he said, bowing his head.

Alex and Caleb exchanged glances.

"Are you alright, sir?" said Alex.

Before Hughes could answer, her phone rang. She took a few steps across the room.

"Jonathan, what's up?"

"Hey. I have some info you might find useful."

"Oh?"

"That Proton Drive had a lot of data on it, some of which we're still decrypting."

"Go on," she said.

He continued. "There are several code names listed. In fact, there are more than a dozen. I was able to tie some of them to identities of individuals and track financial transactions, then match those transactions to comms traffic on email, Telegram, WhatsApp, and places like that."

"And?"

"Your president's chief of staff, Titus Pelletier, is one of the con-spirators."

"Holy shit! Are you kidding me?"

Hughes was watching her intently.

"We've already informed the FBI. They're rounding him up as we speak."

"That's great work, Jonathan," she said.

"There's more. From what I could find, your Eagle character is the linchpin, but their identity still escapes me. Do you remember when we talked about Shadow Guard, and we thought that was the name of an op?"

"Yeah."

"It's not an op—it's a code name for a key player, but I haven't deci-phered that yet, either."

"Stop telling me what you *don't* have and tell me what you *do* have."

"Well, Talon and Eagle have a lot of communication between them. There are discussions between them and conversations with Shadow Guard about disruption ops. We'll be able to tie these comms to the actual operations that have gone on in Finland. At least, I think we will. What I can tell you about Talon is that part of the plan is for them to be in Finland right now."

Damn, thought Alex. *If the conspiracy were home-brewed, as the ev-idence suggests, then the two likeliest candidates high enough in the food chain to be able to implement this kind of operation would be—*

Jonathan was still talking. "But sorry, Alex, I haven't figured out yet who they are," he said. "And I was really hoping to be able to at least identify Talon for you."

Alex's attention was pulled away from her phone by movement in front of her. She looked up and found herself staring down the barrel of a 9-millimeter Beretta held by the president's national security advisor, General Lucas Hughes.

"Don't beat yourself up over it, Jonathan. I know who Talon is."

CHAPTER 53

Rocky and Clare arrived back at the CP shortly after leaving the legislative chamber, where the president had given his address before being whisked away by his Secret Service detail. Moose stood over five stacked Pelican cases, the top one flung open, and was tapping a magazine into the flared well of an M4.

"Something we should know, Moose?" Rocky asked.

Moose grinned. "It's time to put our game faces on, brother," he replied.

Rocky led Clare over to the cases and pulled theirs from the stack.

"You know how to use one of these?" he teased.

Clare didn't reply. Instead, she gave him a sideways look as she donned her heavy ballistic vest and then cleared her M4 before deftly loading it back up with a full magazine and setting it to weapon condition one—safety on, magazine inserted, round in the chamber, bolt forward, ejection port cover closed.

"So that's a yes," he said.

The pair slung their rifles and tucked their service pistols into dropleg holsters before joining Moose over at the comms desk, where he was having a discussion with the Secret Service communications tech.

"President is wheels up," the tech said. "Some of our PPD—the president's protection detail—is heading back here, but the rest is with him aboard Cowpuncher—sorry, Air Force One." He indicated toward the large-screen TV at one end of the room. "That there's what has us scrambling. But the president insisted on being here, and ultimately, he's the boss. Who knew the Russians were going to torpedo a civilian vessel out in the Gulf?"

"Wait, what?" said Clare.

The tech brought them up to speed on what he knew, which wasn't much beyond what the news was reporting. There was no official line or statement from the White House or the Kremlin yet, so he kept it brief, but everyone understood the gravity of the current situation.

"The secretary of state has been evacuated, but we need a detail to return for General Hughes."

"Isn't that where Alpha One and Two are right now?" asked Moose, referring to Caleb and Alex's call signs.

Rocky nodded.

"They're in the MP break room. Top floor, left of the stairs," said the tech.

"Military police?"

"Member of Parliament."

"Fuckin' acronyms," Rocky said. "Why does everybody have to use acronyms?"

"Everybody's got 'em," quipped the tech.

"Right. Let's head up there," Moose said to Rocky. "At least the team will be together."

Rocky keyed his mic. "Bravo One to Alpha One." No response. "Bravo One to Alpha One." He waited a few seconds, but still no reply. "Boss, you copy?" Still no reply. He asked the tech, "You guys jamming comms right now?"

"Nope."

"Any issues with the internet or your comms in the building?"

"Negative, we positioned the IP radio repeaters throughout the building. Our encrypted comms are solid."

"Boss, if you can hear me, we're coming to you."

"Let's go!" said Moose, heading for the door. Clare and Rocky were already ahead of him.

* * *

MEMBERS OF PARLIAMENT BREAK ROOM, PARLIAMENT HOUSE,
HELSINKI

"Hang up," said General Hughes.

For a change, Alex did as she was told.

"What the hell are you doing here anyway?" asked Hughes. She was about to answer, but he cut her off. "It was a rhetorical question, Special Agent Martel."

"What do you imagine will happen here, General?" asked Caleb. "We can't just let you walk out that door."

"I don't think you're reading this room right, Mr. Copeland. I'm the one holding the gun. Hands where I can see them. Both of you."

Through her earpiece, Alex could hear Rocky calling Caleb over the radio, but neither of them could activate their microphone right now.

"He's got you there," said Alex to her partner, raising her hands slightly.

"Shut up, Martel."

"What? I was agreeing with you." She drifted sideways, opening up some distance between her and Caleb, and turned her left side to the general to disguise any movement she made toward her sidearm with her right hand.

"Hold it." The US Army marksman badge she noted on the uniform of this four-star general wasn't lost on her. She stopped shuffling sideways.

"I mean, we could let you go with a *nudge, nudge, wink, wink,*" she said, "but I'm pretty sure you know we can't let that happen."

"You just going to shoot us then, General?" Caleb asked.

Stop giving him ideas.

"I don't see what other option I have."

"You know it's over, right?" said Alex. "No matter what you do next, the jig is up. My friend at Interpol is transmitting the information he's decoded to US authorities at this very moment. I'm sure they're preparing a red notice on you as we speak."

A red notice was an Interpol international alert for a wanted person, like an arrest warrant.

"It wasn't supposed to happen this way. That ship wasn't supposed to sink so fast." The general was clearly upset that his plans—*their* plans—had been ruined by circumstances beyond his control.

"No plan survives first contact with the enemy. Didn't they teach you that at West Point, General?"

"You're pretty bright, Alex, but your smart-aleck mouth is your downfall."

She had heard variations on that theme her whole life, and yet . . .

"We're splitting hairs here, aren't we? I mean, it's only one boat. A nuclear war, on the other hand, would bring about a death toll thousands of times greater than that."

"It would never come to that," he said. "This was all to trigger a *conventional* war—one where the US military would wipe the Russian military off the map on land, sea, and air."

"And did you all think President Sergachev wouldn't have his tiny little finger hovering over that big red button the whole time? Did you calculate his mental state, which, by the way—and I'm no psychiatrist, let's be very clear on this—is batshit crazy?"

"Personally, I think he'd push the button," said Caleb.

"Me too," said Alex, lowering her hand to her Glock. "I mean, the Russian style of warfare is *escalate to de-escalate*. Am I right?"

"I think you're right," said Caleb.

"Stop!" Hughes thrust the Beretta toward her, his finger pressing on the trigger.

Out of the corner of her eye, she saw Caleb spring like a jungle cat toward Hughes. He was fully horizontal when he connected with his tackle, and the general's gun went off.

BOOM!

CHAPTER 54

CENTRAL STAIRCASE, PARLIAMENT HOUSE, HELSINKI

Rocky, Moose, and Clare dodged politicians and other dignitaries as they raced to the second floor.

"What's the plan?" asked Clare, taking two steps at a time.

"Save our team," said Moose.

"Great, as long as there's a plan."

"We'll get to the room and try calling again on the radio," said Rocky.

"And then?"

"We'll figure it out based on whether we get an answer or not."

"Fair enough. Are Caleb and Martel—"

BOOM!

The trio dropped into a crouch behind their rifle sights. The central staircase was a wide, tall marble feature. Not much room for cover.

Rocky keyed his mic. "Boss, we're one minute out."

And they continued up the stairs at a run.

* * *

MEMBERS OF PARLIAMENT BREAK ROOM, PARLIAMENT HOUSE,
HELSINKI

Caleb flew through the air toward the president's national security advisor. General Hughes had always been a buttoned-up soldier, but standing in the break room, explaining himself to them, he'd sounded increasingly unhinged. When he pointed the gun at Alex and began to squeeze the trigger, Caleb had no choice—the general was going to kill her.

Rocky had been talking to him through his earpiece, telling him the team was coming. But who knew how long that might take? One minute? Three? By then, Alex could be dead.

As he crashed into Hughes with his best flying tackle, the general's Beretta went off. Lucas Hughes was a solid man, a former Green Beret and a once-upon-a-time light-heavyweight boxer. And he had packed on some pounds since those days.

As they tumbled across the floor, Caleb saw Alex fall.

Was she hit?

He lingered on that thought too long, and the general pulled an arm back and laid a thunderous punch into the side of his head. Caleb was stunned by the blow, giving the general the chance to climb on top of him. As he blocked the blows raining down on him, he spotted the Beretta on the floor only four feet away. Beyond that, Alex lay still on the carpet.

He bent his knees and tried to pop the general off him, but he was a big man and knew how to keep Caleb pinned. But the bucking had moved them toward the Beretta; now, it was just a matter of who could get to it first.

General Hughes was shouting at him, but he couldn't make out what he was saying. Caleb managed to get in a few punches of his own, and although they weren't particularly effective, they did slow down the beating he was taking.

Then he remembered that he, too, was carrying a pistol. He distracted Hughes with his left hand by landing a couple of glancing blows into his side, wrapping his right hand around the grip of his Glock. He released the catch and yanked the gun free of its holster. Hughes saw and dove to the side to seize the weapon in both hands, bringing his weight down on Caleb's arm and pinning it and the Glock to the carpet.

Caleb sat up and drove his free shoulder into Hughes's chest. He had his finger inside the trigger guard, the pad of his finger beginning to press down. The two men rolled again, and the gun wedged between them. The strain of the fight caused his finger to continue squeezing on the trigger. Then the general thrust his hips to the side, and Caleb was thrown onto the floor, where he lay on his back.

Hughes held Caleb's gun and raised it at him, pointing it at his face.

BOOM! BOOM!

BOOM!

* * *

Alex woke up on the floor in a pool of blood. She remembered General Hughes pointing a gun at her. Caleb diving at him. Then darkness.

Pain seared through her arm and her head. She touched her arm and felt blood on her bicep. She reached back and felt a large goose egg where she must have whacked the back of her head when she was thrown backward.

Her vision was blurry and her ears were ringing, but she could make out Caleb and Hughes wrestling on the floor. Then the general rose up, pointing the gun at Caleb's face.

No, this isn't happening.

"Stop," she said, but it came out as a whisper. "General, no!" she heard herself shout, but Hughes remained unfazed.

BOOM! BOOM!

Alex's Glock spat fire and lead, and a wisp of smoke curled from the muzzle. Her bullets caught the general twice in the center of the chest, but he was still standing, still holding the gun, still a threat.

She lined up her sights for one final shot.

BOOM!

The effect was immediate. General Hughes's head exploded, and he dropped like a heavy sack to the floor just as the door behind her flew open.

Rocky, Moose, and Clare burst into the room, their carbines level, ready to engage any additional threats. But there were none. Just Caleb sprawled out on his back.

And a dead four-star general—the president's national security advisor—on the floor next to him.

* * *

Caleb watched from the floor as General Hughes's finger tightened up on the trigger of his own Glock. But before the trigger broke and released the striker against the primer of the bullet, sending a 135-grain, FlexLock, fully jacketed hollow-point round into his brain, the general shuddered twice, his head exploded, and he fell onto the ornate Persian carpet.

From where Caleb lay on the floor, he glanced over his shoulder. There was Alex, crouched in a tactical fighting stance, her Glock 19 semiautomatic pistol in her hands. Out of breath and breathing heavily from the altercation, and with more than a little adrenaline coursing through his veins, Caleb was speechless. Their eyes met and held each other briefly before the door burst open and the rest of the team entered. Rocky held the unmoving general in his sights while Moose and Clare fanned out around him and cleared the room of any additional threats.

Alex looked at Caleb again. "Are you okay?" she managed to ask in a whisper before collapsing to the floor.

Then Caleb noticed the blood running down her arm. "Shit! Medic!" he shouted.

He ran to her side and pulled her up to support her, his own head and body aching from the altercation with General Hughes.

"I'm on it, boss." Rocky was already on his radio. "We need a medic up here . . . *now!*"

Caleb used his hand to put direct pressure on the bleeder on Alex's arm.

"Moose," he called. "Get over here and fix her up."

"How many times are you almost going to die this week, Martel?" Caleb asked as Moose applied a combat pressure dressing. Alex tried to sit up.

"Hey," Clare said. "Sit still. Let Moose work. Medics are on their way."

"Medics?" Alex looked at the bandage on her arm. "I'm fine—it's just a flesh wound," she said.

Caleb smiled at her. Paramedics entered the room and took over caring for Alex while he stood silently watching them.

"She going to live?" he asked when they appeared done.

The lead medic went over her vital signs with him. Caleb looked at Moose for guidance.

"She'll live, boss," he said.

"Good."

The medics packed up their gear and left the room.

"We have to get back to Washington. We're at DEFCON 2, and I don't know who we can trust anymore," he said once they were gone.

"Well, we have to tell someone what we know," said Alex.

"I'll get a message to both Terry Gault *and* Kadeisha Thomas. One of them will surely get the information to the president. Checks and balances," Caleb said.

CHAPTER 55

Tatiana preferred to travel VIP. It was one of the creature comforts she had become attached to when flying as a special envoy or under unofficial cover as a wealthy businesswoman.

She recognized that her allegiance to the GRU was out of necessity, but she was growing weary of the ineptitude and the dispassionate brutality they employed. How many times had its operations been exposed by amateur sleuths, geolocation experts, and hobbyists alike, not to mention proper intelligence agencies? Poor tradecraft was only half of it. At times, it was almost too embarrassing to endure.

But that is not what motivated her to turn against her country. It was not disloyalty she felt. In fact, it was quite the opposite. She loved Mother Russia. It had raised her with a sense of duty, purpose, and belonging. She was a part of something bigger than herself. But it was and had always been a struggle to stay relevant in an age where young people no longer felt any real purpose.

Conversely, for all its faults, America wasn't the evil empire the Kremlin professed it to be. She saw it as misguided and corrupted by rich and powerful men, yes. Marx and Engels asserted that capitalism was marked by the exploitation of the proletariat by the ruling bourgeoisie. But as bad as Tatiana believed American capitalism to be, the solution wouldn't be found in a nuclear holocaust that would destroy her country and, quite likely, the entire planet and civilization forever.

Seated on the private jet bound for Budapest, she scrolled through her phone. A breaking news notification popped up, and she opened it. A reporter who appeared to be standing on the deck of an American aircraft carrier spoke amid a flurry of background activity, wind, and noise.

"In response to the sinking of a passenger ferry off the coast of Finland, now presumed to have been caused by a torpedo from a Russian nuclear submarine operating in the area, the United States has raised its security level to DEFCON 2, the highest it has been in more than thirty years, and one step away from nuclear war.

"Russia continues to deny any involvement in the sinking of a Finnish ferry called the *Esmerelda*, but, in response to Washington's actions, they have raised their own alert status to their second highest as well. Moscow has scrambled fighter jets into the Gulf of Finland to challenge NATO's presence so close to the Russian border and to protect strategic points around St. Petersburg."

Tatiana looked up from her phone and gazed out the window as the private jet climbed above the Baltic Sea, dotted with warships and danger.

The reporter continued. "Tensions between the superpowers have not been this high since the Cuban Missile Crisis."

Come on, Alexandra. I'm counting on you—do something.

CHAPTER 56

In the command post in the basement of Finland's parliament, the five members of ACCT stowed their gear. Caleb had made his calls, breaking down the information that Alex had discovered on the confiscated phone and that Jonathan had deciphered from the secure cloud drive given to Alex by Tatiana.

"I gotta tell you, Alex, there was a healthy amount of skepticism on that call. Both Mustang and Hacksaw pretty much chewed my ear off."

"But they didn't discount the intel outright. Did they say they'd bring it to the president?"

"They didn't make any promises. As you can imagine, POTUS is a busy man right now, and he's still in transit back to Washington. So, your guess is as good as mine that he'll act on it, or even hear it right away. The fact that his national security advisor tried to kill us, though, works in our favor."

"The intel revealed that Shadow Guard, whoever that is, is somewhere in Virginia, so we need to get there."

"Hold on, Alex," said Caleb. "It's not going to be easy finding this person, let alone arresting them and stopping the operation they set in motion. Intel isn't evidence, and even the evidence will only stand up if a judge allows it. We don't know how high this thing goes, so being guaranteed a sympathetic judge can't actually be guaranteed."

Alex's arm was aching and wasn't quite fully functional. Clare came over to help her with her gun case. "Can you bend your arm any more than that?" she asked.

"Not really," she replied, grimacing with pain at the mere attempt.

The bullet had more than grazed her—it had cut deep. Her arm felt like someone had punched her repeatedly, which made full range of motion unattainable right now.

"It'll be a few hours before we can get a government ride back to DC," said Caleb. "Longer if we go commercial."

"I've got a better plan. I'll message Street."

"Really?" asked Caleb.

"Grow up," she said.

Clare rolled her eyes and walked away from the quarrel to finish stowing her own kit.

Alex tapped a message into her phone, and within seconds had a reply.

"He says he'll have a jet fueled and ready for us at the airport in forty minutes."

"Tell him to make sure there's a full suture kit onboard so Moose can fix you up on the flight home." Alex stared at him. "Seriously, Martel. That's an order."

She sent the message.

Thirty minutes later, they pulled the Range Rovers up to the private terminal and hauled their gear out to a waiting aircraft. Like the helicopter that had flown Alex to Prime Minister Rantala's residence the day before, this one was also decked out in the sea-blue and white colors of Lehtonen Enterprises.

As they stowed their gear in the hold, Street approached and climbed aboard the aircraft.

"Where do you think you're going?" demanded Caleb.

"I go where my plane goes," Street said, smiling.

"We might need his help, boss," Alex said. "He's got skills."

"Hear that?" Street turned to Caleb. "I've got skills."

Well, that came out wrong, thought Alex.

Coming up behind Caleb, Moose gently shoved his boss down the aisle.

"Don't let him push your buttons, boss. We need him alive," said Moose.

Caleb took the seat across the cabin from Alex. Street slid in next to her and grinned at him. Moose pointed finger guns at Street as he passed and pulled the trigger.

Street raised his hands in surrender.

Alex stood. "All of you, grow the fuck up! You're like a bunch of fourteen-year-olds." She shot a look at Moose. "You, too. Stop egging him on." She set her sights next on Caleb. "And of anyone, you ought to know better."

"What does that mean?" he asked.

"Figure it out, dickhead."

Street laughed.

"As for you, ya bloody wee eejit, know when to shut your yap."

She squeezed past him into the aisle and walked up the cabin, taking a seat next to Clare, who smiled supportively.

Five minutes later, the plane took off, its flight path taking it out over the Gulf of Finland before banking west. The sight of dozens of military ships below was surreal and terrifying. How were they ever going to stop this fast-moving train? It had taken on a momentum of its own, and like an out-of-control locomotive that kept gaining speed, it might prove impossible to stop before it ran off the rails.

"Martel!" Moose shouted from the back of the plane. He had donned a pair of surgical gloves and was holding his hands aloft like he was ready for surgery. "Front and center," he said. "This flight's only going to take six hours, so I don't have much time to get this right."

Shit. As she ambled to the back of the aircraft, all eyes were on her.

If ever there was a time to be brave, it was now.

CHAPTER 57

OVAL OFFICE, WHITE HOUSE

Kadeisha Thomas looked around and sat taller in her chair. *I'm in the Oval Office,* she told herself. *The highest office in this great nation.* It was hard not to contrast her surroundings with her living situation during her earliest years.

For the first decade of her life, she had lived with her siblings and her single mother in a double-wide trailer with no running water. But her mother had taught her the value of hard work, a positive attitude, and the need to separate pride from pridefulness. The result of those teachings and the love she received had molded her into a strong and powerful woman, one who knew that her place in the world was wherever she said it was and had the intelligence and determination to back that up.

She stood when President Moore entered the room. She had insisted on remaining in the anteroom until the president arrived, but Moore had instructed his staff that she should be brought in ahead of him.

The man was larger than life. Every time she came face-to-face with the president, she was in awe of his sheer *presence,* that ability to fill a room with—what? An aura? And yet, that's precisely what it seemed—like the man was more than just a man. Moore fit the office of the president, and like the cowboy boots he always wore, the office fit him.

"How was your flight, Mr. President? I hope you got some rest."

"Good," he said. "But let's cut the small talk, Kadeisha. The significance of the intelligence your team has provided is unimaginable. That my chief of staff and national security advisor were both involved in a plot to force us into a wartime footing against our greatest foe, well, that's hard to get my head around. How could I have been so blind?"

"Don't be so hard on yourself, sir."

"Titus Pelletier and Lucas Hughes were my closest advisors. I trusted them implicitly. And now Lucas is dead after trying to kill two of your team members."

"We can't always know what's in the hearts of our adversaries, Mr. President. Some people make it their life's mission to be dishonest. Ambition is a potent drug."

"Hardly reassuring. But I spoke with President Sergachev on the way back to DC. We are both backing things down a little while the information is being processed. And we've agreed to a verification scheme to ensure all the toys are put away and that open communications are maintained until a near-normal status is achieved. But they naturally want to know we've fully cleaned up our mess."

"We're working on that, sir."

"I'm not keen on eating crow, I can tell you that much, Director Thomas."

"Yes, sir. But Titus Pelletier is now in the hands of the FBI, and he gave up Senator Kennington, who we believe is Shadow Guard."

"I understand Titus lawyered up," said the president.

"Yes, sir. Unfortunately, he's now stopped talking," she said. "Maybe the whiff of a presidential pardon might encourage him to get conversational again."

"It might, but I'm not inclined to offer such a pardon just now."

"I didn't say you had to follow through. Hope is almost as powerful a motivator as ambition. Maybe more."

Moore smiled and wagged a finger at her. "You truly are devious, Mustang. I'm glad you're on our side."

"Yes, Mr. President. I most assuredly am."

"Still, I should have seen it coming."

"I'll have to shoulder some of that burden with you. All our nation's intelligence agencies combined missed picking up on this."

"How is that possible?" he asked. "I thought we resolved those issues with the 9/11 Commission."

"Yes, sir. So did I. We in the intelligence community dropped the ball, not you. The point is, you can't go blaming yourself."

"I won't have to. That's what voters are for. They'll do more than enough of that for me. *The president who took us to the brink of a nuclear calamity,*" he said, using his hands to illustrate the words like they were a newspaper headline stretched out between his fingers. "But enough self-pity. Where are we with uncovering the identity of this Eagle character?"

"Working on it, sir. NSA, Interpol, my analysts, we're all running it down. It's only a matter of time."

The president nodded. "It's this Senator Kennington bastard that bothers me so much. That's quite the dossier you compiled on him."

"The information has all been verified by our analysts, sir. Martel helped tie it together with information off the phone she stole from one of the conspirators. That's how we identified Titus as part of the plot. Interpol then helped by providing information that came from a Russian GRU officer who gave that data to Alex."

"So now Alex is recruiting Russian agents for us?"

Kadeisha smiled. "She's a woman of many talents."

"And do we have enough solid evidence to bring down Kennington?"

"Our joint task force is working on it. We've traced him to his ranch in Northern Virginia."

"I never did like that man. He considers himself untouchable. Always has. He has more DC lawyers buzzing around him than a pile of cow dung has flies."

"Yes, sir."

"So, we'll need solid evidence before the Department of Justice can file charges."

"Agreed, but an overinflated ego is a dangerous thing, Mr. President."

"Meaning?"

"Meaning we have a plan."

"Do tell . . ."

CHAPTER 58

Twenty minutes outside Leesburg, Virginia, the Chevy Tahoe turned off US Route 15, passing through miles of farmland before the road narrowed and the bordering forest and mountainside encroached, blocking out most of the daylight.

"I spoke to the CIA and FBI directors a few minutes ago, Copeland." Deputy Director Thomas's voice poured from the Bose speakers. "The bottom line is there's no way we'll get a warrant on this slippery eel with what we have. But, straight from the president, you and Special Agent Duffries are clear to engage him in an interview if he lets you onto his property. Let's see if he's in a sharing mood. Short of an invitation, though, y'all are going to have to return to DC and wait for the evidence to mount."

Caleb looked across at Clare, sitting in the passenger seat.

"You both best mind your p's and q's when you talk to him," she continued. "He's got more friends in the Department of Justice than the president, so do this smartly or not at all. Is that understood, Viking?"

Clare mouthed the word *Viking* back at him like a question. He shrugged.

"Did you hear me?" Thomas asked.

"Yes, ma'am. That's an amen."

"Lord help you, it better be." And with that, she hung up.

As they approached the Kennington Ranch, a vehicle trailing behind them peeled off, leaving them to go it alone from there. The terrain was hilly, with patches of meadow interspersed among the thick Virginia woods. At last, they turned onto a paved lane—more like a two-lane highway than a driveway—and approached the front gates to the compound. A brick-and-mortar guard booth stood next to a set of vehicle intrusion barricades and an automated lift-gate system. Cameras covered every angle as Caleb pulled up to the sentry house.

"Help you?" asked the armed guard stepping out of the booth. A second guard remained inside.

"Here to see Senator Kennington."

"Do you have an appointment?"

"He's expecting us."

"I'm afraid you're not on my schedule, sir."

"I think he'll want to talk to us."

"Don't be so sure. Can I see some ID?"

Clare held up her FBI credentials, but they didn't impress the guard at all, who took her wallet and punched her name into an iPad. Caleb scanned the perimeter and clocked sentry lights, fencing, perimeter alert systems, and at least two teams of roving guards.

"How about yours, sir?"

"I'm with her," he said.

"I'm sorry, sir, but if you don't provide some identification, I can't—"

Just then, the phone in the shack rang. The guard answered it.

"Roger that, sir," he said before hanging up. "You can drive straight up to the main building. Senator Kennington's staff will show you in."

"Thanks," said Caleb insincerely.

He hit the gas, and the Chevy deposited a patch of rubber on the pretty asphalt and roared up the driveway.

The house was smaller than Caleb had expected. It still seemed to be ten thousand square feet or more, but he had prepared himself for something modern and cubist and triple the dimensions. Instead, it was a tasteful, albeit inflated, rendering of a Georgian Colonial, not unlike the Scattergood-Thorne residence on the Calvert Estate at Langley, only vastly bigger.

"What's the plan?" Clare asked.

"Get him to confess."

"Glad we had this discussion."

Caleb wheeled the SUV around the fountain in front of the main entrance. As they climbed the steps, the front door opened, and a man in a suit invited them in. The bulk of a large weapon was visible beneath his unbuttoned jacket.

They followed him down a hallway to an office of warm wood paneling with a coffered ceiling. Once inside, they were surrounded by sports memorabilia.

"Please, make yourselves comfortable," their escort said, indicating they should sit in two wingback chairs before a desk. "The senator will be right with you." With that, he slid the pocket doors closed.

They remained standing. "You want to play good cop, bad cop?" Clare asked.

"How about bad cop, bad cop?"

"You catch more flies with honey."

"Well, how about one cop, no cop, then? I'll follow your lead."

Caleb walked around the office and studied the items inside the cases. He whistled.

"Wow," he said. "This is some high-end sports shit."

Clare shrugged her shoulders. "If you're into that kind of stuff, I suppose." She looked down at the rug. "I'm more into what's on the floor. That's a gorgeous carpet."

"If you're into that kind of stuff, I suppose," he said.

The sound of soft footfalls coming down the hall alerted them to Kennington's approach. He entered the room dressed in gray dress slacks and a white Oxford shirt, sleeves rolled to below the elbows, and a pair of burgundy loafers on his feet. The security escort was with him.

"I'm sorry for keeping you waiting," Kennington said, smiling graciously at the pair.

"Not at all, Senator," said Caleb. "We appreciate you seeing us on such short notice."

"Correction," said the senator. "*No* notice."

"I guess you're right, sir. So even greater is our debt of gratitude."

"And they say I'm the politician." Kennington looked up at his security man and pointed at Caleb. "This one is slicker than a bowl full of snails covered in oil."

The security man smiled.

"Senator Kennington, I'm Special Agent Duffries with the FBI." She presented her badge and creds. But it was performative, as Caleb was sure she knew the senator had already been told who she was by the front gate security detail.

"And you are . . . ?" he asked Caleb.

"A servant of the people, like yourself, Senator."

"Interesting response, Mr. Copeland."

"You *do* know my name. You're well informed, Senator," said Caleb.

Kennington spread his arms to indicate the breadth of his possessions. "It's my dominion," he said. "A man should be in control of all he surveys within his domain."

"Agreed," said Caleb.

"So, I must ask, what is the interest of the CIA in me? If I didn't know better, I'd think I should be calling my attorneys to question the legality here."

"There's no need for that, sir. I'm merely Special Agent Duffries's chauffeur today."

"Of course you are."

Caleb was on his best behavior: clever, charming, friendly.

Alex would be pleased.

"I'm sure you are aware of the events of the past couple of days, Senator," Clare began.

"Who isn't? Troubling times," he replied, pulling a cigar from a humidor behind his desk. "I'm assuming, of course, you're speaking of the events in Finland."

"Yes, sir."

"What does that have to do with me?" He expertly prepped and lit his cigar, opening the window behind his desk. "My wife and grandchildren aren't home today, but I would never hear the end of it if she came back to a house full of Cuban cigar smoke."

"I guess not," agreed Caleb.

"Where were we?" he asked. "Oh, yes. You were implying I might have had something to do with nearly starting World War Three, is that it?"

"No—" began Clare.

"Exactly right, sir," said Caleb. "So, did you?"

"Did I what, exactly? Did I have anything to do with a boat sinking in Finland?"

"Sure, we can start there. Did you? Or, for that matter, any of the events of the past twelve months. Blackouts, ghost ships running aground, that sort of thing."

"Caleb," he heard Clare say.

"Cyberattacks on critical infrastructure. Have anything to do with that? You know a kid died in the hospital in that one."

Kennington's face reddened.

"Did you know what the body count is up to from the ferry sinking? Over four hundred and still rising. It wasn't a Russian torpedo, by the way. Satellite footage shows there was a series of explosions aboard. Analysis shows it likely started with a single bomb aboard the ship."

"And do you honestly think I did that, Mr. Copeland? I flew over to Helsinki and planted a bomb with my own hands next to the engine of a passenger ferry?"

"Interesting bit of detail right there, sir."

Kennington puffed his expensive cigar like an old diesel locomotive chugging uphill. The security man stepped forward, but Kennington held him back with a wave of his hand.

"Did you know the president's chief of staff has been arrested? I think Titus Pelletier will make an excellent witness for the prosecution. Of course, he'll have to since the president's national security advisor took a bullet. Actually, three, but who's counting."

"I think our friendly little conversation has come to an end, Special Agent," Kennington said, staring past Caleb at Duffries.

"I'm sorry to hear that, Senator," Clare said. "You were beginning to reveal so much."

Caleb suddenly liked Clare that much more.

"Brick, see them out."

Caleb looked the man over. "*Brick?* Your mom didn't like you much right from birth, did she."

"This way, please," he said, showing them the door.

As Caleb followed Clare out, he turned to Kennington.

"Oh, Senator, I almost forgot to ask. Does the word *Eagle* mean anything to you? I mean, besides the obvious." Kennington appeared distracted. "Senator?"

"No, it doesn't," he said.

"Thanks. What about Shadow Guard?"

Kennington stared at him and rose to his feet. He walked up to Caleb until they were practically touching.

"Senator? Shadow Guard. Mean anything?"

Finally, the senator let out a breath. "Good day, Mr. Copeland."

* * *

Caleb and Clare sat between the fountain and the front door in his Tahoe.

"I didn't know there was a third option," she said. Off his blank stare, she said, "Good cop, bad cop, and smartass."

"I don't like smug, entitled jackasses."

"I can see that. You might have pushed him a little hard, but truth be told, I'm impressed."

"Oh? Got your federal agent heart all aflutter?"

"Don't you wish."

"It's true you can catch more flies with honey, but you can also poke a sleeping bear into attacking."

"Interesting reference."

"It's not so much a reference as a philosophy."

He hit the start button, and the Chevy roared to life.

* * *

Senator Kennington sat stewing in his study. He stubbed his cigar out in his thousand-dollar crystal ashtray—he'd suddenly lost his appreciation for it.

Copeland was an asshole, but he was right. Titus had been arrested. General Hughes was dead, shot by that other meddling former FBI agent, Alexandra Martel. The president had spoken to the Russian president, and the two men had agreed to step back from the brink and dial down their respective war footings.

Russia had recalled most of her naval vessels, including some of her nuclear subs, and the US and NATO countries were clearing the Gulf of Finland of their military presence. Not only had his ambition to see America reach a level of untouchable global superiority been nullified, but he was likely on the brink of financial collapse, having poured all his liquid assets into the major defense contractors who were seeing a massive collapse in equity. He'd lose vast fortunes if he couldn't relinquish those positions fast. And there was a very real possibility he could be imprisoned. Even in today's social and political climate, it was still possible for someone of his stature to go to jail.

The world has lost all sense of righteousness, he thought.

Plus, he had made promises. He had virtually guaranteed those same companies that war was inevitable, that their stocks would rise exponentially. Now, that was all for naught.

"Brick!" he called.

Brick appeared almost instantly. "Yes, Senator."

"Those two don't get off the property."

"You wish them to be detained?"

"I wish them to be dead."

Brick didn't even blink. "Yes, sir," he said.

CHAPTER 59

Caleb drove the Chevy up the curving lane they had come in on. He drove slowly to assess the terrain and activity. If Kennington *was* guilty—and Caleb knew he was—anything could happen.

"Stay frosty," he said to Clare. He saw her hand drift to her gun side.

One hundred meters from the gate, he slowed.

"What do you see?" he asked.

"Our two guards have company."

"They do indeed."

Two guards pretended to stand nonchalantly beside the guard shack, talking to two other guards, also looking suspiciously nonchalant. The assault rifles up against their chests were a bit of a tell, though.

Caleb crawled forward to within fifty meters and stopped. Two of the guards began to walk toward them.

"It might be nothing," said Clare.

"And I might be a dancing bear on my days off."

"Are you?" she asked.

"I am not."

He could run at them, but the Chevy wasn't armored and would only attract bullets.

"Let's gear up," he said, putting the SUV in park.

He popped the lift gate, and they walked around to the back of the truck. Each threw on heavy body armor with polyethylene ballistic chest plates. Then they strapped on thigh-rig drop-leg holsters and their pistols and slung M4 rifles.

"Ready?"

There was a hint of trepidation in her eyes. "We're defensive until they give us a reason not to be, okay?" she said. "By the book."

Caleb nodded. He was about to give the benefit of the doubt to the boys at the gate and come around the vehicle with his weapon low, but then someone had the nerve to open fire on his newish Chevy Tahoe, punching holes in its side.

"That's it," he said. "No more Mr. Nice Guy!"

* * *

From her vantage point inside the tree line atop a ridge, Alex watched it all unfolding before her. Caleb and Clare got into his Chevy outside the house, sat for a minute, and then proceeded toward the exit. She saw the men gathering at the gate, but Caleb was on top of it.

"You clocking this, Alex?" asked Street, crouched beside her with a spotting scope.

"I am," she said, glued to the eyepiece of her Nightforce scope.

She had opted for this mission to bring along her Barrett MRAD MK22 sniper rifle, the same rifle she had successfully deployed with in operations not so long ago. But instead of the .300 Norma Magnum caliber she had used then, she opted for the smaller 7.62 x 51 NATO configuration considering the closer-range targets she could be engaging. Alex had spent considerable time training on this rifle in this setup and caliber. The setup was ideal for the job at hand.

She had already ranged the guard shack at 280 meters. Now, she added the Tahoe for reference at 335 and rotated the dial on the top of her scope, adding a few more clicks of elevation. She would adjust on the fly using the reticle as needed. The flag on the guard shack hung limp, so the wind wouldn't be a factor in her shots.

She hoped it wouldn't come to that, but . . .

Then, two of the four men at the gate started moving toward her team.

Safety off.

"Alex," said Street.

"I see it," she replied.

Both fit nicely into her scope. She sighted in the man in front.

In, out, rest, two, three.

It was a silly mantra, but it relaxed her and helped prepare her for a shooting engagement.

At first, the men kept their guns low. But then one raised his, and as Caleb and Clare were about to come out from cover, Bozo opened fire.

Squeeze the trigger rearward with the pad of your finger until it breaks.

BOOM!

She let fly with a 175-grain match-grade hollow-point boat-tail round that reached him in the blink of an eye. Bozo was the first to die.

His mate opened fire. She racked the bolt.

BOOM!

"Hit," called Street. "Two down. Two more badgers at the gate behind cover. They have their weapons raised, Alex. Two hundred and eighty-five meters," called Street.

"Copy."

BOOM!

BOOM!

"Moose and Rocky advancing from our three o'clock," he said.

"Copy."

She could see Caleb and Clare behind the Tahoe, back-to-back, as they engaged targets approaching from the side.

Get down! she thought. *Caleb, get down!*

Moose and Rocky made it onto the property and were running toward the west stand of trees. Two bogeys engaged Caleb from that side. Two came at Clare from the other.

Caleb dropped one of the shooters while Clare managed to take both on her side.

"Two more from the west tree line," Alex called into her mic.

"We're on them," answered Moose.

"Find cover," called Street into his radio.

Moose and Rocky dropped both shooters but then took additional fire. Suddenly, Rocky went down.

"Rocky, are you okay?" called Street into his radio.

"I'm good! I tripped on a stump," he said. Alex watched as he recovered and fired on more men in Kennington's little army. Two went down.

Street called out two more bogeys approaching from the north side of the property.

Caleb and Clare shifted around to the front of the Tahoe.

"Three hundred and forty meters, Alex."

She adjusted her elevation a few clicks and sent two more rounds downrange.

"You're high!"

"I know." Her arm ached, but she didn't tell him that.

She swapped out for a new magazine and worked the bolt, feeding another round.

BOOM!

"Hit!" he called.

She worked the bolt and fired again.

BOOM!

"He's down."

Alex stretched her support hand out. This had never felt so difficult.

"Any more targets?" she called.

Street scanned the entire area.

"None," he said. "I think we're clear, minus whatever's in the house."

* * *

The six of them gathered at the Tahoe. Employing the edict *one can never be too careful*, Moose and Rocky made the rounds to the downed bogeys, zip-tying the wrists of the living and the dead. Alex, Caleb, Clare, and Moose fanned out and began their approach to the house.

Rocky had twisted his ankle and stayed with Street on overwatch from the Tahoe, which looked like it had been used as target practice on a gun range. Which it had.

As they approached the house, Kennington stepped onto the porch, his hired gun by his side.

"Hands up!" shouted Caleb.

The men raised them halfheartedly, and the four continued their advance slowly.

"It didn't have to be like this," said Caleb, his rifle trained on Kennington.

"I'm afraid it did, Mr. Copeland."

"Why?" Alex asked.

"Why, Ms. Martel? Because we could be a great nation. Because we once were a great nation. A president like ours spends his day appeasing America's enemies instead of demonstrating our strength and resolve. Our character."

"Look around, Kennington," Caleb said. "You call this strength?"

"Or character?" asked Alex.

From where they stood, she could see the dead and wounded guards.

"Our nation is weaker because of you and those like you," Kennington said. "We have backed away from what should have been the most decisive moment in the history of the world. We could have crushed our foe. But instead, we showed mercy and are lesser for it."

"Lesser by avoiding the total annihilation of the world?" asked Alex.

"We are nothing without sacrificial patriotism and the willingness to risk everything for this great nation. The greater the risk, the greater the reward. You and those like you fight not to win but to achieve a stalemate. Stalemate is losing! Only by utterly crushing our enemies can we achieve checkmate! We could be the greatest empire the world has ever seen. Instead, we satisfy ourselves with mediocrity while we wait for our enemies to rise again because we have given them that opportunity."

He said something to his guard, who tried to argue, but Kennington pushed him toward the stairs.

"Let's see your hands, Brick!" said Caleb.

Brick showed his hands and raised his jacket, turning slowly to reveal that, unlike when they had first encountered him, now he was unarmed.

"Right, come this way."

"Senator Kennington," said Clare. "I'm taking you in for questioning related to the events that have occurred here today. Other investigations are pending. You are not under arrest at this time, Senator, but I assume you'll want your attorney present."

Kennington turned around without a word and went back into the house.

"Stop!" shouted Clare, but the senator ignored her.

When Brick reached them, Clare hooked him up. She and Moose then walked him toward what was left of the Tahoe.

In the distance, Alex heard the sound of helicopters approaching.

"Our reinforcements," shouted Clare over her shoulder, who had called the cavalry after the gunfight had settled down.

Alex and Caleb looked at each other and then at the house.

"Do you think he's gone to put on some coffee?" she asked.

"Hope so."

"Should we go see?"

They took two steps toward the house when the ground suddenly shook, and a massive explosion blew the world around them to smithereens. The concussive shock wave lifted Alex and Caleb two feet off the ground and hurled them backward several meters. They crashed to the ground, their body armor taking the brunt of the impact. A massive fireball curled high into the clear Virginia sky, birthing thick clouds of black smoke as it rose into the blue.

Alex lay stunned in the dirt next to Caleb, who was lying on his back, struggling to take a breath. Around them, the air filled with dust and the acrid smell of smoke. As fiery debris began to rain down on them, Alex rolled on top of Caleb to shield him. The firestorm finally ceased after what seemed like an eternity but was mere seconds. She raised her head to look at the house. What had once been a stately manor was reduced to jagged rubble. Of the entire structure that had formed Kennington's home, few walls remained standing, but the roof and other walls were obliterated. What hadn't blown outward across the estate had fallen inward into burning heaps. Fire raged from the rubble, and pockets of fire scattered across the debris field extending out in all

OUT IN THE COLD   317

directions. She lowered her head down beside Caleb's, her body still covering his.

"Let's just lay here awhile and rest," she said.

* * *

Dozens of emergency vehicles dotted the property and spread across the laneway and adjacent patches of lawn. A helicopter circled overhead while another settled into an open paddock two hundred feet from the burning structure.

Fire crews continued to douse the flames, but the once grand home had been reduced to a smoldering corpse of its former beauty. Paramedics treated the remaining casualties from among Kennington's men, but of those who were still alive, most had already been evacuated to nearby hospitals and a trauma center.

The Loudoun County Sheriff's Office, Virginia State Police, and the FBI were scattered throughout the grounds collecting evidence and interviewing subjects and witnesses from among those not dead and not transported to a hospital. Hours after the explosion, interviews with Caleb's team were finally wrapped up, and they were permitted to leave the scene.

The concussive effect of the explosion had Caleb and Alex feeling like they had been hit by a truck. But other than some lacerations and abrasions, they had miraculously suffered no serious injuries.

Street was hitching a ride to the airport with an FBI agent who was returning to headquarters but offered to drop him off.

Alex walked over to him. "You should stay awhile."

"Nah," he said. "I don't have a green card."

"I'm sure we could arrange a special visa."

"I have to get back. Valtteri left an empire that requires my skills," he said, winking at her.

"Fine." She leaned in and gave him a big hug. "But keep in touch," she said, kissing him on the cheek before stepping off to the side as Caleb approached.

"You're on your way then," Caleb asked rhetorically. "Don't want to hang around for the debrief?"

"I'm sorry I'm going to miss it."

"I'm sure you are," laughed Caleb.

"Listen, it's none of my business," Street said in a low voice. "But look around you. We're all lucky to have survived these past few days."

"And?"

"And if you have feelings for that girl, you should get off your arse and do something about it before it's too late."

Caleb looked over his shoulder at Alex, who was standing with Clare, Moose, and Rocky, still managing a smile after all that had happened.

"You're right, Street. It's none of your business," he said through a friendly smile. "But thanks for your help." He reached out and shook the Scotsman's hand firmly. "And safe travels home."

Street gave him a final salute as he climbed into the FBI agent's car and drove off.

Caleb walked up to his team, all standing together.

"Everything okay?" asked Alex.

He smiled at her. "Much better now."

CHAPTER 60

OVAL OFFICE, WHITE HOUSE

Taylor Moore stood in the center of the gray-blue carpet that stretched clear across his office, the seal of the president beneath his size-eleven custom-made cowboy boots. He listened with rapt attention as Alex and Caleb relayed the action that had occurred the previous day out on the Kennington Ranch.

"Pompous windbag," he said. "I never trust a man that doesn't earn his keep and pay his dues but thinks he's the Lord Almighty himself. That one didn't come to town two to a mule. He's all hat and no cattle."

"He had this planned out for years," Alex said. "If not all the details, then the intention and objectives behind it."

Caleb spoke up. "He didn't seem to care much for the system that brought him to power and kept his family so well-heeled for generations."

"Boatloads of money can distract a person from the more important things in life. Power corrupts," mused Moore, shaking his head. "I want my legacy to be that I brought back the faith of the people in their government. What they get from it should be what they expect of it. We need to ensure that the checks and balances our Founders envisioned and the accountability those systems brought about work again." He paused to look at his audience, needing to get it out and off his chest, then continued. "Government shouldn't be performative. It has to mean something—*be* something—bigger. The oath we swear shouldn't be empty words. But enough of me preaching to the choir. Come, sit by the fire and take a load off."

He led them to the fireplace that burned real logs.

"Well, Alex, I'm glad that wing isn't broken," he said, indicating toward her arm resting in a sling. "But that cheek of yours looks like you've gone a few rounds with Mike Tyson."

"Yes, sir," she said. "Some old, some new."

"Mr. President, I've seen Alex in action a few times now, and frankly, my money's on her every time. But I'm surprised she's still with us."

"We're all grateful for that," he said. "Alex, I understand Secretary General Clicquot is on the road to a full recovery."

"Yes, Mr. President," she replied. "I'm told she was transferred out of the ICU yesterday."

"I imagine you must be anxious to see your former boss."

"Yes, sir. But she's more than just a former boss. She's stuck her neck out for me more times than I can count."

"That kind of leadership is rare," Moore said. "So, when you find it, it's nice to be able to repay those kindnesses. And, if I were her, I would be most grateful for your loyalty."

"Sir, I'm flying back to The Hague tomorrow. I want to see for myself that she's okay."

"That doesn't surprise me a bit, Martel."

There was a light rap on the door before the president's assistant led Vice President Garcia into the Oval.

"Ah, just who I wanted to see. One of our nation's most industrious citizens. Thanks for joining us, Babs," he said, using Vice President Barbara Garcia's seldom-used nickname. "Come in, come in." The VP made her way across the carpet and over to the group. "Alex and Caleb were just regaling me with their exploits over on Randolph Kennington's spread."

"That must have been quite the adventure," she said.

"Adventure?" echoed the president. "That's a lot like calling Old Abe's Gettysburg Address a little fireplace chat."

"Yes, Mr. President," she backpedaled. "Clearly, I'm underrepresenting the heroism of your guests. It's sad that so many lives were lost, though."

"Is it?" he asked.

"Why, yes, sir. It seems Senator Kennington might have been misguided in his approach, but it's hard for me to see him as anything but a patriot in the end. I think he was a man who loved his country deeply but chose a different path to change things into what he saw to be a better version of ourselves, our great nation."

"Are you saying we should accept the instigations of world war as merely a minor annoyance meant to effect change, as long as America comes out on top, Babs? That we should be willing to allow confederacies within our Union to incinerate the planet and all her people so that our own beloved America achieves global supremacy?"

"No, sir. But—"

"It's all academic anyway," Moore said. "Republics need a lot of nurturing to survive, I suppose. But all this talk of conspiracies and global domination gets a little tiresome, wouldn't you say, Alex?"

Alex nodded.

Vice President Garcia only now seemed to notice the arm sling and bandages on Alex's face. Then she assessed Caleb as well, equally battered and bruised.

"Goodness, shouldn't these two still be in the hospital, Mr. President? I mean, look at them."

"They probably should," replied Moore. "But even after their hair-raising exploits yesterday, they were eager to tell me a story."

"Oh? And what story would that be?"

Just then, the door at the side of the Oval Office opened, and in walked two FBI agents.

"I'll let Alex tell you," President Moore said.

Alex turned to Vice President Garcia and smiled. "Hello, Eagle."

ACKNOWLEDGMENTS

Thank you for reading *Out in the Cold*, the second installment in the Special Agent Alexandra Martel thriller series. I know the value of your time, and I appreciate you spending yours with Alex, Caleb, and company. Your support allows me to keep writing; I am thankful for that.

I owe the greatest gratitude, love, and respect to my wife, **Lynne**. She is my first reader, editor, and biggest fan. She is also my life partner, traveling companion, and best friend. Her observations and contributions to the story and characters—especially of Alex and Caleb—make me a better writer and the story richer. Thank you, Lynne!

To my literary agent, **John Talbot**. I have been writing since long before we met, but my publishing journey began with you. Thank you for your encouragement and support. Thank you for believing in me.

Over the years, many authors have become my friends and mentors: **Simon Gervais, Jack Stewart, Ryan Steck, Tessa Wegert, Hannah Mary McKinnon, Samantha Bailey, Kim Howe, Samuel Octavius, Anthony Franze, Drew Murray, Robert Dugoni, Taylor Moore, Brian Andrews, Jeffrey Wilson, Marc Cameron, Mark Greaney, Brad Taylor, Tim Hendrickson, Linwood Barclay, Tess Gerritsen,** and **Jack Carr,** to name only a few. They have been generous with their friendship, advice, support, and conversation, for which I am greatly indebted.

Thanks also to my writer friends who are podcasters and graciously hosted me on their programs: **Sean Cameron, Chris Albanese,** and **Michael Houtz** of *The Crew Reviews* podcast, **David Temple** of *The Thriller Zone* podcast, **Jeff Clark** of the *Course of Action* podcast, and **Hannah Mary McKinnon** and **Hank Phillippi Ryan** from the *First*

Chapter Fun podcast. Thank you for allowing me to talk about my books and reach new readers!

Greater-than-honorable mention goes to **Ryan Steck,** founder of The Real Book Spy website, for being the first to tell the world about *Out in the Cold*, and **Jeff Circle,** purveyor of The Dossier, for including me in your fun and informative project!

To **Barbara Peters** at The Poisoned Pen Bookstore in Scottsdale, Arizona—there's scarcely a thriller writer out there who hasn't benefited from the landscape you helped shape. Thank you for your kindness and support!

While writing and researching *Out in the Cold,* I had the pleasure again of traveling to the various locales in the story. Scenes at the opening of the novel take place aboard a luxury megayacht on the Mediterranean, and several characters make their escape from the ship aboard Axopar Boats. These are among the most dependable vessels on the water. **Noel McAvennie** of Axopar Boats in Finland was gracious enough to talk boats and took Lynne and me boating on the Baltic Sea around Helsinki in his own Axopar. Noel, I am grateful for your kindness and that adventure!

To my friends and former colleagues on the frontlines at **Toronto Paramedic Services, York Region Paramedic Services,** the **Ontario Provincial Police,** the **Ontario Emergency Medical Assistance Team (EMAT),** and **Sunnybrook Health Sciences Centre,** and to those who serve on the frontlines of healthcare, law enforcement, public safety, and the military, I never forget the sacrifices you make and the heroism you demonstrate every day to ensure our safety. I know what it takes to show up in uniform day after day. Thank you for your service!

To the great folks at **Minotaur Books** and **St. Martin's Press,** it is a pleasure working with you. **Stephen Erickson** and **Hector DeJean,** thank you for your contributions and the roads you have paved for me on the marketing and publicity sides of the house. To my former editor, **Sarah Grill,** I am glad we got to work together and grateful for how you helped shape *Out in the Cold.* To **Michael Homler,** my new editor, and his assistant, **Madeline Alsup,** thanks for leaping into the fray and continuing to steward this project. To **Sara Thwaite** and others in copy-editing, thank you! Your keen eye for detail is much needed and greatly appreciated. To the crazy-good **art department,** you nailed the cover again! Thank you, all!

To our children, **Michael** and **Meghan,** you mean the world to me. Not a moment passed that I wasn't the happiest and proudest father in the world. Okay, maybe that one time . . . Never mind.

Finally, to **Mom.** Thank you for always encouraging me to read. I'm forever grateful. The pride you showed in me for my smallest achievements made me always believe I could accomplish so much more. Love you forever!

ABOUT THE AUTHOR

Raph Nogal

Steve Urszenyi was a paramedic in Toronto and a tactical medic with the Ontario Provincial Police, where he was a specialist in SWAT, CBRNE, HUSAR, and public order operations. Steve is also the former commander of the province of Ontario's disaster medical response and all-hazards emergency management team, EMAT, and is a recipient of the Governor General of Canada's EMS Exemplary Service Medal and Bar in recognition of his distinguished service. Steve loves touring on his Harley-Davidson motorcycle with his wife, Lynne. They live in Toronto and have two grown children.